Testing Kate

Whitney Gaskell

little
black
dress

First published in 2006
by BANTAM DELL
An imprint of RANDOM HOUSE, INC., NEW YORK

First published in this paperback edition in Great Britain in 2007
by LITTLE BLACK DRESS
An imprint of HEADLINE PUBLISHING GROUP

A LITTLE BLACK DRESS paperback

2

978 0 7553 4109 2

Typeset in Transit511BT by Avon DataSet Ltd,
Bidford-on-Avon, Warwickshire

Printed and bound in Great Britain by Clays Ltd, St Ives plc

Headline's policy is to use papers that are natural, renewable and
recyclable products and made from wood grown in sustainable forests.
The logging and manufacturing processes are expected to conform to
the environmental regulations of the country of origin.

HEADLINE PUBLISHING GROUP
A division of Hachette Livre UK Ltd
338 Euston Road
London NW1 3BH

www.littleblackdressbooks.co.uk
www.hodderheadline.com

For my dad,
who tried to warn me that I'd hate law school

Author's Note

I'd like to thank the following people, all of whom were instrumental in bringing *Testing Kate* to print:

My editor, Danielle Perez, who is everything you'd want in an editor – talented, kind, and possessing the good sense to know just where things are going wrong;

My agent, Ethan Ellenberg, whose enthusiasm for Kate's story inspired me to keep writing;

Sharon Propson, my publicist, who never makes me feel dumb even when I ask her stupid questions;

Patricia Ballantyne, who helps Danielle do such a wonderful job;

Lynn Andreozzi, for the fabulous cover design;

My fellow Literary Chicks – Alesia Holliday, Lani Diane Rich, Beth Kendrick, Eileen Rendahl, and Michelle Cunnah – for making me laugh every day;

My parents, Meredith Kelly and Jerry Kelly, for their continued support;

My husband, George, who makes everything possible;

And our son, Sam, who makes everything worthwhile.

I was in the middle of writing *Testing Kate* when Hurricane Katrina hit New Orleans. I have a love affair with the city – it's where my husband and I met and married, and lived as newlyweds – and it was heart-wrenching to see the devastation that followed the hurricane. I salute the courage of the residents of New Orleans, and send them my best wishes as they continue to rebuild their wonderful city.

Fall Semester

When I was twelve years old, I froze right in the middle of the three-meter springboard diving competition. I'd been taking diving classes at the local YMCA. When I'd stand at the edge of the rough board, my toes curled over the end, and stare down at the sprinklers spraying over the surface of the water, the whole world would go quiet. And then I'd take three steps back, turn, balance my shoulders over my hips and my hips over my feet, lift my arms out, and then it was three steps back again to the end of the board. With one final bounce, I'd leap straight up and then out, stretching my body into an arrow and slicing into the cold water, feeling like a mermaid.

At the end of the summer, the Y hosted a fun meet called Splash Day. The swimmers raced like a pack of sleek dolphins, and the synchronized swimmers spun around and fluttered their hands in time to a Christopher Cross song, and the divers sprang fearlessly from the board.

But when it was my turn to dive – a forward half-twist dive I'd been practicing for months – I stood at the edge of the springboard, staring out at the crowd, at my parents sitting side by side on the wooden bleachers, and smelling the chlorine in the air, and I just . . . froze. I don't mean that I had a moment of anxiety, or even that I decided not to dive and retreated back down the ladder. Oh, no. I was incapable of movement. I just stood there in my navy blue Speedo suit, shivering a little, my arms wrapped around myself in a hug, and I listened to the crowd first grow quiet and then, becoming restless at the holdup, start to call out either encouragements or barbed jokes, their voices echoing over the water.

'You can do it, honey!' (My mother.)

'Just jump already!' (Mr Hunt, father of Bobby, who for some inexplicable reason wore sweatbands on his wrists when he swam the hundred-meter freestyle.)

'Damn, that water must be *really* cold!' (Mindy's dad, Mr Camp, who thought – incorrectly – that he was hilarious.)

The voices just made it worse. I don't know why. I don't even know what it was that stopped me from making the same dive I'd completed hundreds of times in practice, the dive I'd been so sure would secure the blue ribbon. But even as I told my legs to *jump now*, they refused to obey.

In the end, Ms Hadley, my coach – one of those sturdy, capable women with a square jaw and bushy brown hair cut in a severe bob – had to climb up onto the board, take my limp hand in hers, and lead me down and away. As soon as my bare feet hit the wet tiled pool deck, I dashed for the locker room – disobeying the sign that forbade poolside running – where I sat huddled on the wooden bench while hot tears of shame dripped down my cheeks. It was the most humiliating moment of my life.

Until now.

As I sat in my very first class on my very first day of law school, only one terrified thought had crystallized in my mind:

Which one of us will he call on first?

Actually two thoughts, the other being: Please, please, please, God, please don't let it be me.

Law schools are infamous for their use of the Socratic Method, where the professor singles out a student and questions him or her on the finer points of case law. And despite my performance anxiety, which had been lingering since the diving incident seventeen years earlier, I hadn't worried about the Socratic Method when I first applied to law schools.

Getting called on in class? Big deal, I'd thought as I paged through the glossy admissions catalog.

But as I sat in the too-cold lecture hall for the first time, a queasy, oily fear slid through me. And I wasn't the only one. Everyone around me was sitting a little too straight and rigid; heads were bowed over casebooks, eyes flickering around nervously.

Professor Richard Hoffman had finished his curt introduction to Criminal Law and stood leaning forward against the wood lectern, his flat grey eyes scanning row after row of students, all of whom did their best not to make eye contact with him.

Please don't let it be me, I thought again. My hands tensed into two fists, the nails pressing into the tender skin of my palms. Please, please, please don't let it be me. Not today, not when I hadn't done the reading assignment, or even brought my casebook, for that matter. Not the one day of my academic career when I was completely and totally unprepared.

'The sixth row to the right. The young woman who didn't seem to think it necessary to bring her textbook to class,' Professor Hoffman said.

Which row was I in? One, two, three, four . . . shit, shit, shit. He couldn't possibly be . . . was he really? . . . oh, God . . . he *was* . . .

I looked up and saw that all of my new classmates had swiveled around to face me, a sea of strangers, their faces stamped with relief that they hadn't been singled out as the first member of our class to be called on.

Dumb fucking luck, I thought.

You know those people who fill out a sweepstakes entry form on a lark and end up winning a new flat-panel television, or who always manage to make it to the gate just in time when they're running late for a flight, or who find priceless antiques for next-to-nothing in the back room of a dusty thrift store?

I'm not one of them.

I step in wads of gum the first time I wear a pair of shoes, and get stuck in traffic when I have an appointment I can't be late for, and my first and only new car was dinged by a hit-and-run driver less than half an hour after I drove it off the car lot.

So it really shouldn't have surprised me that I was the very first person to get called on by the professor on the very first day of class. It was just more of the freaky bad luck that had been hanging over me since the day I was born (which just happened to be right in the middle of one of the worst blizzards to hit central New York in forty years).

'Your name?' Hoffman asked.

My skin felt very hot and very tight stretched over the bones of my face, and my throat closed up. 'Kate. Kate Bennett,' I croaked.

'Ms Bennett, please stand.'

'Ex-excuse me?'

Hoffman sighed dramatically. 'If you are not capable of speaking loudly enough for the rest of the class to hear you, you must stand. Up. Now,' he said. He raised his hand, with the palm facing up.

But all I could do was gape back at the professor, while the eyes of my classmates burned into me. And just like that, I was twelve years old again, frozen at the end of the diving board.

Twenty minutes earlier, I'd been standing on the Freret Street sidewalk and staring up at the imposing three-story brick facade of John Giffen Weinmann Hall. The morning sun cut down at a sharp angle, and I had to hold my hand up for shade to get a good look at the building that housed the Tulane School of Law, where I was now officially enrolled as a first-year law student.

I was sweating. Heavily.

Perspiration beaded up on my forehead, rinsing away the

tinted moisturizer I'd so carefully applied that morning, and my white cotton T-shirt dampened under my armpits in two wet crescents.

Great, I thought, shifting my black leather knapsack on my shoulder and plucking the thin cotton of the shirt away from my skin. Nothing like making an elegant first impression.

It was only nine in the morning, but it must have already been ninety degrees in New Orleans. The late August humidity made the temperature even more oppressive, blanketing the city with a heavy wet heat that was causing my blonde wavy hair to rise up from my head in a halo of frizz. And I thought we'd had heat waves back home in Ithaca, those brief summer spells that baked the spring mud until it was dry and cracked. Graham and I would sit in front of an oscillating fan set on high, wet towels wrapped around our necks, and bemoan our lack of air-conditioning for those nine days a year when we actually needed it.

Back home . . . Only Ithaca wasn't home anymore, and I no longer shared an old Victorian house, with a wraparound porch, poky kitchen, and hideous blue floral wallpaper in its one dated bathroom, with Graham.

Now I lived in New Orleans, in a shabby shotgun-style apartment on the corner of Magazine and Fourth, on the second floor of a converted Greek Revival house. The house had probably been grand in its glory days but had long since faded into a state of genteel decay. My apartment had no closets, the toilet ran nonstop, and when I walked barefoot across the narrow-planked wooden floors that ran from the living room to the bedroom, the bottoms of my feet turned black from decades of worn-in grime.

My new roommate was a cockroach the size of a rat, which had leapt out at me the night before when I went into the kitchen for a glass of water. I'd shrieked and dropped my glass, only remembering at the precise moment that it shattered on the black-and-white linoleum tiled floor that I still hadn't gotten around to buying a broom and dustpan.

Afterward, I huddled in my bed, giving myself the heebie-jeebies by wondering if the ticklish feeling on my arm was the roach climbing into bed with me.

'You said you wanted to get out of Ithaca,' I now muttered to myself. 'And this is out. Hell, they even have palm trees here.' Palm trees were exotic, the stuff of vacation resorts and *Miami Vice* reruns.

Students streamed past me, most walking in small chatty clusters, on their way into the law school. I still had a few minutes before class started, so I held back and tried to figure out what the hell I was smelling. It wasn't the sweetly Southern aroma of magnolias and mint juleps I'd expected, but instead an odd odor of burned toast that hung in the air.

Just then, a tall, thin woman strolled by. She had a sleek dark bob that reminded me of Uma Thurman's in *Pulp Fiction*, and she looked effortlessly elegant in slinky jeans, a slim-fitting charcoal-gray T-shirt, and black leather thong sandals. An equally tall skinny guy with spiky brown hair and a nose ring loped along next to her. He was gesticulating wildly as he talked, and the brunette threw back her head in appreciative laughter at whatever it was he was saying. I watched them turn into the law school, disappearing behind the heavy glass doors.

Was I the only person at this goddamned school who didn't know anyone?

'Excuse me,' a voice said. I pivoted around to see who it belonged to.

The man standing there was roughly my age – late twenties, or possibly early thirties – and he was gazing at me expectantly. He had short dark curly hair that rose in peaks over his high forehead. His nose, peeling from a sunburn, was a little too big for his face and his chin was a little too long, but he had the brightest blue eyes I'd ever seen. 'Are you talking to me?' I asked.

'Yeah, actually, I've been trying to catch up with you since we got off the streetcar,' he said.

I had heard someone calling out after me as I'd trekked across campus. But since I didn't know anyone in New Orleans, much less anyone at Tulane, I'd assumed that whoever it was wasn't talking to me.

'I'm sorry . . . have we met?' I said. I looked at him a little closer. 'Actually, you do look sort of familiar.'

'If I had a dime for every time a woman said that to me. I used to think it was because I was starring in everyone's sexual fantasies,' the guy said. 'Let me guess, I look just like the brother of one of your friends. Or the friend of one of your brothers.'

I laughed. 'No, I don't think so. I don't have a brother.'

'No? Really? That's usually it. Well, then maybe it's because we live in the same building.'

'We do?' I asked. I hadn't met any of the other three tenants in my new apartment building. I hoped he wasn't the person who lived in the other second-floor apartment. Every time I stood on the narrow landing at the top of our shared staircase, fumbling with my key and sticky dead bolt, I could smell cat urine wafting out from under his door. And then, last night, while I was trying to fall asleep after my run-in with the gargantuan cockroach, I'd heard what sounded like someone over there tap dancing, their steps reverberating through the cheap hardwood.

He nodded. 'Yep. I live in the bottom right apartment. I saw you leaving today, and we were on the same streetcar. I was right behind you. We both had to run to catch it. . . .'

I nodded. 'Oh, right. That must be it.'

Now that he mentioned it, I did have a vague memory of someone getting on the streetcar right behind me, joking with the driver as he boarded. I'd taken the rattling green streetcar from my stop at Fourth Street all the way up St. Charles Avenue to the Tulane campus, gawking out the open window at the Greek Revival mansions we passed along the way, sitting like dowager queens on their carefully manicured lawns.

'But that's not why I was trying to stop you. You have a . . .' His voice trailed off, and he looked uncomfortable.

'I have a what?'

'A . . . thingy. Um. Something. Stuck to . . .' He made a vague gesture toward my hips. 'On the back of your skirt,' he said. He blushed and averted his eyes.

I reached back, brushing at my skirt, trying to figure out what he was talking about, what was causing him such obvious embarrassment. And then I felt it.

Oh. *Shit*.

There was a maxipad stuck to my ass.

I could feel the blood flooding to the surface of my skin as I peeled the pad off my skirt and stuffed it into my knapsack. It wasn't used – thank *God* – but still. *Still*. I'd just walked across the entire campus with a sanitary napkin stuck to my skirt.

'Ah. Um. Thank you,' I said stiffly, trying to regain some smidgen of dignity. I glanced nervously at the law school, wondering how many of my new classmates had seen me. Would I spend the next three years known as the Maxi Girl? 'Well. Um. I'd better get to class.'

'Are you a law student too?' the guy asked.

Too? Oh, no.

'Please tell me you're not a first-year law student,' I said, briefly closing my eyes in the hopes that he would disappear. When I opened them, he was still standing there, looking a little confused.

'Yeah, I am.'

'Of course you are,' I said dryly. 'Because this wouldn't have been sufficiently mortifying otherwise.'

At this, he laughed. It was a nice laugh, full and deep.

'Don't worry, I won't tell anyone. So you're a One-L too? I don't remember seeing you at orientation,' he said.

'I wasn't there. My U-Haul truck broke down in Pennsylvania. I spent three days outside Pittsburgh waiting for a replacement,' I said.

'You didn't miss much,' he said. 'They made us wear name tags.'

'Yeah, but now everyone knows everyone else,' I said. 'Except for me.'

'You know me.'

'No, I don't, actually.'

'That we can remedy immediately. I'm Nick Crosby,' he said.

'Hi, Nick. I'm Kate. Kate Bennett,' I said. I sniffed again as the burned-toast aroma became even stronger. 'What is that smell?'

'What smell?'

'You don't smell that? It smells like burned toast.'

'Maybe someone burned some toast,' Nick suggested.

'I don't think so. I smelled it earlier, when I was leaving my apartment. Unless people are burning toast all over the city, all at once,' I said.

'Did you know that carob trees smell like semen?' Nick said.

I blinked. 'What?'

'I thought we were having a conversation about things that smell weird.'

'No. Just the one smell,' I said.

'Right, sorry. So what classes do you have today?'

I consulted the slip of paper the school had sent me over the summer. 'This morning I have Criminal Law with Hoffman. And then Torts with Professor Gupta,' I said.

'Excellent. We must be in the same section,' Nick said. When I looked at him questioningly, he explained. 'They break the One-Ls into four sections. Each section has all of their classes together.'

'Just like at Hogwarts in the Harry Potter books,' I said.

Nick laughed. 'Minus the magic and all of the other cool stuff. Come on, we'd better get in there.'

We walked up the steps, and then Nick held a glass door open for me, and I stepped inside. The ground-floor corridor of the law school was bustling with students standing around in groups or winding their way through the crowd en route to class. Up ahead, to the left, there was a student lounge furnished with green upholstered chairs and couches and lined with glowing vending machines that spat out soda cans with a loud clatter.

'We have mailboxes in there,' Nick told me, pointing to the lounge. 'Only they're not really boxes, they're hanging folders; but, whatever, they call them mailboxes. The Powers That Be have ordered us to check them once a day.'

'You see, you did learn something at orientation. Did I miss anything else?' I asked.

'No, not really. They gave us a tour of the building, told us what to expect at lectures, stuff like that. Mostly it was just a chance for people to meet and settle into cliques at the earliest possible point,' Nick said.

'Oh, good. That makes me feel better,' I said, rolling my eyes.

We turned left and walked to the end of a locker-lined hall, where even more students were milling around, some of them shoving heavy legal books into the lockers before slamming them shut. The hollow metallic clang reminded me of high school. The law school smelled like a high school too, that unmistakable bouquet of tuna fish sandwiches, new sneakers, and freshly shampooed hair.

'Do we have lockers assigned to us?' I asked.

'Yeah, but to get one you have to fill out paperwork at the reception desk we just passed back there,' Nick said. 'Give the Powers That Be your student ID, take a blood oath that you won't deal drugs out of it, promise them your firstborn, and they'll give you your combination.'

When I laughed, the tangle of nerves in my stomach loosened.

Directly ahead of us was a set of heavy wooden doors. Just through it was a large, sunken lecture hall, so that when we stood at the doors, we were at the highest point in the room, looking down. At the front of the hall, a wooden lectern sat on a slightly raised platform. Long tables were bolted into the floor across the center of the room, set up in a stadium style, so that each was on lower level than the one behind it. There were two sets of staircase corridors – the one where I was standing, and another to the right of the long tables. The room was already half filled with our new classmates sitting in green upholstered task chairs lined up behind the tables. Their voices, buzzing with excitement and anxiety, echoed around us. The chic dark-haired girl I'd seen earlier was there, I noticed, along with her skinny companion with the nose ring.

'Do you want to sit here?' Nick asked, gesturing to one of the shorter tables just to our left, which was still empty.

'Sure,' I said. We sat down, and I got out a yellow lined legal pad and a pen. Nick unzipped his black messenger bag and pulled out a thick brown textbook with gold lettering on its face: CRIMINAL LAW, 8TH EDITION, ALAN M. HOFSTEADER.

'You already got your textbook?' I asked him.

Nick's eyebrows arched. 'You didn't?'

'No, I just got into town on Saturday, and since then I've been unpacking and getting groceries and things. I figured I'd just go the bookstore today after class,' I said, trying to keep the shrill edge of panic out of my voice.

Nick nodded. 'That must have been your U-Haul parked in front of the house on Saturday. I saw it when I came back from the library.'

'The library . . . you mean you've already started studying?'

'Yeah, we had a reading assignment for class today.'

'*What?*'

'That's right – you weren't at orientation. They posted the first class assignments over by the student lounge. This class was the worst. We had two chapters to read, and the cases were unbelievably boring. I thought Crim Law would have been the most interesting assignment, but apparently not,' Nick said.

'Oh, no,' I said, slumping forward. 'I'm already behind. Stupid U-Haul . . .'

'Don't worry, I'm sure you won't get called on. What are the odds? There must be over a hundred students in here,' Nick said.

'Called on? He's going to start *calling* on people today?' I asked, and when Nick nodded, my stomach did that dropping thing where it feels like you're falling off a tall building. I *never* thought the professors would be calling on us on the first day of classes.

'Hoffman is supposed to be the worst of the worst when it comes to humiliating students in class. The upperclassmen call him Professor Satan. Actually, I think that's him there,' Nick said, nodding at the back of a man cutting through the students.

I turned and saw a middle-aged man making his way down the stairs. He led with his crotch as he walked, and the fluorescent lights shone on his pate. He reached the front of the room, stepped up on the platform, and turned to face us. From where I sat, he didn't look outwardly satanic. Just your average academic type. He wore the hair he had left a bit too long, and his blue oxford shirt was rumpled. His pants were low on his hips to accommodate his stomach paunch. The professor crossed his arms and leaned forward against his lectern, looking blandly disinterested as he waited for the noise level to drop to a nervous buzz before finally tapering off. When silence stretched across the room, he continued to stare back at us for a few uncomfortable moments.

'This is Introductory Criminal Law. I am Professor Hoffman. If you are in the wrong place, please leave. For those of you who are in the right place, I'm going to go over the ground rules. First, do not be late to my class. We will begin promptly at nine a.m. on Monday, Wednesday, and Friday.

'I will be passing around a seating chart. The seat you are now sitting in will be your seat for the remainder of the semester. Locate your seat on the chart and fill in your name in large block letters.

'My system for calling on students is as follows: Everyone will be called on at least once over the course of the semester. If you volunteer to answer a question during class, you will inoculate yourself from being called on for the rest of that week.

'Office hours are Wednesdays from two to four p.m. Do not bother me at any other time, including before and after lectures. And do not waste my time during office hours by asking questions that were addressed during the lecture. If you attempt to do so, I will not be pleased. And I assure you, ladies and gentlemen, you do not want to displease me. Any questions? Good. Open your casebooks to chapter one,' Hoffman said. His biting voice had just the faintest trace of a Northeastern accent. Connecticut? I wondered. Rhode Island, maybe.

Nick opened his book and moved it between us on the table so that I could share it with him. I shot him a grateful look and began speed-reading through the introductory paragraphs of the chapter, praying that I wouldn't be called on.

'Ms Bennett, I don't like to be kept waiting,' Hoffman snapped. 'Stand up now.'

Finally my legs obeyed me, and as I stood shakily, my chair rolled backward, turning as it went, so that the hard, curved plastic of the armrest was pressing into my right thigh. My hands shook slightly as I clasped and then unclasped them, and I tried to resist the urge to wipe my slick palms on the front of my skirt. Nick gave me a tight-lipped smile of encouragement and pushed his book even closer to me.

'Define *mens rea*,' Professor Hoffman said. He continued to stare at me blandly, with eyes that were light and flat, like a shark's.

'I don't know,' I admitted. 'My moving van broke down, and so I missed orientation and I didn't know there was a reading assignment due today. I'm sorry. I'll be prepared next time.'

I started to sit down.

'I didn't tell you to sit. I asked you to define the term *mens rea* for the class,' Hoffman said.

My mouth went dry and my throat was so scratchy, it felt like I'd swallowed a handful of sand. He wasn't going to let me off the hook, I realized. He was going to make an example out of me in front of everyone. I slowly stood back up, my legs shaky.

'Um . . . I don't know. I'll have to pass,' I said lamely. I crossed my arms in front of me, pressing my elbows down so that no one would be able to see my sweaty armpits.

'I don't allow passing in my class,' Hoffman said.

Mens rea, mens rea, I thought wildly. I'd watched every episode of *Law & Order* at least three times. Hadn't Assistant District Attorney Jack McCoy used that term during that episode with the teenager who'd killed his friend? It had something to do with . . .

'Is that . . . does that mean . . . the mental state of a . . . um, criminal . . . person?' I asked, stumbling over the words.

'Are you asking me or telling me?' Hoffman asked.

Asshole, I thought, biting down so hard, the muscles in my jaw twinged.

'*Mens rea* refers to the, um, mental state of a criminal,' I said loudly.

'And why is that important?'

'Because a person's intent when they commit a crime is important for . . . um . . . determining . . . um . . . what kind of a crime . . . it is,' I said, hoping that that made sense. I had a feeling that Jack McCoy had been more eloquent when he was explaining it to the police detectives.

'And what are the four levels of criminal intent under the Model Penal Code?' Hoffman asked.

Four levels? I didn't have the slightest fucking clue. *Law & Order* wasn't going to save me now.

'Ms Bennett?' Hoffman said.

I shook my head. 'I don't know,' I mumbled.

Hoffman strode to the whiteboard behind his lectern, picked up a black Magic Marker, and began writing: PURPOSELY, KNOWINGLY, RECKLESSLY, NEGLI-GENTLY. Then he drew a line under the four words, and below the line wrote: STRICT LIABILITY.

'This is a basic concept of criminal law,' Hoffman said, pointing to the board with the uncapped marker. 'Your inability to answer does not bode well for how you'll do in my class. I gather it would be a waste of everyone's time to ask you for a summary of *Staples v. U.S.*?'

Somehow his bland, sneering tone was worse than if he'd yelled at me.

'Yes,' I said in a small voice.

'You can sit down now. And don't come to my class unprepared ever again,' Hoffman said.

I reached behind me for my chair, sat down shakily, and edged it back toward the table. Resting my hands on my forehead, I stared at Nick's casebook, but the words on the pages didn't make any sense. They just floated around, an impenetrable sea of tiny type.

'That wasn't so bad. Could have been a lot worse. At least you were able to answer a few of his questions,' Nick whispered. His breath was warm on my ear and smelled like mint toothpaste.

I just shook my head at him and tried to focus on the casebook. If that was how Hoffman treated a student who was unprepared, I could only imagine how he'd deal with our whispering in the middle of a lecture. I certainly wasn't about to find out.

I was in the back of the student-union bookstore, where the
law textbooks were shelved, when a giggling female voice
from the other side of the stacks said, 'I heard Professor
Hoffman made a One-L cry in class today.'

I clutched a Torts textbook up to my chest, holding it like
a shield, and crouched down before they could see me.

'He did! She was in my class. It was awful; she practically
broke down right in the middle of the lecture,' her friend
replied.

'I'm so glad I didn't end up with him. I heard he's the
hardest professor in the whole damned school,' the first
woman said. 'You want to go get a coffee?'

'Sure. I just have to buy my Contracts book.'

Great, I thought. I slid down a little farther, until I was
sitting on the ground, leaning against the book stacks, hoping
they'd leave without seeing me. And as if it wasn't bad enough
that they were gossiping about me, they didn't even have their
facts straight. I hadn't broken down. I'd spent the remaining
hour of class staring down at Nick's textbook. Only after
Hoffman had finished – ending his lecture with the menacing
warning, 'I expect everyone will be prepared for Wednesday's
lecture. No excuses this time' – did I pack up my supplies and
hurry out of the lecture hall. I heard Nick call out to me, but
I didn't stop.

Now, sitting on the cold floor in the back of the bookstore,

I sighed and rested my forehead against my bent knees, closing my eyes against the series of mortifying events that had been my day thus far. A little bit of bad luck was one thing, but this was turning into an epidemic.

'I surrender. Just make it stop,' I muttered into my knees.

'It really wasn't that bad,' a voice said.

I opened my eyes. Two thin denim-clad legs were standing in front of me. I tilted my head back, looked up, and saw that it was the *Pulp Fiction* girl. She was peering down at me, her slanting eyes sympathetic.

'Really. In a few weeks, no one will even remember,' she said.

'Do you mean the part where I came to school with a maxipad stuck to my skirt, or the part where the professor called me a simpleminded moron in front of the whole class?' I asked.

She laughed. 'He didn't say that,' she said.

'He implied it,' I said darkly.

She reached down, holding out her hand to help me up. 'It's safe to get up now. Those girls who were talking about you left. Besides, I can see your underwear.' She pointed down at my skirt, which was now gaping open, thanks to my bent knees.

'Of course you can,' I said, accepting the proffered hand as I stood. 'Thanks.'

'No problem. I'm Lexi, by the way. Lexi Vandenberg.'

'Kate,' I said.

'I know,' Lexi said. She grinned impishly. 'Kate Bennett. You're infamous.'

Lexi waited for me as I paid for my textbooks, which weighed a ton and looked like they'd burst out of the over-stuffed plastic shopping bags at any minute. Together we walked out of the student union and across the outdoor patio.

'Hey, you guys! Over here!'

Nick was sitting on one of the benches that flanked the

patio. With him was the spiky-haired guy I'd seen with Lexi earlier. A second woman, who had a long tangle of burnished red hair falling around her shoulders, was sitting cross-legged on the ground in front of them, leaning back on one hand and holding a cigarette in the other.

'Hey, Add,' Lexi called out. 'Come on, you have to meet Addison. He's hysterical. Oh, and that's Jen with them. She's in our section too.'

'Is Addison your boyfriend?' I asked.

Lexi let out a snort of laughter.

'As if,' she said. When I looked at her questioningly, she said, 'Wait until you meet him. Add's a riot, but he's not exactly boyfriend material.'

'We were just talking about what a dick Hoffman is,' Nick said, once we reached them. I dropped the heavy bags on the ground, grateful for the rest. My arms felt like they were being stretched out from the weight.

'*Such* a dick,' the redhead said. She was big-boned, with the wide shoulders of an athlete, and her pale white skin was sprayed with freckles. 'I used to work for a law firm in town as a paralegal, and the lawyers there said that Hoffman has a horrible reputation. Total egomaniac. Oh, I'm Jen, by the way,' she added, smiling at me. There was a slight gap between her two front teeth and a dimple in her right cheek.

'And that's Addison,' Lexi said, nodding to the spiky-haired guy.

'Hi.' I sat down awkwardly on the bench next to Nick, scooting forward so that I could see everyone. Addison looked different somehow. 'Weren't you wearing a nose ring earlier?' I asked him.

'It's a clip-on,' Addison said, holding the gold ring up. 'I was hoping it would keep me from getting called on.'

'How so?'

'I thought facial piercings might intimidate the professors,' Addison said, grinning affably. He had a narrow face and a long beaky nose, and wore black-plastic-framed glasses.

'So why didn't you just get your nose pierced?' Nick asked.

'Because that would really fucking hurt,' Addison said.

'Better that than being called on,' I said, sighing. 'Trust me.'

'I heard that Hoffman married one of his students,' Addison said.

Jen snorted. 'I find that hard to believe. Who would find that man attractive?'

'Someone who's into S&M?' Nick guessed. 'Only instead of being into handcuffs and leather, she gets her jollies by having a middle-aged dork scream at her.'

At this everyone laughed, and I could feel my shoulders relax.

'I can't believe I was the first one to get called on,' I said. 'It was like that dream where you're walking around in your underwear.'

'I love that dream,' Addison said.

'I totally know what you mean,' Jen said, ignoring Addison. 'I was white-knuckling it the whole time, praying he wouldn't call on me next. And the guy he called on after you – What was his name? Mr Sobel? – he didn't do any better.'

'At least he'd read the case,' I said.

'Yeah, but he was so nervous he was stuttering,' she said.

'Where are you from, Kate?' Lexi asked.

'I grew up outside of Albany, New York, in Saratoga Springs. But for the past ten years, I've been in Ithaca,' I said. 'I went to school at Cornell, and then after I graduated, I worked in the admissions office.'

'Married? Boyfriend? Any dark secrets?' Lexi continued.

I shook my head. 'Nope. None of the above,' I said, and tried not to feel guilty about the ease with which I was able to push Graham aside. It wasn't like I was lying. He wasn't my boyfriend any longer.

'So, we're all single. Except for Jen; she's married,' Lexi said. Jen nodded at this, and for the first time I noticed the wide gold wedding band etched with interlocking circles on her finger.

'And we all did something else before coming back to law school,' Lexi continued. 'None of us came here straight from college.'

'Where are you from?' I asked.

'I went to NYU and then worked for Bloomingdale's in their PR department,' Lexi said. She tucked a shiny tendril of blue-black hair behind her ear and smiled. Her teeth were very white and straight. It was as if every last detail on her person had been polished. I suddenly realized that Lexi wasn't quite as pretty as I'd originally thought when all I'd seen were glossy hair, slanted eyes, and a slim figure. Her nose was a little too sharp and her lips were too thin.

'Addison's from L.A., and he's been very mysterious about what he did there,' Jen said.

Addison shrugged. 'It's not a mystery. It's just not that exciting. I worked for a few of the studios, did some location scouting.'

'Compared to being a paralegal, working in Hollywood is exciting,' Jen said dryly. 'Anyway, my husband and I were high-school sweethearts – we grew up in Missouri – and we both came here, to Tulane, for undergrad. Then Sean went to med school, and now that he's finishing up his residency, it's my turn to go back to school.'

'D.C.,' Nick said. 'I worked on the Hill as a congressional staffer. Nothing too serious. Mostly I just brokered deals between the various power players. You know, shaping U.S. foreign policy, keeping my finger on the pulse of the country's epicenter. Stuff like that.'

'Is that what they call being the coffee gofer up there?' Jen quipped.

'Hey, watch it. I have CIA contacts,' Nick joked.

'So . . . we should form a study group,' Lexi said. 'We're all in the same section together, and we're all about the same age.

Older than the average One-L. If we stick together, we'll be able to blow everyone else out of the water.'

'I'm in,' Addison said.

'Me too,' Nick said, and Jen nodded.

They all looked at me. 'Sure,' I said, feeling happy for pretty much the first moment since I'd arrived in New Orleans. It had been one misery after another – from getting lost in the maze of streets that made up the Garden District while I was driving around looking for a grocery store, to having to drag almost all of my furniture up the stairs on my own, aided only by a spacey-eyed guy who told me to call him Jimmy-D.

'Like the sausage,' he'd said happily.

Jimmy-D had approached me on the street while I was unlocking the back of the U-Haul and offered to help me move in for twenty bucks. It'd seemed like a good deal, right up until I discovered that he'd stolen my toaster and three pairs of pink satin Victoria's Secret panties.

'May I join your study group?' a voice asked.

I turned and noticed for the first time that there was a girl sitting on the bench behind us. She looked even younger than the undergraduates milling around, but she was dressed like a junior executive in a tan pantsuit and expertly pressed blue oxford shirt. A gold-toned pin of the scales of justice was fastened to the lapel of her suit jacket. She had a mop of brown corkscrew curls framing a serious, pointed face.

'Are you in our section?' Nick asked her.

The girl nodded. 'I'm sorry Hoffman called on you,' she said. 'Although you really should have read the assignment.'

'Ah . . . you're right, I should have,' I said, waiting for her to smile. She didn't. She just looked at me with solemn eyes and then nodded briskly, as though she was satisfied that I appreciated the gravity of my transgression.

'I heard what you were talking about – forming a study group of older students. I came here straight from undergrad, but I'd really like to join your group. I think older students are more likely to take things seriously,' she said.

'Sure, you can join us,' Nick said, smiling at her.

His instincts were markedly nicer than those of the rest of us, all of whom were staring at this girl, who looked so young she ought to be out shopping for a prom dress or running for student-body treasurer.

'What's your name?' Lexi asked her.

'Dana. Dana Mallick,' she said. And then she did smile, a beaming, confident grin. It was the smile of someone who had never failed at anything in her life, the smile of someone who had won student-council campaigns, led the debate club to victory, and delivered a valedictorian speech.

I'd known girls like Dana at Cornell, both during my time as a student there and the subsequent years I spent working in the admissions office. They were earnest and peppy and threw themselves at their schoolwork and activities with tireless enthusiasm. They'd always sit in the front row at lectures, take elaborate notes that would later be filed in a color-coded binder, and would fling their arms up in the air whenever the teacher asked for a volunteer to answer a question or helm a project. When they sent out college applications, they always requested interviews.

'Cornell is a good school. It's my first choice after Harvard and Yale,' they'd say, with the innocent confidence of one who has never had to resort to the desperate ass-kissing that less confident candidates instinctively fall back on. Usually unsuccessfully.

I joined the others in smiling back at Dana, and we introduced ourselves in turn. And then finally Jen blurted out what we were all wondering.

'How old *are* you?'

Dana had the grace to blush. 'Nineteen,' she admitted, looking down at the toe of a perfectly polished black pump with a sensible two-inch heel.

'Nineteen? And you're in law school?' Addison exclaimed. 'That means you're, like, Girl Wonder.'

'Are you a genius?' Lexi asked.

Dana's cheeks stained even darker, and she shrugged. 'I was accelerated, so I graduated from high school and college early,' she said.

I decided to rescue her from further interrogation. 'When should we meet?' I asked. 'And where? Is there room in the library for study groups?'

Nick nodded. 'There is, but when I was there on Saturday, it seemed like it could be sort of a scene. And the librarian had to chase away some undergrads who were hanging out in the reading room.'

'I say we meet Sunday afternoons,' Jen said. 'That way we'll have all weekend to go over our notes from the week before we get together.'

'There's a coffee shop near my house, the Rue de la Course,' Addison said. 'The Rue, for short. It's in the lower Garden District, on Magazine Street, and it's far enough away from campus that it might not be crowded.'

'Sounds perfect. Sundays at the Rue,' Lexi said. She pulled a white box of Marlboro Light cigarettes out of her leather knapsack, packed them against the heel of her hand, and then pulled one out. She lit the cigarette with a light-pink Bic lighter and took a long, satisfied drag on it. The mannerism was fluid and self-possessed, reminding me of a Parisian woman, the kind whose elegance is so natural she can wear a scarf or hat without looking foolish.

'Cool. I'm sure we'll talk before then,' Addison said. He stood and shifted his knapsack onto a thin shoulder. 'Okay, chickadees, I'm going to split.'

'Plan on coming over to my place next Saturday,' Lexi said to him. She nodded at the rest of us. 'All of you. There's a Bar Review that night. We can hang out at my place and then all go together.'

'What's a Bar Review?' Dana asked, frowning. 'Is it a requirement for class?'

Lexi laughed and shook her head. 'No, it's just a party the law school hosts at a bar near campus. They'll have free beer there for law students. It may be lame, but I thought we could check it out.'

'Oh. I can't drink,' Dana said. 'I'm underage.'

'You could still come,' Jen said.

Dana shook her head. 'No, that's okay. I don't have time for parties. I heard that the only way you can make Law Review is if you study pretty much all of the time.'

Was that true? I wondered. I wanted to make Law Review too. Everyone did. At the end of the school year, the illustrious legal journal extended invitations to only ten One-Ls – those with the highest grade point averages in the class. They also had a writing contest in the fall, but that was an even longer shot; they only took five write-ons a year. Being on Law Review meant a whole hell of a lot of extra work for your second and third years at law school, but it was where the top law firms in the country went to recruit and was pretty much the only route to a prestigious judicial clerkship. I knew that the competition for Law Review seats was intense; I just hadn't expected it to start this early.

'You can't study all the time. You'll get burned out,' Jen said.

Dana stood and grabbed her bag. 'I'm used to it,' she said. 'See you all on Sunday.'

'I should go too,' I said. 'I still have to unpack and catch up with the reading assignments.'

'Are you taking the streetcar home?' Nick asked. When I nodded, he said, 'I'll come with you. Help you carry your books.'

'You don't have to,' I protested, but he picked the bags up as he stood.

'Just consider me your own private pack mule,' Nick said, and he grinned. 'See you guys later.'

'Bye,' I said, waving at Lexi, Jen, and Dana. And then I turned and walked with Nick across the lush green Tulane campus.

'Did you hear a guy in our building tap dancing last night?' Nick asked.

'Yes! You heard that too?'

'I was sleeping right under the dance floor,' Nick said. 'Or, I should say, I wasn't sleeping. I went up and knocked on his back door.'

'What did he say?'

'He didn't. He didn't even answer the door. He just turned off all of his lights and got really quiet.'

'What a freak.'

'No kidding. And I think he has about a dozen cats in there too.'

'Great,' I said gloomily. 'A sadistic Criminal Law professor and a next-door neighbour who's a tap-dancing cat freak. It should make for an interesting year.'

It was early in the semester, but there was already a distinct competition brewing between my classmates over who was studying the most. It wasn't enough to simply read the class assignment; we highlighted important passages in our casebooks, outlined the key holdings, and supplemented the class reading with Nutshells, which were like Cliffs Notes for law school. There were law students lined up at the doors every morning when the library opened at eight a.m., and the staffers always had to shoo us out at closing time, at which point we'd stagger out, bleary-eyed and hyped up on coffee. As we scattered into the night, weighed down by knapsacks full of textbooks, my classmates bragged incessantly about how many hours they'd just put in.

And even though I knew it was mostly bullshit and bravado and just part of the bizzare law-school culture, I couldn't help but feel the flutterings of panic. What if people really were studying as much as they claimed? Was it even possible? When did they eat?

The one saving grace was that my fellow One-Ls had finally – *finally* – stopped pointing and whispering when they saw me. The story of my humiliation in Hoffman's class was losing its legs as people turned their attention to their studies.

One night, about a week after classes began, I was in the main reading room at the library, trying to plow through a Civil Procedure case. It was a large room, with approximately thirty long tables and a bank of floor-to-ceiling windows on one side that looked out over the Tulane campus, now dark and studded with lights gleaming out from dorm-room windows and lampposts. Every sound echoed off the high ceiling and wood-paneled walls. A few days earlier, I'd witnessed a tightly wound One-L woman, whom I vaguely recognized from class, shriek at a guy humming softly along to the music on his iPod. Talking was strictly forbidden in the reading room, theoretically punishable by death.

I'd been up late the night before, studying, and the night before that, and I was exhausted. It was like the weariness was clinging to me, pulling me down. The words on the page I was trying to read began to blur, and my head felt unbearably heavy. Maybe if I just rest my eyes for a minute, I thought. Just one minute . . .

The next thing I knew, someone was jostling my shoulder.

'Five more minutes,' I mumbled, swatting at the hand.

The peaceful darkness of sleep was too seductive to resist, and I could feel myself slipping back under when the hand on my shoulder gave me another violent shake, causing my forehead to bump uncomfortably against the table.

My eyes snapped open, and I became aware of several things at once: the bright, buzzing lights. The inky smell of new books. Whispers. Muffled laughter.

Shit, I thought, sitting up suddenly. I looked around wildly. Jen was standing there – she'd been the one shaking my shoulder – grinning down at me. And she wasn't the only one . . . As I glanced around, I realized that nearly every person in the reading room was staring at me. Some were laughing; others looked annoyed. I blinked in confusion.

And then a thought occurred to me, one that caused my face to flame with embarrassment.

'Please tell me I wasn't snoring,' I whispered to Jen.

She reached out and peeled a square yellow Post-it note off my cheek, a gesture that increased the hilarity among my rapt audience.

'I could tell you that. But I'd be lying,' Jen said.

I closed my eyes for a minute, wondering if anyone had actually ever died from humiliation. I'd snored for years, since I was a kid. My parents, my friends, everyone who ever heard me, teased me mercilessly about it.

'If you ever decide to get married, Katie-belle, you'd better pick a sound sleeper,' my dad had advised me more than once.

I used to hold out hope that my snoring was cute, endearing even, until my college roommate decided to disabuse me of this notion by taping me one night. It was awful – I sounded like a dying rhinoceros.

I opened my eyes and looked at Jen pleadingly. 'Please just kill me now,' I said.

'Come on, let's get out of here,' she advised.

We walked over to P.J.'s, which was still doing a brisk business despite the late hour. We ran into Lexi, also on a study break, and after we'd ordered iced lattes all around, the three of us returned to the law-school courtyard to sit and drink our coffee.

'How late are you staying tonight?' Lexi asked.

'I have at least another three hours of work tonight, and its' already . . .' I checked my watch. 'Shit, it's already nine o'clock. I had no idea I'd been here for so long.'

'That's because the law school is like a black hole. You go in and lose all sense of time,' Jen said. 'In a bad way.'

It was a warm, sticky night out, and the air felt damp against my skin. Lexi and Jen lit cigarettes, and the rich perfume of the tobacco filled the air, mixing in with the smells of freshly cut grass and grease from the nearby dorm dining hall.

'So, Kate, what's up with you guys?' Lexi asked.

'Who?' I asked.

'Who do you think? You and Nick,' she said, and smiled knowingly.

'Nick? Nothing,' I said, shaking my head. 'We're just friends.'

Law school resembled high school in more ways than one. I didn't know if it was the enormous pressure we were under or a result of the microcosm we spent our days in, but everyone seemed to regress. Gossip, especially speculation over who was sleeping with whom, had become a popular topic of conversation. I guess it was more interesting than chatting about the Uniform Commercial Code.

'Oh, come on. You guys are always together. There must be something going on,' Lexi said.

It was true; Nick and I had been spending a lot of time together. It was sort of inevitable. We lived in the same house and had all of our classes together, so we usually carpooled into school or else rode the streetcar together. The night before, Nick had helped me put together the computer desk I'd bought in a flat cardboard box from an office supply store, and the night before that we'd shared a cheap Papa John's pizza, dipping the slices into the greasy garlic dipping sauce.

'Really, we're just friends,' I said again. 'Anyway, I broke up with my boyfriend just before school started. I'm not ready to get involved with anyone right now.'

'Why? What happened?' Lexi asked. She tucked one long slim leg under the other and looked at me with interest.

'What do you mean?'

'Why did you break up?'

It was a good question. And the truth was, I really wasn't entirely sure what had gone wrong between Graham and me.

We had gone out for Chinese on our first date, and by the time we were cracking open our fortune cookies, we both thought that this was It, that the person sitting across the table was The One. We immediately started dating exclusively – dinners out, Sunday-morning pancakes, long walks across the picturesque Cornell campus on crisp autumn afternoons. A year later we were moving into the seventy-year-old Victorian house that had seemed so charming when the Realtor first showed it to us. The lace curtains at the windows, the huge bay window in the living room, the elaborate crown molding.

Graham was the most intensely focused person I'd ever met. He was an academic by profession but a student by nature; he loved to learn about things. His interests changed – in the time we were together, he took up snowboarding, Russian literature, modern architecture, chess, and wood-working. He'd study his topic voraciously and learn every-thing there was to be learned about it. And then, after a time, his interest would burn out and he'd move on to something new.

In the beginning, it was this passion, this intensity, that attracted me to him. I loved watching his face glow with interest while he read, loved how his excitement would light him up. My previous boyfriend hadn't been passionate about much of anything, outside of his softball league. But then I started to tire of feeling lonely even when Graham was sitting next to me, his attention absorbed in a book or paper. It didn't help that our sex life had grown stale, to the point that much of the time it felt like we were more roommates than lovers. And, after a while, one thought kept flitting through my mind: There has to be something more out there. Not some*one*, although, yes, that would be nice too. But some*thing* else – a different career, a different path, a different life.

But that was probably too much detail to go into on a study break.

'Nothing too dramatic. We'd grown apart, and most days it felt like we were more platonic roommates than romantically involved. And then I decided to go to law school down here, and he got a job offer for a tenured position at Arizona State – he's a professor of astronomy. It just seemed like a good time to split up,' I said.

I left out the part where Graham had agreed to come to New Orleans with me – he'd been offered an instructor position at Loyola, a lateral move from his current job at Ithaca College. And for the first time in a long while, I'd felt excited about our relationship again. Maybe this was what we needed – a new city, a fresh start. But then the offer from

Arizona State came through. I understood why Graham wanted to take the job – it meant more money, more prestige, job security. But he hadn't even discussed it with me. He'd just taken the job and assumed I'd change my plans.

'You can go to law school in Arizona,' he'd said.

'No, I can't. It's too late now to apply for the fall semester,' I argued.

'So, you wait a year and go next fall instead. Big deal.'

'I don't want to do that.'

Graham spent another three months trying to talk me into going to Arizona with him – he even started to make noise about "maybe" getting engaged – and when I refused, he withdrew into a tight-lipped silence. The day he moved out, his suitcase packed and the plane ticket to Arizona jammed in his pocket, I wondered if I'd just made the biggest mistake of my life.

'Still. That's no reason to swear off men altogether,' Jen now said. 'I think that will be my goal of the year – finding Kate a new and better man.'

'Shouldn't your goal have something to do with, I don't know, law school? Like getting good grades, or making Law Review?' I asked.

Jen made a face. 'Spoilsport.'

'What about finding me a new and better man?' Lexi asked. 'Although I do have my eye on someone.'

'Addison?' Jen asked. She'd obviously made the same assumption I had.

Lexi laughed, and as she did so, a plume of smoke shot out from her mouth. 'Oh, my God, are you serious? Addison? No way!'

'Well, you two are always together,' Jen said.

Lexi waved her hand, dismissing the idea. 'We just bonded over cigarettes at orientation and ended up in the same section. But, no, I'm definitely not interested in him. I'm not even sure if he's straight,' Lexi said.

'Why, did he tell you that he's gay?' Jen asked.

'No, but he's way too sketchy about his past. I can tell he's trying to hide something,' Lexi said.

'You think he's in the closet?' I asked. 'That's kind of weird, don't you think? He's a thirty-year-old single guy – why not just be up-front about who he is?'

'I don't know for sure. It's just a feeling I got,' Lexi said, shrugging. 'I mean, we've been hanging out a lot, and he's never hit on me. Not once.'

'Nick hasn't hit on me, and I'm pretty sure he's not gay,' I said.

'Addison just seems . . . asexual to me,' Lexi said vaguely. 'Anyway, even if he is straight, he's totally not my type.'

'Who is?' Jen asked.

Lexi leaned in. 'Do you know Jacob Reid?' she asked quietly.

'The name sounds familiar,' I said, trying to remember where I'd heard it. I still hadn't put names to faces.

'Jacob Reid . . . Wait – do you mean *Professor* Reid?' Jen asked, her eyes suddenly round.

Lexi nodded and smiled coolly.

'He's a professor *here*? At the law school? Is that even allowed?' I asked. Romantic relationships between faculty and students had been strictly prohibited at Cornell – in fact, it was pretty much a surefire way for a professor to ruin his or her career.

Lexi shrugged. 'He's not *my* professor, so I don't see what the problem is. It's not like he'd have a conflict of interest.'

'He is really good-looking,' Jen said.

'Isn't he? And he's got an incredible body. I saw him at the gym working out, and I have to tell you, he looks amazing in jogging shorts,' Lexi said. 'While I was talking to him, he lifted up the hem of his T-shirt to wipe his hands, and his abs were rock hard. I think he caught me staring.'

'I don't know who he is,' I said.

'Yes, you do, I pointed him out to you yesterday,' Lexi said. 'When we were in the lounge checking our mail folders.'

'Oh, that guy? I thought he was a student,' I exclaimed.

'He's just here for a year as a visiting professor, but he said that if it goes well, he might be offered a tenured position. He teaches Income Tax and Commercial Paper,' Lexi said.

'Did he seem interested in you?' Jen asked.

Lexi looked at her with an expression that bordered on smugness. *What do you think?* her face seemed to say. But then Lexi's face softened into a smile, and she said, 'I think so. He did tell me that he was going to be at the Bombay Club on Saturday night. He said he hoped to see me there.'

A group of guys exited the law school. We watched as they congregated by the back door, joking with one another and laughing.

'I think they're in our section,' Jen said.

'They are. I recognize the tall blond guy,' Lexi said.

'He's cute,' Jen said. 'His friend too. Is either of them your type, Kate?'

'Please don't try to fix me up with anyone. I'm begging you,' I said, shaking my head.

'What? I was just making casual conversation,' Jen said, although her grin gave her away.

'Hey, you're the girl that Hoffman creamed in class last week,' one of the guys said as he approached us. I didn't recognize him; he was short and broad-shouldered and had the thick, shiny dark hair of a Prell girl.

'That's me,' I said, smiling tightly. My notoriety did not thrill me.

'What's your name?' Lexi asked flirtatiously. She tipped her head to one side and narrowed her eyes.

'Scott,' he said.

Lexi smiled creamily. I watched her, realizing for the first time that Lexi was the sort of woman who reveled in male attention. The type had always made me wary.

'I remember. Mr Brown, right? Professor Legrande called on you in Contracts yesterday,' Lexi said.

'That's right,' he said, grinning at her.

I remembered him too. Scott Brown had remained poised while handling a line of questions. He'd flubbed one of the answers but ended up deflecting it with a joke that amused the class and Professor Legrande. I had no doubt Mr Brown was headed toward a career in a courtroom – I could already picture him in a dark suit and red tie, charming the jury with his sugary Southern accent.

'You're in my section?' Scott asked.

'We all are,' Jen said. 'I'm Jen, this is Lexi, and that's Kate.'

'Kate, right. Man, that was harsh the way Hoffman called on you. The entire time you were standing there, I was just cringing,' he continued.

'Me too,' I muttered.

'Hey, Berk, come here,' Scott called out. A tall, heavyset guy with shaggy blond hair and hangdog brown eyes left the group still standing by the front door and walked over. 'This is Pete Berkus. He's a One-L too, but he's in a different section. Berk, this is that chick I was telling you about, the one that Hoffman demolished.'

'Oh, yeah. You're the one who cried in class, right?' Berk asked.

'I didn't cry!'

'He made her stand up while he grilled her. Man, it was painful,' Scott said. He hooted with laughter.

'Gee, thanks,' I said. My face flushed a hot red.

'Just ignore him,' Jen said, patting my leg soothingly.

'Aw, I'm just teasin'. It could have happened to any of us. Hey, I got called on yesterday,' Scott said.

'Yeah, but you did great,' Lexi said, slanting her eyes toward him. She tossed her dark hair back over her shoulder.

'I'm so glad I didn't get stuck in your section. I've heard that Hoffman is a prick,' Berk said. 'All of my professors seem okay so far.'

'Lucky you,' I said.

4

My parents were married on New Year's Eve. My mom claimed that they chose the date so they'd always be able to celebrate each passing year of marriage with a big blowout of a party. My dad, the more pragmatic of the two, disagreed; he said my mom just wanted to make sure he'd never forget their anniversary.

Even so, the New Year's Eve/anniversary party became a family tradition, going back as long as I could remember. My parents' friends – and, later, my friends too – would come over to our house every year to celebrate. My mom always served fondue, a nut-encrusted cheese ball, and meatballs that were basted in grape jelly and chili sauce and then kept warm in a Crock-Pot. My dad would pull out his old Dave Brubeck and Bill Evans Trio records. Everyone drank too much and got a little loopy.

Their twenty-fifth wedding anniversary fell in the middle of my sophomore year of college, and my mom was planning to go all out for the party. This year, there would be a caterer and a bartender and waiters circulating with trays of chicken saté skewers and sea scallops wrapped in bacon. A pianist in a tuxedo and tails would play jazzy show tunes. The engraved invitations would request that everyone dress in formal wear. It would be, my mother proclaimed, an Event.

'Guess what?' Mom said one night. It was midway through the fall semester at Cornell, and she'd called me at my dorm, interrupting my Modern American History homework.

'What?' I asked, only half listening as I scanned the reading assignment on the Civil Rights Movement.

'I ordered new furniture for the living room,' Mom announced. Her voice was breathy, as if she'd been running laps around the house before she called. 'It got here today. Oh, Kate, it's gorgeous. The sofa is sage green chenille, and there's an armchair and ottoman, both of which are covered with the most beautiful striped fabric that coordinates with the sofa. I can't wait until you see it.'

'That sounds nice,' I said without much enthusiasm. 'I didn't know you were redecorating.'

'It's for the party.'

'You got new furniture just for a party?' I asked.

'I want the house to look nice. And we needed new living-room furniture anyway. I thought this was a good time to do it,' Mom said.

'Oh,' I said. And as I lay on my narrow bed, looking up at a poster of Monet's *Water Lilies* stuck to the puce cinder-block wall opposite me, I silently promised myself that I would never be as boring and suburban as my mother.

The party was a huge hit. Everyone had a great time drinking too much (including the pianist, who guzzled down a bottle of bourbon and then passed out, face-first, on the piano) and dancing late into the night. My mom wore a sparkly black sequined cocktail dress and had her hair and makeup professionally done. Just before midnight, my parents hooked their elbows together as they drank a cham-pagne toast. I snapped a picture just as they lifted the flutes to their lips, but it didn't come out well; in it, both of my parents have sallow yellow skin and glowing red eyes.

Five weeks later, on a chilly February night, a young doctor left his bachelor party after downing an untold number of Martinis and lost control of his BMW when he hit a patch of black ice. The car went careening into the oncoming lane. My parents were on their way home from the movies, and

though my father had likely seen the car coming, the investigating officer told me there probably hadn't been time for
him to swerve out of the way.

'It would have happened very quickly,' the assistant
medical examiner later told me. 'They wouldn't have felt
anything.'

I just nodded and stared down at my scuffed L.L. Bean
duck boots.

How do you know what they felt? I wanted to say as anger
bubbled up through the heavy blanket of grief. *You didn't even
know them.*

The Bar Review that the law school threw for us at Tipitina's
was the first chance I'd had to see what my classmates were
like outside the pressure cooker of law school. The answer:
They were pretty much the same.

Everyone was still posturing, still trying to impress one
another. The free beer lubricated things, though, and eventually conversations moved on from who had started their class
outlines (normally phrased to freak out anyone who hadn't:
'You mean you haven't started outlining yet? Are you serious?') and early speculation on who would make Law
Review, to the more normal topics of where people had gone
to college and what had brought them to Tulane.

I had a beer and spent most of the night hanging out with
Jen, Nick, and Addison. We didn't see much of Lexi; she was
too busy flirting. Pete Berkus in particular seemed besotted
with her and looked visibly annoyed whenever she talked to
another guy.

Lexi intercepted me on my way to the bathroom.

'What are you doing after this?' she asked.

'I'm so tired, I'm just going to head home. But I think Nick
and Addison, and maybe Jen, are going to check out a bar
called the Maple Leaf. It's over near campus,' I said.

'I'm going to go to the Bombay Club,' Lexi said casually.

'By yourself?' I asked, but then suddenly I remembered

that the professor she was interested in was going to be there. 'Oh, that's right. Have fun. But be careful.'

'Always am,' Lexi said. She gave me a saucy wink.

When I returned from the ladies' room, a perky blonde coed wearing a pink sparkly cutoff shirt and low-slung jeans that showed off a diamond belly ring had joined our group. She was holding on to Nick's arm, laughing up at him.

'I think you have some competition,' Jen said.

I glanced at the giggling blonde and shook my head. 'I already told you, there's nothing going on between us,' I said.

'Nothing going on with whom?' Addison said.

'No one,' I said.

'Nick,' Jen said.

'Nick? I thought you said Kate had the hots for that Scott guy.'

I turned to Jen, my mouth open. 'What?' I said.

'I didn't say that,' Jen said, giving Addison a warning look. 'I just said I thought you'd make a cute couple.'

'Jen wants to marry everyone off,' Addison said.

'I have my eye on someone for you too,' Jen said.

'Oh, yeah? Who?' Addison asked eagerly.

Jen nodded toward a tall, good-looking black guy I recognized from our section. He had wide shoulders and a shaved head and was wearing a white polo shirt.

'What . . . *him*? Are you kidding me?' Addison stared at her, aghast.

'You think he's out of your league?' Jen asked sympathetically.

'I'm not gay!'

'You're not?' Jen looked confused. She frowned. 'But Lexi said . . .'

'Lexi told you I was *gay*?'

'Well, no, not in those exact words . . .'

'Because I'm not,' he said hotly.

'Okay,' Jen said.

'I'm entirely one hundred percent hetero.'

'Fine,' Jen said soothingly. She looked to me for help, but I just grinned.

'Serves you right for trying to play Cupid,' I told her.

'I just want my friends to be happy,' she said. 'And you have to admit, Add, that guy is hot.'

'I admit no such thing,' Addison said. 'And now, if you'll excuse me, I'm going to go find a woman to hit on.'

He stalked off in the direction of the bar.

Nick drove me home in his little Mini Cooper.

'This car is so cute,' I said.

Nick shot me a dirty look. 'It's not "cute." Babies are cute. Kittens are cute. This car is cool and hip,' he said.

'And don't forget fuel-efficient,' I said. 'So, who was your girlfriend?'

'Who?'

'The blonde teenager who was dry-humping you at the bar,' I reminded him.

'Ah. Tiffy,' Nick said fondly. 'She's actually a sophomore at Loyola. She said she's majoring in Pre-Law, but what she really wants to do is move to Las Vegas and be a showgirl.'

'It's good to have a dream,' I said.

'She gave me her number,' Nick said. He held up his hand, where a phone number was written in black ink on the back, along with TIFFY–CALL ME!!! She'd dotted the 'i' in 'Tiffy' with a heart-shaped bubble. 'She said she wants to get together sometime so I can tell her what law school is *really* like.'

'Jesus,' I said, rolling my eyes at the blatant come-on. 'Tell her it's like the army: First they grind you down, and then they build you back up. Only instead of soldiers, they turn us into humorless robots set to destroy mode.'

'I take it you're not enjoying school,' Nick said.

'I don't think anyone with a soul enjoys law school,' I said.

'So why do it?'

'It's a means to an end,' I quipped, mostly because the

truth – that I'd undergone some sort of quarter-life crisis, where I felt an inexplicable urge to Make A Change Before It Was Too Late – sounded silly and juvenile. Normal people, adult people, don't quit their jobs, break up with their boyfriends, and move across the country, only to spend several years of their life and many thousands of dollars embarking on a career they've only been exposed to through movies and television shows. In fact, when I thought about it, which wasn't often, that was what my future career felt like – something distant and vague, something that was going to happen to someone else. The only thing I was sure about was this: A law degree meant I'd always have a job, and a relatively well-paying one at that. A law degree meant safety.

'Hmmm. That's an enigmatic response,' Nick said.

'Well . . . I have to believe that practicing law will be more rewarding than law school has turned out to be,' I said.

'Believe . . . or hope?'

'Right now, believe. And please don't ruin it for me; it's all I have to cling to,' I said.

He drove around Lee Circle and then up St. Charles, making a left on Third Street and a right on Magazine Street. He pulled up in front of our apartment building and shifted the car into park.

'Thanks for the ride,' I said.

'Are you sure you don't want to come to the Maple Leaf with us?' Nick asked.

I nodded. 'I have to study tomorrow. I don't want to be up too late.'

'We all have to study. Some of us are just in denial about it,' Nick said.

I laughed and turned toward him. His face was shadowed, backlit by the streetlamps along Magazine Street and the occasional passing car, but I could tell that he was smiling at me. I was suddenly reminded of my first kiss. I was a freshman in high school and had gone to see *Uncle Buck* with John Sissal, a junior I'd had a crush on for ages. John had parked his car in my driveway, and just before he leaned over to kiss me, darkness and light had played across his face in much the same way.

And for a moment, I wondered if there *was* something there between Nick and me. A spark of interest, a sign that maybe this wasn't just a platonic friendship after all. And then Nick leaned forward, and I thought, *He's going to kiss me*, and excitement flared inside me.

But he didn't kiss me. He was looking out the window past me, up at the house.

'There's a man on our porch,' Nick said instead.

I turned, looking to see what Nick was talking about. He was right. There was a man loitering on our raised porch. He was of medium height and build and wearing tortoiseshell glasses that were too large for his narrow face.

I recognized those glasses. In fact, I recognized everything about him.

'It's Graham,' I said faintly.

'Who?' Nick asked.

'My ex-boyfriend.'

5

The Rue de la Course occupied a large storefront on Magazine Street in the Garden District. The coffee shop had dark, creaky wooden floors, tall windows, and rows of charmingly mismatched tables and chairs. Along the back of the store, there was a long coffee bar, complete with a stainless silver espresso machine and a glass counter full of decadent desserts. Two dozen ceiling fans rotated lazily above.

Lexi and Jen were already at the Rue when I arrived on Sunday afternoon. They'd pulled a few tables together so there'd be enough chairs to go around, and I sat down with them, placing my steaming white latte mug on the table in front of me.

'Hi,' I said.

They both looked at me expectantly. I quickly surmised that Nick had spread the news of my surprise visitor. It was going to be hard to keep a secret with this group.

'So . . .?' Jen asked. She was wearing a pink-and-green-striped rugby shirt, khaki shorts, and pink Dr. Scholl's sandals.

'So what?' I asked innocently.

'Come on, just tell us,' Lexi said. 'We know your ex made a surprise appearance last night.'

'Oh, that,' I said. I took a sip of my latte; it was so hot, it burned my tongue. 'Well . . .'

*

'Graham . . . what are you doing here?' I'd asked, when I reached him on the porch.

'Hi, Kate,' Graham said, pulling me into an embrace. He kissed the side of my neck, his lips lingering against my skin. It was something he'd done a thousand times in the past, but that was before – before we broke up, before we moved apart.

I stepped back, moving away. Nick was still idling at the curb, waiting to make sure everything was okay. I waved at him, and he nodded and waved back and then drove off uptown.

'Who was that?' Graham asked.

'Nick. My neighbor. And you haven't answered my question. What are you doing here?'

Graham gazed at me, his green eyes intent on my face. With his high, carved cheekbones, thick eyelashes, and full mouth, Graham was handsome – extremely handsome – but in an almost feminine way, which I knew he hated. The clumsy glasses and closely cropped hair were an attempt to draw attention away from his sensually soft features.

'I came to see you. I've missed you,' Graham said. And then he leaned over to kiss me, his lips pressing against mine.

'Are you getting back together?' Lexi asked, after I finished.

I shrugged. It had been so late, we'd put off any serious discussion of our relationship, and Graham had spent the night on the couch – at my request.

'I don't know. Maybe,' I said.

'I suppose this means I'll have to tell Scott that you're not interested in him after all,' Jen said thoughtfully.

'Huh?' I said.

'I saw Scott Brown at the library this afternoon,' Jen said. 'Your name came up.'

'Please tell me you didn't try to set me up with him. Please,' I said.

'Oh, no, nothing like that. I just got the feeling he was into you,' Jen assured me. 'Anyway, Lexi was filling me in on her new romance when you got here.'

'That's right, I forgot. What happened with the professor?' I asked.

'Shhhh,' Lexi said, glancing around to make sure we weren't overheard. The Rue was empty, except for a couple of college kids sitting at one table and a pair of young mothers camped out with their offspring at another. 'No one can know. Jacob could get in trouble for dating a student.'

'So I take it things went well,' I said.

Lexi grinned, looking enormously pleased with herself. 'Very, *very* well.'

'Berk is going to be brokenhearted,' I said.

'What?' Lexi looked puzzled.

'Berk. You know ... Pete Berkus. The guy you were hanging out with at Tipitina's last night. He was really into you,' I said.

Lexi shrugged this news off. 'Anyway, after Jacob and I left the bar, I went over to his place, and ...'

'You didn't tell me that!' Jen exclaimed.

'I was just getting to it when Kate came in,' Lexi said.

'What happened?' Jen asked breathlessly. She was on the edge of her seat, leaning forward.

'Nothing. I mean, we kissed a little, but mostly we just talked and listened to some music. But it was still really romantic. Jacob is amazing. Smart, funny, and – unlike every guy I've ever dated – he's a real grown-up.' Lexi sighed happily.

'You two are so lucky,' Jen bemoaned. 'I miss romance.'

'I don't know if having an ex-boyfriend camped out on my couch really qualifies as romance,' I said.

'Oh, yes, it does. Especially the part where he came to find you because he couldn't bear living without you,' Jen said.

'That's not exactly what he said,' I replied.

'Just showing up is a romantic gesture,' Jen insisted.

'Sean isn't romantic?' Lexi asked.

'Once you get married, you never get to have a first kiss again. Or that nervous butterfly feeling in your stomach when you see someone you have a crush on. And romance . . .' Jen paused to snort. 'Unless you find it romantic to pick your husband's dirty clothes up off the bedroom floor for the four hundredth time – because, despite the fact that he graduated with honors from medical school, he can't grasp the concept of a laundry hamper – you're shit out of luck.'

'Hey, chickadees. Shit out of luck about what?' Addison asked, slinging his knapsack on the ground and sitting down at the table. He was wearing a faded black Pink Floyd concert T-shirt, gray sweat shorts, and his black-rimmed glasses.

'Nothing,' Jen said. 'Just girl talk.'

'Do you want to know what I figured out today? Three hundred and fifty-seven thousand dollars,' Add said.

We looked at him.

'That's the answer. It's like *Jeopardy!* You're now supposed to say, "What is *blank*" ', Addison explained.

'I don't know . . . Is it the salary of a big-firm attorney?' Lexi guessed.

'Not an associate,' I said. 'Not even Manhattan associates make that much.'

'It's the amount I'll end up shelling out in the thirty years it takes me to pay off my law-school loans,' Addison said.

Jen sucked in her breath.

'That much?' Lexi asked. She dropped her pen on her notebook and gave a little shiver.

'If you borrow the maximum for the entire three years that we're here. And that's not counting undergraduate loans,' Addison said.

'Oh, my God,' Lexi said. 'That's what I'll owe too.'

'That's the upside of being married. I only had to take out loans for tuition, not living expenses,' Jen said. 'Which is a good thing, since Sean's med-school loans are huge.'

The three of them looked at me, and I flushed.

'My parents . . . well, they had a life-insurance policy,' I said. 'It wasn't huge, but it's enough for me to get through school.'

This was met with silence, which I understood. It wasn't exactly as though they could respond with *Lucky you*.

'Am I late?' Dana asked, scraping a chair back from the table and sitting down. Her face was flushed, and her hair was pulled back into a high curly ponytail, like Pebbles from *The Flintstones*.

'No, Nick isn't here yet,' Lexi said. 'Why didn't he drive over with you, Kate?'

'I don't know what happened to him. I knocked on his door before I left, and he wasn't there. His car wasn't in its usual spot either,' I reported.

'I didn't see him at the library this morning,' Addison said.

'I think he hooked up last night,' Jen said. 'When we were at the Maple Leaf, Nick spent the entire time playing pool with some chick. I think she was a med student. A med student with breast implants.'

'Mmmm, breast implants,' Addison said dreamily.

'Should we start without him?' Dana asked, ignoring our gossip.

Lexi looked at her, eyebrows arched. 'Were you at church or something before you came here?'

Dana's face colored. She was wearing a navy blue short-sleeve sweater over a long blue-and-yellow-floral skirt, while the rest of us were wearing jeans or shorts. I hadn't even bothered brushing my hair that morning and instead just put on a black baseball hat.

'I was at the library,' Dana said defensively. 'I like to wear real clothes when I study. It helps keep me focused.'

'What did I miss?' Nick asked, appearing beside the table. He looked like he hadn't slept or showered – or even changed his clothes from the night before. Sporting a day's worth of stubble and smelling strongly of smoke, he collapsed into the chair next to me.

I wrinkled my nose. 'No offense, Nick, but you smell like a bar. And not in a good way.'

'Coffee . . . I need coffee,' he croaked.

'Kate tells us you didn't make it home last night,' Jen said, winking at me.

'Keeping tabs on me?' Nick asked irritably.

'Don't be so cranky. I just stopped by your apartment before I came over, and you weren't there,' I explained.

'So . . . let's have it?' Lexi asked, tipping her head coyly to one side.

Nick shook his head. 'A gentleman does not kiss and tell,' he said piously. 'Unless someone wants to buy my virtue with a cup of coffee.'

'I'll go,' Addison said. 'Anyone else want anything? Dana?'

'Just a glass of water, please,' Dana said. 'I try to stay away from caffeine; it makes me jittery.'

Lexi pulled a face, which irked me. Dana was a little different, if for no other reason than she was younger than us, but that was no reason to be unkind to her. And to Jen's credit, she ignored Lexi's eye roll, and said, 'Smart girl, Dana. Caffeine is poison.'

'You don't want anything, Jen?' Addison asked.

'A large cappuccino, please,' Jen said, handing him a five-dollar bill. She shrugged. 'What can I say, I'm addicted.'

Lexi and I both shook our heads when Addison looked at us questioningly, and he went off to stand in line.

'So, spill it, Nick,' Jen ordered.

'Not until I've had my coffee.'

'At least tell us this: Did you spend the night at the med student's place?' Lexi asked.

Nick looked sheepish.

Jen hooted with laughter. 'I knew it! I would never have guessed you were such a player.'

Nick looked affronted. 'I am not a player. She forced me back to her apartment, where eventually I passed out. When I woke up this morning, I didn't know where the hell I was.

But here's the really scary part – this chick is obsessed with Justin Timberlake. She had posters of him up all over her room. Do you have any idea how scary it is to wake up to Justin Timberlake's face staring down at you?' Nick shuddered. 'I don't think I'm ever going to get over it.'

'Are you going to see her again?' Lexi asked.

'God, no,' Nick said. 'Hopefully never again. Didn't you hear what I said? Justin Timberlake?'

'But that's so . . .' I trailed off, grasping for the right adjective.

'Piggish,' Lexi finished for me.

Jen nodded in agreement. 'Disgusting,' she said.

Nick looked hurt. 'I am not piggish. And besides, how do you know she wants to see me again?'

'Of course she would,' Jen said. 'You're a total fox.'

'I am?' Nick asked, looking so pleased, I rolled my eyes.

'Yup,' Jen said, ruffling his hair. 'In a brotherly sort of way.'

'That's the kiss of death,' Nick complained.

'Did she give you her phone number?' Lexi asked. Nick nodded. 'Then of course she wants you to call her.'

'I thought that was just morning-after etiquette. You exchange phone numbers, make promises to call, and then hope like hell you never bump into each other ever again,' Nick said.

'What did I miss, what did I miss?' Addison asked. He handed steaming mugs of coffee to Nick and Jen, a glass of iced water to Dana, and then sat back down at the table.

'Nick hooked up last night,' Lexi said. 'He was just telling us about it.'

'Way to go,' Addison said. 'The hot girl you were hanging out with? Give it up, my man.'

The two guys bumped fists.

'You think she was hot?' Jen asked.

'Um, yeah,' Addison said.

'But she was so . . . obvious,' Jen said.

'In a good way,' Addison said. 'That's the thing women

never understand about men. We *like* one-night stands. We revel in them. And you don't want to have one with the girl next door. You want someone . . . dirty.'

All of the females at the table, including Dana – who up until that moment had been trying hard to ignore the conversation while she reviewed her notes – wrinkled our noses.

'Dirty?' I repeated.

'Ew,' Lexi said.

'Dirty as in diseased?' Jen asked.

'No, dirty as in twelve hours later she doesn't even remember your name,' Addison said. He held two pens up like drumsticks and began to tap on the edge of the table with them.

'Oh. My. God,' I said.

'You are so gross,' Jen exclaimed, whacking Addison on the arm. 'Both of you are.'

'Easy there, tiger. No need to get hostile,' Addison said.

'Leave me out of it,' Nick said. He slouched down in his chair.

'Coward,' Lexi said.

'Hey, I'm just telling the truth,' Addison said. He winked lasciviously.

'I thought men were supposed to like women who play hard to get,' Dana said.

Addison shrugged. 'Some men might. But all guys appreciate an easy score now and again,' he said.

'This is why I'm not dating guys my age anymore,' Lexi said, pointing across the table accusingly at Addison. 'Jacob was a perfect gentleman last night. He didn't even try to get me into bed – he said he wanted to get to know me better before we took our relationship to the next level.'

Addison and Nick exchanged a knowing look, their eyebrows raised.

'What?' Lexi demanded.

'He's totally playing you,' Nick said.

'He'd already figured out you weren't going to sleep with

him the first night, so he was laying the groundwork for Phase Two. It was a tactical decision,' Addison said.

Lexi crossed her arms. 'There are some men in this world who are interested in a woman for something more than sex,' she said.

'Yeah. They're called *gay*. Which, by the way, Lexi, I am not,' Addison said, shooting her a pointed look.

'Oops,' Lexi said, laughing as she took a sip of coffee. 'Who told you?'

We all looked at Jen.

'What?' Jen said, spreading her hands, palms upward. 'Like everyone doesn't gossip when they drink.'

Addison pretended to look hurt. 'And here I thought I came across as a manly man.'

'You do, you do,' Lexi said, so unconvincingly, we all sniggered.

'Oh, come on. Really?' Addison asked. 'What do I have to do? Carry around power tools?'

'For starters, don't ever refer to yourself as a manly man,' Jen said.

'Maybe you should rethink your glasses,' Lexi said thoughtfully.

'What's wrong with my glasses? I love these glasses,' Addison exclaimed.

'They're nice, but . . .'

'But what?'

'They're just a little . . . feminine-looking. In fact, I think they might be women's frames,' Lexi said delicately.

'No, they're not! Are they? Shit. They were on the men's side of the eyewear store,' Addison said. He took off his glasses and squinted down at the black plastic frames.

'Come on, let's get to work. We're never going to get through the Torts assignment,' I said.

'Kate, let me share your book. I didn't get a chance to go home before I came here,' Nick said.

*

After we'd gone over Torts and Crim, we decided to pack it in for the afternoon.

'Did you drive?' Nick asked me as I stacked my books and notepads up.

I nodded.

'Can you give me a ride home? I left my car at the bar last night,' Nick said.

We said good-bye to the rest of the group and began the two-block walk to where my Civic was parked.

'I feel like shit,' Nick said. 'I'm so hungover. Hey, can we go to Burger King?'

'We could, but why would we want to?' I asked.

'The Whopper is the world's best hangover cure. Especially when accompanied by a chocolate shake,' Nick said. He glanced at me and frowned. 'What's that?'

'What's what?'

'That thing on your back,' he said.

'What, my knapsack?'

'It's enormous. It looks like the kind that people use when they climb mountains,' Nick said.

'Yeah, I think that's what it's for. It's from L.L. Bean. It just arrived yesterday. My leather one wasn't big enough to fit all of my textbooks in it,' I explained.

'Do you have a pup tent in there? A month's supply of beef jerky?'

'Well, if I do, smart-ass, I'm not sharing it with you,' I said.

'I love it when you sweet-talk me,' Nick said, and I punched him playfully in the arm.

Twenty minutes later, I pulled up in front of our house. Nick was clutching a greasy Burger King bag in his hand as he got out of the car.

'What are you doing now?' Nick asked as we climbed the steps to our shared front porch. 'There's a *Magnum, P.I.* marathon on cable. Want to come over and watch it with me?'

'Can't,' I said. I nodded toward my door. 'My ex – Graham – is waiting for me.'

Nick's eyebrows arched up, and he looked at me for a moment. 'I'm sure there's a whole long story there, huh?'

'Probably. Although I don't know what it is yet.'

'Well . . . good luck finding out,' Nick said. He turned and unlocked his door.

'Thanks,' I said.

And then I went up to see Graham.

'I think we should get back together,' Graham said.

We were sitting on either end of the couch, half turned to face each other. Graham's arm was draped over the back of the couch.

'But . . . why?' I asked. I didn't realize how abrupt the question sounded until I saw the frown pull at his face.

'I've missed you. I miss us,' he said simply. 'Don't you?'

'Sometimes,' I admitted. 'But things weren't going that well between us before.'

Graham nodded. 'I know. I think we were both too passive about our relationship. We got lazy.'

Was that it? I wondered. Everyone always says that you have to work at a relationship, that you have to make an effort to keep things spicy. So how do you know when you have something worth saving, worth holding on to, something good that's only gotten stale through neglect . . . and when you don't?

'A lot of the time I felt really alone,' I persisted. 'And also that I was less important to you than the other things in your life. Your work, your hobbies.'

Graham shook his head. 'You were always the most important thing in my life, Kate. Always. And if you didn't know that . . .' He closed his eyes for a minute. 'Then that just makes me the world's biggest asshole.'

I smiled. 'You're not an asshole.'

'Will you give me a second chance?'

'But now you're in Arizona, and I'm here,' I said.

'I know it won't be easy. But we can do the long-distance

thing, and if it works out, one of us will move,' Graham said.

'Meaning you want me to move to Arizona,' I said, deliberately – churlishly – picking at the scab of the well-worn argument.

Graham shrugged. 'Yes, maybe. Or maybe I'll get as good a job here. Or maybe we'll wait until after you graduate and move somewhere else together,' he said, sounding so reasonable, I felt guilty for my earlier flash of temper. I rested my hand on his, by way of apology.

Graham reached for me, sliding across the couch to close the distance between us. He wrapped his arms around me, and I relaxed into the embrace. And for the first time since law school began, I felt safe. The tide of strangeness – the new people, and schedule, and crushing workload – ebbed and receded, and normalcy returned. I buried my head into Graham's shirt, sniffing in the sameness of him. He smelled of fabric softener and bar soap and oranges.

'Can we try?' Graham asked softly.

I nodded. A second chance. 'Yes,' I said. 'I'd like that.'

6

I sat in class, doodling on a yellow legal pad, while my thoughts drifted to Graham. He'd left Tuesday morning, flying back to Arizona. We'd slept together the night before he left, and it was . . . nice. Quite nice. Maybe it wasn't the sort of epic romance Jen had been imagining, but how often did that happen in real life, anyway? It wasn't like Graham was going to stare soulfully at me while I popped chocolate-covered strawberries in his mouth.

I glanced up at the clock. Twenty more minutes until Crim class ended, and then I was free from Hoffman for the week-end. Despite my poor performance on the first day of class, Hoffman hadn't called on me again. Instead, he seemed to delight in picking on different students every day, mocking them when stage fright caused them to stumble over the answers. So far, though, no one else had been caught unpre-pared or been forced to stand while Hoffman grilled them, so I still held that special distinction among my classmates.

He's such a sadistic prick, I thought. *He probably tortures small animals in his free time. I wonder if the cats that live in his neighborhood have a tendency to go missing. Or, maybe—*

'Ms Bennet?'

The sound of my name cracked across the room like a whip. I looked up, horrified to see that Hoffman had turned his flat shark eyes on me. *Shit.* It was as if the asshole had been reading my thoughts. My stomach roiled nervously, and

I had to force myself to meet his gaze while I waited for the interrogation to commence. But this time I was ready for him – this time I'd not only read and reread the assignment, I'd taken careful notes, complete with the fact pattern, case summary, and holding of every case. This time I wouldn't make a fool of myself. I folded my hands in front of me on the table and waited for the question.

'Well, Ms Bennett, don't keep us all in suspense.'

Huh? Why was he looking at me so expectantly? Wait . . . why was everyone in the room looking at me? Oh, no . . . oh, no no no no no. Had he asked the question when I wasn't paying attention? Oh, God. That must be it. Of all the times to zone out . . .

'Would you mind repeating the question?' I asked, barely recognizing the high, thin voice as my own.

Hoffman gave an exaggerated sigh. 'Yes, actually, I would mind. This lecture is for your benefit, not mine. If you aren't prepared to come to class and listen, Ms Bennett, then I would suggest you not bother coming at all. I don't care if you waste your own time, but I take great offense at your wasting mine and everyone else's,' he said in a cold, biting tone that had its intended effect of making me feel like shit on a stick. 'Mr Fournier, please repeat the question for Ms Bennett.'

Mr Fournier – I had no idea what his first name was – sat in the front row of class and was exactly the sort of law student who gave the rest of us a bad reputation. He constantly volunteered in class, took an obvious and annoying pleasure in hearing the sound of his own voice, and shamelessly brown-nosed all of the professors.

Mr Fournier now cleared his throat, and said, 'You asked, "Is the failure to act included in the principle of *actus reus*?"'

'Thank you, Mr Fournier,' Hoffman said. Mr Fournier beamed up at him sycophantically.

I breathed a sigh of relief. I'd just gone over this last

night. Surreptitiously, I flipped back a few pages in my notes and read over them quickly before I began to speak.

'No. Although *actus reus* is not specifically defined in the Modern Penal Code, the basic requirement is that there be a willed act. Therefore, an omission to act wouldn't be included under the commonly held definition,' I said.

As soon as I heard Nick suck in his breath sympathetically, I knew I'd screwed up.

'Is that so?' Hoffman asked. He looked at me the way a snake might look at a mouse just before consuming it whole. My stomach turned and dipped in a way that made it feel like it was falling out of my body.

Oh, *shit*, I thought grimly.

'A mother is mopping the floor. Her small child comes upon the bucket of water and falls into it, headfirst. The child begins to drown, flailing his little arms and feet around helplessly,' Hoffman said, in the disinterested monotone voice one might use to read a weather report aloud. 'The mother turns and sees that the child is struggling. But instead of re-trieving the child from the bucket, she walks out of the house, sits on the front porch, and proceeds to smoke a cigarette while the toddler drowns. Did the woman commit a crime?'

I hesitated. 'Yes,' I finally said.

'Please do enlighten us, Ms Bennett – what was the crime?' Hoffman persisted.

I don't know what happened. Everyone was staring at me, their faces alternating between sympathy and smugness. I could hear the *tap-tap-tap* of someone typing notes directly into a laptop. The fluorescent overhead lights buzzed. A woman coughed. And try as I might, I couldn't remember one thing about *actus reus*, criminal law, or just about anything else that would resemble an answer. In fact, it felt like my mind had been stripped clean of all knowledge, except, bizarrely, for the lyrics to Milli Vanilli's song 'Girl, You Know It's True.'

It was the diving competition all over again.

Girl, you know it's true, ooh, ooh, ooh, I love you.

Think, damn it, THINK! I thought desperately. Surely, leaving your child to drown in a bucket must be a crime . . . right? Or was it a trick? I looked down at my notes, praying they'd hold the answer, but I couldn't make sense of anything I'd written.

'Um. She committed a crime by . . . leaving the bucket of water out?'

'Are you asking me or telling me?' Hoffman said.

'She committed a crime by leaving the bucket of water out for her child to fall into,' I said more firmly.

'No!' Hoffman screamed. He hit his hand on the top of the lectern, and the cracking sound echoed around the classroom. The sudden movement caused a strand of his hair to break loose from its comb-over and fall forward over his shiny forehead. 'No, Ms Bennett, that was *not* the crime! Dear God, it's as though my students get dumber with every passing year!'

This statement deflated some of my smugger classmates. They stopped smirking at me and turned back to their case-books.

'If you had done your reading – you are capable of reading, are you not? – you would have known the answer. Your pitiful response can mean only one of two things. Either you didn't do the assigned reading, or you did and you were too stupid to understand it. Which was it?' Hoffman continued, his hissing voice echoing across the lecture hall.

Still there was nothing. Just a big, sucking emptiness where my brain used to be.

Girl, you know it's true, ooh, ooh, ooh, I love you.

'Well, Ms Bennett? Are you now also incapable of speech?' Hoffman sneered.

'I did do the reading. And I thought I understood it,' I said shakily. I couldn't believe it. I was nearly thirty years old, and I was being screamed at and condescended to by a middle-aged prick with a severe case of megalomania. Anger pressed at my chest and buzzed in my ears. 'If I didn't, I apologize. But I thought that's what class was for. To learn material we don't yet know,' I added, my anger emboldening me.

'Do you think you can come into my class unprepared and I'll just spoon-feed you the syllabus? Is that right, Ms Bennett?' Hoffman said. He was no longer shouting, but in a way, this new, icier tone was even more menacing.

'Isn't that your job?'

There was a collective gasp from my classmates. Under his breath, Nick muttered, 'Jesus, Kate.'

I don't know how it happened. I hadn't meant to say it out loud, I really hadn't. It was as though the words had been spit out of my mouth beyond my control. Was it possible I had multiple personalities? Specifically, an evil multiple personality intent on ruining my life?

Sybil, I thought. I'll call my evil multiple personality Sybil. At least now I finally have someone to blame for all of my bad luck.

'Are you trying to embarrass me?' Hoffman asked, biting the words out.

'No! No, of course not . . .' I said, willing myself to apologize, although the words stuck in my throat like stones.

Should I tell him about Sybil? I wondered. No, he'll just think I'm crazy. Although maybe that wasn't so bad at the moment. An insanity defense would be apropos for Crim class.

Hoffman stared at me with his pale malevolent eyes in a way that made my skin crawl.

'Every year,' he said in a soft, menacing voice, 'I have one student who is convinced that he or she knows more about the subject of criminal law than I do.'

I shook my head vigorously from side to side. No, no, no, that was the last thing I thought. I know nothing about the law. *Nothing.* Less than nothing.

'And, interestingly enough, every year that student always ends up getting the lowest grade in my class. Something for you to think about, Ms Bennett,' Hoffman continued. He turned to the lectern, picked up his notes, and then strode down off the teaching platform. No one moved as Hoffman stormed up the stairs, heading straight toward me.

Is he going to hit me? I wondered, horrified and yet unable to move. Unable to look away.

But Hoffman was not coming for me, he was simply exiting the room, abruptly ending class early. He pushed open the door and then suddenly wheeled around.

'Come Monday, Ms Bennett, perhaps you will be so kind as to take over the lecture. I'm sure we'll all be thrilled to hear more of your brilliant insights into criminal law.'

And then he turned and left the room, the door banging behind him.

No one moved or spoke for a few beats. It was as though we were all expecting him to come storming back into class. But as one moment passed, and then another, and yet another without his reappearance, the silence began to break. A nervous giggle here, a loud whisper there, the thud of a few dozen textbooks closing.

I exhaled a shaky breath and turned to look at Nick. His face was gray.

'You are so fucked,' he said, shaking his head from side to side.

And only then did I realize the extent of my trespass: I'd turned the meanest, most sadistic professor in the school into a personal enemy.

Once again, I was the favorite subject of One-L gossip. After class, as I made my way to my mail folder, I could hear the buzz of chatter surround me as news of my second disastrous standoff with Hoffman spread.

'He, like, totally took her apart,' I heard a tall blond guy with vacant eyes and a surfer-dude drawl say.

'It was ugly,' a woman with the sharp, pointed features of a rat agreed.

I gritted my teeth and pushed through the crowd of congregating students.

'That's her,' I heard Rat Girl say. 'Is she crying?'

I paused for a minute, my back stiffening. No one could blame me for beaning her over the head with my Crim textbook, right? But then I sighed and pressed on. Violence never solved anything, as satisfying as it might be.

There was nothing of interest in my mail folder. I looked up at the corkboard and saw the usual assortment of multicolored flyers posted there. One announced a Bar Review next week at the F&M Patio Bar. Another advertised the Public Interest Law Foundation's bake sale. One had been posted by a Two-L eager to sell his One-L course outlines, claiming that he'd used them to grade onto Law Review. And then my eyes settled on a plain note card with a carefully handwritten message: RESEARCH ASSISTANT NEEDED. IF INTERESTED CALL ARMSTRONG MCKENNA. 555–7823.

Armstrong McKenna. I knew the name, of course. McKenna was the historian and biographer who had, in recent years, penned the best-selling biographies of Thomas Jefferson and Benjamin Franklin. He was a frequent guest on the Sunday-morning talk shows that Graham was so addicted to (and which I only half listened to while I worked on the crossword puzzle). I hadn't known he lived in New Orleans, though. And now he was looking for a research assistant.

I reached up, pulled the note card down, and stuffed it into the outer pocket of my knapsack.

At four o'clock that afternoon, I was driving down Prytania Street looking for the address that Armstrong McKenna had given me when I called about the research-assistant position. I knew that with my current study load it was crazy to even think about a part-time job, but just the thought of working for McKenna sent a ripple of excitement through me. To have something of my own, something outside the stifling confines of law school, was just too tempting to pass up. And I'd always been a history buff; I'd even majored in American History in college. I'd considered going on for my master's degree, but there wasn't exactly a thriving job market for history grad students.

I'd been surprised that McKenna had wanted to see me so soon, but he'd insisted.

'What are you doing now?' he'd asked in a thick Southern accent over the phone.

'Wh-what . . . You mean right now?' I asked.

'That's precisely what I mean.'

'I have a class this afternoon. Civil Procedure,' I added, unnecessarily.

'Then come by after you're done,' McKenna said breezily. He gave me his address and rang off, and it was only after we'd disconnected that I realized he hadn't asked what time that would be.

Now I was crawling along, trying to find the house number he'd given me, although none of the houses on the damned street appeared to be marked. Still, it was a lovely neighborhood, just off Prytania, with cobblestone sidewalks and large Greek Revival homes.

'There it is!' I said triumphantly. The only house on the entire street with a number on the mailbox just happened to be Armstrong McKenna's. I felt a little burst of triumph.

'Maybe my luck is finally starting to turn,' I said aloud as I shifted the car into reverse to pull into the only curbside spot available on the street, which just happened to be located right in front of his house.

I felt a thump, the soft resistance of my back tires hitting something.

'What the . . .' I started to say.

And that's when the howling began. It was an awful noise, like the scream of a banshee hell-bent on revenge. Goose bumps actually broke out over my chest and arms.

I leapt out of the car and ran back to where the source

of the screeching was coming from. There, lying on the pavement with all four of its stumpy legs waving up in the air, was the fattest basset hound I'd ever seen. The dog had limpid eyes, long ears, and a brown-and-white coat. I crouched down next to the hound, looking in vain for any obvious signs of blood or injury. But still, he might have internal injuries. I was going to have to get him some help.

I looked a bit grimly at Armstrong McKenna's enormous periwinkle-blue Greek Revival home. Showing up on his doorstep with an injured dog in tow – particularly one that I had just run over – was not going to make the best of first impressions. But what choice did I have? I started to reach forward, ready to pick up the basset hound, but quickly realized it wasn't possible. This was a dog who liked his kibble, and there was no way I was going to be able to lift him, much less heave him all the way up McKenna's front walk.

'I'll be right back,' I told the dog, and I ran up to McKenna's front door. A gas lamp hung next to the door, the light already glowing, even though sunset was still hours off. I rang the bell and could hear the chimes – which, bizarrely, sounded like the first few bars of the *William Tell Overture* – and waited.

The door swung open, and there was Armstrong McKenna. He was a small man – short with a slight frame – but extremely elegant. I guessed that he was in his fifties, although his thin face was youthful. His hair was streaked with gray and brushed back off his face, and he was wearing a beautiful blue broadcloth shirt – which looked, even to my uninformed eye, as though it had been hand tailored – tucked into pressed khaki chinos. He grinned at me.

'Kate Bennett, I presume,' he drawled.

'Yes. I . . . I just hit a dog. Out on the street. I think he's going to need a vet. Could you please call someone?' The words came out of me in a great rush.

'Who, Elvis?' he asked.

'What?' I replied, puzzled, and then noticed the crystal glass in his hand, half full of what looked like bourbon.

Oh, great, I thought with dismay. McKenna must be drunk. So drunk he was suggesting we call a dead rock star. Obviously, I was going to be on my own in this crisis.

My thoughts must have been reflected in the incredulous look I was giving him, because Armstrong McKenna shook his head impatiently and gestured with his glass. 'Elvis is my dog. Well. He's a dog that lives in my house, in any event,' he said.

My heart sank. I had just run over my prospective employer's dog. Just when I thought this couldn't get any worse.

'He's standing right behind you,' Armstrong continued.

I whirled around. The brown-and-white hound was standing on the front walk, gazing at the stairs disconsolately with red watery eyes.

'He hates climbing stairs. He's always trying to talk me into lifting him up, but he's gotten so damned fat, I can hardly budge him these days.'

'But . . . but . . . I hit him! Or, at least, I think I did. And when he was lying on the road, he seemed like he was in a lot of pain,' I exclaimed.

'It happens all the time,' Armstrong said. 'He's been hit at least ten times that I know of. He likes to nap in the middle of the street, the old fool. You'd think he'd have learned his lesson by now.'

'But shouldn't we take him to a vet and have him examined?' I asked.

'He looks fine to me,' Armstrong said.

Elvis had tired of waiting to be lifted up onto the porch and began slowly climbing the stairs. When he reached the top, the hound sighed heavily before passing through the front door.

'Come on in, darlin',' Armstrong said to me. 'You're just in time for cocktail hour.'

I glanced at my watch. It was not yet four-thirty.

'I'm here for the interview,' I reminded him.

'We'll get to that. But you can't get to know someone properly until you've seen what they're like after a few drinks,' Armstrong pronounced, and waved me into the house. 'You do drink, don't you? I can't abide teetotalers. Or vegetarians or yoga fanatics, for that matter. You're not any of those, are you?'

'Um, no,' I said, wondering if this was part of the interview.

'Thank God for that.'

The house was large and opulent – and looked like it had been furnished by a color-blind lunatic. It was stuffed near to bursting with enormous crystal chandeliers, heavy Victorian furniture upholstered in garnet-red velvet, gilded candlesticks and tiny Limoges boxes gathering dust on every tabletop, and fussy silk draperies swathed on every window. Just two steps in the door and I immediately felt overcome by a choking claustrophobia.

'I know what you're thinking,' Armstrong McKenna said. 'It looks like a French whorehouse.'

'I wasn't thinking that,' I said. Actually, I imagined French whorehouses were more tasteful than this.

'Ironic, no? A gay man living in a whorehouse? Of course, it wasn't really ever a whorehouse, just emblematic of my dearly departed mother's hideous taste. Although I'm not sure that makes it any better,' he said, frowning for a minute. 'I just moved back in last month, so I haven't had a chance to de-chintz and de-pouf most of it. Maybe that's something you can help me with.'

'Sure,' I said gamely, wondering if this meant that I had the job . . . and if he really expected me to know how to decorate.

'Let's go back to the library. It's the only room in the house that I can sit in without becoming constipated,' Armstrong said. He crooked his arm at me in a courtly gesture. 'Shall we?'

*

'I'm famished. Let's go get a nibble,' Armstrong (which he'd insisted I call him) said an hour later. He'd had two more bourbons, which didn't seem to be affecting him at all. I'd been nursing one glass of white wine and felt a little lightheaded.

Since we'd arrived in the library and settled down on a pair of twin black leather Chesterfield sofas, Armstrong had spent most of the time regaling me with the history of the house. It had been decaying and rotted through when his parents bought it thirty years earlier, and they'd spent the next ten years – 'And the lion's share of my inheritance,' Armstrong said dryly – restoring it to its former glory.

'I kept the house after they died, and I decided to move back to New Orleans when I retired last year,' he concluded.

'Aren't you going to interview me?' I finally asked.

Armstrong looked surprised. 'For what?' he asked.

'The job. I thought you were looking for a research assistant,' I said.

'Oh, that. The job is yours,' Armstrong said, waving his hand as though it were all a foregone conclusion. 'You're the only one who responded to my advertisement.'

I thought of his note card, folded in the pocket of my knapsack, and felt a stab of guilt.

'But . . . don't you at least want to know my qualifications?' I said. 'I majored in History as an undergrad at Cornell, and—'

'No, that's okay. You'll do fine,' Armstrong said, interrupting me. 'I liked you the moment I saw you. I like your face. You remind me of a young Doris Day.'

'Um, thanks. I think,' I said. Wasn't Doris Day the one who had her hair curled into a stiff flip and was always wearing a pillbox hat?

'Besides, it's not like the work is going to be particularly hard.' Armstrong made a face. 'It's just a book. I could write it in my sleep.'

'May I ask you a question?'

'Fire away,' Armstrong said.

'Why was your card up at the law school? Wouldn't you rather have a history graduate student help you?' I asked.

Armstrong snorted. 'Absolutely not. I taught at the University of Virginia for twenty-five years, and I'm sick to death of history graduate students. They're all sanctimonious as hell.'

'I'm not sure law students are much better,' I said. 'In fact, I'm pretty sure they're even worse.'

'Well, that's a risk I'm just going to have to take. Now, let's go over to Jacques-Imo's for a nosh. They have the most fabulous banana cream pie,' he said.

7

On Monday morning, I went straight to Hoffman's office, planning to apologize for my outburst. I arrived a half-hour before class started and stood outside the door, tentatively tapping on the frosted glass pane. I could hear him moving around – there was a distinct cough and then he took a phone call – but he ignored my knocks. And then after my last knock, he'd yelled, 'Go away!'

And so I did.

I went to P.J.'s for an iced coffee and then waited just outside the lecture hall, planning to intercept him before class. Students streamed by me on their way in, many of them looking at me with the sort of ghoulish interest motorists pay to cars burning on the side of the road. To avoid making eye contact with anyone, I rummaged through my enormous knapsack, pretending to evaluate my supply of legal pads and Uni-Ball black pens while glancing down the hall every five seconds to see if Hoffman was on his way. I studied some of the homemade campaign posters taped to the wall, painted in block letters on large, brightly colored sheets of poster board with ARCHER DAVIES FOR 3L CLASS PRESIDENT ... MAKE NO PROMISES, BREAK NO PROMISES and RACHEL KATZ FOR ETHICS COMMITTEE – VOTE EARLY, VOTE OFTEN.

'Why are you out here?' Nick asked, appearing beside me. He was wearing jeans and a navy blue polo shirt and had his black messenger bag slung casually over one shoulder.

'Hoffman wouldn't see me in his office, so I'm waiting for him here,' I said.

'Yikes,' Nick said.

'Thanks, that makes me feel loads better.'

'You want my advice?'

'No,' I said. 'Go away.'

'What's going on?' Jen asked, walking up with Addison at her side. She was eating an orange. Between dainty bites, she swept tendrils of burnished red hair back from her face.

'Nothing,' I said.

'Are you plotting to kill Hoffman?' Addison asked. 'Because this morning when I was driving here, Hoffman was crossing Freret Street and he walked right in front of my car. I could have nailed him, and since he wasn't in the crosswalk, I would have totally gotten away with it.'

'I don't think it works like that,' Nick said.

'Really? I thought that if you hit someone outside a crosswalk, it's a freebie,' Addison said. He reached over and stole an orange segment from Jen. She swatted his hand.

'Easy, tiger,' Addison said, popping the orange into his mouth. 'Anyway, that reminds me. I was talking to a Three-L the other day, and she told me that when she had Hoffman her first year, he wasn't such an asshole.'

'So what happened to him?' I muttered.

'His wife died. She was hit by a drunk driver while she was out walking the dog.'

He said it matter-of-factly, but the words cut into me, making it hard to breathe for a minute.

'Oh, God, that's awful,' Jen said. 'When?'

'Last year, I guess. I don't think he was ever anyone's favorite teacher, but from what I hear he got a lot worse after that happened,' Addison said.

As they talked, I stared down at my plastic cup of iced

coffee, bending the plastic straw back where it poked through the lid, while I digested this new detail about Hoffman. I'd previously thought that he was a one-dimensional embodiment of pure evil. But now . . . now it turned out that we had more in common than I'd ever imagined.

'He's coming,' Nick said, nodding in the direction of the stairwell.

Hoffman had turned down the hallway and was walking toward us. His hands were in his pockets, and he was whistling tunelessly.

'Evil approacheth,' Addison whispered. 'A chill wind blows through the air, animals take cover, flowers wilt—'

'Shhhh,' I hissed.

'Okay, okay, we're going. Come on, guys, let's leave Kate to her groveling,' Nick said, and he herded Jen and Addison ahead of him into the lecture hall. Jen looked back over her shoulder and gave me what I'm sure was meant to be an encouraging smile, but it had the effect of making me feel like I was on my way to an execution. *My* execution.

'Professor Hoffman,' I said. 'May I talk to you for a minute?'

Hoffman stopped whistling and looked at me without interest. For a minute I thought he might not recognize me.

'I'm in your Crim class,' I said helpfully.

'I know who you are, Ms Bennett,' Hoffman said, overpronouncing the syllables in my name, rattling them off like verbal bullets.

'I just . . . I just wanted to . . . apologize. For what I said . . . for what happened in class on Friday,' I said.

Hoffman continued to stare at me.

'I wasn't trying to embarrass you,' I said. And even though I was using his words, the very accusation he'd thrown at me on Friday, I knew immediately that it had been just the wrong thing to say.

Hoffman's lip curled with disgust, and he regarded me in

much the same way I had looked at the dead cockroach I'd found on my kitchen floor that morning.

'Embarrass me? Ms Bennett, considering your shoddy case analysis and obvious lack of preparation for my class, I would advise you to spend more time worrying about how much you embarrass yourself with your ineptitude. In fact, I'm beginning to think that perhaps law school isn't the right place for you. Being a student here requires a certain amount of mental discipline, a drive, the ability to process information – all of which you seem to lack,' Hoffman said coldly. And then he turned and walked past me into the classroom. The door shut behind him with a muffled thud.

The blood rushed to the surface of my skin, and I pressed my fingers to my cheeks to cool them. I felt a little dizzy and realized that I'd been holding my breath, catching it in my chest.

'That's it. There's no fucking way I'm putting up with this any longer,' I muttered under my breath.

I marched down the hallway, up a flight of stairs, and straight into the administration offices, which were housed on the second floor of the law school. The door from the hall opened into a gray-carpeted reception room, furnished with expensive-looking cherry office furniture. Behind the reception desk sat a middle-aged woman with a soft blonde bob and bored blue eyes. She was focused on her computer screen, frowning as she typed. I marched over and stood at her desk.

'Excuse me,' I said. 'I'd like to see the Assistant Dean of Students.'

The receptionist continued to type. 'I'll be with you in one minute,' she murmured, holding up a finger and not looking at me. An unflattering shade of tangerine lipstick was smeared across her mouth.

I waited while she continued to whack away at the keys, ignoring me as she worked. Finally, after an unreasonably long time had passed, she stopped typing, clicked the mouse a few times, and then printed something out on a laser printer behind her. She removed the papers from the printer, neatly tapped them into a stack, stapled them, and dropped them in a metal out-box sitting on the corner of her desk. Only then did she look at me and say, 'May I help you?'

I struggled to keep my temper in check. It never pays to piss off the gatekeepers, and right now I had bigger problems than difficult receptionists.

'I'd like to see the Assistant Dean of Students,' I repeated in as pleasant a tone as I could muster.

'Do you have an appointment?'

'No.'

'Well, let's see.' The receptionist flipped through a desktop calendar, the kind with the long columns that allow you to schedule every minute of every day. 'Hmmm. No, that won't work. Maybe . . . no, that's not going to work either. I can give you an appointment on November the twelfth,' the receptionist said, looking up at me expectantly, pencil poised over the book.

I shook my head. 'No, I need to see her today. Now, if possible.'

The receptionist clucked her tongue and shook her head regretfully. 'I'm sorry, but Ms Sullivan doesn't see anyone without an appointment. This time of year is quite busy, what with the new semester just starting.'

'The semester started weeks ago! And I can't wait more than a month to see her,' I said.

I dropped my oversize knapsack on the receptionist's desk, where it landed with a thud that made her jump, and began to rifle through it, until I found the orientation material Tulane had sent to me before I left Ithaca.

'See? Here on this pamphlet, it says that if we have any problem – *any problem at all* – to see Teresa Sullivan, Assistant Dean of Student Affairs, who – and I quote – *is responsible for counseling and advising students*.' I waved the pamphlet at the nonplussed receptionist. 'And I am a student in need of counseling!' My voice grew high and cracked on the word 'counseling.' Suddenly, to my horror, hot tears began stinging in my eyes and my hands shook uncontrollably. 'I need to see her *now*.'

The receptionist looked at me with complete disinterest. She shook her head firmly and opened her mouth to speak, but I held up a hand to stop her.

'Do *not* tell me she can't see me now. In fact, don't say anything – *nothing* – unless the next words out of your mouth are that you'll pick up your stupid phone and tell Dean Sullivan that there's a student out here in need of counseling,' I hissed.

The tears were now streaming down my cheeks, and I angrily wiped them away with the back of my hand. I glared down at the receptionist, whose lips were now pursing with irritation. It was lucky for me that this was a university and not a corporation, where a squad of efficient ex-military security guards with crew cuts and beefy biceps would be marching in right about now to restrain me.

'It's okay, Ruth,' a calm voice said. I looked up to see a petite woman, elegantly dressed in a professional navy blue suit, standing in the doorway. Her dark hair was cut short in a pixie, and the freckles on her face made her seem younger than she probably was. Despite the conservative cut of her suit, she had on tan leather pumps with very high heels and pointy toes. 'Please, come back into my office.'

I grabbed my knapsack and managed to abstain from shooting Ruth a triumphant smile as I skirted around her desk. No sense in rubbing it in.

'Close the door and have a seat,' she said.

I closed the door and made my way to one of the visitors' chairs, which was upholstered in cobalt blue fabric. I glanced around the office. It was standard institutional stuff – a desk and credenza similar to the reception furniture, a metal lateral file, a bookshelf on the wall opposite the desk. But Sullivan had added some personal touches, including an oriental rug, watercolor paintings on the wall, and family photos on the shelves featuring her, a smiling man with thinning red hair who I took to be her husband, and a beaming coltish girl with a wide smile and curly pigtails.

'I'm Teresa Sullivan. And you are . . .,' she said. She arched her eyebrows.

'Kate. Kate Bennett,' I said. 'I'm a One-L.'

'And what can I help you with, Kate?' she asked.

I didn't know if she hadn't noticed my tear-streaked cheeks or if she was just too polite to comment on them. I drew in a shaky breath. 'I need to transfer out of my Crim class,' I said. 'My professor hates me.'

'Why do you think that?'

'I have Professor Hoffman. He called on me the first day of class and I wasn't prepared – I had some problems with my moving van on the way down here, and I missed orientation, so I didn't know about the reading assignment – and he ridiculed me in front of the entire class. And then he did the same thing last Friday, although I was prepared then, I just got . . . nervous, I guess. So then I tried to apologize to him about it before class today, and he was awful,' I said, the words falling out of me in a great rush.

The assistant dean nodded. 'Hoffman can be tough. But sometimes new law students who aren't used to the Socratic method of guided questioning feel that their professors are being antagonistic, when in reality it's just a teaching tool, a way to help you develop necessary critical-thinking skills.'

'No, it's not that. He mocked me and told me I lacked the discipline to be a student here,' I said, shaking my head emphatically. 'Trust me, Hoffman hates me. You have to move me into another class.'

'I can't do that. First years aren't allowed to change sections, barring some sort of extraordinary situation.'

'I would think having a professor who despises me, who

has a . . . a . . . personal *vendetta* against me, would qualify as an extraordinary situation.'

Teresa Sullivan folded her hands on her desk. 'The first year of law school is always difficult. I remember it all too well – the stress, the workload, the competition. Sometimes the cumulative effect of all of that pressure can make some problems seem unmanageable,' she said.

'He's going to fail me,' I said, remembering Hoffman's ominous claim that the student who stood up to him in class always ended up with the lowest grade. It had sounded like a threat.

'No, he can't. Not purposely, anyway. All of the testing at Tulane is anonymous.'

'Okay, so he's just going to make my life a living hell for the rest of the semester.'

'I'll tell you what. Give it a few more weeks. And after that, if you still feel uncomfortable in his class or feel that you're being singled out, I'll talk about your concerns with you again at that time,' Sullivan said.

'I can tell you right now he's going to continue to target me. Can't I switch into another section now, when it's still early enough in the semester that I can get caught up on the reading assignments?' I asked.

'No. I'm sorry, Kate, but please try to understand our position. If we switched every first year who was unhappy, it would be complete chaos. Everyone would want to move around. We have to limit schedule changes to only the most extreme situations,' Sullivan said. Suddenly she smiled at me. 'I promise you, Hoffman's not as bad as you think. In a few weeks you'll get used to his teaching style, and you'll stop feeling so shy when you're called on in class. You'll look back on this and laugh.'

'If you say so,' I said. I felt hollow, as if the anxiety had left behind a sickly, sour emptiness.

'It will get better. It just takes time. After a while you'll get so used to talking in class, you won't even remember why it made you so nervous to be called on in the beginning. It's not as though you're graded on your answers . . . so try to embrace it as a learning tool, as a way to gain a deeper understanding of the course material. Okay?'

I'll have to take her word on that, I thought darkly. But I nodded, and stood.

'Thanks for your time,' I said.

'Anytime. My door is always open,' she said.

After the waitress took our order, I surreptitiously checked the time.

'That's the fourth time you've looked at your watch since we sat down,' Nick complained.

'I just don't want to be late for my first day of work,' I said.

I was supposed to meet Armstrong at an address on Magazine Street, a few miles uptown from my apartment. Over our heavenly dinner at Jacques-Imo's, Armstrong had told me his plan to write a book about D-Day. It was part of the reason he'd decided to return to New Orleans after his retirement from the University of Virginia. There was an enormous D-Day museum downtown, and the curator had agreed to grant Armstrong liberal access to the collection. World War II history had always fascinated me – I'd done my undergraduate thesis on the workforce of women who manned the factories during the war – and the idea that I was going to be instrumental in researching a book on the subject was thrilling.

Armstrong hadn't said what we were going to do that afternoon, but I was so keyed up, I couldn't settle down to study. So when Nick had swung by to see if I wanted to grab some lunch, I readily agreed. Although now that we'd gotten to the restaurant – a grimy little hole-in-the-wall with sticky Formica-topped tables, hard-faced waitresses with tattoos covering their arms, and Southern rock playing over the radio – I wasn't so sure I'd made the right decision. I didn't really have the time to deal with a bout of food poisoning. I decided to play it safe and ordered a BLT. Nick, braver than me, ordered something called the Mudbug Platter.

'You're nuts to be doing this. No one can hold down a job, even a part-time one, during their One-L year,' Nick said.

'I heard that one of the Two-Ls is a stripper,' I said.

This piqued Nick's interest. 'Oh, yeah? Which one?'

I shrugged. 'No idea. And it might just be an urban legend of the law school variety.'

'I bet it's that redheaded girl. The one who always wears really short skirts. She was giving me the eye at the last Bar Review,' Nick said dreamily.

I snorted. 'Why am I not surprised?'

'What?'

'I don't know a nice way of putting this, but you're sort of a slut,' I said. It was true. Nick hooked up nearly every weekend, always with a different woman he met out at a bar or party.

'It doesn't work that way,' Nick said, shaking his head. 'I'm a man. Men can't be sluts. I'm just following my biological predisposition.'

'Which is?'

'To spread my seed, thus propagating my genetic line,' Nick said.

I opened my mouth, trying to think of something to say to this, and then thought better of it. I closed my mouth, pressing my lips together with disapproval, and shook my head.

'What?' Nick asked.

'I knew a guy in college like you. He scammed on every girl he saw and hooked up constantly. And do you want to know what he told me?'

'He enjoyed every minute of it?'

'He said that one morning, after he'd had yet another meaningless one-night stand with yet another anonymous girl, he was in her bathroom, planning his escape, and he caught sight of himself in the mirror. And in that moment he was so filled with self-loathing, he actually spit at his own reflection,' I said.

'So he not only snuck out on the chick, he also messed up her bathroom? Can you imagine having to clean someone else's spit off your bathroom mirror?'

'That's so not the point of the story,' I said.

'There was a point?'

'Yes! It's that sleeping around may not be making you as happy as you think it is,' I said.

'God, you really don't know men at all, do you?' Nick said.

The waitress slapped our plates down on the table. My BLT looked nonthreatening, but the platter in front of Nick held what looked like forty miniature lobsters, complete with eyes, antennae, and claws, boiled to a revolting shade of reddish-brown and served with a mountain of curly French fries.

'What are those things?'

'Mudbugs. Also known as crawfish,' Nick said.

'How do you eat them?' I asked.

'Like so,' Nick said. He picked up one of the crustaceans, twisted off its head, and sucked out the contents of its body. It was possibly the most revolting thing I'd ever seen in my life.

'Ça c'est bon,' Nick pronounced in a surprisingly good Cajun accent.

'I think I'm going to throw up,' I said, pushing my sandwich aside as Nick picked up and beheaded another crawfish.

'Do you want to try one?' he asked.

'Um, no.'

'Your loss,' Nick said happily. 'Hey, have you done the Contracts reading assignment yet? Is it bad?'

'Brutal.'

'Great,' Nick sighed. 'Tell me again why I decided to go to law school?'

'Actually, I don't know. You never told me,' I said. I picked up my sandwich and nibbled at an edge. As long as I didn't focus on Nick's slurping – which was hard to do – I thought I might be able to choke it down.

'To Kill a Mockingbird. I wanted to be Atticus Finch,' Nick said.

'Really?'

Nick shrugged. 'No. But it sounds good, doesn't it? Atticus Finch was the ultimate good guy. He was smart and socially conscious and an ace marksman.'

'So if it wasn't Atticus, how did you end up here?'

'Paternal pressure. My dad talked me into it.'

'Oh, right. He's a lawyer, isn't he?'

Nick nodded. He tossed the carcass of a crawfish into a plastic basket the waitress had thoughtfully provided. 'He's a tax and estate lawyer in D.C. He wants me to join his firm when I get out of school.'

'At least you have a guaranteed job lined up,' I said.

'In tax? I don't think so. But I have a few years to break it to him,' Nick said.

'Will he be upset?'

'Definitely. Good old Dad. He likes getting his way.'

'What kind of law are you going to practice?' I asked.

I had no idea what sort of practice I was going to end up in. Litigation? Transactional? The district attorney's office? Probably whatever I could get a job in, I thought darkly. First I had to pass Hoffman's Criminal Law class.

'I'm going into supermodel law,' Nick announced.

I rolled my eyes. 'Yeah, like that even exists.'

'Models need legal representation too, don't they? And I'm just the guy for the job. Seriously, I have it all planned out. And then I'll write a best-selling autobiography called *Supermodel Lawyer*, and it will be made into a movie starring Will Smith.'

'Will Smith?' I asked dubiously.

'Why not? I know what you're thinking – I'm white and he's black, so he's not the obvious choice. But that's what artistic license is for.'

'No, I'm just shocked that you think someone as talented, good-looking, and funny as Will Smith would be the actor chosen to play you in the movie of your life,' I said, and then shrieked when Nick picked up a crawfish and thrust it at me, pretending to let it nibble my hand. 'Ugh, get that thing away from me.'

Nick just laughed and popped the mudbug's head off.

'Where do you want me to drop you?' Nick asked. He was threading his way through the slow-moving traffic on Magazine Street in his Mini.

I looked down at the piece of paper Armstrong had given me. 'He just gave me the address,' I said. 'I assume it's a museum or historical house or something.'

'I don't see anything like that around here,' Nick said. 'Just stores.'

Both sides of the street were lined with shops, most advertising that they sold 'genuine' antiques. Some were housed in converted cottages, others in newer construction, but all were cute and busy. Shoppers bustled around from store to store, spilling out onto the sidewalks with arms full of shopping bags.

'Wait! There he is,' I said, pointing to a spot on the sidewalk where Armstrong was standing. He was wearing a seersucker suit today over a pressed white oxford shirt, looking every bit the Southern gentleman.

'That's Armstrong McKenna? He's shorter than he looks on television,' Nick said. He pulled over to the curb. 'Here you go. Service with a smile.'

'Thanks for lunch,' I said.

'Oh, yeah, it was great. First you called me a male slut, then you disparaged my food. That Graham is a lucky guy, all right,' Nick said. He poked me in the side to show he was just kidding.

'Wish me luck,' I said, surprised at how nervous I actually felt.

'Good luck,' Nick said. 'Although I'm sure you won't need it. You'll do great.'

'Was that a beau?' Armstrong asked, after Nick drove off.

'Who, Nick? No, just a friend.'

'What a pity,' Armstrong said, turning. We started to walk down the sidewalk, passing through throngs of tourists and shoppers all out taking advantage of the beautiful fall weather. 'He had a nice smile. Very sexy.'

'He's a goofball. But you may be right about his smile. A lot of women seem to fall for it.'

'But not you?'

I shook my head. 'No. I have a boyfriend.'

'Ah, that's right. But he doesn't live here, correct? What did you say again? He's an archaeologist in Utah?'

'Close,' I said, with a laugh. 'He's an astronomy professor in Arizona.'

Armstrong shuddered. 'Bad idea. You should never get involved with an academic. They're all insufferable.'

'You're an academic,' I pointed out.

'I *was* an academic. That's how I know. Trust me. Trade him in for the young man with the sexy smile,' Armstrong said. He took a sharp left and started down the walkway of a one-story white shotgun house with black shutters. A white sign hung by the door, with the words BIG EASY ANTIQUES and a fleur-de-lis painted on it in black.

'So is there a museum around here or something?' I asked, looking around. 'I thought you said you wanted to do some research today.'

'I do,' Armstrong said. 'Tables.'

'Tables?' I repeated.

'Obviously, I need to redecorate. I can't live in a whore-house forever. So I thought I'd start with a new dining-room table,' he said. As though this made all the sense in the world.

'And you wanted me here because . . .' I said, my voice trailing off in a question.

'I need a second opinion,' Armstrong said.

'We're going shopping?' I asked, crestfallen that we weren't going to start researching Armstrong's book.

'That we are, darlin'. That we are.'

When I was in the sixth grade, my father gave my mother a Betamax videocassette recorder for Christmas.

The gift did not go over well.

My mom looked at the VCR, sitting on a pile of discarded green wrapping paper dotted with tiny red poinsettias, the same way she might have if he'd gotten her a vacuum cleaner or a mop. Her face tightened with anger, her cheeks reddening and her mouth pursing up. Not only was it wholly impersonal, it was really meant for family use, and thus, to a woman who had been coveting a gold necklace from Tiffany's, the VCR was a truly shitty present.

I have a very clear memory of that Christmas. My mom carefully avoided speaking to, or even looking at, my father for the rest of the day. She and her younger sister, my aunt Caroline, had a whispered conference in the kitchen, but I couldn't hear what was said, even when I pressed a glass to the wall (a technique I'd learned about in a Nancy Drew novel), not with my baby cousin Jenna running around like a shrieking monkey. But it was pretty clear: My mom was pissed. And dinner was even worse.

'What is this we're eating again? Osso buco? Oh, how . . . innovative,' Grandmother Bennett had said. She poked at the osso buco with her fork.

Jenna squawked when she upended her milk right into the

green-bean casserole. Caroline, who was pregnant, excused herself to throw up in the toilet.

'More wine, anyone?' my father asked, looking grim.

Later that night, when my father started to unpack the VCR so that we could watch the Clint Eastwood movie he'd rented, my mother stopped him.

'That,' she said firmly, 'is going back tomorrow. Leave it in the damned box.'

My dad ordered her the necklace the next day, along with a matching pair of earrings.

But the VCR stayed. And when we went to the video-rental store to pick out movies each weekend, I had to fish behind the bulky VHS tapes for the compact Betamax ones that played in our VCR.

'Why couldn't we get one that played VHS tapes?' I asked my dad, when – yet again – the sole copy of *Sixteen Candles* in Betamax was checked out, although there were three VHS copies sitting right there on the shelf.

'Betamax is a superior technology. Just wait and see – it'll only be a matter of time before VHS is phased out and everyone has a Betamax,' my dad predicted.

He was a broad man, with a round face that was always ruddy – in the summer from the sun, in the winter from the wind – but he wasn't fat, just solidly built. His sweaters always smelled like cedar chips, and his voice was deep and full, like a news anchor's. I loved his voice, loved it when he'd read to me when I was a little girl. I'd rest my head against the crook of his shoulder and listen to the words vibrating through his chest.

My dad resisted buying a VHS player for years, caving in only after the local video store stopped carrying Betamax movies altogether and refused to special-order them for him.

Later, after the accident, when Caroline and I set about packing up the house, making decisions about what to keep, what to donate to charity, I found the Betamax squirreled away high on a closet shelf, the cords wrapped up in neat, symmetrical coils. I ran my hand over the black plastic, leaving a trail in the dust that had settled there, and knew that my father had stashed it away so that when Betamax videotapes made their triumphant return to the store shelves, he'd be ready.

My dad never gave up hope. It wasn't in his nature.

By the time I got to the Rue, I was exhausted. My shoulders and neck ached, my back had a crick in it from bending over my books, and my head hurt so much, it felt like someone was sticking needles into my temples. At least now that it was October, the muggy heat was finally starting to break, although the seventy-degree temperature still seemed ridiculously warm to me. When I was a kid living in central New York, we had to wear snowsuits under our Halloween costumes.

Everyone was already at the Rue when I got there. Dana, Lexi, and Jen were sitting at our usual table, and Nick and Addison were over talking to Scott Brown and Pete Berkus, who had also started studying at the coffee shop.

'Does that work?' Lexi was asking Dana as I arrived at the table.

'Does what work?' I asked. I pulled out my books and notepad and dumped them on the table in front of me.

'I bought a book-on-CD version of a Criminal Law study guide, and I play it while I sleep,' Dana explained. She shrugged. 'I don't know if it's helping yet, but I figure it can't hurt.'

'Studying while sleeping. Now, that's hard-core,' I said.

'I've thought about sleeping with my casebooks under my pillow,' Jen said.

'What good would that do?' Lexi asked.

'I thought that the case law might seep in through osmosis,' Jen said.

Nick and Addison walked back over.

'Oh, good, all of my chickadees are here,' Addison said. 'So, I was thinking of starting a harem. Anyone in?'

'In your dreams,' Lexi snorted.

'Hey, Kate,' Nick asked. 'I stopped by your place before I came over.'

'I wasn't there,' I said.

'Yeah, I noticed. When did you get here?'

'Just a few minutes ago. Sorry I'm late. I was at the library, and I lost track of time,' I said.

'See, I told you. Law school is like a black hole,' Jen said.

'It's a whirling vortex of insanity,' Addison said. 'Finals are still months away, but people are already freaking out.'

'The library was packed. Every seat in the reading room was taken,' I said.

'I can't study when it's like that,' Jen said. 'It's too distracting.'

'Hey, Nick, can I see your Contracts notes from Friday's class?' Scott called across the coffeehouse. A few of the patrons glanced up from their papers and books and looked at him disapprovingly. Scott, oblivious, bounded over to our table.

'Hi, Scott,' Lexi said, smiling at him.

'Hey, guys,' Scott said. He was wearing a white baseball cap that was turned around backward. Tufts of shiny dark hair poked out over the plastic adjustable strap.

'You should borrow Kate's notes. She's more thorough than I am,' Nick said.

Scott looked at me. 'Do you mind? I only need them for a few minutes. I'll give them right back.'

I rifled through the stack of binders in front of me and pulled out the black one. 'Sure, here you go,' I said, holding it out to him.

Scott stepped around the table and took the folder.

'I like your hair like this,' he said, holding on to my ponytail. He pulled it playfully, so that I had to tip my head back, and then rested his other hand on my shoulder.

'Um, thanks.'

Scott began kneading my shoulders. 'You're really tense,' he remarked. 'You need a massage.'

His thick fingers dug painfully into my skin. I shrank away from him, but his hands moved with me.

'Yeah, I know,' I said. 'I've probably had too much coffee.'

Scott stopped rubbing, but his fingers lingered on my shoulders. 'What did everyone do last night?' he asked.

'Nick and I went to the Boot again,' Addison said. 'And I went home alone.'

Addison looked at Nick in a pointed way that made it clear that Nick had not left the Boot on his own. Nick grinned, but the tip of his nose turned pink.

'Laundry,' Jen said.

'Studying,' Dana said.

'I had a date,' Lexi said, still smiling flirtatiously at Scott.

'I stayed home,' I said. Armstrong and I had spent the afternoon shopping again – this time for a sofa for his living room – and then I'd curled up in bed with my Torts text-book. Big excitement.

'I thought Graham was flying in this weekend,' Jen said.

'He had to cancel. He's cowriting a paper with another professor, and they had to work on it all weekend,' I said. I still hadn't seen Graham since the weekend we'd decided to get back together. We tried, but we were both so busy, it wasn't as easy to fit in the weekend trips as we'd initially thought.

'Who's Graham?' Scott asked.

'My boyfriend. He lives in Arizona.'

'Oh, right – your *boyfriend*,' Scott said, with a wide grin, taking his hands off my shoulders. He winked at me. 'Thanks for these,' he said, gesturing to my notebook. 'I'll bring them back in a minute.'

After he was out of earshot, I muttered, 'Okay, that was weird. Did he think I was lying about having a boyfriend?'

'Jen, care to fill her in?' Lexi said.

Jen cleared her throat and suddenly became absorbed in her notes.

'What?' I asked. 'What's going on?'

'Nothing,' Jen said, still refusing to meet my stare.

'Tell me!'

'Well . . . Scott might have sort of, kind of gotten the idea that you might . . . be into him,' Jen said. She took a sip of her hot chocolate.

'*What*? Why?'

'Because . . . I . . . uh . . . sort of told him you were,' Jen said. Her pale skin flushed, and she finally looked up at me, her expression sheepish. 'It just slipped out.'

'Slipped out? But I'm *not* interested in him!' I said. 'Why would you tell him that?'

'Because I thought you guys would make a cute couple,' Jen said.

'She thought that if Scott was under the impression that you were interested in him, he'd ask you out,' Lexi explained.

'It was weeks ago,' Jen explained.

'Nice,' Addison commented.

'Jen! You have to go tell Scott that I don't like him,' I said.

'I just had a flashback to the seventh grade,' Nick said.

'Why, did a little girl tell you she liked you and then do a take-back?' Lexi asked, smiling at Nick.

'No, all the little girls loved me. I used to get notes shoved in my locker all the time,' Nick said. 'They were decorated with bubbly hearts and would say things like *Kelli thinks you're cute!*'

'Huh, I never got notes,' Addison mused. 'Although there was this one chick who kept calling my house. She'd giggle when I answered, and say, 'I love you!' But then she'd hang up on me.'

'Yeah, that used to happen to me too. Those little girls can be really aggressive,' Nick said.

'You guys!' I said, louder than I meant. I noticed that Scott was looking over at me. He grinned and nodded when he saw me looking at him. I waved weakly, and then hissed, 'Jen, undo whatever it is you've done.'

'I can't do that,' Jen said. 'It will hurt his feelings.'

'Besides, it sounds insincere,' Nick said. 'If I heard a chick liked me, and then the same friend who told me she liked me came hustling over and told me no, it was just a mistake, I'd assume it was bullshit.'

'Which part?' Lexi asked.

'The part where she did the take-back. I'd think that she was still really into me but was worried that I didn't return her feelings,' Nick said.

'I wouldn't think that,' I argued. 'I'd just assume that it had all been a misunderstanding.'

'That's because you're a woman,' Nick said smugly. 'Men are always ready to believe that women are interested in us. We also don't sit around asking each other if our jeans make our asses look fat.'

'I don't do that,' Dana said.

'You are infinitely more sensible than most women, Dana,' Addison said, and Dana blushed from the praise.

I finally survived a Socratic grilling by Hoffman without humiliating myself. I answered all of his questions until he grudgingly moved on to his next victim. After class, Jen and Lexi took me to the student union to celebrate.

'I was terrified Hoffman was going to call on me today. I didn't do the reading,' Jen said, once we sat down with our pizza slices and sodas.

'I thought you were going home last night to study,' I said. I'd seen Jen just before she left the library the night before, with Addison – who shamelessly sponged rides off all of us – in tow.

Jen shrugged. 'I was tired, so I went to bed early,' she said shortly.

I looked at her. Jen had been preoccupied all morning and hadn't been her usual chirpy self. 'Is everything okay?' I asked.

'Fine,' Jen said, giving me a quick smile before gazing at a group of undergraduate men at the next table. They were wearing fraternity T-shirts and flip-flops and kept calling each other 'Dude!' in loud voices.

'Hot-guy alert,' Jen said.

'They're babies,' Lexi said.

'*Hot* babies,' Jen replied.

'I'm off the market,' Lexi said smugly.

'When do we finally get to meet the mysterious Jacob

Reid?' I asked. I'd seen Lexi's law-professor boyfriend around school but hadn't yet been introduced.

Lexi made a face.

'I tried talking Jacob into coming out with us one night, but he's worried about how it would look if someone saw us together,' Lexi said.

'Then why is he dating you?' I asked. 'If he's so worried that it will get him into trouble?'

Lexi smiled happily. 'Because he can't help himself. He's smitten,' she said.

It occurred to me – not for the first time – that Jacob might just be using Lexi. As far as I could tell, their relationship boiled down to her going over to his apartment and sleeping with him.

'Don't look now, but you'll never believe who just came in,' Lexi said in a hushed whisper.

I turned . . . and felt a jolt of dread. Professor Richard Hoffman. He was waiting in line to order food.

'He's the last person I want to see right now,' I said.

Hoffman stood with his arms crossed and his pelvis shifted forward and looked peevish as usual. He glanced around the room, and when his eyes fell on our table, we all jumped a little and quickly looked down at our slices of pizza.

'Did he see us staring at him?' Jen asked.

'God, I hope not,' Lexi said. 'It's bad enough that he's seeing us with Kate.'

'Hey!' I said.

'No offense, but Hoffman hates you,' Lexi said. 'And I don't want him to associate me with you.'

'Who's that with him?' Jen asked.

'I've never seen her before. I don't think she's a law professor,' Lexi said.

I looked up and saw that a petite woman had joined Hoffman in line. She was wearing a brown suit with a nipped-in waist and pencil skirt, and a pair of killer brown crocodile high heels.

'Oh, my God,' I whispered. 'That's Dean Sullivan. I saw her a few weeks ago. Remember? She was the one I talked to after Hoffman told me that law school wasn't the right place for me.'

'Really? They look awfully . . . cozy. Do you think they're dating?' Lexi said.

'I think she's married,' I said, remembering the family photos I'd seen in her office.

'That doesn't necessarily mean they're not seeing each other,' Lexi said.

We scrutinized the pair, looking for signs of romantic interest. Sullivan kept finding reasons to touch Hoffman's arm, I noticed, and he laughed heartily at something she said, throwing his head back as he guffawed. It made him look almost . . . jolly. In a creepy way. And while we watched them, I started to feel an uneasiness spread through me. I'd trusted Sullivan. I'd told her how much I hated Hoffman, how I knew he was gunning for me. Even worse, I'd *believed* her when she said she'd help me if Hoffman continued to harass me. But now that I knew that at the very least she and Hoffman were good friends, and possibly even more. For all I knew, her relationship with him was the reason she hadn't done anything to help me. Or . . .

'Oh, no,' I groaned.

'What?' Jen asked.

'Do you think she told Hoffman that I told her he's out to get me? And that I tried to get transferred out of his class?' I asked.

'No. I'm sure she wouldn't,' Jen said soothingly.

'Well,' Lexi said, a knowing look crossing her narrow face, 'what would you do if you were sleeping with someone, and a third party came to you with a complaint about your lover. Would you tell him?'

We all pondered this for a minute.

'Yes,' Jen said finally.

I nodded in agreement. 'Yeah, I probably would too. Which means I'm screwed.'

'Not necessarily,' Jen said. 'Up until today, he hadn't called on you in weeks.'

Sullivan and Hoffman had moved up to the counter and were ordering their food.

'It's definitely a date,' Lexi said knowingly. 'He's paying for lunch.'

'Not necessarily,' Jen argued. 'Colleagues treat each other all the time.'

We were still watching them closely when Hoffman and Sullivan turned, each carrying a tray with a salad and beverage cup. Their eyes scanned the room for an empty table, and then, at the same time, they both looked directly at us. Lexi, Jen, and I all froze. This time we'd definitely been caught staring openly at them.

'They're coming this way,' Jen whispered weakly.

Hoffman was walking toward us, Sullivan right behind him. Neither one looked particularly guilty about being seen out together.

'Ladies,' Hoffman said graciously, nodding his head toward us as they passed by to claim the booth just behind ours.

'Hi,' we chimed together, each one sounding more guilty than the other.

Teresa Sullivan smiled pleasantly at me. I returned her smile, although my cheeks felt hot and tight as I did so.

I was so unbelievably screwed.

T he first time I saw Graham, I instinctively didn't like
  him. *What a pompous ass*, I thought, taking in the almost
too-pretty face, the vintage tan corduroy jacket with leather
knot buttons on the sleeves, the haughty pinch to his lips.

I was on my lunch break, eating a bowl of watery onion
soup in the Cornell student union cafeteria, when I spotted
him. He was crossing the room, striding between two rows of
tables with a Styrofoam cup of coffee in one hand and a
leather folder tucked under his arm.

'Wow, he's gorgeous,' my friend Donna, who worked in
the admissions office with me, breathed. She looked at him
wistfully, brushing her dark curls away from her round face.

'You think?' I said noncommittally. I'd never been
attracted to pretty men, so I couldn't see the appeal.

'Uh, yeah,' Donna said.

Graham didn't look our way, didn't seem to notice any of
the women who were glancing at him. He sat down and
pulled out a newspaper, oblivious to the attention.

He was probably used to it, I thought. What must it be like
to go through life as one of the beautiful people, to have
people like you and want to be near you just because you
were blessed by a genetic quirk?

'I think I'm going to be sick,' I heard a voice behind me
say. I turned and saw a thick, meaty guy with a buzz cut stand
up, his hands gripping his stomach, his face a pasty white-

green and damp with sweat. He'd been sitting at a table with four other guys, all of them large and muscular. Athletes, I assumed. They began to laugh at their friend's distress.

'Here it comes,' one of them crowed.

'Fire in the hole!' another hooted.

'Hey, Fitz, you shouldn't have done all of those Jägermeister shots last night!'

I think it was the mention of the liquor that did it. The expression on Fitz's face as he turned toward me held a mixture of nausea and horror as he realized what was about to happen. And then his body convulsed, and he started to gag, and a second later he was bent over and hurling up the five slices of pepperoni pizza and forty-two ounces of orange soda he'd just consumed.

Right down the front of my shirt.

I stared down at my vomit-soaked body. I could feel the sticky wetness seeping through the fabric onto my skin, and I plucked the top away from my body, trying to keep it from touching me.

'Ack,' I said, wondering if I was going to start vomiting too. The smell alone was enough to make me feel sick to my stomach. 'Gah.'

'Sorry, dude,' Fitz mumbled, before running off in the direction of the men's room.

'Oh. My. God,' Donna said, staring at me. She looked like she might throw up too. I had a vision of the entire cafeteria tossing up their lunches, in a grotesque chain reaction.

'I have to get out of here. I have to change,' I said desperately.

'Kate, why do these things always happen to you?' Donna asked, shaking her head in bewilderment. 'You have the worst luck of anyone I've ever met.'

'How the hell should I know?' I snapped. 'It's not like I asked for him to vomit on me.'

Fitz's friends, still at the next table, were howling with laughter. I turned to glare at them, but that just made them laugh even harder. Their faces were practically purple, and one had lowered his head down onto folded arms, his shoulders quivering with mirth.

'Assholes,' I hissed.

'Here, put this on.'

I turned, and the pretty guy was standing there, holding out his corduroy coat. He nodded toward the ladies' room. 'Go on in there and put it on. It buttons all the way up.'

I started to protest but realized that I didn't really have a better alternative. It was either take him up on his offer or walk all the way across campus back to my office covered in vomit. And then I'd obviously have to go home early, which was so not going to thrill my boss, who thought that if he was in the office – even if he arrived early or stayed late – the staff should be there too.

'Thanks,' I said gratefully, accepting the coat. 'You'll have to give me your name and number so that I can return it.'

'I'm Graham,' he said.

A week later, after I had the coat laundered, I called Graham to arrange to return it to him, and we ended up talking on the phone for nearly two hours. Graham had recently taken a biking tour through Ireland – he actually did stuff like that – and he made me laugh when he told me about a supposed bed-and-breakfast he'd stayed in, where his room turned out to be the very pink and very frilly bedroom of the proprietor's teen daughter. The girl in question was in a sulk over being forced to sleep on the couch, and she and her mother spent most of the night screaming Gaelic curses at each other over the din of the television.

At the end of the call, Graham asked me out to dinner, and I accepted. And, much later, after we'd moved in together, Graham confessed to me that when he was a young boy, school bus bullies had routinely called him a faggot, sneering at his finely chiseled cheekbones and full, pouting mouth. He'd started habitually pressing his lips together, trying to make them less pronounced and less noticeable; it was a habit he carried into adulthood.

It turned out Graham wasn't vain after all. Not even a little bit. He was just as self-conscious as the rest of us.

Jen and I went jogging together around Audubon Park, shaded by the arching branches of one-hundred-year-old oak trees. The park was located across St. Charles Avenue from the Tulane campus, and since it was a sunny but cool Sunday afternoon, there was a busy throng of people out walking, running, bicycling, even picnicking.

I had a theory that if I got into shape, it would give me more stamina for studying. When I mentioned it to Jen, she volunteered to go running with me.

'I have got to start exercising,' she'd explained. 'My ass is getting big.'

We met in the Magazine Street parking lot. After stretching for a few minutes, we started at a light trot, moving in a counterclockwise circle around the pavement loop.

'Did you go out last night?' I asked Jen. There had been a Bar Review at the Columns Hotel, but I'd passed on it. Instead, I went shopping yet again with Armstrong, this time for a sleek new bedroom set at a furniture store out in Metairie. Afterward, he took me out to dinner at an Italian restaurant that was – creepily – located in a converted funeral home. We had yet to do any actual work on his book, but I'd started to really look forward to my time with him. It was refreshing to be with someone who wasn't attached to the law school in any way. And Armstrong was a born story-teller, particularly knowledgeable in Southern mythology, so hanging out with him was a bit like spending time with a gay Mark Twain.

'Yes . . . Bar . . . Review,' Jen wheezed.

She's in even worse shape than I am, I thought.

'Who did you go with? Lexi?'

'Can't . . . breathe,' Jen wheezed.

She came to a sudden stop and folded herself over, bracing her hands against her knees.

'I need to take a break,' she gasped.

I glanced at my watch. We'd only been running for three minutes. But Jen staggered off the pavement and collapsed on a wooden bench overlooking the duck pond. I sat down next to her. It was a pretty place to stop and rest, except for the rank odor of bird shit.

'Yeah, Lexi and I went to the Columns with Addison and Nick. And guess who was there,' Jen said, once she could breathe again.

'Who?'

'The mysterious Jacob Reid,' Jen said.

'No, really? Did he hang out with you guys?'

Jen shook her head. 'Not at all. I don't think he knew there was going to be a Bar Review that night. He was with some friends at the bar when we got there. And as soon as he saw Lexi, he went all pale and quiet, and then he left ten minutes later without even saying a word to her.'

'Are you serious?' I asked. I knew Jacob was worried that someone at the school might find out about their relationship, but even so. Leaving without speaking to Lexi was pretty low.

Jen nodded. 'Lexi was pissed. She ended up downing about five Martinis and spent the rest of the night flirting with Addison. Which he just loved, of course.'

'I thought she said she wasn't interested in Add,' I said.

'She's not. She was just using him to make herself feel better.'

'You know, I've had a bad feeling about Jacob from the beginning,' I said. 'I thought he might just be using Lexi for sex.'

'You could be right. I know he called her on her cell phone, late, like right when we were getting to leave, and asked her to come over,' Jen said.

'Please tell me she didn't go.'

Jen nodded. 'Addison drove both of us home, and she had him drop her at Jacob's apartment.'

I sighed. 'Lexi's smart enough to know better.'

'I don't know if any of us are really smart when it comes to relationships,' Jen said darkly.

'Maybe you're right,' I said. 'What happened to Nick?'

'What do you mean?'

'You said Addison drove you and Lexi home. Did Nick go with you?'

'What do you think?'

'Don't tell me he hooked up again.'

Jen nodded. 'He's like some sort of a superhero when it comes to meeting women. And you wouldn't think it to look at him. He's cute, but still. He isn't even that big of a flirt. I think it's the All-American guy-next-door thing he has going on. Women are naturally drawn to that, don't you think?'

'I guess so,' I said, not convinced. 'So who was it this time? I hope not someone from the law school. The last time he hooked up with someone from school, he spent the next few weeks skulking around campus, trying not to run into her.'

'Actually, yeah. He left with Hannah Green,' Jen said.

'Who's that?'

'She's a One-L, although she's not in our section. She's pretty. Very thin, light-blonde hair. You know, the one Addison calls "Cameron Diaz," although I don't think she looks anything like her.'

'I know who you're talking about. Addison must have been beside himself. He's in love with her.'

'Really? He didn't seem to care. But, then again, he had Lexi to distract him.'

We sat quietly, watching the ducks glide along the small pond. One of the ducks looked back at me, his small eyes bright with interest, as he waited to see if I'd toss him a saltine.

'How's your love life going? You and Graham, I mean.'

'Oh . . . good. I guess.'

'What's going on?' Jen asked. 'You have to tell me; I get my vicarious thrills living through my single friends.'

I snorted. 'I haven't even seen Graham in over a month. Not since that weekend he surprised me.'

'But he decided he couldn't live without you and came and found you. That must have been incredible. Make-up sex always is.'

'I've always thought that make-up sex is overrated.'

'And to think I had this vision of the two of you all tangled up in bed, feeding each other cut-up pieces of mango and papaya,' Jen said.

I looked at her, my eyebrows raised.

'I told you, I live vicariously through my single friends,' she said, and laughed. Jen had a great laugh, deep and froggy and completely unself-conscious.

I kicked the grass in front of me with the toe of my running sneaker. A man clasping the hand of a towheaded girl appeared beside us. The little girl wore her hair in two sloppy pigtails and was dressed from head to toe in bright Crayola purple.

'Here, give the ducks some bread, Lyssa,' he said.

Lyssa clasped the slice of bread her father handed her and winged it like a Frisbee into the pond. The ducks all paddled furiously over to the soggy, sinking bread slice, bossing each other in loud honks as they fought over who would get the prize.

'Honey, you're supposed to break it into crumbs first,' the father said gently, handing her another slice.

'Okay, Daddy,' she said, and this time she shredded the bread into confetti before she dumped it into the water. Lyssa clasped her plump hands together, eagerly waiting to see what would happen next. She gurgled with laughter as the ducks dove again and again, grabbing the bread bits. It startled me when I looked at the bland fleshy face of Lyssa's father, as he watched his daughter indulgently, and realized that he was probably only a few years older than me. Parents weren't supposed to be *my* age.

'The weird thing is that I hadn't planned to get involved

with anyone this year, much less get back together with Graham,' I said.

Jen nodded. 'But you can't control who you fall in love with. Or when.'

'True,' I said. 'Do you think Lexi is in love with Jacob?'

'I don't know. I think she thinks she is. I don't know what she was like with guys she's dated in the past. Although it's hard to believe that only a few months ago, none of us knew each other. Now I feel like I know you and Lexi as well as I do my old high school friends. Better even.'

'Boot camp is supposed to be like that too,' I said. 'Although the army would probably be a cakewalk compared to law school.'

'No joke. Did I ever tell you that the first time I saw you was when you and Nick came into Crim together? I thought you guys were a couple,' Jen said.

'I thought the same thing about Lexi and Addison,' I said.

Suddenly Jen sighed, and the smile vanished from her face. 'God, sometimes I really wish I was still single.'

'Why?'

'Why what?' Jen asked, looking startled. I realized that she'd been spacing out and I'd intruded on her thoughts.

'You said you wish you were still single,' I reminded her. 'Are you and Sean having problems?'

'Oh . . . no. There's nothing to talk about, really,' she said, although tension dragged at the outer corners of her eyes, and her mouth curled into a frown. 'We're fine. Sometimes marriage is just . . . well, it's not what you think it's going to be,' she said carefully.

I looked at Jen, not saying anything. The conversation had suddenly become too serious to gloss it over with any of the idle gossip about our classmates that usually occupied us. Who had hooked up with whom at the latest Bar Review. Whether the guy who had fallen out of his second-story window had been drunk. Whether it really was true that one of the Two-Ls was putting herself through law school by stripping at a club in the Quarter. But I had never been married, so I didn't have any real insight into what Jen was going through. Was it something serious, like her husband cheating on her? Or was it just that being around her single friends made her feel confined?

But then Jen grinned at me. 'Don't pay any attention to me,' she said. 'Everything's fine.'

I studied her pale face – the high forehead, the keen eyes, the snub nose, the wide mouth. She might not have been a traditional beauty, but Jen was really quite pretty in her own way. I even liked the slight gap in her front teeth; it gave her a witty, offbeat look.

'Come on, let's walk,' Jen said, standing suddenly.

'I thought we were running.'

'God, are you trying to kill me? And I can't smoke if we run,' Jen said, pulling a pack of Marlboro Lights and a plastic banana-yellow lighter out of her pocket. 'Hey, watch where you step, there's a pile of dog shit right there.'

12

'Okay, this is it. Our last official study group before finals,' Nick announced.

Addison hummed the theme music to *Jaws*.

'I thought we were meeting next weekend,' Lexi said.

'Only informally,' Nick replied.

'As opposed to what?' I asked. 'It's not like our study groups have been run with military efficiency up until now.'

'This is the last time we're going to go over the reading assignments,' Dana explained. 'Next Sunday we're going to exchange outlines, and then we're all on our own.'

'When was this decided?' I asked.

'We took a vote while you were in the bathroom,' Jen told me.

'Oh, okay, then. As long as it was decided democratically,' I said.

'And, as an initial matter of business, don't forget you're all invited over to my house for Thanksgiving,' Jen said.

Finals started eleven days after Thanksgiving, so almost everyone was staying in New Orleans for the long weekend. Everyone but me, that was. Graham and I were spending the holiday with my aunt and her family in suburban Philadelphia. And although I was looking forward to seeing everyone and getting away for a few days, I was starting to regret my decision to travel.

Up until now it had seemed like our first year would drag

on forever (a truly twisted version of the fabled fairy-tale curse where instead of being able to sleep for one hundred years like lucky Sleeping Beauty, I'd spent what felt like the same amount of time stuck in a library cubicle). But now that finals were just a little over two weeks away – just two weeks! – I really didn't have the time to spare for holiday festivities.

'Are you cooking?' Lexi asked.

'As if. Sean's going to do all of it while I lock myself away to study. But don't worry, he's a pretty good cook,' Jen said.

'I'm in,' Nick said.

'I never pass up a free meal,' Addison said.

'I can't,' I said. 'I'm going to Philadelphia, remember?'

'Oh, right. I keep forgetting you're leaving,' Jen said.

'I wish I wasn't,' I said. No matter how much studying I tried to fit in while I was away, there was no way it would be as much as if I just stayed in town. Panic flared, causing a tight, unpleasant pinching in my stomach. 'I don't know why I agreed to do this. It's a crazy time to go away.'

'At least you'll get to see Graham,' Lexi said.

I flew into Philly on the day before Thanksgiving and met Graham at the airport. He didn't seem at all pleased to see me. In fact, he looked pretty pissed off.

'Jesus, Kate, I've been waiting for hours,' he said. 'You were supposed to be here at two.'

'Sorry. The plane's air-conditioning system broke. We were delayed leaving New Orleans,' I apologized. I kissed him hello, and he hesitated for a minute – not yet ready to forgive me – but finally he relented and kissed me back.

'I've never met anyone who runs into as many problems flying as you do. Every time it's something new,' he said as we made our way to baggage claim.

'I know,' I said ruefully. It was the bad luck. When Graham and I were on our way back from Italy a few years earlier, I'd been detained at the airport and strip-searched. It turned out that they were on the lookout for an infamous drug courier who just happened to match my exact description. Just the sight of rubber gloves still gives me the heebie-jeebies.

'Mom locked herself in the bathroom with a bottle of wine,' Jenna announced when she opened the door.

'She's mad at Jenna,' Christy added from behind her.

Jenna, nineteen, was two years older than Christy, but the two looked almost like twins. They were both tall and rangy, and both had a tumble of blonde-streaked hair, although Christy's chin was squarer, and Jenna's eyes were hazel rather than blue.

'She is not,' Jenna retorted. 'You're the one who got her upset.'

Christy snorted. 'Yeah, like your getting a tramp stamp was my fault.'

What the hell is a tramp stamp? I wondered. I wasn't that much older than my cousins, but sometimes it seemed like they were talking a different language.

'You're the one who told her!' Jenna huffed.

'How about a hello?' I asked my cousins. While they bickered, Graham and I were still standing on the front step, shivering against the frigid wind. I'd forgotten how freaking cold it got up here.

'Sorry,' they chorused sheepishly, and stepped aside to let us in. My cousins hugged me hello, and I noticed that when Graham kissed them each on the cheek, Christy blushed. She'd always had a crush on him.

'Your mom's in the bathroom?' I asked, once the door was closed and we'd shrugged out of our coats.

My cousins nodded.

'She's been up there for ages,' Jenna said.

'Although maybe she'll come out now that you're here,' Christy added.

'I'll go find her,' I said. I glanced at Graham.

'Go ahead,' he said. 'I'll deal with our luggage.'

I went upstairs, crossed the master bedroom, and knocked on the bathroom door.

'Go away,' my aunt called out.

'It's me. Kate,' I said.

'Kate!'

The door swung open a moment later, and then my aunt was there, folding me into her arms. Tears blurred in my eyes, surprising me.

'I'm so glad you came,' my aunt said. She pulled back and grinned at me. The girls had taken after her – she had the same blonde hair and athletic build. A faint cobweb of lines was fanning out from her blue eyes, but other than that she looked younger than her forty-seven years. 'Is Graham with you?'

I nodded. 'He's downstairs.'

'Did you hear about Jenna's tattoo?'

'No!' I exclaimed. 'Christy said something about a "tramp stamp," but I didn't know what she was talking about.'

'A tramp stamp? Is that what it's called? Oh, dear God.' Caroline shut her eyes and shook her head slowly. 'Give me strength.'

'I take it you're not pleased?'

Just then we heard a stampede of footsteps thundering up the stairs. My aunt frowned, pulled me into the bathroom, and locked the door behind us.

'Mom!' Christy's voice was muffled through the door. 'Let us in!'

'We want to see Kate too!' Jenna yelled.

'Go away!' Caroline bellowed. She collapsed back on a Lucite vanity stool in a dramatic swoon and took a swig of wine. 'Here's some advice, Kate: Never have a teenage girl.'

'I heard that,' Jenna called out.

'And what exactly is a "tramp stamp," young lady?' Caroline called back.

There was a pause, which Christy filled by giggling. 'A tattoo on your lower back,' she said.

'Shut up!' Jenna said.

'Ow, don't push me,' Christy complained. 'Mom, Jenna just pushed me.'

'They're seventeen and nineteen years old,' Caroline said, widening her eyes with dismay.

But the familiarity of their bickering warmed me. Some things never changed.

'Go downstairs and keep Graham company,' Caroline yelled through the door at her daughters. The girls protested but eventually could be heard padding away and thumping down the stairs. Caroline had a half-empty bottle of wine on the edge of the sink. She poured some into a glass tumbler and handed it to me. She held her glass up in a toast. 'Here's to being home for the holidays.'

'Cheers,' I replied.

We clinked glasses together.

'So, what's the deal with the tattoo?' I asked.

Caroline's lips twitched as she tried to suppress a smile. 'She didn't show it to you?'

'Not yet,' I said.

'It's a butterfly. Or it's supposed to be a butterfly. But it hurt so much that she stopped the tattoo guy halfway through,' Caroline said. 'So there's the outline of a butterfly, but only part of one wing is colored in. It looks awful.'

I couldn't help laughing. 'Why'd she do it?'

'I have no idea. Why do teenagers do anything? I just can't believe my daughter has something called a "tramp stamp" permanently affixed to her body,' Caroline groaned. She tipped her head back and downed the last of her wine. Then she fixed her gaze on me. Uh-oh. I knew that look. It was the same one my mother had perfected during my teen years. I was about to be interrogated.

'How's school?' Caroline asked.

'Fine. You know . . . hard. But it's supposed to get better after the first year.'

'You look thin,' she said.

'I do?' I asked, pleased.

'Too thin,' she said. 'You're not eating enough.'

'I'm eating just fine.' I nudged her with my foot. 'You don't have to worry about me, you know. I'm a big girl.'

'Yes, I do. If it had been the other way around . . . If it had been me who . . .' Caroline pinched her lips together and swallowed. 'Your mother would have worried about Jenna and Christy.'

I nodded, and looked down at my tumbler of wine, and tried to ignore the lump in my throat.

'I know she would have,' I said softly.

After Thanksgiving dinner, Jenna and Christy wanted to go see a local Christmas light display.

'Christmas lights?' Graham asked dubiously.

Graham had been in a difficult mood all day. He wasn't outright rude to anyone, but he wasn't going out of his way to be chatty either. He'd spent most of the afternoon sacked out in front of the television with my uncle Jim, not making any effort to help with dinner preparations. It was what he always did on Thanksgiving, and it had always irritated me. And I'd expected more from him. I thought that part of our getting back together would mean that he'd try harder, that we'd *both* try harder, to change things, to improve our relationship. But instead, we'd slid right back into the same patterns, only instead of living under the same roof and never having sex, we lived several states apart and never had sex.

And we certainly weren't going to be having any sex this weekend. One of Caroline's house rules was that Graham slept on the couch, while I bunked in the guest room.

'We always go see the Christmas lights,' Jenna said. 'It's a tradition.'

'You all go ahead. I think I'll just watch the end of the game,' Graham said.

'Will you excuse us for a moment?' I said. I pulled on Graham's sleeve, and he got up and followed me out of the dining room and into the front hall.

'What?' he asked.

'You *know* what,' I snapped.

'Oh, God. I hate this conversation,' Graham said. He rolled his eyes.

'What conversation? Why are you acting like this?'

'Yep, this is the one.'

'You're acting like a jerk,' I said. 'You know, I really should have stayed in New Orleans this weekend and studied, but you said it was important to you that we spend Thanksgiving together.'

'It was. I mean, it is.'

'Then why are you spending the whole weekend sitting in the living room watching television?' I asked.

'One afternoon doesn't constitute the whole weekend,' Graham said. 'And I've been working hard too.'

'We all have. But that didn't stop the rest of us from cooking all day.'

'I thought it was a woman thing. I figured you all wanted to talk about girl stuff,' Graham said.

I cocked an eyebrow at this. 'Girl stuff?'

'Yeah, girl stuff. Shopping and shoes and things.'

'Caroline's a pediatrician. I'm in law school. Jenna's majoring in business. We are capable of talking about something other than shoes,' I said, nettled at his generalization.

'So what were you talking about?'

I thought back. Actually, we'd spent much of the day discussing what stores were having sales on the day after Thanksgiving and if any of the advertised specials were really worth waiting in line for. And then Christy had showed off the new sequin-covered flats she'd just purchased.

'Politics,' I said loftily. 'We were talking politics.'

'Like what?'

'Like . . .' I stopped to think of something that he'd believe, although I hadn't even watched the news in months. 'I don't know. Why are you interrogating me?' I asked crankily.

A smile twitched at Graham's lips. 'Politics, huh?' he said.

I sputtered, trying to think of a comeback. But before I could respond, he leaned in and kissed me.

'Okay,' Graham murmured. 'Let's go see the Christmas lights.'

'Hey,' Graham said. He stepped into the guest room and closed the door quietly behind him. 'What are you doing?'

It was late on Saturday night, but I was still sitting up in bed, an afghan wrapped around me to ward off the cold, reading my Contracts casebook.

'Studying,' I said. 'And you're not supposed to be in here.'

'Everyone's in bed. Except for your uncle. He fell asleep in front of the TV,' he said, as he crossed the room and sat down on the edge of the bed. Graham reached for my hand, curling his fingers around it. I immediately recognized the glint in his eye.

'Oh, no. No way,' I said, pulling my hand back.

'But you look sexy in your flannel pajamas,' Graham said, plucking at the plaid fabric.

'No, I don't. And my aunt would kill us both if she knew you were in here.'

'We lived together for three years. I think she's aware that we've had sex.'

'It's not my virtue she's worried about. She doesn't want the girls to think she's a hypocrite. Telling them to wait, while letting us stay here together,' I explained. Graham unbuttoned the top button of my pajama top. 'Stop that!'

Graham popped open the next button. 'Make me,' he said, and he leaned forward and nuzzled against my neck. His lips felt warm and dry against my skin, and for some reason the sensation was more annoying than it was sensual.

I hesitated for a moment, not sure what to do. On the one hand, Graham and I hadn't seen each other in months. Even during our driest of dry spells, we'd never gone this long without sleeping together. But I didn't want to purposely break my aunt's rules while I was staying in her house. And even if she didn't find out, I really just wasn't in the mood. I don't know if it was stress or lingering irritation at Graham, but all I wanted to do was finish my reading assignment and then go to sleep.

'Stop,' I said. I gently pressed the palm of my hand on his shoulder.

'Come on, Kate. We're flying out tomorrow, and then we won't see each other until Christmas break,' Graham murmured against the side of my throat. He slid his hand up my pajama top and pinched one of my nipples. Hard.

'Jesus, that hurt!' I said, and this time I pushed him hard, shoving him away from me.

'What the hell?' Graham said. He snatched his hand back and used it to straighten the glasses sitting askew on the end of his nose. 'What's wrong with you?'

'How would you like it if I pinched one of your nipples?'

'Is that an offer?'

'No! I told you,' I said irritably. 'My aunt—'

'Won't know a damned thing. She's sound asleep by now,' Graham finished. He stood up and glared down at me.

'Fine, then. I just don't want to!' I was too annoyed to feel guilty.

'I guess I'll go back to my couch,' Graham said coolly, turning toward the door. And before I could call him back, he was gone.

'Shit,' I said softly. I didn't want this fight. Except for the Thanksgiving Day flare-up, the long weekend had passed amiably enough, and I wanted for us to be on good terms before we flew back to our new respective towns. Now that we were living apart, we couldn't let these arguments fester the way we used to.

I should go find him so we can make up, I thought. And he's right, we should make love. Even if I'm not in the mood now, I'm sure that will change once we get started. It usually does, with a bit of effort.

I looked back down at my Contracts book. I only had about six pages left to read.

I'll go down when I finish, I decided.

But a half hour later, when I padded downstairs in my bare feet, Graham was already asleep. A book on photography – his latest passion – lay open across his stomach. Graham's head was turned to one side, and his chest rose and fell rhythmically. I watched him for a minute, and then I lay down next to him on the couch, turning on my side to fit into the few inches of available space, and rested my head on the flat plane below his shoulder. Graham shifted, curling his arm around me and sleepily kissing the top of my head.

'Hi,' he mumbled.

'Shhh. Go back to sleep,' I whispered.

I felt him relax back into sleep, and I sighed, contented. I knew I couldn't stay here all night, that I'd have to return to my room before my family woke up. But for now, with the length of my body touching Graham's, and my breath matching his, I felt so calm and at peace, I didn't want to move.

13

Finals were hell.

My diet consisted of vending-machine food, and I ingested so much caffeine my hands shook and my stomach hurt. Personal-grooming habits slid too. I showered when I remembered but went days at a time without washing my hair.

I wasn't the only one. Nick stopped shaving and walked around looking like a lumberjack. Lexi almost never left her favorite cubicle on the top floor of the library, holing up with every practice test she could find. Jen did most of her studying outside, sitting at one of the courtyard tables, chain-smoking and yelling at anyone who talked near her. Addison disappeared entirely. Only Dana seemed more or less her usual self.

'I feel ready,' she said, when I asked her how she was staying so calm.

'I wouldn't admit that to anyone else,' I advised her.

On the morning of our first exam, the Contracts final, I was shaking with nerves when I sat down in my usual seat at the back of the classroom – we didn't have to sit in our assigned seats for the exam, but I thought I'd be more comfortable staying with what was familiar – and began to set up for the test, lining up my various supplies across the table in front of me. My outline (the test was open book). My casebook.

Scratch paper. Ten pens (in case nine of them ran out of ink over the course of the three-hour exam). Earplugs. Bottled water. Granola bars. A banana. Aspirin. Kleenex. Tums. I was wearing my favorite faded black sweatpants and a long-sleeve charcoal-gray T-shirt, and I had my hair pulled back in a tight ponytail.

'Hey,' Nick said, sitting down next to me. His face was pale under the stubble of his beard, and his blue eyes were watery and bloodshot.

'Did you sleep last night?' he asked.

I nodded. 'Sort of. I kept dreaming that I was oversleeping, and then I'd wake up in a panic. Finally I just got up at six and came down here early.'

'I knocked on your door but you'd already left,' Nick said. He yawned widely. 'I barely slept. I took a practice test yesterday and totally froze. It freaked me out, so I stayed up most of the night cramming.'

Lexi came in, followed by Jen and Addison. They all looked nervous, although Jen had thrown her head back and was laughing at something Addison had said. I noticed Addison was wearing his clip-on nose ring, like a good-luck charm. They waved at Nick and me but sat down in the front row. I glanced around to see if Dana was there, and she was, sitting to the right of the room, looking unnaturally calm as she chatted with a small, dark-haired woman whom I knew only as Ms Bianchi.

Some of our classmates buzzed nervously, discussing in loud voices what they expected would be on the test, while others sat quietly, their hands clenched in fists. A few looked like they might actually be sick, something that was not an uncommon occurrence during first-year finals. Rumor had it that at least one student every semester ended up racing for the toilet, undone by the sickening anxiety that simmered in us all.

One of the heavy double doors opened, and we all fell instantly silent as Professor Legrande entered the room, carrying blue books and a stack of legal-size papers.

'How's everyone feeling this morning?' Professor Legrande asked in a strong Cajun accent, smiling kindly around. He was my favorite professor, not because his lectures were particularly scintillating – this was Contracts, after all – but because he seemed to be a genuinely nice man. He was younger than most of the professors, probably in his early forties, but was already mostly bald and carried about fifty extra pounds on his broad frame. During lectures, when he was probing one of the students on the drawbacks of a particular policy, if the student answered, 'Increased litigation' (a popular One-L answer), Legrande would clap his hands together and bellow, 'No! You're a future lawyer; increased *litigation* is a good thing!'

'I always wear my lucky tie to finals,' Legrande said, holding up the tie for us to see. It had a picture of Bugs Bunny silk-screened on it. There was a rumble of nervous laughter from the class. 'All right, here's what I'm going to do. I'm going to pass out the blue books and the exams. When you get your exam, please lay it facedown on the table. Once everyone has an exam, I'll start the clock and give you the go-ahead, so that y'all will start at the same time.'

A swell of nausea rose inside me. This was it.

Nick glanced over and gave me a tight-lipped smile. 'Good luck,' he said, holding out his fist.

'You too,' I said, bumping my fist against his.

'Before you hand in your test, don't forget to sign the Honor Code statement printed on the back of each blue book,' Legrande said. 'Are you ready? You may begin. Good luck, ladies and gentlemen.'

My heart lurched and then began to race. I flipped the test over, and I started to read the directions, even though I already knew them by heart from having gone over Legrande's back exams that were kept on file in the library.

So far so good, I thought, as I finished reading the instructions and moved on to the first question. And, just like that, my ability to read suddenly left me. My eyes wouldn't focus, and the typed words swam around the page. My neck and back seemed to stiffen, and a sharp pain throbbed in between my shoulder blades. My lungs felt like they were shrinking to the size of grapes.

Relax! I screamed at myself, as though silently berating myself could possibly have that effect. You have to calm down! Relax! Focus! Concentrate! You can do this!

And somehow – miraculously – it worked. The words came back into focus, and suddenly I was reading a hypo- thetical question about a wholesaler of tiles and a sub- contractor who installed them. The question went on for eight long paragraphs, but as I was reading it, I began to make sense of the issues. I wiped my moist palms on my T-shirt, popped the earplugs into my ears, picked up my pen, and began to take notes on a sheet of scratch paper.

I was so absorbed in the exam that – even though I was just finishing my answer to the last question when Professor Legrande gave us the fifteen-minute warning, his voice muffled by my earplugs – I was startled and dropped my pen. Most of the people sitting around me were bent over their desks, scribbling furiously in their blue books. I took a deep breath and flipped back through the test, luxuriating in the extra time I had to recheck my work.

And then Legrande was suddenly calling time, and we all put down our pens and passed our papers back to the ends of the rows. We weren't allowed to speak until all of the exams and blue books had been collected, which seemed to take an inordinate amount of time. When Legrande was satisfied that he had all of the papers, he smiled at us and said, 'Contracts One is now officially over. Good luck on the rest of your exams, ladies and gentlemen.'

'How'd you do?' Nick asked, as we stood stretching muscles that were tight from sitting still for three straight hours.

'All right,' I said, breathing out. 'I think.'

But then I heard someone behind me say, 'Did you get

that unjust-enrichment angle in Question Two? I almost missed it and didn't notice it until I was going over my work,' and a tremor of terror shook me. Unjust enrichment? Had there been an unjust-enrichment angle in Question Two?

'Was there an unjust-enrichment issue in Question Two?' I asked Nick, my voice dropping to an anxious whisper.

He nodded and looked serious. 'Yeah, I think so. You don't remember that part?'

'No, I don't think I wrote anything about that.' I groaned. 'Oh, God. I am so screwed.'

Nick shook his head. 'You don't know that. Let's get the hell out of here. It's not going to help to hear everyone rehashing the test,' he said.

I threw all of my test supplies into the knapsack that I'd stashed by my feet. Nick was striding ahead of me, walking quickly and not stopping to talk to anyone. I hurried after him. I was glad when I saw that Lexi and Jen were huddled around Addison while he looked up something in his text-book book and they didn't notice us leaving. Nick was right – the last thing I wanted to do was relive the exam.

'How'd you do, Kate?' Scott Brown called after me.

I shrugged and smiled but didn't stop to talk. Outside in the hall, Nick had finally slowed down and was waiting for me, watching our classmates trickle out of the lecture hall in groups of two or more, chattering loudly about the test.

'Everyone's going insane,' he said, looking disgusted. 'They're all just torturing themselves.'

'No, they're trying to make themselves feel better,' I said as we turned and walked down the hall and out the front doors of the law school together.

'Where did you park?' Nick asked as we turned east down Freret.

I shook my head. 'I didn't dare drive this morning. I took the streetcar.'

'Probably a smart move. Come on, I'll give you a ride.'

'What are you doing now? Are you going to study?'

'No way. I'm too burned out after that exam,' Nick said. 'I should probably take a nap, but I'm too revved up to sleep. Hey, you know what I want to do?'

'No, what?'

'Go to a movie,' Nick said. 'You want to?'

'We can't,' I said immediately, although when Nick said, 'Why not?' I couldn't think of a good answer.

The idea did have enormous appeal. The idea of being able to hide in the darkness and zone out to a celluloid fantasy while gobbling down handfuls of buttery popcorn sounded heavenly.

'Okay, let's go,' I said happily.

The movie theater was mostly empty when we arrived for the one o'clock showing of a horror movie starring glossy young actors who were all ten years younger and thirty pounds lighter than me. It wasn't the type of movie I'd normally see, but it was the only thing playing that wasn't a melodrama or a cartoon, and Nick and I had been in agreement that we couldn't take anything too heavy.

Nick bought my ticket, and when I protested, he simply smiled and said, 'It's okay. You get the popcorn and we'll be even.'

We stopped at the concession counter, where I bought the biggest tub of popcorn they sold, with extra imitation-butter topping, along with two sodas and an enormous box of Milk Duds.

'I can't believe we're doing this,' I said. 'It feels so . . . so reckless.'

'Wow, you really do know how to walk on the wild side, don't you?'

I elbowed Nick playfully in the side. 'You know what I mean. Most of our class probably went home and started studying for Torts on Friday,' I said.

'There's no point in studying right now. My brain is fried,' Nick said.

We sat in the middle of the row, halfway up the theater, and both of us slouched back in our seats as we waited for the movie to start. Now that the tension was starting to leave my body, my neck and back ached.

'I'm starving,' he said, his voice muffled through the mouthful of food.

'Milk Dud?' I offered him.

'Definitely. There's a secret to the ultimate movie-theater snack that not many people know about. But I'm going to let you in on it,' Nick said.

'Tell me.'

'The secret is to first take the popcorn.' Nick stuffed a handful of popcorn in his mouth. 'Then add the chocolate.' He tossed a few Milk Duds in. 'And then chase it down with a splash of Coke.' He slurped some Coke through the straw.

'That's the secret?'

'Yup. Popcorn plus chocolate plus Coke,' he said through his popcorn and candy-stuffed mouth. 'It's the patented Nick Crosby Movie Snack.'

I shook my head in disbelief. 'Do you really think you're the only person who's figured out that popcorn, chocolate, and soda taste good together? Popcorn, chocolate, and soda make up three of the four pillars of the concession-stand marketing strategy. Of course they taste good together; they're supposed to,' I said.

'That may be true, but they taste better when you eat them in the patented Nick Crosby Movie Snack sequence.'

'Stop saying that.'

'You're just jealous. What's the fourth pillar? Nachos?'

'No.'

'Hot dogs?'

'Eww. No. Twizzlers. Actually, all of the synthetic-fruit-based candies, as opposed to the chocolate-based candies. Twizzlers, Sour Patch Kids, Jujubes.'

'All inferior.'

'Be that as it may, they're still the fourth pillar.'

He stuffed another round of popcorn and Milk Duds into his mouth, and then sucked up some Coke through a straw. 'The fourth pillar isn't holding its weight,' Nick said.

The Torts exam on Friday and the Civ Pro exam on Monday were pretty much what I expected, although they left my brain feeling numb.

'One more test and then we're done forever,' Jen said as we dragged ourselves out of the Civ Pro exam.

'You mean until next semester, when we get to do this all over again,' I said.

'Don't remind me,' she sighed.

'Hey, chickies, wait up,' Addison called, jogging to catch up with us. 'What did you guys put for Question Two-B – the one about the plane crash in Brazil?'

'No! No postmortems! It's too depressing,' I said.

'And I can't even remember. I think that was around the point where I lost my mind,' Jen said desolately.

We walked outside into the law-school courtyard and sat down on one of the cement benches. Jen pulled out a white box of Marlboro Lights and smacked it against the heel of her hand.

'Let me bum a smoke,' Addison said.

'What a surprise,' Jen muttered. 'I hate Social Smokers. They never want to buy their own cigarettes, because they think that will make them a Real Smoker, so they just mooch off those of us who are honest about our bad habits.'

'I'll buy you a pack if you give me two cigarettes now,' Addison bargained.

'Deal,' Jen said. She flipped open the box, pulled out two cigarettes, and lit one. She handed the lit cigarette to Addison and then lit her own.

'That was traumatic,' Lexi said as she exited the law school. She looked dazed as she sat down next to Jen and sighed heavily. 'May I have a cigarette?'

Jen rolled her eyes heavenward but produced a cigarette

for Lexi. While Lexi lit her cigarette, Nick and Dana walked up. Nick looked absolutely awful – dark rings under his eyes, a heavy beard, and wearing rumpled sweats and a faded T-shirt that looked as though he'd slept in them. Dana, in stark contrast, was serene. She was wearing ironed khakis and a black sweater, and her curly hair was caught back into a neat ponytail.

'Brutal, huh?' Nick asked.

'We're not discussing it,' I reminded him.

'I just mean in general,' he said.

I shrugged. 'It was about what I expected,' I said.

'Well, it kicked my ass,' Jen said.

'Mine too,' Addison agreed. He blew out a big puff of smoke and sighed mournfully.

'I'd seen it before,' Dana said.

'What? How?' Lexi said, staring at her.

'It was the exact same test that Professor Vega gave to his Civ Pro class a few years ago,' Dana said.

'But how did you see it?' I asked her.

'It was on file with the rest of the tests in the library. I finished going over all of Chandler's old tests, so I started going over Vega's,' she said.

'But that's *cheating*,' Lexi said sharply. Her voice had a shrill edge to it.

'No, it's not,' Addison said. 'The tests are there for whoever wants to look at them. Just because Chandler was too lazy to come up with a new test doesn't mean Dana cheated.'

Dana looked at Addison as though he'd thrown his body between her and an oncoming bus, gratitude shining in her brown eyes.

'It just doesn't seem fair,' Lexi grumbled.

'Kate, do you need a ride home?' Nick asked suddenly.

I nodded and stood. We said good-bye to the others and then walked down toward Freret, where Nick's car was parked.

'Lexi can be such a bitch,' Nick said, once we were out of

their hearing. 'You don't accuse people of cheating like that. She's just jealous because she didn't think to look at the practice tests from other classes.'

'Who would, other than Dana? I didn't get through all of Chandler's old tests. Hell, I didn't get through half of them.'

'I didn't either,' Nick said. 'But that's probably why Dana's been cruising through finals, while the rest of us look like shit.'

'Hey! Speak for yourself,' I said, hitting him lightly in the arm.

We reached Nick's red Mini Cooper, parked on a side street.

'Why didn't you get the Mini Cooper with the British flag painted on top of the car?' I asked, once we were settled in and Nick was maneuvering down Freret and turning right on State.

'Hmm. Don't know. Maybe because I'm straight and American?' Nick asked.

'I'd drive one, and I'm straight and American,' I said.

'Yeah, but you're a chick. You can get away with it,' Nick said. 'Anyway, what's up with Addison and Dana?'

'I don't know,' I said. 'I don't think there's anything going on. Why, is Addison interested in her?'

'Actually, I think he's into someone else.'

'Who?'

'I can't tell you. It would go against the Guy Code of Honor.'

'Oh, come on. You have to tell me. You know you're incapable of keeping a secret.'

'That's not true,' Nick said.

I leaned over and poked him in the ribs.

'Hey! Don't do that, I'm driving,' he exclaimed.

I poked him again.

'Stop! Okay, fine, fine, I'll tell you, just stop poking me. I think Add likes Jasmine West,' Nick said.

'Who's that?' I asked, trying to remember. The name

sounded familiar, but exams were frying my short-term memory.

'You know. She sits in the first row in Torts and raises her hand all the time? Long curly hair and rather well endowed in the, um, chest area.'

'The *Sweaty Girl*? Add has a *crush* on the *Sweaty Girl*?' I asked.

'The Sweaty Girl – why do you call her that?'

'Duh – she's always sweaty,' I said. 'Always. Every time I see her. It looks like she sprays herself down with water before class.'

'I think she just works out a lot.'

'I've seen her sweaty at eight in the morning,' I said.

'Women are so critical,' Nick said, with an annoyingly superior air of resignation.

'I can't help it if I notice she has perspiration issues,' I said. 'And how is that any worse than you noticing how big her boobs are?'

'Because I was just appreciating the natural beauty of the female form.'

'Ha!'

'It's true. How burned out are you on studying?'

'So burned out, I don't know if I'm going to make it through Crim,' I said. 'And, knowing Hoffman, it's going to be a bitch of an exam.'

'Do you want to study together? Without the others, I mean. Jen and Addison joke around too much, so I never get anything done when they're there. And Dana's way too prepared. Studying with her would just freak me out,' Nick said.

'And Lex?'

Nick shook his head. 'No, I can't deal with her right now. If I hear her talk about her stupid boyfriend one more time in that annoying sticky-sweet tone of voice, my head might actually explode.'

'Okay. Where do you want to study? My place or yours? Or the Rue?'

'Let's start at the Rue tomorrow when we're fresh, but if it gets too noisy, we'll head back home.'

'It's a date,' I joked, because the only thing less datelike than studying for exams would be if Nick accompanied me to my yearly gynecological exam.

The day before Hoffman's Criminal Law final exam, a cold front came through New Orleans. Initially I dismissed how panicky the weathermen were acting, as they reminded their viewers to bring in their plants and pets, to cover their pipes, and advising that any possible school closings would be listed on the morning news.

'This is the Deep South,' I laughed scornfully, when Graham called to wish me good luck on my last exam. 'How cold could it possibly get? The temperature's barely going to dip below freezing.'

'The houses around here weren't built to withstand the cold. I've seen your apartment. It isn't exactly well insulated. Every window and door lets in a draft,' Graham said.

'At Cornell we'd be sunbathing on the middle of campus when the temperature got up into the forties. I think I'll survive one night of thirty-two-degree temperatures,' I scoffed.

'Even so, don't forget to put an extra blanket on your bed,' Graham advised.

'Don't worry,' I said. 'I should probably get back to work, though.'

'Okay. I'll call you tomorrow after your test,' Graham said.

'I won't be coming home right away. Some of us are going out to celebrate after finals are over,' I said. 'I'll call you when I get back, okay? Oh, but wait – would you do me a favor?'

'Of course.'

'Will you call me tomorrow at seven a.m.? I'm worried I'm going to oversleep,' I said. 'I need a wake-up call. I know that's, like, five your time. . . .'

'No problem. I'm getting up early to run tomorrow anyway.'

'Thanks,' I said. 'I'll talk to you tomorrow.'

'I have never been colder in my life,' I said, through chattering teeth.

'Are you kidding me?' Nick asked. 'You used to live in Ithaca. It's like Antarctica up there for a good six months of the year.'

It was so cold out, the Rue had closed early, so we were back in my apartment, camped out in my living room.

Unlike our other finals, which were all open-book, Hoffman had limited us to a two-page outline for the Crim exam. He wasn't even letting us bring in scrap paper; he said that we could always take notes on the exam itself, which was ridiculous, because there was hardly any room to write, except around the margins, and no one could outline their answer in such a small space. And all the outline page restriction meant was that everyone was coming up with creative ways for shrinking their text down and reducing the margins, so as to fit all crucial information onto the two sheets. I had my outline down to a six-point font, although I had to squint to read it.

'Yes, and in Ithaca we had houses with insulation and real heating systems,' I said, looking at my window unit with disgust. It was turned on high and was about as effective as a hair dryer would be at warming the room. 'I'm thinking of lighting a campfire right here in the middle of the floor. Look at this, my fingers are actually turning blue.'

'So what do you want to do?'

'I'm getting under my covers.'

'You're done studying for the night?' Nick said.

'No. Gah. Not even close. Come with me, and bring the books. Oh, and the Doritos,' I said. I rubbed my hands together, which were becoming stiff with the cold. The frigid wind was swirling around the house, finding its way into my apartment through every last creaky floorboard and crooked windowsill. 'Look at this. It's so cold, I can actually see my breath, *inside* my apartment.'

When I got to my bedroom, which was at the front end of the apartment, I pulled open a dresser drawer and rifled through it, pulling out extra sweaters, sweatshirts, and a pashmina scarf that I could use to layer, and then I jumped into bed and pulled the comforter up around me.

'Brrrr,' I said as I waited for my body heat to fill the cold layer between the blanket and me.

'Where should I go?' Nick asked, as he came into the room with our pile of books and notebooks, a half-eaten bag of Doritos and an unopened package of Oreos resting on top of the stack.

'You can get under the covers too,' I said.

Nick's eyebrows went up. 'In bed? With you?'

'These are exigent circumstances. And besides, I have so many layers of clothes on, even if you wanted to get fresh, you wouldn't be able to get to me,' I said.

'Is that a challenge?' he asked, leering comically. But he climbed into bed and wrapped the other half of my comforter around him.

'Okay, where were we?' I asked.

'Conspiracy and attempt,' Nick said. He ran a hand through his hair, so that the curls stood up at wonky angles. 'I will never get this.'

'It's easy,' I said. 'You're just overanalyzing. Let's go through it again.'

I woke up to the phone ringing. Loudly. In my ear.

'What? Phone?' I mumbled incoherently.

'Are you going to answer that?' a voice asked. A male voice. More specifically: Nick's voice.

That got my attention.

I sat up straight in bed, and everything began to click into place. We were studying for Crim. Must have fallen asleep.

Oh, God, the test's *today*. What time is it? Am I late? Where's my clock? Seven. That's a.m., right?

The phone rang again.

I grabbed the black cordless phone and clicked the on button.

'Hello?'

'I was starting to worry that you were sleeping through my wake-up call,' Graham said.

'Oh, right, I totally forgot,' I said, slumping back against the pillows. 'I fell asleep studying, and when the phone rang, I was disoriented.'

I looked at Nick, who had pushed himself up into a sitting position and was staring at me bleary-eyed. 'What happened,' he mouthed to me. I shrugged and shook my head.

'Are you awake now?' Graham asked.

'As awake as I get without having coffee,' I replied.

Nick got out of bed. A minute later, I heard him softly close the bathroom door. Without thinking it through, I covered the phone with the heel of my hand so Graham wouldn't hear the floorboards squeaking under Nick's feet or the sound of muffled gargling coming from the bathroom.

This is ridiculous, I thought. Why am I hiding Nick's presence from Graham? It's not like I was cheating on him. . . . Nick and I just fell asleep studying. Graham wouldn't care; he isn't the type of guy to blow something so trivial and harmless out of proportion.

'Are you still there?' Graham asked.

'Sorry, yeah, I'm here. It was so weird, last night –' I began.

But Graham had also started to talk at the same time. 'Good luck on your test today. I love you,' he said.

'Um, yeah, you too,' I said, and then I cringed painfully. I'm not known for my witty repartee first thing in the morning.

There was an awkward pause.

'Okay, well . . . call me after your exam. And good luck,' Graham said.

'Thanks. I'll talk to you later.'

'Bye.'

I pulled the covers up over my head and groaned. Did I really respond to his 'I love you' with 'Yeah, you too'? And I hadn't told Graham that Nick spent the night, which meant that if I told him later, it would look like I was trying to hide something.

'Kate?'

I pulled the blanket down slightly and looked at Nick with one eye.

'Yes?' I said.

'Is everything okay?'

I nodded. 'Mmm-hmm. Do you want some coffee?'

'Gallons. The Crim exam starts in two hours,' Nick said grimly. 'Are you ready?'

'I guess I'm as ready as I'm going to be,' I said, swinging my legs out of the bed. It was still freezing in my apartment, and the shock of cold air slapped me awake.

Not that it cleared my thoughts, which were tumbling around my head like mismatched socks in a clothes dryer: Nick spent the night in my bed. I have to take my Criminal Law final in two hours.

This last thought made my stomach lurch. I could only guess what kind of a final exam Hoffman would dream up. I had a sudden vision of him crouched over his desk, chuckling maniacally to himself as he conjured up bizarre and terrifyingly hard hypothetical scenarios to test us on.

'You okay?' Nick asked. He frowned, concerned, and took a step closer to me.

'Coffee,' I croaked, stepping back. 'I need coffee.'

14

'**Y**ou will have three hours to complete your Criminal Law exam. When I call time, put your pen down immediately. Anyone who continues to write after I have called time will receive a failing grade. Do I make myself clear? Good,' Hoffman barked, as he stood at the front of the lecture hall, his arms folded over his chest, looking out at the sea of tired, worried faces.

'Asshole,' Nick muttered under his breath.

'The Honor Code is absolute,' Hoffman continued. 'Honor Code violations will result in expulsion. Keep that in mind before you even consider cheating. Eyes are to remain on your own papers, and you are limited to a two-page outline for this exam. All other books, notes, and papers should be stored out of sight and stay there for the remainder of the exam period.'

Once Hoffman finished issuing his list of threats and ultimatums, he finally got around to handing out the tests and blue books. I was staring down at the back of my test packet, wondering what hell was waiting inside, when Hoffman said, 'Begin.'

I drew in a deep breath, flipped the test over, and began to read. The first question had to do with a woman who stabbed her husband when he walked in the front door of their house. In her interview with the police, the woman claimed that her husband had beaten her earlier that night and, before he left to go out drinking with friends, issued threats that he'd kill her when he returned home. The question directed us to list all the charges that could be brought against the woman and any possible defenses she could raise. I picked up my pen and began to write as fast as I could.

I finished the exam with time to spare. When Hoffman gave the twenty-minute warning, I'd already removed my earplugs and was in the process of checking over my answers. But I was too numb to make much sense of anything I'd written, so I finally gave up. I closed my blue book, stacked it neatly on top of the examination book, and stood up. Hoffman didn't look up as I walked to the front of the room to hand my test in. I wasn't the first to leave; there was already a short stack of blue books and exam papers messily piled on the folding table where Hoffman sat. I carefully added my papers to the two stacks.

It's over, I thought, and somewhere deep inside, despite the stress and mind-numbing exhaustion of the past few weeks, happiness stirred and then bubbled up inside me. I did it: I made it through my first set of law-school exams. And I will never have to suffer through another Hoffman lecture ever again.

'Done so soon, Ms Bennett?' Hoffman murmured.

When I looked up, I saw that he was staring at me levelly. I nodded.

'I'll look forward to reading your exam, then,' Hoffman said, so softly, I doubted that anyone – even those sitting in the front row, still hunched over their blue books, hands scrawling wildly as they raced the clock to get every last bit of legalese crammed into their answer – could hear him.

And then Hoffman reached forward and marked the corner of my blue book with a single, tiny dot.

'What are you doing?' I asked, more loudly than I meant to. Several of my classmates looked up, bleary-eyed and irritated. Adam Keeley, who was sitting in the front row, hissed, 'Shhh!'

'Did you just mark my blue book?' I whispered to Hoffman. I could feel the blood rushing to my face, my heart pumping hard and fast.

'Of course not, Ms Bennett. The exams are graded anonymously, even you must know that,' Hoffman drawled, but the look of triumph that flashed across his face was unmistakable.

'It's an Honor Code violation for you to know whose paper you're grading,' I said.

'That's right, it would be. If I did know,' Hoffman said.

I stared at him, but Hoffman had tired of me. He returned to the law journal he was reading, not looking up even as I turned and stalked out of the classroom.

'Are you sure you weren't just seeing things?' Jen asked, raising her voice so that I could hear her over the din of the streetcar rattling up St. Charles Avenue. A large portion of our One-L class was also on board the streetcar. We were all riding uptown to a bar-slash-bowling-alley on Carrollton Avenue called the Mid-City Lanes, although it was more affectionately known as the Rock 'n' Bowl, since it was as popular for its live music as it was for bowling.

My classmates were laughing and yelling back and forth along the length of the streetcar, so relieved to be done with exams that for once they couldn't even muster up the energy to obsess over how their answers compared to everyone else's. Excitement spread through the trolley car, and the stress that had been building for months exploded into an exhausted, euphoric giddiness.

I wished I could share in the fun. But every time I thought of Hoffman's cold, victorious smile as he dotted my blue book, defeat pressed down at me. All of my hard work, all of those tedious hours spent poring over casebooks and practice exams, had been wasted. My shot at grading onto Law Review, my entire legal career even, had been torpedoed by one sadistic boil of a man.

'He put a dot on the corner of my blue book. I saw him do

it,' I said for about the four hundredth time since the test ended, as I slumped back against the uncomfortable wooden seat. Jen was seated next to me, Dana and Nick were directly in front of us, and Lexi and Addison sat across the aisle from them.

'Maybe he was just screwing with you,' Jen suggested. 'It's the last time you'll ever have him as a professor, so maybe he was just trying to get one last dig in.'

'I hope so,' I said, unconvinced. I looked down at my hands. There were blue ink splotches all over the fingertips, and my nails were jagged and raw from where I'd chewed them.

Jen nudged me and nodded to Lexi and Addison. Addison was sitting sideways on the bench, leaning back against the window, and Lexi was facing him, her head tilted coquettishly, her hand resting playfully on his knee.

'I take it she and Jacob are on the outs again?' Jen whispered into my ear, cupping her hand over her mouth like a little girl telling secrets on a school bus.

I shrugged. 'I don't know. She hasn't said anything to me about it.'

'What are you two whispering about?' Addison asked, watching us.

'Nothing,' I said, but Jen just folded her arms and looked annoyed.

Even though it was just after lunch when we got there, the Rock 'n' Bowl was already filling up, mostly with law students ready to blow off steam. There were bowling alleys directly ahead and a bar and stage to the side, where, Jen informed us, bands set up when they played there. Framed autographs of movie stars who'd made the pilgrimage to the Rock 'n' Bowl were mounted on the wall: Tom Cruise, Nicole Kidman, Ashley Judd, Liv Tyler. Zydeco music blared from the ceiling-mounted speakers.

'Come on, the shoe rental is over there,' Jen said, herding our small group along.

'Shoe *rental*?' Lexi said, wrinkling her nose. She was holding on to Addison's arm as though he were her father giving her away on her wedding day.

'Don't worry, I'll make sure they give you a nice, sweaty pair,' Addison teased her.

Once we'd tied the grubby laces of our rental shoes, we claimed a middle lane and started to bowl. Which, once I got into it, was actually kind of fun.

'I haven't bowled in fifteen years, maybe more,' I said, standing up to take my turn. I selected a marbled red ball from the stand and fit my fingers into the smooth holes.

'I would never have known,' Nick deadpanned. 'Your technique is so polished.'

'Hey! What's wrong with how I bowl?'

'Nothing . . . but I think most pro bowlers use only one hand,' Nick said.

'That's what I'm doing,' I protested.

'What are you talking about? You use two hands, and you start from between your legs. Like a granny,' Addison said. He stood up to demonstrate my so-called technique, spreading his legs, leaning all the way down, his butt stuck comically up in the air, and rolled an imaginary bowling ball in front of him.

'I don't look like that when I bowl!'

'Oh, my God, that's a perfect imitation. He looks just like you, Kate,' Jen giggled. She sipped at a cup of tepid beer, poured from the plastic pitcher we'd chipped in for at the beginning of the game.

'Dana, back me up,' I protested, but she just shook her head and shrugged.

'I'm the scorekeeper. I have to stay neutral,' she said.

Dana looked especially cute today. She was actually wearing jeans – a first for her – and an apple-green cardigan sweater buttoned over a slim-fitting white T-shirt. Her hair, freed from its barrette, fell down to her shoulders in shiny curls. Her lips were glossy, and I noticed that her eyes kept flickering over to Addison, who was, as usual, treating her like his kid sister.

'I've got Dana in my pocket,' Addison bragged. 'I bribed her with a hot dog, so she's throwing all of the close calls my way.'

'There are no close calls in bowling, you dork,' Jen said.

'Still, it doesn't hurt to have the official scorekeeper on your side,' Addison said, swinging an arm around Dana's shoulders. She giggled happily and tucked a loose curl back behind her ear.

Nick took his turn, bowled a strike, and pumped his arm in the air.

'Woo hoo! I'm still winning, right?' he said, and then sat down next to me while we watched Lexi take her turn. As in all things she did, Lexi bowled elegantly, rolling the ball with a fluid sweep of her arm. She watched her ball sail down the lane and take down four pins, and clapped happily. I turned and noticed that Nick was watching me.

'You okay?' he asked softly.

I nodded and sighed. 'Yeah. I'm absolutely sure I saw Hoffman mark my paper, but I guess there's nothing I can do about it.'

'You can go talk to Dean Sullivan again,' Nick suggested.

'Because that helped so much last time?'

We watched Addison select a black ball. He waited for the pins to reset and then took a running start, stopped suddenly, and threw his ball down the lane. When all of the pins fell with a loud clatter, he whooped.

'I am the golden god of bowling!' Addison announced, raising his hands above his head in triumph.

'This is different. Flagging your blue book is a serious violation of the Honor Code,' Nick said.

'Who do you think she's going to believe – him or me? And before you answer, remember that I'm not the one Teresa Sullivan is crushing on,' I said.

'Thanks for that image,' Addison said, interrupting us. I

hadn't realized he'd been eavesdropping. 'You and Dean Sullivan wrapped together in a passionate embrace . . .'

I rolled my eyes. 'What is it with men and their lesbian fantasies?'

'Two great tastes that taste great together,' Addison joked.

'Add, stop being such a pig,' Jen said with disgust, although Dana giggled.

'Are you going to talk to her?' Nick asked.

'No, I am most definitely not going to talk to her,' I said, putting down my plastic cup of beer and standing up. 'And it's my turn to bowl.'

'Just think of the bowling pins as ten little Hoffmans,' Addison yelled after me.

As the afternoon wore on, the crowd at the Rock 'n' Bowl got larger and louder. It was still predominantly law students, but our presence was gradually diluted, first by undergrads from Tulane and Loyola and then, a little later, by people getting off work wandering in for happy hour. We ate cheese fries and buffalo wings and drank beer and listened to the music, which rotated among classic rock, R&B, and zydeco. When we grew tired of bowling, we handed in our rental shoes and migrated back to the bar.

'Come on, let's dance,' Jen said. I shook my head, but Lexi, Addison, and even Dana joined her on the dance floor. Addison danced with all three women at once, twirling them around one after another and striking poses like John Travolta in *Saturday Night Fever*.

'How long are you going to stay?' Nick asked, once he and I were alone, perched on bar stools gathered around a high table.

'I don't know, I'm getting a little tired of being here. The smoke is hurting my eyes,' I said. 'And either the music is too loud or I'm too sober.'

'Do you want to go home?'

'No, not really.' I thought that I should probably call

Graham – I'd told him I would – but I also wasn't really in the mood to do that. I felt cagey and out of sorts and not yet ready to return to the comfortable corner of my life that Graham occupied.

'Let's go down to the Quarter,' Nick suggested.

'Now?'

'Why not? We don't have anywhere else we have to be.'

'Okay. I'll get the others,' I said, but Nick shook his head, grabbed my hand, and started to pull me toward the exit.

'We're just going to leave without saying anything to them?' I asked.

'Yes, we are. Because otherwise they might come with us, and I've had about enough of the love quadrangle,' Nick said.

'Love quadrangle?' I frowned, trying to figure out what he was talking about.

'Dana, Lexi, Jen, and Addison,' Nick said, as though it explained everything.

I looked at him quizzically and then shrugged, shaking my head.

'Dana has a crush on Addison, and Lexi's flirting with him, probably because Jacob's not here and she's feeling put out by his absence,' I said. 'How does Jen fit in?'

'I think she's into Addison too,' Nick said.

'Jen?' I was incredulous. 'But she's married.'

'Even so,' Nick said, shrugging. I glanced back at the dancers, but the rest of our study group were still gyrating to the techno beat of 'Everybody Dance Now,' which had incongruously followed the rock anthem 'Love the One You're With.' I followed Nick out the door and down the stairs, and a moment later we were out in the bright, chilly late afternoon.

With the afternoon rush-hour traffic clogging St. Charles Avenue, the streetcar ride down to the Quarter took over an hour. By the time we got to Bourbon Street, the sky was darkening and the brilliant lights from the bars lining each side of the street were spilling out, illuminating our way as we walked. Bourbon Street was closed to car traffic, so Nick and I walked right down the center of the street, careful not to step in the puddles of vomit that wouldn't be hosed off until the morning. The music changed from bar to bar – pop, jazz, more zydeco – but it was all loud. The strip clubs featured photos of their women – or, in some cases, men in drag – and were guarded by bored bouncers with thick necks and arms like ham hocks. It was a Thursday evening, but the streets were already crowded, mainly with tourists sporting garlands of Mardi Gras beads around their necks, even though Fat Tuesday was still over two months away. In the Quarter, every night is Mardi Gras and New Year's Eve all rolled into one.

Nick and I walked along in a companionable silence. Neither of us was inclined to join in the fray or tempted by one of the karaoke bars or touristy jazz clubs, which required all patrons to buy a minimum of two overpriced, watered-down drinks apiece.

'Are you hungry?' Nick asked.

'Not at all,' I said. The oily bar food was shifting uncomfortably in my stomach, and the tinge of a future hangover started to press at my temples. If I ever ate again, I decided, I'd only consume clean-tasting foods, like salad and lemon Jell-O.

'I'm not either. Let's go over that way,' he said, pointing with his chin.

We headed toward Jackson Square, sidestepping a guy in his late twenties, well past the age when his muscle had started to be replaced by fat, hunched over and puking on the street while his friends watched and hooted with laughter.

'Now you've got room for more beer,' one of them shouted.

'*Laissez les bons temps rouler,*' Nick said. 'Let the good times roll.'

The music faded behind us as we entered Jackson Square. There were still throngs of people milling around the park, admiring St. Louis Cathedral and grouping around a man behind a hot-dog-shaped booth, who yelled, 'Lucky dogs! Get yo' lucky dogs!'

Around the perimeter of Jackson Square, enterprising artists were selling paintings and photographs and drawings. Some weren't bad; others were awful. I stopped by one artist, who was starting to pack up his paintings now that night was falling.

'Those are amazing,' I said, admiring the vivid canvases. They were painted with bold modern stripes of scarlet and gold and violet, color combinations that probably should have looked discordant but didn't.

'That's one of my favorites,' the artist said, nodding at the canvas I was admiring. It was red, with horizontal slashes of gold and black through the middle. 'I'll make you a good deal on it.'

I turned and smiled apologetically at him, only then noticing that the artist was so gaunt, his clavicle bones looked like they'd cut through his skin. He was wearing one of those Russian fur hats with the flaps that come down over the ears and a heavy wool cardigan sweater. He was ill, I realized, maybe even terminal. Sympathy stabbed at me, along with a flash of guilt. There were worse fates in life than getting screwed on a law-school exam. It was so easy to lose perspective.

'I'm sorry, I'm not really in a position to buy right now,' I said. 'I'm a student.'

'What do you study?'

'Law, at Tulane.'

'That's impressive,' the man said.

Was it? I thought, wondering why it didn't feel that way.

'HIV?' Nick murmured in my ear once we'd moved on.

I nodded. 'Or cancer,' I said, and my throat closed up.

When we reached the far end of the park, we paused. If we kept walking straight ahead, we'd be heading down a dark and isolated street. It wasn't a smart idea to start wandering blindly around the French Quarter at night.

'If we're not going to go to a bar or a restaurant, what do you want to do? What else is there to do down here?' I asked.

'Get our fortunes read,' Nick said, nodding to a woman sitting off to the side at the corner of the park. There was a cart beside her, adorned with stars and pictures of cards and voodoo dolls and stenciled in black letters:

HAVE YOUR FORTUNE READ BY A GENUINE VOODOO PRIESTESS.

'Oh, please,' I scoffed.

'Come on, it'll be fun,' Nick said. He stepped toward the so-called voodoo priestess, a dark woman with smooth skin that didn't betray her age. I couldn't tell if she was thirty or sixty, or somewhere in between. She was dressed in a long orange skirt and black shawl, and a flowing red scarf topped her braided hair. 'How much to have our fortunes read?'

The voodoo priestess appraised us, her lips pressed tightly together.

'Ten dollars each,' she finally said.

'Nick, come on,' I said, pulling his shirtsleeve. 'That's a total rip-off.'

'No, I want to find out how I did on my finals,' Nick said. He pulled out his wallet and handed the voodoo priestess a twenty-dollar bill.

'This is what comes of drinking in the middle of the afternoon,' I commented.

'Don't mind her, she's a nonbeliever,' Nick told the priestess.

The voodoo priestess wasn't paying much attention to either of us. She plucked the bill from Nick's hand and tucked it into her skirt pocket. Then she pulled a deck of tarot cards from another pocket and began to shuffle them on the cart. Nick sat down in the folding wooden chair on the opposite side of the cart and waited. When she finished shuffling, she handed the cards to Nick.

'Cut the deck,' she said.

Nick did so and then handed the deck back to the priestess. She dealt out four cards, facedown, in a diamond arrangement. She turned the cards over one by one and examined them.

'Be straight with me – how long do I have to live?' Nick joked.

The woman gave him a stern look. 'The tarot can be a powerful tool, but only if its powers are believed,' she said.

Nick nodded and looked chagrined, although when the priestess bent back over the cards, he winked at me.

'This is the Fool card,' the priestess said, tapping her finger on the card at the top of the diamond.

I snorted. 'Maybe there is something to this after all.'

'Hey now,' Nick said. 'What does it mean?'

'That you are living in the moment and letting go of expectation. It can also mean you're accepting your fate,' the priestess said.

'So, I should accept that my fate is to be a lawyer and give up my dream of becoming an astronaut?' Nick asked, straightfaced.

'You wanted to be an astronaut?' I asked.

'Yeah. Either that or a ninja,' Nick said. 'Either one would be a kick-ass job.'

'This card here,' the priestess said, as though Nick had not spoken, 'is the Magician. It signifies understanding your intentions and taking action. This one, the Six of Cups, is the innocence card, which indicates contentment of childhood or indulging in play.'

'She's got you pegged,' I remarked.

'And, finally, the Knight of Wands,' the priestess said. She tapped the final card before her. 'That's an emotional card. It stands for one who is charming and capable . . . or it can mean that the bearer is daring and foolhardy.'

'If it's all the same to you, I think I'll take charming and capable,' Nick said.

'What a surprise,' I said.

The priestess looked at him, her face impassive, and didn't say anything.

'So?' Nick said.

She spread her hands apart, palms facing up. 'That is all,' she said.

'But you didn't tell me anything,' Nick protested. 'All you said was what the cards stand for. That doesn't tell me anything about my future. I want to know how I did on my final exams.'

'The answers are all there. Sometimes it just takes time to see what they mean,' the priestess said. She raised a finger of warning. 'But that journey is for you alone to take.'

'Huh. Well, if you put it that way,' Nick said, standing up. 'Your turn, Kate.'

'That's okay,' I said. 'I'll pass.'

'Come on, don't be a chicken,' Nick said.

'I'm not afraid . . . I just don't believe in fortune-telling,' I said. I looked at the priestess. 'No offense.'

She smiled at me. 'I understand your reluctance. The future can be hard to see.'

'Didn't Yoda say that?' I asked.

' "Difficult to see. Always in motion is the future," ' Nick said in a high, froggy Yoda voice.

I rolled my eyes at him, but sat down on the folding wooden chair. 'Okay, let's see what you've got.'

The priestess gathered the cards back up, shuffled them, and handed them to me. I cut the deck, and she again went through the motions of laying the cards out in a diamond, facedown, and then flipped them over one at a time. She studied the cards for a long time, frowning down at them while she bridged her hands together, fingertips pressed together.

'This is a difficult reading,' she finally said.

'Why? What does it say?' I asked.

'The cards contradict one another. This one here, the one at top, is the Hanged Man.'

'That doesn't sound like it bodes well for your Crim grade,' Nick said.

'It signifies a reversal or letting go,' the priestess said, ignoring Nick. 'And that contradicts this card, the Four of Pentacles, which indicates maintaining control and blocking any change.'

'So which one wins?' I asked.

'Impossible to tell. Perhaps the cards signify different points in your life, or perhaps they foretell a struggle you'll go through,' the priestess said. 'This card here is more troubling – it's the Nine of Swords, a card of negative energy. It signifies worry, anguish, guilt, or grief. But perhaps that won't come as a surprise to you.' She looked at me then, her eyes zeroing in on mine.

I swallowed and said nothing. I was afraid that if I did, I'd start to cry. I shook my head slightly, trying to shrug off the sadness that was pressing at me.

It's just nerves, I told myself. Nerves and exhaustion.

'And, lastly, this card. The Wheel of Fortune,' the priestess said.

'She's going to be on a game show?' Nick asked.

'Nick, shhh,' I said. 'What does that mean?'

'It signifies destiny, or a turning point. Or perhaps that you'll become more aware,' the priestess said.

'Aware of what?'

'Others, yourself, life,' she said.

I nodded and inhaled deeply, trying to calm the emotions welling up inside me.

'Thank you,' I said, standing up abruptly.

The priestess nodded dismissively and turned her attention back to gathering up and shuffling the deck of tarot cards. Nick and I walked aimlessly away. We passed through the arched entrance of Jackson Square and walked up to the statue of General Andrew Jackson in the middle. I perched on the edge of one of the wrought-iron benches facing the statue, gripping the seat on either side of me. Nick sat next to me. He leaned back and stretched his long legs in front of him, crossing one foot over the other.

'You okay?' Nick asked.

I nodded. 'It just gave me the creeps. I felt like she was . . . I don't know, reading my thoughts or something.'

'She can't really tell the future,' Nick said softly. 'You know that, right?'

'I guess. It's just all that she said about conflict and guilt . . .'

'Those are emotions that every person has at some point in their life,' Nick pointed out. 'Any of the things she said could be applied universally. That's why it's just for fun.'

'I've probably just had too much to drink,' I said, and wrapped my arms around myself. 'It's getting chilly.'

I'd dressed up today, wearing my nicest jeans and a pink cashmere cardigan over a fitted black T-shirt to the Criminal Law final, knowing that we'd be going out afterward. But now I was wishing I'd thought to bring along my jacket, which I'd left behind in my school locker along with my knapsack and books.

'Here,' Nick said, putting his arm around me and pulling me toward him. 'We'll keep each other warm.'

The air seemed to thicken. There was suddenly a tension between us – one of expectation and challenge. I sensed that I had only a few seconds to keep everything from permanently changing between us.

'Nick . . .,' I said, turning toward him, but before I could finish, he kissed me.

His lips were soft against mine, and his breath tasted faintly of beer. I hesitated and then kissed him back, and when I felt his tongue flicker against mine, it sent a jolt of heat running through me. I closed my eyes, and the world around us seemed to recede. I could just barely hear the shouts of the drunken Bourbon Street revelers, the strains of zydeco music, the clip-clop of hooves from the horses dragging buggies full of tourists around the Quarter.

But then Nick's lips began to press harder – too hard, his teeth felt like they were cutting against my lips – and then his hand slid up from my waist, cupping my breast over my T-shirt.

'Nick, don't,' I said, pulling back. I pushed his hand away.

'Sorry,' Nick murmured. He leaned back toward me, and his hand felt heavy on the back of my neck.

'No, I can't,' I said. I stood up and folded my arms in front of me.

'Why?'

'You know why.'

'Graham?'

'Yes, Graham. My boyfriend,' I said. The words felt foreign and unwieldy in my mouth. I turned away from him to face the impassive General Jackson, forever frozen in time. An inscription on the statue read,

THE UNION MUST AND SHALL BE PRESERVED.

I felt Nick stand and move so that he was standing behind me.

'Kate . . .'

I shook my head. 'Let's just forget this ever happened. We both drank too much, we've been under a lot of pressure, things just sort of got away from us. Okay?'

'No. It's not okay,' Nick said. He turned me around to face him and held me there, his hands resting heavily on my shoulders. 'I want this to happen.'

'What?' I said, confused.

'I've had feelings for you for a long time. I thought you knew that.'

'What? No. How would I?' I said, shaking my head. Nick had hooked up with every eligible woman who fell in his path. Christ, that's what I was now. He was drunk, and I was available. And I'd almost fallen for it.

I stepped back out of his reach, tripping over something.

I looked down and saw a broken strand of cheap plastic Mardi Gras beads lying at the edge of a dirty puddle.

'Kate,' Nick said.

An electronic beeping cut off whatever else he was going to say. I pulled my cell phone out of my pocket. The keypad was glowing blue as it continued to beep insistently. The caller ID announced the caller: Graham.

I clicked the on button. 'Hello?' I said, pressing the phone against my ear.

'Hey,' Graham said. He sounded like he was trapped in a box, his voice echoing against the sides. 'How did it go, babe?'

It took me a minute to remember what he was talking about: the Crim exam. It seemed like I had taken the test ages ago.

'Oh . . . fine. Pretty much what I expected,' I said.

'Good. Are you and your friends having fun?' Graham asked.

'Yeah,' I began, and glanced over at Nick. He had folded his arms in front of him, and his blue eyes were hostile, challenging me to . . . I don't know what. I turned away from him. A white-faced mime was performing just in front of the cathedral. A crowd circled around him, eager to be entertained, laughing as he began to juggle purses and hats and even sneakers donated from the crowd.

'Look, I'm going home right now. Can I call you back when I get to my apartment?' I asked.

'Sure. Where are you?'

'The Quarter.'

'Really?' Graham laughed. 'You guys are partying, huh?'

'Just walking around,' I said weakly.

'Have fun. Call me when you get home.'

'Okay, bye,' I said, and clicked the off button on the phone. I slid it into my pocket and then turned back to Nick. 'I have to go,' I said.

'Was that him?' Nick asked.

I nodded. 'Look, Nick –'

'Forget about it. At least now I know,' Nick said. He turned and stalked off, his hands thrust in his pants pockets, his shoulders hunched forward.

'Wait,' I called after him, raising my voice to a shout. I could hear the tinge of desperation in it and wondered, as Nick paused for a moment, if he'd heard it too. But then he just kept walking away, toward the frenzy of Bourbon Street, until the crowd swallowed him out of my sight.

He didn't look back.

Spring Semester

15

'Jen! Lexi! Wait up,' I said, sidestepping a crowd of Two-Ls congregating by the first-floor elevator, and skirting past Professor Legrande, who was carefully guarding a steaming paper coffee cup from P.J.'s as he walked to class. It was the first day of classes after the holiday break, and the law school was buzzing with activity – squealed greetings, raucous laughter, the hollow metallic clank of lockers slammed shut.

I'd just come in from the bright, chilly morning and spotted the backs of two familiar heads – one with a sleek dark bob, the other a tousled auburn – bobbing away down the crowded hallway.

'Jen! Lexi!' I called out as I wormed past the students gathered around the Public Interest Law Foundation's breakfast table, where they sold doughnuts, stale bagels, and weak coffee.

Lexi stopped and turned around. When she spotted me, she grinned and waved. I hurried forward to greet them.

'Kate!' Jen said. She opened her arms and gave me a big hug. Her long tangle of red hair smelled like roses and cigarette smoke. 'When did you get back in town?'

'Yesterday,' I said.

'You should have called me. I'd have picked you up,' Jen said.

'I didn't know if either of you was around, so I just took a cab,' I said. 'And besides, my plane was delayed. There was hail in Arizona.'

'They have hail in Arizona?' Jen asked.

'Planes don't fly in hail?' Lexi asked.

'Apparently. At least, not when the hail is the size of tangerines and coming down with a wrath-of-God vengeance,' I said. More bad luck. And maybe the saddest part was that I was coming to expect it. Even though the weather had been perfect when we left for the airport, I'd packed an extra paperback just in case.

'So, how was your trip?' Jen asked.

'It was fun,' I said, but then hesitated. 'Well . . . mostly.'

I'd spent the holiday break visiting Graham in Arizona. We'd bought and trimmed a Douglas fir, watched *A Charlie Brown Christmas*, and gone to see the local ballet company perform *The Nutcracker*. On Christmas morning, I made eggs Benedict and Bloody Marys for breakfast, and we ended up getting loopy and going back to bed. Graham's main gift to me had been a surprise – a four-day vacation to Key West during spring break.

I'd been unprepared for his other gift – it was the snapshot I'd taken of my parents' toast at their last anniversary party. Graham had scanned the photo into his computer and retouched it, successfully getting rid of the red eyes my parents had sported in the original. He also changed it to a black-and-white print to disguise the bad coloring, and finally blew it up and had it matted and framed. It was beautiful. My parents looked so happy, so ethereally beautiful frozen in black and white.

I stared at it, speechless.

'Do you like it?' Graham asked anxiously.

'How did you do this?' I whispered.

'I've been learning about photography and all of the new methods for digitally enhancing photos. Is it okay? Because if

I didn't get it right, I can try again,' Graham said, reaching to take the photo back.

But I pulled it away, cradling it against my chest. 'I love it,' I said fiercely. 'I don't want you to change a thing.'

We were living in a bubble, away from the stresses of daily life, and were able to connect in a way we hadn't in years. For the first time since we'd gotten back together, it felt like we were a real couple. And not just any couple, but the kind of couple who's so well matched, so happy, so sitcom-perfect, that they cause other people to gaze wistfully after them, wondering if they'll ever have that sort of relationship for themselves. The kind of couple that appears on those diamond commercials filmed in an arty black-and-white format, staring at each other longingly before the man slips an enormous, sparkling engagement ring onto the woman's finger, while a symphony orchestra plays in the background.

But then on the night before I left, we got into a huge, messy fight, thus destroying the whole perfect diamond-commercial-couple image. Even worse, the fight was entirely my fault.

Graham had been keeping me company while I packed my suitcase. Or at least he said he was keeping me company. In reality, he was sitting on the bed, hunched over, foot in hand, clipping his toenails. There was a look of intense concentration on his face as he positioned the clippers, followed by a loud cracking sound and a thin sliver of nail flying through the air. And with every crack, I grew just that much more irritated.

'Do you have to do that here?' I asked through clenched teeth.

'Do what?'

'Your toenails. You're getting clippings all over the sheets.'

'I'll clean them up,' Graham said.

Crack! A chunk of toenail flew through the air and hit me in the face.

'Jesus Christ!' I exploded.

Graham started, and looked up. 'What's wrong?'

'I just got hit by your disgusting toenail!'

'Oh. Sorry,' Graham said. He leaned back over his foot, poised to clip yet another nail. I stared at him, feeling the anger swell up inside me like helium inflating a balloon. And then I leaned forward and snatched the clippers out of Graham's hand.

He looked up at me again, perplexed. 'What are you doing?'

'Stop. Clipping. Your. Nails,' I fumed. And then I took the clippers and threw them across the room, where they pinged against the wall and fell with a satisfying thump. I went back to folding a stack of shirts into my suitcase. Graham stared at the spot on the wall, speechless.

'I can't believe you just did that,' he finally said.

'I can't believe you don't listen to me.'

'How am I not listening?'

'I just asked you not to clip your nails in bed. Or when I asked you not to leave the bathroom door open when you're using the toilet. Or yesterday, when I asked you not to put my dry-clean-only sweaters in the washing machine.'

'I said I was sorry about that.'

'You washed them on hot! They shrank!'

'Why are you yelling?'

'Because I'm just so sick and tired of living like this,' I exploded. I stopped folding and started just piling the clothes into the suitcase in a messy heap.

'Then I guess it's a good thing you're going back to New Orleans tomorrow,' Graham said. I looked at him and saw that his face was stiff and angry, and his arms were crossed in front of his chest. Regret washed over me, dousing out the anger. I closed my eyes and took a calming deep breath.

'I'm sorry,' I said.

Graham didn't say anything.

'I shouldn't have lost my temper,' I said, trying again. 'I shouldn't have thrown your nail clippers.'

'It's okay,' he said, shrugging. But his face was stony, and his voice was cool.

Eventually the argument blew over, and we went to a Japanese steakhouse for a farewell dinner. But even as we talked and sipped wine, there was still a tension between us that hadn't been there before. And I knew it was my fault. Why should being near Graham grate on my nerves so much? Had it ever bothered me before that he made a weird throaty noise when he gargled with mouthwash or that he never used a sponge in the shower, which meant that I was constantly finding his pubic hair embedded in the bar of soap? Or had I gotten so used to his tics while we were living together that I didn't even notice them?

And, if so, why were they bothering me so much now?

'What did you end up doing over the holidays, Jen?' I asked as we checked our mail folders. Before break, her plans had been up in the air, depending heavily on the rotation Sean would have at the hospital.

'We ended up only going to St. Louis for Christmas weekend. Sean was on call after that,' Jen said. 'So basically I spent the rest of the break stuffing myself with leftover Christmas cookies and catching up on *Oprah* reruns.'

'What about you, Lex? How was your vacation?' I asked.

'Amazing. I visited my mom and stepdad in Seattle for two weeks, and then I got back here in time to spend New Year's Eve with Jacob,' Lexi said.

'I wanted to go to the French Quarter for New Year's Eve, but they wouldn't go out with me,' Jen grumbled. 'They're so lame.'

'People shoot off guns in the Quarter at midnight on New Year's. Jacob told me some woman was killed when a falling bullet hit her a few years ago,' Lexi said. 'And anyway, we just wanted to stay in and have a quiet night alone. And then on New Year's Day, we drove out of town and spent a few days at a bed-and-breakfast at this gorgeous old plantation.'

'Jacob takes her to a romantic B&B to celebrate New Year's. My husband takes me to Chili's,' Jen said. She sighed dramatically. 'It's so unfair.'

'I don't know. Chili's fajitas are pretty damned good,' I said. Lexi snorted, but Jen just rolled her eyes.

'Ha-ha. Can you believe that classes are already starting? It seems like we were just in finals,' Jen said. 'Who do you have this semester?'

I consulted the scrap of paper the law school had sent me.

'Cook for Property, Contracts Two with Washington, Ethics with Yanni, and Constitutional Law with Chai,' I read. 'Con Law is my first class this morning.'

'Yeah! We're all in the same section again,' Jen said. 'Addison and Nick too. No one's seen Dana yet, though.'

'Oh . . . is Nick here?' I asked, trying to sound casual.

I hadn't seen Nick since that night in the Quarter. He'd left for his parents' house in Virginia the next morning, and although I could hear him through the thin walls of our house when I dragged my suitcase up the stairs the previous evening, he hadn't come up to see me. I hadn't told anyone about the kiss – not even Graham. I'd meant to tell him, but then the moment passed, and later it seemed that confessing what happened would only upset Graham and ruin what little time we had together.

'Haven't you seen him? He and Addison went in early to save us seats,' Jen said.

'Did you hear that grades are coming out today?' Lexi asked me.

My stomach turned and plummeted, as if I'd just taken a particularly steep plunge down a roller coaster. I'd known that I'd have to face my first-semester exam grades eventually – I just hadn't expected to get hit with them on the first day back.

'Are you sure?' I asked anxiously. 'Today?'

Jen nodded. 'They're going to be in our mail folders by lunchtime. We just overheard Dean Spitzer telling some students about it outside. Come on, class is about to start. We'd better go in.'

The roller coaster in my stomach banked around a corner before whooshing down again. I was about to see Nick. How would he and I act around each other? Could we pretend that we hadn't kissed, that he hadn't touched my breast? I'd played the scene over and over in my head, until I'd memorized every last detail, from the feel of his lips against mine to how his eyes had darkened when he leaned in to kiss me. I closed my eyes and willed the images away.

'What's wrong, Kate?' Jen asked.

'What?'

'Are you feeling okay?' Jen looked concerned.

'Oh . . . yeah. I'm fine. I just have cramps,' I lied.

Our Con Law class was in the largest of the law school's lecture halls, located on the ground floor next to the student lounge. We walked through the heavy double doors and looked down over the sea of chattering One-Ls, some sitting, some leaning on the tables, while everyone waited for the spring semester to officially begin.

'Where did Nick and Add go?' Jen asked.

'There they are,' Lexi said, pointing.

I saw Addison first. He was leaning back against a table, facing the rear doors, with a hand raised in greeting. I smiled at him. He was wearing new glasses, rectangular silver ones, and his hair was extra spiky.

And sitting just next to Addison . . . was Nick. He leaned back in his chair, his long legs sprawled out in front of him, and he was wearing the navy turtleneck sweater that brought out his blue eyes. His cheeks looked a little red, as though he'd been in the sun. Addison leaned over to say something to Nick, and then Nick turned and looked right at me. Everything else seemed to go still and quiet, even though I was peripherally aware of Lexi lifting her chin to show off the silver Tiffany bean necklace Jacob had given her for Christmas and Jen complaining that the only thing Sean had given her was a blender.

'It wasn't even a particularly *nice* blender,' Jen said. 'And *he's* the one who likes to make fruit shakes, not me.'

I forced the corners of my lips up into a stiff smile, while Nick just stared at me. But then, just as I faltered, he grinned back, and relief melted through me.

'This is going to be a big class. We'd better sit down before someone takes our seats,' Jen said. She trotted down the stairs and dropped into the empty seat next to Addison. I hesitated, not knowing if I should claim the empty seat to Jen's right – or sit next to Nick, as though everything were normal between us. But then Lexi headed down in front of me and took the seat next to Jen, and I was left with no choice.

'Hey, babycakes,' Addison said, reaching out and grabbing my arm as I passed by. 'Give me some sugar.'

I hugged him, and he kissed me wetly on the cheek. 'How was your break, Add?' I asked.

'So good I almost didn't come back,' Addison said. He pulled out the green task chair and sat down, looking glum. 'It sucks being back. It's almost like we never left.'

'Hey,' I said softly to Nick as I sat next to him, dropping my enormous camping knapsack on the table.

'Hey,' he said.

The silence swelled between us, and after an awkward moment we both rushed to fill it.

'Did you go skiing after Christmas?' I asked as I pulled out my new Con Law book with the dark green cover, along with a lined yellow pad and two Uni-Ball pens.

'I stopped by your apartment yesterday,' Nick said at the same time.

We paused, and then both started speaking again.

'You did?' I asked.

'Yeah, I went to Colorado with some of my college buddies,' Nick said.

Nick laughed, and I bit my lip and shook my head.

'You go first,' Nick said.

'You stopped by my apartment?' I asked.

Nick nodded. 'But I didn't think you were back yet.'

'I didn't get in until around seven.'

'I was going to see if you wanted to drive in to school this morning together,' he said.

'I came in early,' I said. 'I went to the bookstore before class started, and then I did the reading assignment over at the student union. You know . . . avoid my mistake from last semester.'

'No Hoffman this semester,' Nick said. He raised his hand, and I slapped it lightly.

'Thank God,' I said.

'Hey,' Dana said, dropping breathlessly into the empty seat to my left.

'Hey, Dana. How was your . . .' My voice trailed off when I turned to look at her. Dana had her dark hair back in cornrows, like Bo Derek wore in the movie *10*, exposing lines of pale white scalp. There were beads on the end of each skinny braid that clattered as Dana busied herself getting out her class supplies. 'Ummm . . . I take it you went to the Caribbean?'

Dana nodded happily. 'My parents took me to Jamaica for Christmas,' she said. 'I got my hair braided on the beach. What do you think?'

'It looks nice,' I said, hoping I sounded more sincere than I felt.

'I'm only going to keep them in for a few more days,' Dana said, shrugging. 'Although, actually, it's a really effective way to keep my hair out of my face when I study.'

'You could just shave it off,' I said. 'You'd look cute bald.'

'Mother of God,' Addison said, sounding aghast.

'What?' I asked, turning back toward him.

But then I saw what was spooking Add – and my mouth sagged open in horror.

Hoffman.

Professor Richard Hoffman was walking to the front of the class, in all of his pouched-belly and balding-head glory, the familiar worn leather folder that held his lecture notes tucked under his arm. Hoffman stepped up onto the raised platform, dropped the folder on top of the metal lectern, and then turned to the erasable pen board. With a thick black marker, he began writing on the board: CONSTITUTIONAL LAW, PROFESSOR HOFFMAN.

What the . . . ?

No way . . . no *fucking* way.

'No way,' Nick whispered, echoing my thoughts. He pulled his schedule out of the front pocket of his messenger bag and unfolded it, smoothing the creases in the paper. 'It says right here that our Constitutional Law professor is supposed to be Chai. Doesn't it? Doesn't it say that *right here*?' Nick asked. He shoved the piece of paper at Addison, looking a little wild-eyed as he did so.

'Maybe Hoffman came into the wrong classroom by mistake,' Addison whispered back. 'Maybe he had some sort of an emotional breakdown and can't remember what class he's supposed to teach.'

'Stop talking,' I hissed at them. The first rule of surviving Professor Hoffman was to never, ever bring attention to yourself.

I'd learned that one the hard way.

'Welcome to Constitutional Law. I am Professor Hoffman. If you are in the wrong place, please leave. For those of you who are in the right place, I'm going to go over the ground rules. First, do not be late to my class. We will begin promptly at ten-thirty on Monday, Wednesday, and Friday mornings. If you walk through those doors even a minute late, you will not be permitted to stay for the lecture that day,' Hoffman announced. A hush had fallen over the class when Hoffman began to speak, although it was a charged silence, full of a shared dread and horror.

It was like some sort of an awful time warp that was looping me back to that first day of law school, when Hoffman had forced me to stand up in front of my gaping classmates and proceeded to humiliate me.

'Excuse me, Professor?' a loud voice to my left said.

I startled and then froze when I realized that the voice belonged to Dana. I immediately reverted to jungle law and tried to avoid making any sudden movements that might cause Hoffman to take notice of me. I slid only my eyes in Dana's direction. She was sitting at the edge of her green task chair, her back straight and her hand waving slightly as she held it up over her head.

'What is she doing?' Nick hissed.

I didn't dare answer. Hoffman had stopped cold and turned on Dana, his features contorting with a just barely concealed rage at the interruption. I'd seen that expression before and knew what it meant: danger.

'Excuse me, Professor Hoffman?' Dana said again. This time her voice quavered a bit. Hoffman had never targeted her during Crim – Dana's voluntary participation in class had earned her his grudging approval – so she'd never fully appreciated the force of his withering scorn.

'Ms Mallick, is that you? I hardly recognize you with your new hairstyle,' Hoffman said. His voice was dripping with condescension.

Dana smiled serenely, as though completely unaware that he was mocking her. 'Excuse me, sir, but my schedule says that I was assigned to this lecture hall for Con Law, but I'm supposed to have Professor Chai. Am I in the wrong place?'

For a moment, hope dawned. Maybe it was all just a clerical error – right class, wrong teacher. Please let it be a mistake, I prayed.

'Professor Chai has had to take a medical leave of absence, and I was asked to take over this class in her place,' Hoffman said. 'And today we'll begin by examining the limitations the Constitution imposes on governmental power.'

I groaned inwardly. It wasn't just some dreadful – but fixable – error. We were actually going to be stuck with Professor Satan for another semester.

At least this time I knew my foe. Ducking my head down

in an obvious attempt to avoid eye contact would alert Hoffman that I didn't want him to call on me. So instead I drew in a deep breath and forced myself to look right at him. His pale eyes slid from Dana's face to mine, and I saw his thin lips twist up into a malevolent smile that made my fingers tingle with dread. But I forced myself to stay steady, and even raised my chin up a few millimeters in a silent challenge.

I dare you to call on me, I thought. I dare you, you son of a bitch.

My bluff worked. Hoffman's eyes continued to slide past me.

'Ms Jans, give us the Court's holding in *Marbury v. Madison*,' Hoffman said, calling on a chunky brunette sitting in the row in front of me.

I exhaled slowly and deeply, uncapped my pen, and started taking notes.

'Grades are out.'

The announcement spread through the Con Law class almost immediately after Hoffman had finished his lecture. My stomach lurched, and my heart felt like it was thudding against my rib cage. This was it.

'Did you hear that?' Nick asked, turning to look at me.

I nodded slightly.

'What?' Dana asked.

'They're saying that grades are out,' I said, jerking my head toward the back of the classroom, where, I assumed, the rumor had started when the students sitting in the last row had heard the chaos break out in the student lounge.

'Oh, good,' Dana said, standing up briskly, swinging her knapsack over her shoulder.

'You're not nervous?' I asked.

Dana shook her head and looked surprised. 'No. I don't want to sound conceited, but I've always gotten good grades.'

'We all have,' Nick said. 'Everyone who gets into this school was at the top of their undergrad class. We're all A students.'

'And now some of us are going to be B or C students,' I

said. My throat felt like I was trying to swallow a handful of sharply edged stones.

'Or worse,' Addison said cheerfully, also standing. 'Let's go get the verdict.'

The buzz in the room was louder, more manic than usual, as we filed out of the room.

'I heard that they give out only one A in every class,' Dutch Jackson muttered as he stacked up his books.

'No, they give out more than one A per class, but there are more Cs than As and Bs combined,' Alicia Ramirez replied.

Nick turned and rolled his eyes comically, mocking our classmates who were desperately trying to quell their own anxiety by freaking out their friends.

'I heard that Hoffman gave out three Ds this year,' Brad Sobel said.

'Aw, man, then I'm doomed,' Scott Brown replied in his thick Southern accent, grinning good-naturedly. He nodded at Nick and winked at me.

Three Ds.

I remembered the dot that Hoffman had placed on the corner of my blue book and felt queasy.

It seemed like the entire One-L class was gathered around our hanging mail folders, jostling to pluck the crisp white envelopes out. I saw a broad-shouldered black student with a shaved head whom I recognized from one of the Bar Reviews – he was the guy Jen had wanted to set Addison up with – tear his envelope open and unfold the paper within. His shoulders sagged, and at first I thought he was getting bad news, but then he turned and I saw that he was smiling, the relief etched on his face.

'Here, I got ours,' Jen said, appearing out of the crowd that she'd pushed her way into. She handed the envelopes out to Lexi, Dana, Nick, Add, and me. I looked down at mine. It felt light and insubstantial in my hand. My name was visible through a window in the envelope: BENNETT, KATE E.

Lexi started to tear at hers and then hesitated. 'Let's go

outside,' she said. 'I don't want to do this in front of everyone.'

A woman I didn't recognize burst into tears and sat down in one of the armchairs that lined the student lounge, staring disbelievingly down at the paper in her hands. Her friends squatted down next to her, patting her arm, but the woman was inconsolable.

'My life is over,' she wailed.

'Yes, outside,' I agreed, and our group moved quickly to get away from the frenzied crowd. The shouts of triumph were as disconcerting as the bitter moans. I clutched my envelope a little tighter, so that it creased in my hands, and wondered what it contained. A plum job at a top law firm, or years spent slogging it out with a firm of ambulance-chasers that ran cheesy commercials during daytime television and officed in a strip mall?

'Out here,' Jen said, and she darted to the left, into the center courtyard of the law school. I'd never been back here before. The patio was full of wrought-iron garden tables and chairs, and apart from the six of us, it was deserted.

'Are we supposed to be back here?' Dana asked doubtfully.

'Not really,' Lexi said. She dropped her leather bag on a table and tore open her envelope, hesitating before she pulled the paper out. 'Come on, you guys, don't watch me. Don't you want to open your own grades?'

I looked down at the envelope. No, I did not want to open it. But my shaking fingers started to tear at the seal, acting all on their own. I heard the quiet sound of envelopes ripping around me, and I turned, so that my back was to my friends, before I pulled out the paper containing my grades and unfolded it.

BENNETT, KATE E.

TORTS, *Gupta*	A–
CONTRACTS I, *Legrande*	A*
CRIMINAL LAW, *Hoffman*	C
CIVIL PROCEDURE, *Chandler*	A

I stared at the paper, my eyes running over the list of grades again and again.

Hoffman had given me a C.

In theory, the As should have cushioned the C, but I'd never gotten a C before in my life. . . . The lowest grade I'd received in college was a B in my Mythology class the semester my parents had died, when I'd been walking around in a thick cloud of grief, wondering if I should have, as my adviser urged, taken the semester off.

'So who's going to go first?' Addison's voice cracked through the silence. 'Should we go around in a circle, or just announce it all at once?'

I turned around, taking in the pale faces, the tight jaws, the hands clenching the thin papers that foretold our future more surely than a deck of tarot cards ever would. Dana alone was folding her paper back up and tucking it into the outside pocket of her knapsack.

'I have to go,' she said abruptly, turning and walking quickly to the door that led back into the interior of the law school.

'You okay, Dee?' Addison called after her, but she didn't respond or look back, and we watched silently while the door closed behind her.

'Maybe one of us should go after her,' I said.

Addison shook his head. 'She'll be fine. She's tougher than she looks,' he said.

I looked at him quickly, but Addison's face was closed. If he knew any of Dana's secrets, he wasn't sharing them.

'Shit,' Jen said softly. She was staring down at her paper. 'This isn't good. I got two Cs and two Bs. That gives me a solid 2.5 GPA. Guess I'm out of the Law Review race, not that I had any hopes I'd be in it.'

'I didn't do much better,' Addison said. 'I got a C-plus – in Contracts, that exam kicked my ass – a B-minus, and two Bs. Thankfully, they're not going to tell us what our class rank is until the end of first year. I can only take so much bad news in one day.'

'I actually did okay,' Lexi said. Her voice was thin with relief. 'An A-minus, two B-pluses, and a B. I can't believe I actually got an A-minus from Hoffman. I was sure I'd bombed that test.'

A poisonous stream of jealousy snaked through me. Lexi had done better than me in Criminal Law? I'd studied twice as hard as she had. Hell, I'd been the one who outlined Crim for our study group. Lexi – who'd never even gotten the principles of Resulting Harm down – had used *my* outline to get a better grade than I had.

'Nick? Your turn,' Jen said.

Nick colored, but he was smiling. 'I did pretty well,' he admitted. 'I got an A in Contracts, two A-minuses, and a B-plus.'

Addison whistled. 'Dude, that's amazing.'

'You're going to make Law Review,' Jen said.

'I don't know about that,' Nick said, but I could tell that he was pleased.

'All right, Kate, your turn,' Lexi said.

'Hoffman gave me a C,' I said tightly. 'And that was the class I was the most prepared for.'

Jen sucked her breath in sympathetically as she lit a cigarette. The smell of butane from her Zippo lighter – a Christmas present from Addison to make up for all the cigarettes he bummed off her – floated through the air.

'He's an asshole,' Lexi said. 'He's been after you since the first day.'

'How else did you do?' Nick asked.

'Better,' I admitted. 'I got an A in Civ Pro and an A-minus in Torts. And I think I got an A in Contracts, although there's an asterisk next to the grade, and I don't know what that means. Maybe it's provisional or something.'

'You got an *asterisk*?' Lexi asked, her voice sharp. I glanced at her, startled by the tone. Her lips were pinched up and her thin nostrils were flaring.

Jen stared at me, shaking her head. She exhaled a plume

of smoke and sat down heavily on one of the metal chairs. 'You don't know what that means?'

'It means you fucking rocked the class,' Addison said. 'You got the highest grade.'

'What?' I asked, staring back at the paper. 'How do you know that?'

'They told us at orientation,' Nick said.

'I wasn't there,' I said.

'It's a big deal. They give you an award for it,' Jen said.

'Congratulations, Kate. That's great. I'll see you guys later, have to get going,' Lexi said abruptly. She tucked her shiny dark hair behind her ear and stalked out of the courtyard. I stared after her.

'What's up with her?' I asked. 'She did really well.'

'But you did better,' Nick said.

'And now she's angry at me?'

'Not angry. Jealous,' Nick said quietly.

16

When I was in the fifth grade, my school held a fire safety assembly. The local squad of firefighters was there, wearing the pants and black rubber boots of their uniforms strapped on with suspenders, their helmets perched on their heads. The fire chief had a thick Boston accent and dotted his speech with a lot of 'ums' and 'ahs' that suggested a lack of experience with public speaking. He explained to us how to check a closed door for fire on the other side, how to wedge damp towels at the bottom of the door to keep smoke from leaking in, and how second-story bedrooms should all have an emergency exit ladder rolled up in the closet. And then he gave us a handout, faded from the copying machine, to plan our family's fire strategy.

When I got home from school that day, I set myself up at the kitchen table with my drawing tablet and markers and drew a picture of our house, carefully labeling the exits and where everyone slept. My mom sat with me, sipping from a mug of chamomile tea, and we planned out what our emergency exit path would be and which of our neighbors' driveways we would meet in.

'We're supposed to have a fire drill,' I'd said. 'One night when we're all asleep, you have to hold a match up to one of the smoke detectors, so that we can practice how to get out. We're also supposed to get out our fire ladders, to make sure we know how to use them.'

This was the exciting part. It's not every day that you get to climb out your bedroom window.

'We don't have a fire ladder,' my mother had said. She blew on her tea, her breath making tiny ripples across the surface.

'Then we *have* to get one,' I'd insisted. 'The fire chief said that every second-story bedroom should have a fire ladder stored in the closet. He said it can make the difference between life and death.'

'Don't worry, we'll get one,' Mom said, and she smiled at me with that distant look that I knew from experience meant she wasn't really listening to me anymore. What did she think about when her thoughts wandered? Was she wondering what direction her life would have veered off in if she had accepted that postcollege job offer in Los Angeles instead of turning it down in favor of my dad's marriage proposal? Or was she contemplating whether she should paint over the border of stenciled-on pineapples that circled the kitchen walls?

I wish now that I'd thought to ask her.

My parents never did get a ladder for my bedroom, and we never had an emergency fire drill. And for years after, I'd fall asleep worrying that someone would leave a candle burning too close to the drapes or that the toaster would spontaneously burst into flames, and we'd be totally unprepared for it. My parents wouldn't remember which emergency exit they were supposed to take, nor where we were all supposed to meet up together outside, away from the danger of the fire.

And I decided that if I had to get out my window, I'd knot my sheets together the way the fire chief had instructed, tie a corner to the bedpost, and lower myself down one inch at a time.

'I thought I'd find you out here,' Nick said.

I looked up at him from the faded orange plastic chair I was curled up in, a throw blanket warming my lap. Nick was standing at the French doors that led out to my petite balcony overlooking Magazine Street. It wasn't much of a view – there was a boarded-up Cuban restaurant directly across the street, and next to that a burned-out storefront. There were some lovely homes nearby, but to see them I'd have to lean way over the balcony, and I didn't have enough faith in my landlord's maintenance of the wrought-iron railing to risk it.

Nick sat down in the mate to my chair and glanced at the mug I was holding in my hands.

'Coffee?' he asked. 'I didn't see any brewing when I came in.'

Graham – who'd apparently memorized every crime statistic about New Orleans – nagged me to keep the doors to my apartment locked at all times, but I'd gotten in the habit of leaving the back door unlocked. All four tenants in our house shared the small paved backyard, and Nick and I could visit each other by climbing up and down the flight of wooden steps that led up to my back door. And since Nick shamelessly sponged coffee off me, it was easier to just leave the door unlocked for him, rather than get up every time he knocked.

'Wine,' I said, nodding to the bottle of merlot resting next to my chair.

'Pass it over,' Nick said. I handed him the wine, and he took a swig right from the bottle.

'You're all class,' I said. 'Just don't backwash.'

The late afternoon was chilly and getting even colder as the sun shrank down from the sky, but I didn't care. I didn't want to go back inside, where I knew I'd just end up staring at my grades, which I'd left facedown on my desk, as though that would somehow lessen their power.

Lexi's jealousy aside, I didn't understand how I'd managed to get the highest grade in Contracts class. Of all my exams, that was the subject I'd been the shakiest on. My strongest subject had, ironically, been Crim. Fearing Hoffman's wrath, I'd prepared for his class twice as thoroughly as the other classes and knew the case law inside and out. There was no way I could have done better in Contracts but so much worse in Criminal Law.

Unless, of course, I was right and Hoffman had flagged my exam and purposely marked me down. Over the past few weeks, I'd tried to convince myself that I'd just imagined the whole thing, but now it seemed that my worst fear had been realized. It could have been worse, I thought. I could have gotten one of the three Ds Hoffman was rumored to have given out. But somehow that didn't make me feel much better.

'Congrats on your grades,' Nick said. He held up the bottle in a toast, and I clinked my mug against it.

'You too,' I said. 'You really did amazing. I haven't heard of anyone who's done better.'

Nick shook his head. 'I'm sure that's not true. And you did just as well. Even better, Asterisk Girl.'

'Did you talk to Dana?' I asked.

'No, but Add saw her later. She told him she did fine. All As and Bs,' Nick said.

'So why was she so upset?'

'I don't think she's used to getting anything other than straight As.'

'At least she didn't get a C,' I said ruefully, taking a swig of wine.

Nick was quiet. 'You should talk to Dean Sullivan about your Criminal Law grade,' he finally said.

'No way.'

'Then why don't you talk to someone else in the administration? Like Dean Spitzer?'

'Because he wouldn't take me seriously. No one would. They'll want to know why I didn't make the Honor Code complaint right after the Crim exam. It'll sound like I'm only complaining now because I got a low grade. Which is true,' I said.

'Maybe they'll talk to Hoffman. Or transfer you into a different Con Law class,' Nick said.

'It didn't do any good to complain last time,' I said. I

stretched my legs out, so that one white Tretorn sneaker poked out from underneath the blanket, and balanced my foot against the black metal bars that surrounded the balcony. 'I'm just going to try to stay out of Hoffman's way this semester. Not give him any reason to go after me.'

'Sounds like the safest course of action,' Nick said.

His words hit me the wrong way. 'What's that supposed to mean?'

'Just what I said,' Nick said.

'No, you said it in a pointy way.'

'No, I didn't.'

'Yes, you did.'

'I just think . . . you like to stay in your comfort zone,' Nick said.

'Doesn't everyone? In fact, isn't that how you'd define "comfort zone"?' I asked sarcastically.

'Yeah, but you sort of take it to an extreme.'

'Are we still talking about my Crim grade, or are we talking about what happened between us in the Quarter that night?' I asked. The wine was making me bolder than I'd have otherwise been.

Nick was quiet again. 'Is there anything to talk about?' he finally asked. 'Or can we just pretend that I had too much to drink and exhibited shockingly bad judgement as a result?'

I smiled. 'We can.'

'Good,' Nick said. 'Because now that you've proven yourself to be a legal genius, I'm counting on you to get me through Property. That class is going to be a bitch.'

'You're on,' I said.

La Crêpe Nanou was a French bistro nestled on a side street in the upper Garden District that specialized in, not surprisingly, crêpes.

'Yum,' I said, digging into one of the dessert crêpes that was filled with fudge sauce and topped with coffee Häagen-Dazs ice cream. 'This is the best thing I have ever tasted.'

'Are you going to share that?' Armstrong asked. We were supposed to be splitting the dessert, but he'd been sipping an espresso while I greedily attacked the crêpe.

I grudgingly moved the plate a quarter inch closer to him.

'Did you get any work done on the new book while I was gone?' I asked.

Armstrong looked guiltily down at his coffee cup.

'You still haven't started, have you?' I said accusingly.

'I told you, it's a process. The creative juices have to flow for a while,' Armstrong said. He brightened. 'Although I did get the most fabulous carpet for the living room while you were gone. And I finally boxed up all of Mother's Limoges miniatures and sent them off to Goodwill.' Armstrong shuddered. 'Good riddance. Elvis ate one of the boxes, and I had to take him to the animal emergency room.'

'Did they pump his stomach?'

'No. We had to wait for him to crap it out,' Armstrong said. 'It took three days.'

I could have lived without that mental image.

'That's it,' I said firmly. 'We're getting to work on the book tomorrow. Real work. No more shopping.'

'Bossy pants. I'll have you know I happen to be a world-renowned historian,' Armstrong said.

'A world-renowned historian who never actually works.'

'I just have a slight case of writer's block,' Armstrong corrected me. He sipped his coffee. 'How was your first day back at school?'

'Oh! I forgot to tell you – I have Hoffman again this semester,' I announced. Armstrong knew all about my tortured history with Hoffman.

'Not by choice,' Armstrong said, his eyebrows raised.

'No, of course not. I was supposed to have another professor for Constitutional Law – Professor Chai – but she didn't show up. My friend Addison said he heard she's an alcoholic and had to go to rehab. Hoffman took over her class,' I said. I shook my head, the horror of it washing over me anew. 'I can't believe I'm saddled with that asshole for another semester.'

'Can't you drop the class?' Armstrong asked.

'No, we aren't allowed to change classes. But want to know what else Addison told me? It's juicy.'

'What?' Armstrong set down his coffee and leaned forward eagerly. He loved gossip, even if he didn't know any of the people involved.

I gave a little wriggle of happiness. 'Supreme Court Justice Ginsburg was in town last year giving a talk at the law school. Hoffman sat next to her at a luncheon and apparently ate some bad shrimp, *and* . . .,' I hesitated, reveling in the climax of the story, 'Hoffman ended up getting food poisoning and *threw up* right on poor Justice Ginsburg.'

'What do you mean on her? On her shoes?' Armstrong asked.

'No! On her lap,' I crowed triumphantly. I could picture it vividly – hell, the same thing had happened to me four years earlier when Fitz upchucked on me at the Cornell student union – Hoffman's stomach heaving, his pale eyes watering. The moment of panic he must have had when he first realized what was going to happen. He'd probably been turning to get up, ready to race to the men's room, but didn't make it out of his seat in time. 'He must have been humiliated. I'd have given anything to see it.'

'Good evening, Ms Bennett,' a familiar voice said.

I froze.

Oh, no. Oh, please no.

This wasn't happening.

I looked up, hoping that the person who had suddenly materialized at the edge of our table was not who I thought it was – even though I wouldn't have mistaken that voice anywhere. It was the very voice that mocked me in my dreams, sneering at me coldly, ridiculing me for my incompetence.

Hoffman.

He was standing next to our table, staring down at me with

his flat, malevolent eyes. He looked much the same as he did in class – the windblown hair, the button-down blue oxford shirt with the rolled-up cuffs, the wrinkled khakis hanging down over his flat ass (which I couldn't see at the moment, since he was facing us, but I knew it was there).

'Um, hi,' I said, wondering if I looked as wild-eyed as I felt. Had he heard me? *Had he*?

'Are you having a nice dinner?' Hoffman asked, as though we were just old friends meeting up.

'Yes. Yes, we are,' I said. I looked at Armstrong. 'This is Armstrong McKenna. Armstrong . . . this is, um' – Don't say Professor Satan, don't say Professor Satan – 'Professor Richard Hoffman. He teaches at the law school.'

'It's nice to meet you,' Armstrong said pleasantly, extending his hand out to Hoffman.

'I know you by reputation, of course,' Hoffman said. He smiled thinly. 'And how do you know Ms Bennett?'

'She's my research assistant,' Armstrong said. 'And my right arm. I've been lost without her for the past three weeks.'

'How . . . extraordinary,' Hoffman said dryly. I considered stomping on his foot. 'Are you out celebrating, Ms Bennett? I know grades came out today. I hope you were pleased with how you did,' Hoffman continued. And this time when he looked at me, I could have sworn I saw a malevolent glitter in his eyes. I gaped up at him. Was he *gloating*? Should I confront him? Maybe if he was so eager to let me know what he'd done, he'd come right out and admit to violating the Honor Code.

The silence stretched awkwardly between us until it was verging on the point of rudeness. And then, just when I thought things couldn't get any worse, Hoffman's pale eyes suddenly slid down . . . to my cleavage. I glanced down and saw that an extra button on my black oxford shirt had come undone, offering a glimpse of my lace-edged bra.

I flushed with embarrassment, a red stain that started at my cheeks and crept down until it covered the exposed skin.

I wanted to button the shirt back up – in fact, button it all the way to my neck – but I resisted the urge. It would be like handing Hoffman a victory.

'We *are* celebrating,' Armstrong said, apparently unaware that Hoffman had just graduated from asshole to lech. 'Kate received the highest grade in her Contracts class.'

'Did she indeed?' Hoffman said, his eyebrows arched up, and I blushed even darker, now with fury at the insinuation that he wouldn't have thought it possible for me to shine academically.

'They're ready to seat us, Richard,' a woman said, appearing at Hoffman's side and tucking her arm around his. His date, I presumed, although I wondered where that left Dean Sullivan. The woman was blonde and pretty. She looked glamorous in a black sweater ringed with a fur collar and charcoal gray pants, although she'd made the mistake of encircling her mouth in mauve liner that was a shade darker than her lipstick, which gave her a slightly tacky, Jersey Girl look.

'It was nice to meet you, Dr. McKenna,' Hoffman said to Armstrong. He nodded to me. 'Ms Bennett. Oh, and by the way . . . I didn't eat the shrimp. I just had the flu.'

Oh, *fuck*.

And then Hoffman turned and followed the hostess and his date off to their table while I stared after them, open-mouthed and horrified.

'What a pompous asshole,' Armstrong said as he glanced at the bill the waitress had left on the table.

'Oh. My. God. He heard me telling you about how he *puked* on Justice Ginsburg,' I whispered. 'Hoffman *heard* me making fun of him. I'm doomed. *Doomed*. He already hates me . . . now he's going *destroy* me.'

'It's remarkable, if you think about it.'

'What is?' I asked. The veal and *pommes frites* I'd just consumed were sitting in my stomach in a heavy, congealed mass.

'Do you know what the odds are of randomly bumping into someone in a city, much less of being overheard by the very person you're gossiping about? Statistically, it's practically an impossibility.'

'Not for me,' I said grimly. 'I'm cursed. No one believes me, but I am. I have the worst luck in the history of bad luck.'

'Which reminds me,' Armstrong said. He pulled a small wrapped package out of his jacket pocket and pushed it across the table toward me. 'A late Christmas present.'

'You already gave me a present,' I protested. Armstrong had given me a ridiculously high bonus. Since we hadn't actually done any work yet, I'd tried to refuse the bonus and all of my paychecks, but Armstrong had insisted.

My fingers were still shaking with horror after the exchange with Hoffman, but I managed to unwrap the paper. A snowy white rabbit's foot on a chain fell into my hand.

'Um . . . a foot. Thanks,' I said, without any enthusiasm. What was he going to get me for my birthday, a stuffed bird?

'For luck,' Armstrong said. He rolled his eyes heaven-ward at my ignorance. 'What are they not teaching you in school these days? Don't you know a lucky rabbit's foot when you see it?'

'Oh,' I said, realization dawning. 'Because of my bad-luck streak.'

'Because of your bad-luck *epidemic*,' Armstrong corrected me. 'And after your run-in with Professor Prick back there, you're going to need this more than ever. Keep it close. Tuck it in your brassiere.'

I sputtered with laughter. 'Thanks, but no matter how bad my bad luck gets, I'm not going to start stuffing my bra with dismembered rabbit parts.'

'Suit yourself,' Armstrong said, shaking his head.

Just to be safe, though, I slipped the rabbit's foot into my purse.

17

'That's the worst thing I've ever heard in my life,' Jen said. She turned so pale, the spattering of freckles covering her nose and cheeks stood out prominently against her paper-white skin. We were all sitting in the courtyard after a painfully boring Property lecture, and while Jen and Addison chain-smoked, I recounted my run-in with Hoffman at La Crêpe Nanou.

'Are you going to drop out of school? Move away? Change your name?' Addison asked.

'Add,' Lexi said warningly. I was glad to see that her anger – or jealousy, if Nick was right – from the previous day had passed.

'What? That's what I'd do,' he said. 'Hoffman's going to slice and dice her in class tomorrow.'

'Addison! That's not helping!' Jen exclaimed, glaring at him.

'What are you going to do?' Nick asked.

'What can I do?' I said, hating the way my chest was pinching and swelling. I took a deep, ragged breath, hoping to quell the tears before they started leaking out. 'I can't take it back. I can't get out of his class. I can't do anything.' I shrugged helplessly.

'You have to talk to Dean Sullivan,' Nick said quietly.

'And say what?' I asked. 'That Hoffman overheard me making fun of him? Yeah, I'm sure that will go over well.'

'Was his date really that attractive?' Lexi asked, frowning.

'She looked like a slightly tacky interior designer – very well groomed, although not with the greatest taste. Look, I don't want to talk about it anymore,' I said. I stood up and heaved my knapsack, laden down with textbooks, onto my shoulder. I had Con Law tomorrow and knew with a sickening certainty that Addison was right: Hoffman would be gunning for me. I had to be prepared for him, even if that meant throwing my shoulder out from lugging all of my textbooks home with me.

'Do you want a ride home?' Dana asked. She'd been sitting quietly, perched on the edge of the stone bench. Her hair was still braided, although some of the brown curls were starting to escape, rising up in kinky wisps over the cornrows.

'You're leaving?' I asked, surprised. Dana usually camped out at the school library all day. She even had claimed her own cubicle on the second floor of the library, tucked back behind the stacks. It was well known within our study group that if you needed to get ahold of Dana, it was far more reliable to leave a Post-it note stuck to the wall of her cubicle than to leave a message on her answering machine.

Dana nodded. 'Didn't I tell you? My parents gave me a puppy for Christmas,' she said, grinning. 'I'm going to have to start studying at home, because he doesn't like being alone for that long.'

'A puppy! Really? What kind?' I asked.

'A poodle,' she said. 'I named him Oliver Wendell Holmes.'

Holmes had the worst breath I'd ever smelled. It was like something that had crawled into a garbage dumpster and fermented there until even the cockroaches were offended. But it was hard to hold it against the little guy. From his bright coal eyes to his tail, which whirled in constant motion, he was a charming little dog. I held my breath while he attacked me with stinky puppy kisses, licking my face as though it were a hamburger iced with liver-infused frosting.

'He's adorable,' I panted, when Holmes had turned his attention back to Dana and I was able to breathe freely again.

'Thanks,' she said happily. Dana gathered the squirming mass of black fur into her arms and hugged him to her chest. 'I've been wanting a dog forever, but my mom is allergic so I couldn't have one growing up.'

'What made you choose a poodle?' I asked.

'They're really smart. And clean,' Dana said.

'I can see why you got him. It's hard to be stressed out when he's around,' I remarked, watching Holmes, who had squirmed free from Dana's embrace, begin to spin in circles, chasing his tail. I'd have to take her word for it on the 'smart' part.

'I thought the same thing,' Dana said. She watched Holmes scamper about, her face shining with happiness.

'I should probably get home, though. I have to be prepared for Hoffman tomorrow.'

'I've never had a problem with him,' Dana said. 'He's always been pretty nice to me. Well, maybe not *nice*, but . . .'

'I know what you mean. He hasn't targeted you,' I said. 'But you sat in the front row last semester and raised your hand a lot.'

'Maybe you should try doing that.'

'I can't sit in the front row. The seating chart's already been drawn up.'

'No, but you could try raising your hand more,' Dana said.

'But . . .,' I began, and then stopped. Because as much as I wanted to dismiss her idea – volunteer in Hoffman's class? It was suicide! – maybe she did have a point.

'Hoffman always goes easier on the students who volunteer a lot. I've noticed that,' Dana said.

'It could be too late. I may have already pissed him off too much,' I said.

'Maybe,' Dana said. She scooped Holmes back up and

giggled as he writhed toward her, his long pink tongue out-stretched. 'But what do you have to lose?'

'How did Chief Justice Warren define *justifiability* in *Flast v. Cohen?*' Hoffman queried.

'What are you doing?' Nick whispered.

I stretched my hand farther up into the air and ignored him. I didn't even dare pass notes in Hoffman's class, much less carry on a whispered conversation.

'Put your hand down,' Nick hissed.

Hoffman's flat eyes swept over the class. I thrust my hand up a little higher to catch his attention. Hoffman stared at me for a long moment. I returned his gaze, keeping my hand up in the air.

'Kate, are you insane?' Nick asked. He was still whispering, but the room was so quiet, his voice carried.

'Mr Crosby, are you volunteering?' Hoffman asked mildly.

Shit. Nick had just been trying to help me. I raised my hand even higher, so that one butt cheek was actually lifting up off my chair, and I waved it around a bit, the way I'd seen Dana do.

'Yes, Ms Bennett, I see you. You can put your hand down now,' Hoffman said, the words laced with acid. I lowered my hand and glanced at Nick, who seemed to have frozen. I'd never seen him have such trouble being called on before. He'd even suffered through a withering Hoffman examination during our first semester and lived to joke about it afterward.

'I don't know,' Nick said softly.

'Speak up, Mr Crosby, the rest of the class would like to hear you.'

'I don't know,' Nick said. 'I . . . I didn't read the assignment.'

Hoffman looked at Nick with a sour mixture of amusement and scorn. 'Is that so? Perhaps you should rethink your friendships, Mr Crosby. It seems that Ms Bennett's lackadaisical approach to her studies is rubbing off on you.'

To my surprise, Nick chuckled. 'I'll take that under advisement,' he said, shooting me a self-assured grin. The class tittered. Hoffman's lectures weren't normally ripe for a laugh, so we'd take what we could get.

Hoffman, however, was not amused.

'There's nothing humorous about incompetence, Mr Crosby. Or bad judgment,' Hoffman snapped. 'Perhaps some of Ms Bennett's other friends will be more helpful. Mr Quinn,' Hoffman said, his eyes snapping over to Addison, who was suddenly sitting up very straight in his chair. 'The holding of *Flast v. Cohen*, please.'

By the time class was over, Hoffman had grilled Addison, Jen, and Lexi, sneering at their responses and goading each of them in turn. And even though I raised my hand with each question – although now instead of trying to win his favor, all I wanted to do was to draw his attention away from my friends – Hoffman studiously ignored me. It was awful.

'Well. That was fun. I guess I better read up for Friday,' Nick said cheerfully, tossing his books into his black messenger bag.

'I'm so sorry,' I whispered. I felt sick, actually physically ill. Bile churned in my stomach. 'I know he only went after you guys because of me.'

'Don't worry about it, chicky,' Addison said, shrugging. 'It had to happen sometime. He didn't call on me once last semester, so I was overdue.'

But Lexi and Jen weren't so forgiving. Jen had been hit especially hard when she wavered on the holding in *Village of Arlington Heights*. Hoffman needled her until she fell silent, unable to say anything else. Now that class was over, she stood up and hurried from the room without a word to any of us. Before she left, I could see tears shimmering in her eyes.

Lexi turned and looked at me. 'Jesus, Kate, why did you have to go and piss him off again?' she huffed, and then she left too, tossing her hair as she stomped off.

'Forget them,' Nick said.

'Yeah, it's not your fault. I should never have told you the shrimp story,' Addison said.

'No, I'm glad you did. It was a good story,' I said miserably.

It was for my friends' sake, and not my own, that I went to see Teresa Sullivan again. This time I made an appointment ahead of time.

'Kate Bennett?' Teresa Sullivan said when she walked into the reception area where I was waiting for her. Her face arranged itself into a polite smile that made me wonder if she remembered me.

I followed Sullivan back to her office and sat in the same chair I'd occupied on my first visit there. The pictures of her husband and pigtailed daughter were the same, although there was a new one of the family standing in front of a Christmas tree. I wondered if the handsome husband with his chiseled jaw and confident stare suspected that his wife was having an affair with a middle-aged prick. And what would happen to the little redheaded girl if her parents ended up divorcing over Hoffman? Would she be forced to pack her Barbies into a pink overnight bag and spend the rest of her childhood schlepping back and forth to each parent's house, per the terms of the custody agreement?

'We've met before, correct,' Teresa Sullivan said. It was less of a question than a statement.

I nodded. 'At the beginning of the fall semester,' I said.

Teresa Sullivan consulted an unmarked manila folder sitting on her desk. 'Oh, right. You were concerned about Professor Hoffman's treatment of you,' she said.

I nodded. 'Unfortunately, that's why I'm here again,' I said.

And then I told her. All of it, even the part about Hoffman putting the dot on the cover of my blue-book exam and the stupid story about Hoffman throwing up bad shrimp on Justice Ginsburg's lap.

'And now he's started targeting my friends. In fact, for the past three classes, he's called on my friends almost exclusively, mocking them, berating them,' I concluded.

Teresa Sullivan looked at me thoughtfully. While I'd been talking, she'd kicked off her high heels – today they were black crocodile with four-inch needlelike heels – and tucked one of her stockinged feet up under her leg.

'As unfair as it may seem, Professor Hoffman is free to run his class as he sees fit, even if that means calling on some students more than others. But marking a blue book – that's a serious accusation,' Teresa Sullivan said. She flipped open the folder and began writing something on a sheet of paper within.

'I . . . I know that you and Professor Hoffman are friends,' I said hesitantly. 'So if you don't feel comfortable handling this, I can talk to another member of the administration.'

'I don't understand,' Sullivan said, frowning a little as she looked at me. 'I wouldn't say I know Professor Hoffman especially better than any other member of the faculty.'

'But . . . I saw you having lunch together that one day,' I said.

'Oh, right,' Sullivan said, realization brightening her face. 'That wasn't a social lunch. Did you know that Dean Spitzer is retiring at the end of this year?'

'No,' I said, surprised. 'I hadn't heard that.'

'Well, he is, and I'm on the search committee to find a new dean. Professor Hoffman asked me to lunch that day so that he could tell me, informally, that he would like to be considered for the position.'

It took a minute for this to sink in.

'Hoffman . . . as dean of the law school?' I whispered. The idea was horrific. I pictured a totalitarian administration, complete with library police and random locker searches. 'But he's *evil*.' The words slid from my lips before I could stop them.

A smile twitched at Sullivan's mouth. 'When I was in law

school, I thought my Contracts professor was out to get me. He once called on me every single day for two weeks straight,' she said.

'What happened?'

'I ended up doing really well in his class. All of that extra studying I did to be prepared for class, I guess. Years later I ran into him at a conference, and we ended up having a drink together and laughing about it,' Teresa Sullivan said breezily.

'Well, I can tell you right now, Hoffman and I will never, ever end up laughing together over a drink,' I said darkly.

'No, perhaps not,' Sullivan said. 'But in any event, you don't have to worry about my ability to handle this inquiry with impartiality.' She scribbled down a few final notes on the paper, and when she finished, she looked up at me. 'Is there anything else you can remember?'

I shook my head. 'No. What happens now?'

'Now we look into the allegations you've reported,' Teresa Sullivan said.

'But . . . you're not going to leave me in his class . . . are you? Or my friends?' I blurted out.

'For the time being, yes. If you have any further problems, please let me know,' Teresa Sullivan said, in a tone that clearly indicated that our meeting was over.

I sighed, puffing out my cheeks, even though I wasn't surprised. This may not have been a wise move, I thought. If Hoffman found out about the investigation – as he surely would – he'd hate me that much more. And now that I knew he was going after the deanship, there was even more at stake.

18

Mardi Gras fell in early March that year. We had that week off – Graham and I were scheduled to fly into Miami the day after Fat Tuesday – but the festive spirit permeated the law school the week before the break, and everyone, even the professors, visibly relaxed. Some students began showing up to class with Mardi Gras beads hung around their necks. Even Hoffman was less of a bastard than usual, or, at least, he wasn't being as aggressively antagonistic. Ever since my meeting with Teresa Sullivan, he hadn't called on me or any of my friends, other than Dana, but that was only after she volunteered.

I'd promised Graham that I wouldn't bring any law books with me on our trip to Key West, so I planned to spend most of the weekend studying. But my friends had a different plan for me.

'There's no way you're studying today,' Jen said, as she swept in through my back door without knocking, Lexi in tow.

It was the Saturday morning of Mardi Gras weekend, and I was sitting at my kitchen table, eating a carton of blueberry yogurt and contemplating whether or not to shower before I tackled the enormous Con Law reading assignment that Hoffman had saddled us with over spring break.

'Come on in,' I said belatedly. Lexi poured herself a cup of coffee and Jen rummaged through the refrigerator.

'You don't have any beer?' Jen complained.

'It's nine in the morning,' I said. 'Isn't it a little early for you?'

'It's already nine?' Jen checked her watch. 'We're going to be late. Kate, you better change.'

'I'm not going anywhere. And I'm not changing,' I said defiantly, when my friends looked at me critically. I had on my comfiest old sweatpants and my Tulane Law T-shirt.

'You can't go out like that,' Lexi said critically. She was wearing a lemon-yellow T-shirt with short, flutter sleeves, fitted Levi's, and pink Adidas sneakers, and Jen had on a short-sleeve black turtleneck over khakis and black high-heeled ankle boots.

'Yeah, you have to change. If you look like that, no one's going to throw you beads,' Jen said. She leaned out my back door and yelled, 'Hey, Nick! Kate doesn't have any beer up here! Bring what you have!'

'Jen! Keep it down. My neighbors are going to complain,' I said.

'No, they're not. It's Mardi Gras, dahlin',' Jen said, grinning. 'Now, go shower.'

An hour later I was standing on the St. Charles Avenue curb, drinking warm beer out of a red plastic cup and getting elbowed by the crowd milling around me. Nick and Addison had walked over with us, and even Dana had come out, leading her little black poodle puppy on a purple nylon leash. There were people everywhere, so many they were spilling off the sidewalk onto the street. Most were drinking out of plastic cups, but some flouted the open-container laws and held cans of beer or bottles of Jack Daniel's. Many of the crowd were wearing garlands of fat plastic beads they'd scored at parades the night before, and some even wore silly hats – purple and green court-jester hats, towering red-and-white-striped Cat-in-the-Hat hats. I saw a few guys wearing those stupid caps that hold two beer cans with straws snaking down for hands-free drinking. Kids sat above the crowd, perched on seats affixed to stepladders so that they'd have an unobstructed view once the parade floats started rolling by. Vendors walked through the crowd, hawking everything from beads to bags of popcorn. Music boomed from portable stereos, and the crowd sang and danced along, hooting and cheering and waiting to be entertained.

'Here it comes,' Jen said excitedly. She had brought a disposable camera and dashed forward to snap a photo of the approaching floats. One of the mounted policemen preceding the parade blew his whistle at her and gestured at her with a white-gloved hand.

'Step back, ma'am,' he yelled. Jen blew him a kiss and ducked back.

'I got a great picture of the krewe captain on horseback,' she said breathlessly when she returned.

As the parade drew closer, the crowd began to cheer. The captain and his escorts wore elaborate robes and face masks, and they waved to everyone as they passed by, tossing plastic gold coins, which the kids pounced on. Next up was a high-school marching band and a troupe of teenage girl dancers boogying along in silver-sequined leotards.

'They must be freezing,' Lexi commented.

The theme of the parade was 'Under the Sea.' The first float was covered with blue metallic paper and cutouts of fish, and the masked krewe members – all male – were dressed up as mermen. They wore shiny green tails and many were shirt-less, with glitter rubbed over their hairy chests and soft bellies. Some of the men carried plastic tridents that they waved triumphantly overhead. They were all throwing things down from the float – beads and plastic cups and more colorful coins. The float was taller than I thought it would be – two stories high and holding fifty or more members of the krewe. The kids up on the ladders were just the right height to catch the eyes of the second tier of mermen, and they waved their arms wildly, yelling, 'Throw me something, mister!'

A strand of beads smacked me in the face, stinging the tender skin around my eye and at the top of my cheek.

'Ow!' I exclaimed.

'Keep your hands up,' Jen yelled in my ear.

I raised my arms, holding them protectively in front of my face, and even though I wasn't really trying to collect them, there were so many beads raining down from the sky, I soon had a dozen strands of them around my neck. The parade had paused while the band and dancers up ahead performed a number, and the merman float had stopped right in front of us.

'These beads suck,' Jen complained. 'They're just the cheap ones.'

'What other kinds are there?' I asked.

'All kinds. You can buy them all over town, but that's no fun. It doesn't count unless you catch them,' Jen said. 'Like those! I want *those* beads!'

I looked up. One of the mermen was holding out a strand of beads shaped like Mardi Gras masks. He shook them at me, grinning broadly. I put my hand up, reaching for them.

'Let's see 'em!' he yelled at me over the crowd.

'What is he talking about?' I asked Jen.

'He wants you to flash your boobs at him. He's not going to give you the beads unless you do,' she shouted back.

'No way,' I said, and I shook my head at him. 'Not a chance in hell.'

'No tits, no beads,' he said, and started dancing like a fool, taunting me with the beads.

'I want those beads!' Jen yelled. I looked at her, and my jaw dropped open. She'd pulled her black turtleneck up, exposing a red lacy bra that just barely contained the round heft of her breasts.

'Jen!' Lexi said.

'Wow,' Addison said, sounding impressed. He leaned in to get a closer look.

'All the way!' the masked merman said, dangling the beads just out of Jen's reach.

Jen shrugged, pulled down the edges of the bra. Her weighty breasts spilled out. They looked vulnerable and pale in the late-morning sun, and the pink circles of her areolas stood out prominently.

'Tits! Tits! Tits!' the krewe members cheered wildly, and suddenly they were all flinging armfuls of beads down on Jen and, by our proximity to her, on us. Jen grabbed the Mardi Gras mask beads and then held them over her head triumphantly, while she tucked her boobs back into her bra.

'These are the coolest beads I've ever gotten,' she said, grinning broadly.

The rest of us were all staring at her, openmouthed.

'It's not even ten-thirty in the morning,' I said slowly.

'Jen, I can't believe you just did that. There are kids here,' Lexi said, gesturing to the children perched on their step-ladder seats.

'And Dana,' Nick said.

'I'm not a kid,' Dana said. She'd scooped Holmes up at the beginning of the parade, worried that the surging crowd would trod on one of his dainty paws, and she was now cuddling him up in front of her. 'In fact, give me a beer. Please,' she added politely.

'Only if you promise not to get drunk and start flashing your breasts,' Addison said. He popped open a can of Budweiser and handed it to her. 'I don't want to be responsible for corrupting your virtue.'

'It's Mardi Gras,' Jen said, taking a swig of beer. 'If she's ever going to be corrupted, now is the time.'

Three parades later, I was slightly buzzed and tired of standing outside. I also had to pee, and there wasn't enough antibacterial soap in the world to tempt me into using one of the foul-smelling Porta Potties that were chained in groups to the street signs. Rather than warming up, the day had gotten cooler as it wore on. Low dark clouds rumbled in and hung heavily over the city, threatening to start spitting down rain at any minute. The air was thick with humidity.

'I'm going to head home,' I said, yawning widely.

'Not yet, there's another parade coming,' Jen protested. She'd bared her breasts three more times and was now weighed down with more beads than the rest of us combined. One strand was made up of beads shaped like hot peppers, and another had enormous purple, green, and gold orbs the size of walnuts. Men all around us had stopped watching the parades, instead fixing their bleary drunken eyes on Jen while they waited for the next display of her nipples.

'No, thanks. I've seen enough,' I said. The beads I'd collected – nothing like Jen's riches, mine were chintzy and small – were heavy around my neck, and I had a stack of cheap plastic drinking cups printed with the names of the krewes that had passed by. Why I was collecting these, I don't know. It seemed to be the thing to do.

'But we're going down to the Quarter,' Lexi said. 'You have to come down with us; a whole bunch of One-Ls are meeting up at the Cat's Meow.'

'What's that?'

'A karaoke bar on Bourbon Street.'

'Thanks, but I'll pass,' I said, yawning again. This time I didn't bother to cover my mouth.

'I'll walk home with you. I need a nap if I'm going to go out later,' Nick said.

'Me too,' Addison said. 'Dana, can you give me a ride home?'

Dana lit up and nodded. 'Sure! I parked right in front of Kate's apartment,' she said.

'Cool. Thanks, chicky,' Addison said.

'Why don't you just take a nap at Nick's place?' I suggested to Addison.

Nick and Addison both stared at me.

'Um . . . because that would be gay?' Addison said.

'Guys don't nap together,' Nick said.

'Oh, good grief. Are you twelve? Fine, Add, you can nap at my place if you want,' I said.

'No, I want to go home. I'm not wearing my going-out clothes,' Addison said.

'I don't mind driving him,' Dana said. She wore her hope on her face, shining so brightly, I had to look away.

'Okay,' I said, shrugging my defeat. It wasn't like I was worried that Addison was going to seduce Dana on the way home. Surely he had more sense than that, I thought. I glanced over at Addison. He had reinserted his fake nose ring and was talking to a tourist in a fake British accent.

Okay, maybe not.

Lexi and Jen wanted to stay for the next parade, so we left them behind as we walked back to Nick's and my apartment building. We cut over to Fourth Street, and then meandered down the uneven brick sidewalk, passing by the various candy-colored Garden District Creole cottages and Greek Revival houses. Dana had put Holmes back on the ground, and the tiny poodle was mincing smartly down the sidewalk, darting after the odd squirrel that crossed our path. Dana had twisted a pink bow onto the black poodle's curly head, and it now flopped loosely to the side, giving Holmes a slightly demented look.

In some of the yards there were people out barbecuing or pumping beer from iced kegs on the front porch. Mardi Gras flags flapped in the wind, and wreaths of purple, green, and gold adorned front doors. As we passed by, the revelers smiled and called out, 'Hi, y'all!' or 'What will you give me for these beads?' and we waved back, grinning. It was like a citywide frat party.

When we got back to the apartment house, Dana and Addison climbed into Dana's gold Mercedes sedan, a hand-me-down from her mother.

'A Mercedes, huh? We're styling,' Addison said as he climbed in.

'My parents wanted me to have a safe car,' Dana explained, blushing.

Addison raised his stack of empty plastic cups he'd collected at the parades in a mock toast. Nick and I stood on the front porch and watched them drive off.

'Just how drunk is he?' I asked Nick.

'Pretty drunk,' Nick said.

'So drunk that he'd hit on Dana?'

Nick shrugged. 'I don't know. Dana's cute. Why would someone have to be drunk to hit on her?'

'She's a baby,' I said.

'No, she's not. She may be young, but she's an adult. And she's capable of taking care of herself,' Nick said.

But, still, I watched as they drove off down Magazine Street, and I offered up a little prayer to the hook-up gods that Addison would have the sense to abstain.

'Happy Fat Tuesday,' Nick said, as he waltzed into my kitchen, unannounced. He collapsed into one of my ladder-back kitchen chairs.

Nick looked awful – his skin had a greenish tinge, and his beard was stubbly. His normally brilliant blue eyes were blood-shot. And he smelled dreadful, like a bar at closing time. Stale cigarette smoke and fumes of liquor rose up from him. It was what Pigpen from *Peanuts* would look like if he were twenty years older and coming off a bender.

'Good God, what happened to you? And where have you been? I haven't seen you in days,' I said.

'Coffee . . . I . . . need . . . coffee . . .,' Nick said, leaning dramatically on the table. 'I am so hungover. I'm never going to drink again.'

'Isn't that the whole point of Mardi Gras? A day of debauchery before the Lenten fast?' I said.

'Stop using big words and pour me some damned coffee.'

'This isn't a diner,' I said pointedly, but he looked so woebegone, I finally took pity on him and poured a cup. 'You didn't answer my question: Where have you been? I haven't seen you in days.'

'All over. I think I've been drunk for three straight days,' Nick said. 'Can I have some milk?'

I stared at him until he hauled himself up out of the chair and retrieved the milk out of the refrigerator. 'Saturday night we went down to the Quarter. Sunday we went to some parades, and then Jon Barry – you know, that guy who was in our section last semester? – had a party. And then yesterday we pretty much spent the whole day in the Quarter,' Nick said. 'What have you been doing?'

'Studying,' I said briefly. I'd burned out on Mardi Gras pretty quickly. Once I saw two moms get into a fistfight over a strand of green metallic beads at one of the parades on Saturday, I knew I'd had enough.

'Are you going out today?' Nick asked. I shook my head. 'Good, let's hang out.'

'I have to work,' I protested.

'No one works on Fat Tuesday. Not even you,' Nick said.

I hesitated. I was tempted. Studying while everyone else was out having fun was starting to make me seriously cranky. 'What do you want to do?'

'I have some videos. Come down and watch them with me. You know you want to,' Nick said, smiling.

'What movies do you have?' I asked.

'It's a surprise,' Nick said, perking up. 'Come on, it'll be fun.'

'*Star Wars?*' I asked flatly.

'And *The Empire Strikes Back*. And *Return of the Jedi*. Even though *Jedi* sucks. But still, if you're going to watch the Holy Trilogy, you have to include it,' Nick enthused. 'It'll be a triple feature.'

'I'm going back upstairs to work on my Contracts Two outline,' I said.

'Come on, it'll be fun,' Nick said. 'I don't want to watch them alone, and I'm too hungover to study today.'

'But I'm going out of town tomorrow,' I said.

'Oh, right, your big trip to the Keys. I forgot about that. Just stay for the first movie. And after that, if you want to go back and study, I won't try to stop you.'

I thought it through. It was true, no one else had spent the weekend handcuffed to their desk. Not even Dana, who, Nick reported, was going out with the rest of the gang to the Quarter that afternoon.

'Really?' I asked, surprised. Dana didn't usually go out on a normal Saturday night, much less on the Superbowl of party days.

'Yeah. And . . . I know something else, which you probably don't want to hear,' Nick said.

'What?' I asked.

'I can't tell you.'

'You can't do that,' I protested. 'Now you have to tell me.'

'I think Addison and Dana hooked up,' Nick said.

I gaped at him. 'Did he tell you?'

'No. I just know he hooked up with someone this weekend, and he wouldn't tell me who it was. So it must have been Dana. Who else could it be?' Nick said.

I sat there, huddled on his sofa under his plaid comforter – Fat Tuesday was another chilly, windy day – trying to absorb this information.

'Wow,' I finally said. 'I hope he doesn't end up hurting her.'

'And that's not the only shit that went down this weekend,' Nick said.

'What else happened?'

'I heard Jacob and Lexi broke up.'

'Really?'

'Jen told me that when she and Lexi were coming down to meet us in the Quarter yesterday, they bumped into Jacob, and he was out with another woman,' Nick said.

'Maybe it was just his sister.'

'Not unless he kisses his sister. With tongue,' Nick said.

'No!' I gasped.

'Yup. Jen said Lexi was *pissed*.'

'I'd be furious too,' I said. Then I thought of something. 'Maybe that's who Addison hooked up with. Lexi always flirts with him when she's mad at Jacob, and you said he didn't want to say who he was with.'

But Nick shook his head. 'Whoever Add hooked up with, it happened on Sunday night, before Lexi saw Jacob out with the other chick. And she spent all of last night hanging out with Scott Brown from school.' Nick smiled. 'You know, that guy who thinks you like him.'

'Stupid Jen. I can't believe she told him I was interested in him,' I growled. 'Do you know that he actually patted my ass the other day? I couldn't believe it. I was just checking my mail folder at school, minding my own business, and boom – my ass gets grabbed.'

'That's just Scott. He's even grabbed my ass a few times. Anyway, I think Lexi's taken him off your hands. He seemed pretty starstruck at the attention she was giving him. And before I left, I saw them swapping spit.'

I eyed him. ' "Swapping spit"? What are we, back in the ninth grade again?'

Nick grinned. 'Yeah, pretty much. Hadn't you noticed? Come on, let's start watching the movies, before it gets too late.'

We ate buttered microwave popcorn and leftover pizza while we watched *Star Wars*.

'It's freezing in here,' I complained as the final credits rolled. I'd draped the comforter around my shoulders like a shawl and wrapped the edges around me, trying to seal in my body heat.

'You're supposed to be the Yankee,' Nick said. 'The one who weathered snowstorms for nine months of the year.'

'Yeah, but we have insulation in our houses up there. We might as well have the doors and windows open in here, for all the good they're doing us.'

'Can I have a corner of that comforter?' Nick asked.

'No,' I said.

'Come on, Kate, I'm freezing my 'nads off.'

'That's a lovely image,' I said. 'Okay, here, take this half.'

'You're going to have to move closer,' Nick said.

I slid to the center cushion and, pulling the comforter down off my shoulders, spread half of it over Nick.

'Ahhh. That's better,' he said.

'For you. Now I'm freezing,' I said, wrapping my arms around myself, shivering. 'Don't you have the heat on?'

'It's on high, but those window units don't do a damned thing. Come here,' Nick said, stretching his arm out, inviting me to cuddle in. I looked at him. 'No funny business, I promise. This is strictly for survival,' he said.

The wind began howling again, and rain splattered against the door. I couldn't believe anyone would actually want to be down in the Quarter in this weather, even if they were warmed by an excessive amount of alcohol. I leaned back into Nick's arms, resting my back against his chest, and pulled the comforter up to my chin.

'Better?' Nick asked.

I nodded. 'Uh-huh. Go ahead and start the second movie.'

Nick hit the play button, and the prologue to *The Empire Strikes Back* began scrolling up the screen. I could feel the tension starting to leak from my body as I relaxed back against Nick, warmed by his body and the heavy comforter. I started to blink drowsily sometime around the point where Luke meets Yoda, and by the time Han and Leia reached Cloud City, I slid easily into a heavy, dreamless sleep.

I woke up to someone stroking my arm. Fingers trailed down the soft skin of my inner arm, the same way my friends and I used to do it when we were in middle school and trying to give each other the shivers. I opened my eyes and looked up into Nick's. If he had smiled or made a joke or did his awful Yoda impersonation, the fragile connection would have broken. But he didn't. Instead, he leaned forward, and as he did, I lifted my face to his, and we kissed.

Nick's lips were soft, almost hesitant as they brushed against mine, and so I was the one who leaned toward him, running the edge of my tongue over the inside of his lower lip. Nick's left hand cupped the side of my face as his right hand moved under my sweatshirt to cover my breast, first gently brushing against me and then flickering a finger over my nipple, pinching at the delicate pink skin. The touch widened its path, circling around to cover all of the soft flesh before moving downward.

My breath quickened with excitement as Nick's fingers pushed under the waistband of my sweatpants and peeled back the hem of my panties. He pushed down, thrusting into the soft wetness. As his hands moved against me, stroking and touching, I lost myself in the swirling sensation. At one point I gasped, breaking off our kiss, and I pulled back to look into Nick's face, searching for a confirmation that we really wanted to do this. His eyes were glittering and unreadable.

Wordlessly, Nick stood. He leaned down and pulled off my sweatpants and panties. I lay limply back, my head propped up against a throw pillow, and watched as Nick unbuckled his jeans and let them fall to the ground with a soft rustle of fabric. And then all at once, he was on me, inside me, pushing toward me. We kissed again, and Nick's lips pressed down on mine, his tongue thrusting into my mouth. I wrapped my legs around his, pulling him closer to me.

And then suddenly I thought of Graham – safe, reliable Graham, who I'd just spoken to last night. His allergies were bothering him, and he'd been planning on going to bed early in the hopes of warding off a sinus infection. And just before we hung up, he'd said, 'Only two days until I get to see you.' His voice had been so warm and comforting, I wanted to wrap myself up in it. And it was at that moment, when Graham's face was floating through my thoughts, that Nick suddenly stiffened, gasped, and pushed into me one last time, before collapsing down on top of me.

We lay there, hot and sticky, while I waited for Nick to catch his breath. Finally, when I couldn't bear it anymore, I closed my thighs, pushing him away, up out of me, and he pulled back, holding himself up in a push-up position and looking down at me hazily. Sweat was beaded up on his forehead.

'Wow,' Nick said, panting slightly.

I didn't say anything. I just wanted things to be normal between us – but how could they ever be again? Now, every time I saw Nick, I'd think: He was inside me.

'Are you okay?' Nick asked. He reached down, touching me again.

'Stop,' I said tersely, batting his hand away.

'It's just, I know you didn't . . . I want you to . . .,' he said. He was still breathing heavily, and I was suddenly struck with how ludicrous we must look. Both of us half dressed, our hair mussed. I was still wearing my sweat socks, although the right one was half off. The room smelled thickly, pungently of sex.

'It's okay. Just . . . don't,' I said, and I pushed myself up, propping myself on my arms and then pulling my legs out from either side of him. I grabbed my sweatpants.

'I have to use the bathroom,' I said, and walked shakily back to Nick's bathroom, turning the old-fashioned latch on the door. I looked at my reflection in the mirror. My face was flushed, and my hair was standing up in furious messy curls. The mascara I'd put on that morning had smudged around my eyes, and I looked strung out and hungover, even though I was neither. I remembered my college friend and his story of spitting at himself in the mirror, and I understood how he had felt – and just how much you could despise yourself.

I'd cheated on Graham, and I wasn't even drunk. Not that alcohol would make it acceptable, but at least it would be an excuse. And not only had I cheated, I'd slept with Nick, the biggest scammer I knew. Jesus, how many women had he hooked up with just this year? And here I was – stupid, foolish me – just another notch in his bedpost.

One thing was for certain: I had to get out of here. I had to get into my own space, breathe my own air.

Pack for my trip to Key West.

My trip with Graham.

'What have I done?' I said out loud.

I quickly dressed and then splashed cold water over my face. I used Nick's comb, sitting neatly in a glass jar at the edge of the sink, to untangle my hair. I could hear Nick outside, his footsteps creaking against the floorboards, the dishes clanking in the kitchen sink, the sound of water running. I took a deep breath and opened the door.

He was in the kitchen. As I walked through the living room, I saw that he'd already set the couch back to rights – straightening the cushions, busing our dishes away. Nick's apartment was set up the same as mine, with his office and bedroom in the front two rooms, the living room and kitchen at the back. Four small rooms, stacked up in a row. I paused at the door to the kitchen and watched Nick. His back was to me, and he was washing out the popcorn bowl and rinsing the tomato sauce off the plates, then carefully stacking them on a dish rack at the edge of the sink.

'Hey, do you want to get some takeout? I'm pizza-ed out,' Nick said.

'No . . . I should get going,' I said. My voice sounded thin and artificial, the way it does on my answering machine.

Nick shut the water off and turned to look at me. 'Why?'

I nodded. 'I have to pack.'

'For what?'

'My trip. Remember?'

'Wait . . . you're not still going to Key West?' Nick's voice was incredulous, and he frowned at me, disbelief flushing over his face.

'I have to go,' I said, which was probably not the strongest argument I could have made, I realized too late.

Nick's face changed. His eyes hardened, his jaw tightened. He looked at me coolly and shrugged.

'Well . . . have a good trip,' he said.

'Nick,' I began, but I couldn't think of anything to say. I swallowed, hard, trying to push down the ache that had started throbbing in my throat.

'Bye,' I said quietly. And I left.

It took me most of my childhood to figure out that I had rotten luck. For a long time I thought I just suffered from the same growing pains all girls have to deal with, even when faced with the steady stream of incidents that proved me wrong.

So what if the clasp on my very first bra broke right in the middle of our square-dancing unit in gym class? Embarrassing, yes – particularly since the elastic snapped with a loud, audible *ping* right when I was dancing with Jason Baum, who later lied when he told everyone that he'd used the opportunity to feel me up – but not unheard of.

When I lost the election for high-school freshman-class vice president by one measly vote, I sucked it up and tried to be a gracious loser. Even though I knew that the Wells twins – Jessica and Jacqueline – would have voted for me if they'd been in school that day. It was just an unfortunate co-incidence that they both had to have their tonsils out. At the same time. On election day.

No, it wasn't until my junior year in high school, when I came down with the triple whammy of mononucleosis, strep throat, and bronchitis two days before the junior prom, that I realized something else might be going on. Bad juju, black kismet, whatever you wanted to call it, it all came down to one sour truth: I was really freaking unlucky.

But I couldn't help but think there were even larger

karmic issues than my congenital bad luck at play when my trip to Key West began with the airline losing my luggage and the car-rental company running out of cars. And then, after we'd finally found a sketchy independent company that agreed to rent us an ancient, sputtering Taurus, the car blew a tire thirty minutes after we left the Miami airport right in the middle of a downpour.

The universe was sending me a message: I was on its shit list for sleeping with Nick.

'It's all my fault,' I said miserably, standing behind Graham in the rain as he changed the tire. He was getting covered with grease, and we were both drenched.

'Shit!' Graham yelped as he scraped his knuckles against the hubcap. A bright line of scarlet sprang up from the scratch.

'See? It's my bad luck. I'm cursed. It's probably not even safe for you to be near me.'

'I'm a scientist. I don't believe in bad luck,' Graham said.

Just then an eighteen-wheeler thundered by. It barreled right through a huge puddle and, with a great swishing splash, sprayed me from head to toe.

'Ack!' I shrieked. I held my arms out in front of me as I stared down at the damage. I was filthy. My pink boat-necked shirt and jeans were soaked through with muddy water. Even my face was splattered; I could taste oily grit on my lips.

Graham looked at me solemnly. He looked liked he was trying very hard not to laugh.

'See? Bad luck,' I said, through clenched teeth.

'You have a little mud right here,' Graham said, pointing to my cheek. I reached up to brush it off and only succeeded in smearing more dirt on my face. Graham couldn't hold back his laughter any longer and began to snicker.

'If you need me, I'll be back behind the car,' I said with as much dignity as I could muster.

*

'Everything okay? Besides the mud bath, I mean,' Graham asked, once he'd gotten the spare tire on and we were back en route. I'd used one of his T-shirts to wipe off as much of the mud as I could from my hands and face, although my clothes and hair were still a mess. At least the rain had finally stopped, and the sun looked as if it was trying to break through the heavy gray clouds.

'Just dandy,' I said.

'You've been really quiet,' Graham said.

It was a bland remark, but I cringed anyway and turned to gaze out the window of our rented Taurus before he could see my face.

'I'm sorry,' I said automatically. Guilt flooded through me every time I looked at Graham. I worried that he'd be able to sense that I'd cheated on him, maybe even smell Nick's scent still clinging to my body. I'd showered three times – twice last night and once again this morning – but maybe I'd missed a spot on the hollow of my throat or the small of my back that was still imprinted with Nick.

'Don't be,' Graham said, smiling at me. He reached out and took my hand, entwining our fingers together. He brushed his lips against my curved knuckles and then rested our hands on the seat between us.

The drive from the Miami airport down to Key West wasn't what I had expected. For some reason, I thought that the entire trip would be over water, one long bridge stretching out across the ocean. But most of the interminably long drive south on U.S. 1 was over land. One key blended into the next, a blur of fast-food restaurants, kitschy hotels, and gas stations. 'The Girl from Ipanema' hummed on the radio, and I stared out the window at the occasional stretch of teal-blue water and wondered for the umpteenth time what in the hell I'd been thinking of the day before.

'This should be fun. I've never been to Key West before,' I said, trying to force myself into the spirit of things.

'I was there once, but it was years ago. I've been wanting to come back ever since,' Graham said. He glanced at me. 'Come on, tell me. What's wrong?'

'Wrong? Nothing. Nothing's wrong,' I said.

'I know you better than that. Something's obviously on your mind.'

Great. I'd cheated on my boyfriend, and I was terrible at hiding things. Note to self: Learn how to lie.

After we checked in to the hotel, Graham went out to buy me something to wear to dinner, while I got in the shower and did my best to scrub the mud out of my hair. He was already back when I emerged from the steam-filled bathroom, wrapped in one of the hotel's white, fluffy robes and feeling slightly more human.

'That was fast,' I said.

'There's a T-shirt shop just next door. I wasn't sure what you wanted, so I just got you a T-shirt and shorts,' he said, handing me a red plastic bag.

'Great, thanks. I guess we won't be able to go anywhere dressy for dinner.'

'The concierge told me there's a really good casual Italian place nearby. I'm just going to hop in the shower, and then we can go eat,' Graham said.

As Graham showered, I emptied the shopping bag that contained my new outfit onto the bed. And I learned something new about my boyfriend: Either he was color-blind or he just had terrible taste. The shorts and T-shirt he bought me were a garish orange cotton knit screen-printed with sparkling blue fish. When I put them on, I looked like an eighty-year-old woman going on a cruise. Even worse, the only shoes I had to wear were the high-heel zebra-print mules I'd worn on the plane. The shoes were adorable with jeans, but when paired with orange cotton cabana-wear they made me look insane. I examined my reflection in the full-length mirror. It was even worse than I thought.

I need a drink, I thought. A *big* drink.

'I'm going to the hotel bar,' I yelled through the closed bathroom door.

'I'll be out in a few minutes,' Graham called back.

The bar was poolside, forcing me to walk by a herd of glamorous bikini-clad women reclining by the pool. They looked me up and down and smirked.

Gah, I thought.

When I reached the bar, there were two men sitting on bar stools. One was tall with thinning blond hair, and the other short and stocky with a wide nose and a thatch of dark hair. Both were sunburned. They were drinking frozen margaritas with salt around the rim and thick wedges of lime bobbling amid the melting ice cubes.

'Yeah, that guy is a prick,' the blond man said.

'No fucking kidding,' his friend agreed with a bark of laughter.

I slid onto a bar stool, careful to leave an empty stool between us.

'What can I get you?' the bartender asked, sliding a beverage napkin and small white bowl full of Goldfish crackers toward me.

'Gin and tonic, please,' I decided.

'Put her drink on our tab,' the dark-haired man said, leaning across the bar to get the bartender's attention.

'No, that's okay,' I demurred.

'I insist,' he said, waving my objections away.

'Oh . . . well, thanks,' I said, accepting the tall, sweating glass from the bartender. I took a sip and winced. It was a bit heavy on the gin.

'Are you here on vacation?' the blond man asked.

I nodded.

'Us too. Came down on a fishing trip. Left the wives and kids behind,' the blond man said, and I relaxed. Men who are trying to hit on you, no matter how loaded, normally don't bring up their wives. 'Where are you from?'

'New Orleans,' I said. My answer, although technically true, felt artificial.

'No kidding! The Big Easy, huh? I was down there for a bar convention two years ago. I got so drunk on those . . . whadyacallems, hurricanes, I don't know how I got back to my hotel. I spent the night praying at the porcelain altar,' the dark-haired man said, guffawing at the memory. 'I'm Larry, by the way. My friend here is Ray.'

'Nice to meet you. I'm Kate,' I said. 'So . . . you're a lawyer?'

'We both are. We're partners. We have a med malpractice in Grand Rapids,' Ray said.

'I'm in law school,' I admitted. 'I go to Tulane.'

'Great school,' Larry said. 'I wish I'd gone there; what a blast that would have been.'

'You'd have failed out the first semester,' Ray said.

'Yeah, probably. Ha! I would have ended up blowing all of my tuition money down at the French Quarter,' Larry replied.

I shook my head. 'I think it's pretty much like going to law school anywhere. You spend most of your time in the library.'

'Yeah, those were the days,' Ray said fondly.

'Are you crazy? It's awful!' I exclaimed.

'You don't know what awful is. Just wait until you start practicing. I'd rather be a law student than a law-firm-associate any day. At least when you're in school you get to see daylight once in a while,' Larry said. 'When I was an associate, a whole week would go by when I didn't see my wife awake. I'd leave for work before she got up in the morning and get back after she'd gone to bed.'

'I missed the birth of my son,' Ray said.

'You did?' I asked. 'Why?'

'I was stuck at a deposition in Lansing, with no one to cover it.' He chuckled, and gave Larry a sideways glance. 'Maribeth was pissed.'

'I bet. How'd you dig your way out of that one?' Larry asked.

'She got the new car she'd been wanting; I got to keep my

testicles. All in all, I think it was a good trade,' Ray said, and they both guffawed.

'But now that you're partners it's better, right?' I asked.

Larry looked at me, the smile sliding from his face. He shrugged. 'I guess. I know a lot of guys – and gals, excuse me – who are good at what they do and who earn a shitload of money. But I don't know anyone who actually enjoys it.'

'You just live for the time off. And the satisfaction that you're providing for your family,' Ray said, falling into the same melancholic state as his friend.

'Would you want your boy to go into the practice?' Larry asked.

'Hell no,' Ray said. 'I'm trying to talk him into going to business school.'

'But the whole point of having a law degree is the security – it means that you'll always be able to get a job, you'll always be able to make a living,' I said. I wasn't able to keep the shrill note of panic from my voice.

'Hey, honey,' Graham said, walking up behind me. He was wearing a linen shirt, shorts, and flip-flops, and his hair was still damp from the shower. Unlike me, he looked fantastic. Graham slid a protective arm around my waist, which I knew was meant to discourage Ray and Larry from any plans they might have to hit on me.

I introduced Graham to my new acquaintances. 'They're lawyers,' I explained. 'They were telling me about their practice.'

'Let me give you some unsolicited advice,' Ray said. 'Get out now, while you still can.'

And even though he smiled as he said it and held his margarita up in a mock toast, there was a desperate note in his voice that made me shiver.

On our last day of vacation, my luggage showed up. Finally dressed like a normal person, I went into town alone to browse through the tourist shops, where I bought T-shirts for my aunt and cousins and a perfect pink conch shell. Graham was by the pool, lying on a chaise longue and baking in the sun when I got back. He was bare-chested and slicked with oil, and I was struck by what good shape he was in. He smiled when he saw me, squinting up, one hand shading his eyes.

'That's some hat,' he said.

I touched the brim of the pink sunhat I was wearing.

'I have a fair complexion,' I explained.

'Do you have on sunblock?'

'SPF sixty-five.'

Graham laughed. 'That should do it,' he said.

'You should put some on,' I said.

'I have some oil on,' Graham said, pointing to the tube of SPF 4 lying on the ground next to his chaise.

'SPF four? I didn't even know they made it that low anymore,' I said, dropping in the chaise longue next to him. 'You're going to get skin cancer.'

'You worry too much.' Graham stood up and kissed me. He smelled like coconut oil. 'Want to go for a swim with me?'

'No, that's okay. I'm going to sit here with the new issue of *Vogue*, and maybe even get one of those tropical drinks that come with a little umbrella,' I said, stretching out contentedly.

Graham waded into the water and then dove in with a splash. When he popped out, his hair was plastered down against his scalp, and his legs and red swim trunks were warped by the water, making him look like a Picasso painting. I saw two women, sitting at a table on the opposite side of the pool, watching him. One whispered something to the other, and they both giggled, never taking their eyes off my boyfriend. They were pretty, but in a hard, artificial way, and both wore tiny little bikinis to show off their surgically enhanced bodies. But Graham didn't notice them. He swam a few laps, his arms cutting capably through the water, and then he stood up at the shallow end, shaking his head like a dog.

'Kate, you should come in, the water's fantastic,' he called out to me. I waved at him but shook my head.

'No, thanks. I'm in the middle of an article about fall hemlines,' I said. 'It's riveting stuff.'

Graham laughed, and recommenced his laps. I glanced at the implant twins, who were pouting that he hadn't paid them any attention and were now eyeing me jealously. I just smiled at them from behind my magazine.

That night we went down to the rocky beach to watch the sunset. It was fabulous, a symphony of pinks and corals, smudgy grays and pastel purples. Graham slid his arms around me, and for the first time since we'd gotten to Florida, I relaxed back against him. The gorgeous sunset, the white-capped waves roaring in toward us, the warmth of Graham's chest . . . it was perfect, right out of a vacation brochure.

'I've been thinking about something,' Graham said.

'What's that?'

I felt Graham's hand move away from me as he reached into his pocket. And then he was holding an object out in front of me. I looked at it, confused.

A ring box.

'Will you marry me?' Graham's voice was a low, warm buzz in my ear. I took the box in my hands and opened it up.

The ring was beautiful. Three princess-cut diamonds in a platinum setting, a large stone flanked by two smaller ones. With shaking hands, I pulled the ring out of its white satin box. The diamonds winked and glittered up at me.

It was heavier than I thought it would be.

I was quiet. A pelican soared just over the water, trailing his wings slightly against the wake. The sun continued to sink down toward the horizon. Graham wrapped his arms tighter around me and nuzzled his nose into the curve of my neck.

'You're the one, Kate,' he said, so softly, I could just barely hear him over the surf. 'I love you.'

I turned and snaked my arms around his waist, squeezing him tightly and burying my head against his chest. I kissed the triangle of skin bared by his polo shirt. He tasted of sunlight and salt.

I could see our life together unfolding so clearly, I could almost touch it. We'd have two blond children we'd take to the beach in the summer, and Graham and I would sit on low folding chairs, our hands clasped together absentmindedly, while we watched our kids romp around on the sand. Every Christmas we'd get a big tree, and the scent of evergreen would mix with the cinnamon from the holiday baking. We'd have a glass of wine together in the evenings and talk about our days. On weekends we'd plant flower beds and go out to dinner.

It would be a good life, a sturdy life.

A safe life.

I'd be a fool to pass it up.

I looked up. Graham's face was close to mine, so close that I could see the web of faint lines by his eyes and the small mole on his right cheek.

'Yes,' I said softly. And I slipped the ring on my finger.

20

Late Sunday morning, we drove back up to the Miami airport and caught our respective flights to Arizona and New Orleans. I made it back in time to meet the others for our weekly study group at the Rue, but I decided to pass. The last person I wanted to see was Nick. I didn't know if I'd ever be able to see him again without remembering what he'd looked like leaning back on his couch, wearing only a T-shirt.

With everything down below sort of . . . hanging out.

No, I thought fiercely. No more thinking of Nick, naked or otherwise.

I was too restless to study, so I drove over to Armstrong's house. The windows were dark, and his car wasn't in the driveway. I rang the bell – the *William Tell Overture* rang out, making it sound like the Lone Ranger was galloping through the house – and when Armstrong didn't answer, I let myself in with the key he'd given me.

When I walked in, Elvis the Guard Dog was asleep in the front hall, lying on his back with his feet sticking straight up. I'd never seen a dog sleep like that before, but Elvis could hold the position for hours.

'Hi, Elvis. Don't worry, I'm not here to rob the place,' I said.

Elvis opened one eye, looked at me blearily, and then farted.

'Lovely,' I said.

I headed upstairs to Armstrong's office and settled in to my work. We'd finally started on the book research, and since I worked irregular hours, Armstrong had gotten in the habit of leaving me a list of the articles he wanted me to pull off the Internet and skim for content. Elvis followed me up the stairs and found the climb so exhausting, he collapsed on one of the leather sofas with a loud sigh.

The work was interesting, but not grueling, and I felt my stress begin to melt away as I fell into the rhythm of reading through the research. The only distraction was Elvis's constant gas. It got so bad, I finally had to throw open the French doors that led onto the second-floor balcony to air the room out.

'What has Armstrong been feeding you? Baked beans?' I asked Elvis.

'Butter pecan ice cream,' Armstrong said from the doorway. 'Never again. He's been windy for two days now.'

I hadn't heard Armstrong come in, and the interruption startled me. I shrieked and threw my pen up into the air.

Armstrong raised his eyebrows. 'Heavens, child, if you keep that up, the neighbors are going to call the police.'

'You scared me,' I said.

'So I gathered,' Armstrong said.

It was only then that I noticed that Armstrong was swaying from side to side, and he was slurring his words. I looked at him more closely. Definitely drunk. His eyes were red and unfocused, and his normally impeccable clothing was rumpled. I'd seen the man put away three bourbons straight up on an empty stomach without showing the slightest sign that the alcohol affected him. I couldn't imagine how much he must have drunk to be swaying and slurring. I glanced at the clock; it was after midnight.

'God, how did it get so late?'

'Time has a way of moving on,' Armstrong said sadly. 'One day you're dancing with David Bowie at Studio 54, and the next you're an old man living in a whorehouse.'

'You danced with David Bowie?' I asked.

'No. But it makes for a good story,' Armstrong said, collapsing on the sofa next to Elvis.

I stood up, stretching. 'I had no idea it was so late. I'd better get home.'

'First tell me how your trip with the academic was. Wait – what's that I see on your hand?' Armstrong demanded. His Southern accent got stronger when he drank. Right now he sounded like Foghorn Leghorn.

I looked down shyly at my ring. It still felt foreign on my hand, like a piece of borrowed jewelry.

'We got engaged,' I said.

'So I see. To the academic, I take it?'

'Of course,' I said. 'And how can you disapprove of Graham when you've never even met him?'

'Who said I disapprove?'

'You keep telling me I should break up with him.'

'That doesn't mean I disapprove,' Armstrong said. I looked at him. He shrugged. 'Okay, so I disapprove.'

'At least meet him before you decide to hate him,' I said, as I gathered my keys and papers together.

'Have a drink before you go,' Armstrong said.

I hesitated. He looked like he'd already had more than enough to drink.

'We have to celebrate your pending nuptials,' Armstrong said, waving two empty glasses at me.

'Okay, one drink. And then I have to get home. I have class tomorrow,' I said.

I sat back down while Armstrong poured a bourbon for him, a glass of wine for me.

'If you're going to live in the South, you're going to have to learn how to drink bourbon one of these days,' Armstrong said, handing me my glass. 'So tell me all about it.'

I filled him in on the trip, and Graham's proposal, and how we'd gone out to dinner afterward for lobster ravioli and champagne. Graham – still enthralled with photography – had taken about a hundred photos, ensuring that the whole magical evening would be captured on film.

'It was perfect. Very romantic,' I said.

And it was. I remembered my mother telling me a story about how the daughter of one of her friends was proposed to while she and her boyfriend were watching a football game on television. At the commercial break, the boyfriend had turned to her and said, 'So . . . wanna get married?' And she actually accepted. Ever since I've lived in fear that I'd receive a similarly dismal proposal. I mean, really. How can you marry someone who proposes on a commercial break?

'Ah, to be young and in love,' Armstrong said. The slur was becoming more pronounced, and his head lolled back on the sofa. 'Have I ever told you about Hunter?'

'A hunter? Like the kind that killed Bambi?'

Armstrong gave me a dirty look. 'No. That was his name: Hunter.'

'Oh . . . no. You've never talked about him.'

'He was the love of my life,' Armstrong mused. 'And he broke my heart.'

I could feel the weight of his words settle between us.

'What happened?' I asked gently.

He shrugged. 'Whatever generally happens. I was neglectful, he was bored. He resented my success. I resented his . . . indiscretions.'

'I'm so sorry,' I said.

Armstrong set his empty glass on the coffee table. When he leaned back against the sofa, he shut his eyes. People usually look younger when they relax into sleep, but Armstrong seemed to age. Without the usual vivaciousness lighting his face, his skin grayed and the lines fanning out from his eyes and mouth became more pronounced.

'Love is not so easy to come by, Katie,' he murmured. 'Be careful with it.'

His breath slacked off into a low rumbling snore. I took a

throw blanket from the back of a chair and tucked it around him, and then let myself out.

The next day I noticed that my engagement ring was starting to leave a rash on my finger. The skin under it was rising up in itchy red bumps.

Great, I thought, scratching my finger. I was allergic to my engagement ring. I hoped it wasn't a sign.

I considered leaving the ring at home in my jewelry box, but it seemed disloyal. So I smeared some cortisone cream on the rash, slid the ring back on, and went to school.

I got in early so I'd have time to read Hoffman's assignment before class. Even though it was gray and muggy, and the air was so humid my skin felt clammy, I couldn't bear sitting in the airless library. Instead, I claimed a bench outside on the student-union patio, sitting cross-legged with my Con Law book open on my lap.

Just as I was finishing, two figures loomed in front of me. I looked up. It was Jen and Lexi, standing side by side and grinning down at me with knowing smiles.

'Hi,' I said.

'Is there something you want to tell us?' Jen asked.

'How did you find out?' I asked. I knew what the gossip network was like at the law school, but the only other people who knew about my engagement were Graham and Armstrong, neither of whom knew anyone I went to school with.

'I can't believe you thought you could keep it a secret,' Lexi said.

'I didn't. I'm wearing my ring, after all,' I said, holding up my left hand to show off the diamond.

'What?' Jen gasped.

'You're engaged?' Lexi chimed in.

'To who?' Jen asked.

'Graham. Who do you think? Wait . . . what were you guys talking about?'

Lexi and Jen looked at each other.

'Nick,' Jen said.

I went cold. Nick told them we slept together? The idea that they'd all talked about me – that *he* had talked about me – made me queasy. I knew Nick's reputation, of course, knew that he probably saw me as just another conquest, but *still*. I'd assumed he'd keep our interlude to himself for the sake of our friendship.

'What did he tell you?' I asked quietly.

'Nothing,' Jen said. My sick dread must have been reflected in my face, because she blanched and sat down next to me. 'Oh, no, Kate. It wasn't like that. He didn't tell us anything. Nick was upset, so Addison took him out and got him drunk to cheer him up, and that's when Nick told Addison what happened. Addison told me, and I told Lexi. We were just going to tease you about it.'

'Why was Nick upset?' I asked.

Jen and Lexi exchanged another meaningful look.

'What?' I asked.

'Kate, Nick really likes you. I think that he thought that after you two . . . well, you know. He thought you were going to get together. That you'd be a couple,' Jen said.

'And then you went off to the Keys with Graham,' Lexi said.

'No. You're wrong,' I said, shaking my head. 'Nick doesn't like me. Not seriously. You know what he's like. He's a player.'

'Actually,' Jen said thoughtfully, 'I can't remember the last time Nick hooked up with someone. Well. Someone other than you, I mean. Lexi, can you?'

'Last semester, maybe?' Lexi said, furrowing her brow as she thought it over. 'Addison was teasing him about it one night when we were all out. Nick said he was a changed man.'

'Oh, my God!' Jen exclaimed, so suddenly that I started.

'What?' I asked.

'What if you're the reason why? What if he's fallen so madly and deeply in love with you he's given up all other women?'

I had to admit, it was a flattering thought. Flattering – but unlikely.

'I seriously doubt that,' I said.

'I'd ask you how your trip was, but I'm guessing it went well,' Lexi said. 'Are you going to tell us what happened?'

'Yes, tell us everything! How did he propose? What did he say? What did you say? I can't believe you're engaged!' Jen chirped.

And just as the words were leaving her mouth, Nick appeared. I hadn't seen him approach, because all of a sudden he was just *there*, standing in front of us. When my eyes met his, my stomach dipped and dropped. I knew he'd overheard Jen, but I couldn't tell what he was feeling. Hurt? Surprise? Indifference?

'Nick,' I said. 'Um . . . hi.'

'Hey. I've got to get inside, class is starting,' Nick said. He turned and strode off toward the law school.

'Damn. Shit,' I said. I pressed the heels of my hands to my forehead. 'I didn't want him to find out like this.'

'Oh, Kate. God, I'm sorry,' Jen said. She looked stricken.

'It's not your fault. It's just my bad luck again. And it's getting worse. Do you see this?' I took out the lucky rabbit's foot Armstrong had given me and waved it at them. 'This doesn't work. In fact, if anything, my luck has gotten even worse since I started carrying it. It's probably cursed. I have the only cursed rabbit's foot in existence.'

'You think it's bad luck to have two great guys in love with you?' Lexi asked curtly.

I looked up at her, surprised by her biting tone. But then I remembered: Jacob. I'd been so caught up in my own drama, I'd forgotten all about hers.

'Oh, Lex, I'm sorry. I can't believe I'm being so self-centered,' I said, grabbing one of her hands and squeezing it. 'I heard about you and Jacob. Are you okay?'

Lexi paused, and then she slipped her hand from mine. She tossed her hair back, gathered it in a ponytail and secured it with a black elastic.

'Oh, *him*,' she said disdainfully. 'He's an asshole. I'm so over that.'

'You're not upset?' I asked.

She laughed without humor. 'Of course not. It's not like I was ever that into him. Come on, we'd better go in. We don't want to be late for Hoffman.'

I looked at Jen, and she shrugged and briefly shook her head, silently warning me not to push Lexi. However Lexi had really felt about him and the sudden demise of their relationship, the subject of Jacob Reid was closed for discussion.

21

Nick didn't look at me when I sat down next to him in class. He bent over his notes, his head resting on one hand.

'Good morning, ladies and gentlemen.' Hoffman's nasal voice filled the room. 'When we last left off, we were discussing the Commerce Clause, limping along at an excruciatingly slow pace, thanks to Mr Chesney's feeble analysis.'

I glanced at Brian Chesney, who had endured a scathing interrogation during the last class before spring break. He now looked down at his book, his puggish face red and his shoulders sagging.

'Today we'll be covering the civil-rights cases. I hope you're prepared, because we're going to be moving through the material quickly to catch up to where we should be,' Hoffman continued. 'First up will be *Heart of Atlanta Motel*. Let's see . . . who haven't we heard from in a while,' Hoffman mused aloud while he consulted his seating chart. I saw his eyes flicker toward me, and I immediately raised my hand.

'Ms . . . Mallick,' Hoffman said, his flat eyes sliding past me and onto Dana.

Dana inhaled sharply, and she began paging through her textbook with shaking hands. I glanced at her, not sure what was wrong. It wasn't like she hadn't done the reading. Dana was always prepared. Always. She'd even come to class when she had the flu.

'Ms Mallick, we're waiting,' Hoffman said, his voice louder and more peevish.

I looked back to Dana. She'd turned a sickly shade of white and looked on the verge of tears.

Oh, my God, she doesn't know the answer, I realized. Dana – the academic Girl Wonder – had actually shown up unprepared. And now it looked like she was going to be sick right then and there.

I closed my eyes, gritted my teeth, and then thrust my hand back up in the air.

'Ms Bennett, put your hand *down*,' Hoffman said. He didn't raise his voice, but his tone was dangerously cold. 'Ms Mallick. *Heart of Atlanta Motel.*'

'I didn't read the case,' Dana said, so softly I could barely hear her.

'We can't hear you, Ms Mallick. Please stand up,' Hoffman said.

Dana looked at him fearfully but didn't move. I could see tears shimmering in her wide brown eyes, and her lips were pressed so tightly together, they were ringed with white.

'Ms Mallick, are you deaf or merely dumb?' Hoffman said.

'Leave her alone!' I said, my voice cracking across the silent room.

'Kate,' Nick breathed, the word a warning. But it was too late. Everyone's eyes were on me, just as they'd been on that first day of Criminal Law class. But this was worse, I knew. Then I'd only been yet another timid law student for him to bully. The transgression of openly confronting him in class was far more serious.

'I beg your pardon?' Hoffman's voice was more incredulous than angry.

'I said, leave her alone,' I replied, trying to keep the quaver out of my voice.

Hoffman and I stared at each other, and for a moment it was as though we were alone in the room. Nick's presence,

Dana's sniffling – they were both pushed to the periphery of my consciousness as I waited.

'Ms Mallick. Stand. Up. Now.'

Dana pushed her chair back and, bracing her hands against the edge of the table, she pulled herself up.

'Thanks to your friend Ms Bennett, you will be in the hot seat for the remainder of class, Ms Mallick,' Hoffman said. 'Now. The Court's holding in *Heart of Atlanta*.'

'I . . . I didn't read it,' Dana said again, this time a little louder.

She held on to the edge of the table. Her eyes were wide with fear and her mouth gaped open, giving her a vaguely fishy appearance. Hoffman stared back at her, his face cold and foreboding. I closed my eyes for a moment, took a deep breath, and then stood up.

'In *Heart of Atlanta*, a hotel owner sought to have the Civil Rights Act of 1964 held unconstitutional,' I said loudly. 'The Court rejected this claim, and—'

'Ms Bennett, get out of my class,' Hoffman snapped.

Hoffman glared at me, and as I looked into his cold, pale eyes, I wavered. What the hell was I doing? Was I crazy? Had I finally snapped under the pressure? I wondered.

'The Court held that Congress had the power to pass the act, because the motel's business had an effect on interstate commerce,' Nick suddenly said. He stood up too, so that we were shoulder to shoulder.

'Mr Crosby. How nice of you to join us,' Hoffman said. 'You've also bought yourself a ticket out of my class.'

But Nick's help bolstered my courage.

'The Court struggled with the fact that their holding was a pretext but concluded that the ends justified the means,' I said, projecting up from my diaphragm so that my voice rang across the room.

'I want the two of you out of here now. Get out of my fucking class!' Hoffman shouted. He banged his fist against the lectern, and his notes flew up into the air and scattered on the ground. Wisps of Hoffman's hair floated up over his face, which was turning a violent shade of purple.

The silence that had been holding the class broke in a swell of gasps and murmurs. The noise seemed to snap Hoffman out of his rage, and he visibly struggled to gain control of himself. He smoothed his hair back down with one hand, gripped the edge of the lectern with the other.

'Before your continued presence disrupts us any further,' Hoffman continued, his voice cold and tight.

'Fine,' I said, and I leaned over and grabbed my notepad off the table and shoved it into my knapsack. Dana looked at me fearfully, and I shook my head at her. Walking out of the room right now pretty much guaranteed not being able to return, and there was no reason for Nick and me to drag Dana down with us. 'Just sit back down,' I whispered to her, and she sank into her seat.

The class went silent again as I walked down the aisle and up the staircase, Nick following behind me. The room was thick with scandal, and it seemed to take forever to reach the exit. When we finally got there, I held the door open for Nick and then followed him out into the corridor. The hallway was empty, except for a group of Two-Ls who were sitting in the student lounge, so when the door shut behind us, the loud clatter echoed ominously.

I paused just outside the door, pressing my hands against my cheeks to cool them. What the hell had I just done? I was doomed. *Doomed.* Nick too. What had he been thinking jumping in like that?

Nick hadn't waited for me. He kept walking down the short hall toward the front door of the law school. His shoulders were squared, and his step was determined. He seemed intent on getting away.

'Nick!' I called out. When he didn't turn back or even break his stride, I hurried after him and grabbed his arm.

'Hey,' I said. 'You didn't have to do that.'

Nick just looked at me as though I were a stranger. As

though we hadn't spent nearly every day together for seven months. As though he hadn't just seen me naked less than a week ago.

'Neither did you,' he said.

'What do you think Hoffman's going to do?' I asked.

He shrugged. 'I don't know. But I can't think about it now. I have too much work to do.'

'Yeah, me too.' I tried to think of something to say, something that would dispel the strangeness between us. I wanted my friend back.

'I hear congratulations are in order,' Nick said casually.

'What? Oh. Thanks,' I said. I touched my engagement ring self-consciously. 'Look, Nick—'

'I've really got to get going. I'll catch you later,' Nick said. He turned and strode off down the hall, rounding the corner out of sight.

The reprisals came almost immediately. When I got to school the next morning, there was an official-looking missive on school letterhead waiting for me in my mail folder. It notified me politely, but tersely, that I was to report to Teresa Sullivan. Immediately.

I remembered the last time I'd been summoned to a dean's office.

It had been back in my undergrad days at Cornell. A phone call from the Dean for Student Affairs had woken me up so early on a Saturday morning, I'd incorporated the ring of the telephone into my dream at first before it shook me awake. When I finally did answer, I fumbled with the receiver before finally hitting the on button.

'Hello . . . is this Kate Bennett?'

I hadn't recognized the voice. It was male and sounded older, official.

'Who is this?' I'd asked groggily. I was hungover from the Amaretto sours the night before. My head pounded and my throat felt dry and fuzzy.

'My name is David Bell. I'm the Dean for Student Affairs . . . I need to see you immediately,' he'd said. My mouth went dry with fear when he added, 'It's . . . it's very important.'

I'd never crossed campus so early before. The sun was just starting to rise as I hurried across a freshly salted walk-way from my sophomore dorm to the administration office building. The winter light was weak and the freshly fallen snow was as yet unmarred by footprints, giving the campus a beautifully eerie look. The wind had been bitterly cold, and it stung at my eyes – the only part of me not bundled up in a coat or scarf or hat – causing them to water so much I could hardly see where I was going.

I'd known even before Dean Bell had emerged from his office to greet me in the empty reception area that something was terribly wrong.

'Kate,' he'd said, taking my hand in his and looking down at me through thick glasses. He was mostly bald, except for some white fringe hanging about his ears, and there was a large liver spot covering his prominent forehead, like Mikhail Gorbachev's. Despite the early hour, the dean was dressed in a natty three-piece gray flannel suit and a blue-and-red-striped Brooks Brothers tie. A power tie, I'd noticed, like the kind the President wears.

'Your parents were in a car accident. They . . . they didn't make it. I'm so sorry,' the dean had said.

Those words cracked open my world, and everything familiar slipped away.

Whatever happens this morning with Dean Sullivan, at least it can't be as bad as that meeting was, I reminded myself. When I looked back down at the letter her office had sent me, I saw that my hands were shaking, gently rattling the linen paper.

I climbed the stairs to the second floor of the law school and crossed the hall to the administration offices. The same obnoxious receptionist was manning the front desk. She was examining her teeth in a makeup compact when I entered.

'I'm Kate Bennett. Teresa Sullivan asked me to come see her this morning,' I said.

'*Dean* Sullivan will be with you shortly,' the receptionist corrected me. She snapped the compact shut.

Before I even had time to sit in one of the cherry wing chairs, the door to Sullivan's office swung open and Nick walked out, looking incredibly pissed off.

'What happened?' I asked him softly when he passed by on his way out the door, but Nick just shook his head.

'It's total bullshit,' he said. He didn't look me in the eye.

'Kate, come right this way,' Teresa Sullivan said. She was standing in the doorway, her arms crossed in front of her. Today she was wearing a red suit with big black buttons and black patent pumps squared off at the toe. She waited at the door, closing it after I'd entered her office.

'Go ahead and take a seat,' she said.

Once Sullivan had settled back down behind her desk, I said, 'So . . . am I expelled?'

'No. But you are on probation, which means that any further incidents could result in expulsion,' Sullivan said. She sighed, and shook her head. 'Why did you go out of your way to provoke him, Kate? I'm not supposed to tell you this, but both you and Nick are at the top of your class after last semester. You both have an excellent chance of grading onto Law Review. Why screw it up over an egomaniacal professor?'

I didn't know what startled me more – that I was in the running to grade onto Law Review or that Sullivan had actually just called Hoffman an egomaniac.

'So, you know what he's like? Then why haven't you done anything about him?' I asked, the words tumbling out.

'Because if we fired every professor for egotism, we wouldn't have much of a faculty left,' Sullivan said, allowing herself a thin-lipped smile.

I shook my head. 'None of my other professors is as bad as Hoffman,' I insisted. 'He just goads and picks at you, waiting for you to screw up . . .'

'But he didn't overstep the line. You did,' Sullivan said.

'How can you say that? He was ridiculing Dana.'

'I heard what happened. And no, not just from Professor Hoffman,' Sullivan said, interrupting me before I could protest. 'But even if he was being a jerk, he was acting within the boundaries. However, when you stood up and interrupted his questioning of Ms Mallick, *you* violated the Code of Student Conduct.'

'What happens now? Do you put me in law-school jail?' I asked, my mouth twisting.

'Would that I could, if it would keep you out of trouble,' Sullivan said, and this time her lips curved up into a genuine smile. 'Professor Hoffman has decided that the two of you won't be returning to his class. Which means that there are only two options open to you. One, you receive a failing grade for the course and then retake it next year. There's little chance that you'd still make Law Review.'

This grim possibility hadn't occurred to me. I'd have an F on my transcript, which every law firm I ever interviewed with would see.

'What's my other option?' I asked.

'You can take the final at the end of the semester,' Sullivan said. 'You'll have to study on your own, but at least you'll still have a shot at Law Review that way.'

It really wasn't choice at all. And, actually, being able to study on my own was far more appealing than having to sit through any more of Hoffman's sadistic lectures. My friends would surely let me copy their notes, and there were plenty of commercial study guides available that would cover the rest of the material.

Although there was the obvious downside to this option.

'Will Hoffman be the one to administer the exam?' I asked.

Teresa Sullivan looked at me and nodded once. 'I looked into your charges that Hoffman marked your blue book, and there was no conclusive evidence that it happened,' she said.

'Did you see the actual blue book?' I asked.

'Yes, but I didn't see any sort of a marking on it that would obviously flag it as yours.'

'But you saw the dot.'

'It was inconclusive.' Sullivan raised her hands, holding the palms out toward me, fingers spread. 'I'm telling you, Kate, there's nothing I can do. Hoffman has control over his own exam. If you opt to take it, you'll have to follow the same protocol as every other student in his class.'

'Then I guess that's what I have to do,' I said. The meeting seemed to be over, so I stood, swinging my heavy knapsack up onto my shoulder. 'Is Nick taking the test?'

Sullivan nodded. 'He wasn't happy with the options. He thought you should both be able to transfer into another Con Law class.'

This idea had enormous appeal. No Hoffman . . . a fair shot at a decent Con Law grade.

'That sounds good to me,' I said hopefully.

But Sullivan shook her head. 'This wasn't my call. Dean Spitzer made the final decision, after consulting with Professor Hoffman about how he wanted to handle the situation.'

And there it was. Hoffman had engineered the punishment. We'd be stuck taking his exam, and he'd screw me – or perhaps both Nick and me – on the grade. 'Great,' I said without enthusiasm. 'So he's going to get away with it.'

'I know you're not happy about this, Kate. But if you have any further problems with Professor Hoffman, come to me and I'll be fair about how I handle it,' she said.

I nodded.

'It could have been worse,' Sullivan said gently. 'You could have been expelled. Next time please think before you lash out. You don't want to ruin your career before it even begins.'

22

The call came on Saturday at two o'clock. I'd just started the Contracts reading assignment when the shrill ring interrupted me. I was expecting a call from Graham – he'd said he'd phone when he got back from the gym – but when I answered, it was a woman's voice.

'Is Kate Bennett there, please,' she said.

'This is Kate.'

'I'm calling from Tulane University Hospital. Dana Mallick listed you as her emergency contact, so I'm calling to notify you that she was admitted to the hospital this morning.'

'Dana? What's happened? Is she okay? What's going on?'

'I'm not authorized to give information out over the phone. I can tell you that she's in stable condition,' the woman said.

Stable condition? The words should have been reassuring but weren't.

'May I see her?'

'We have visiting hours daily until six p.m.'

Twenty minutes later I was striding through a hospital corridor lit with rows of fluorescent bulbs and smelling of desperation and industrial-strength cleaner. I passed by an orderly who was wheeling an elderly man in a wheelchair. A family, clutching vases of carnations and Mylar balloons with *Get Well Soon!* printed across them in bubbly purple script, was in a whispered conference at the side of the hall. One of the women was crying, and another younger one – her daughter, perhaps – was rubbing the older woman's back soothingly.

Just past the family was the nurses' station. A stout bleached blonde wearing mint-green scrubs and a rail-thin black woman with an elaborate updo and pink scrubs stood behind a chest-high counter.

'Can I help you, hon?' the blonde asked me. She had enormous breasts, and her white-blonde hair was teased up high. The plastic name tag clipped to her scrubs said RENEE.

'I'm here to see Dana Mallick. The information desk downstairs told me she was on this floor, that she'd just been moved here from ICU.'

'Dana Mallick . . . Dana Mallick . . . oh, yes,' the nurse said as she ran a fuchsia nail down the patient list attached to the clipboard. 'That poor baby.'

'Please, what happened? They wouldn't say over the phone,' I said. My voice was high and spiked with fear.

'Are you family?'

'No, a friend – but Dana has me listed as her emergency contact. My name is Kate Bennett,' I said.

'Right, here you are. Well . . . I'm sorry to tell you, hon, but your friend attempted suicide this morning,' Renee said.

Suicide?

It took a moment for the word to sink in, and when it did, I wasn't prepared for how my lungs froze and my legs began to shake. And even as my body started to react, my mind couldn't seem to process Renee's words.

Dana tried to commit *suicide*. . . .

I opened my mouth, wanting to voice the questions that were firing from my thoughts – *Why? How? When?* – but I couldn't seem to draw in a deep-enough breath to speak.

'Are you okay, hon? Here, sit down right here.' Renee bustled around the nurses' station, grabbed my arm, and guided me to an empty wheelchair parked nearby. 'Just take in a deep breath. No, don't try to speak just yet. Just inhale in . . . and out. . . .'

Renee rested a plump hand on my shoulder as she instructed me to breathe. I stared down at the light-gray industrial-tile floor and wondered why everything suddenly seemed too pronounced – the lights were too bright, the tip-tapping of a passing woman's high heels too loud, the smell of ammonia too strong.

'Feeling any better?' Renee asked.

'Yes,' I finally managed. 'What happened to Dana?'

'I don't know all the details. She cut her wrists and then apparently changed her mind, because she called 911 herself. An ambulance brought her in,' Renee said.

'And . . . is she okay? I mean, obviously, she's not *okay*, but is she going to be?'

'She lost a lot of blood before the ambulance got to her,' Renee said. 'The cuts were horizontal, but they were deep – she was very lucky not to have hit a vein. But her condition is stable. She'll be admitted for a psych evaluation; that's hospital protocol.'

I nodded. That made sense. They couldn't exactly bandage her up and send her back home to an apartment full of scissors, razors, and knives.

'Are you a good friend? The reason I ask is that she hasn't put down any contact information for her family. Do you know how to get ahold of them?'

'We go to school together. At Tulane,' I said. 'I don't know her parents, but I can talk to someone in the administration office. They probably have contact information there.'

'Good. She shouldn't have to go through this alone,' Renee said.

A new wave of horror washed over me. Would I have to call her parents? What would I say to them? *You don't know me, but I'm calling to tell you that your daughter tried to kill herself.*

But Nurse Renee saved me from this unpleasant task. 'We can't call her parents directly anyway – it's against the rules – but we can call Tulane, since she's a student there. The universities always get students to sign a permission form allowing them to contact the family in emergency situations,' she said.

'I doubt there's anyone in the administration offices over the weekend.'

'They all have emergency numbers for these types of situations. This isn't the first time this has happened, after all,' Renee said kindly. 'Would you like to see your friend now?'

I nodded, although a cowardly part of me wasn't at all sure that I really did.

Renee helped me to my feet, and I followed her down a hospital corridor lined with medical equipment and empty transport beds. Renee stopped at a door to our left. The room inside held two beds, but only the one closest to the windows was occupied. Lying there, propped up at a forty-five-degree angle, was Dana.

She looked awful. Her skin was waxy and white, as though when she'd cut her wrists, all of the blood had been drained from her face. The purple-rimmed circles under her large brown eyes stood out viciously, like bruises. Her hair was messy and her lips were flaky. Her thin wrists, resting limply to either side of her, were bandaged. She was looking out the window, although as I drew closer, she turned suddenly and smiled wanly at me.

'Let me just check your IV,' Renee said, inspecting an udderlike bag filled with clear liquid hanging on a metal rack next to Dana's bed. A tube snaked from the IV into a needle taped to the back of Dana's hand. Renee pressed the plastic bag with her fuchsia-tipped fingers. 'This looks just fine. I'll check back with you in a bit, hon.'

Renee bustled from the room, leaving Dana and me alone.

'You came,' Dana said.

'Of course I came. Are you okay?' I asked, and then closed my eyes for a minute. What a stupid question. Obviously she wasn't okay.

'I've had better days,' she said wryly, lifting her bandaged wrists up as explanation. Dana seemed remarkably composed. More so than me.

'Do you need anything?' I asked, sitting down on the edge of an orange visitor's chair at the foot of her bed.

'Actually, yeah, I do. Holmes is home alone. Would you mind taking him until . . . well, until whenever?' Dana asked.

My head nodded like a bobble-head doll, I was so eager to be given a task.

'Yes, of course I'll take care of him. Of course,' I said. 'I'll take him home with me.'

Dana smiled, looking almost obscenely serene. 'Thanks,' she said. 'I've been worried about him.'

But not so worried, I thought, that it kept you from doing this.

And then the picture clarified in my mind – Dana sitting on the edge of her utilitarian white ceramic bathtub, the rectangular razor held pincerlike in her right hand, Holmes curled up on the plastic-backed hunter-green bath rug, yawning or maybe investigating an itchy spot on his belly, completely unaware that Dana was about to do something so . . . final. Violent and final.

'Dana, what were you thinking?' I asked.

The smile faded from her pale face, and she looked away, staring out the window with glassy eyes. While I waited for her answer, I stayed as still as I could, as though scratching my arm or bouncing my foot would have imposed on her sanctuary. But Dana did not speak, and we sat there like that for a long time, so long I thought she might have fallen asleep. But when I checked, looking over the pointed little face framed by a mess of brown curls, her eyes were still open and fixed on something in the distance. I glanced around and bitterly wished I'd thought to stop at the store for a get-well bouquet to brighten up the depressingly sanitized room.

'I'm cold,' Dana suddenly said, her voice cracking across the silence.

'I can get you an extra blanket,' I said.

She shook her head slightly. 'No, that won't help. It's the IV. Whatever they're pumping into me is making me cold on the inside,' she said. She began to tremble.

'I'll go get the nurse.'

'No, don't. I . . . Look, I'm not some kind of an unstable wack-job,' Dana said.

I laughed. I didn't mean to – it was probably about the most inappropriate response I could have had – but the gurgle of laughter popped out before I could stop it.

'I'm sorry . . . it's just . . . you're one of the most stable people I've ever met. So if you're a wack-job, we're all in trouble.'

'That's nice of you to say, but obviously false in light of the current circumstances.' Dana sighed. 'I wish I could say something that would make you understand why I did it, but the truth is, I don't know why myself. I really don't want to die. I knew that as soon as the blood started. I used my teeth to tie tourniquets around my arms and then called 911.'

I swallowed, these details adding themselves to the slide show already flickering through my mind.

'Then why?' I asked. 'What made you cut yourself? Was it . . . Addison?'

Dana frowned. 'Addison? What do you mean?'

'I thought . . . I mean, I wasn't sure, but I wondered if . . . the two of you were . . . involved,' I finished lamely.

'Are you kidding? Addison thinks I'm his kid sister,' Dana said wryly. She shrugged, her narrow shoulders rising up pathetically against the bulk of the pillows stacked behind her head. 'It wasn't because of Addison. I just didn't want to do it anymore, any of it. Study, go to class, worry about finals, worry about grades, worry about my future . . . I didn't want to have to worry anymore,' she said.

'Are you really that worried about grades? I thought you did really well last semester.'

'No, I lied. I didn't do well. I got . . .' Dana began, and then stopped, looking pained. She swallowed and continued on in a tiny, ashamed voice. 'Two Bs, a B-minus, and a C-plus. It put me completely out of the running for Law Review.'

'Law Review – so that's why you hurt yourself? Over Law Review? I know everyone makes a big deal about it, but it's not worth *dying* over.'

'You don't understand,' Dana said. Her face pinched up.

'I want to. I'm trying to.'

'I'm the smart one. That's who I've been my whole life. I've always had the best grades and gotten more academic awards than anyone else. I was even a member of Mathletes in high school,' Dana said. 'When people pointed me out they'd say, "There's that smart girl, the one who skipped three grades." '

'And you think that if you don't make Law Review, you're not going to be that person anymore?' I asked.

'Well, I wouldn't be, would I? I'm just average now, somewhere in the middle of the class. I'm nothing special anymore . . . nothing at all,' Dana said, and then she began to cry, the tears leaving silver-red tracks down her hollowed-out cheeks. As I watched her, my heart felt like it was folding in on itself. I wanted to hold Dana's hand but didn't know if it would hurt her wrists if I did, so instead I patted her leg.

'What will my parents think?' she wailed. At first I thought she meant what would they think about her suicide attempt, but then she said, 'It was bad enough when I didn't get into Harvard Law. My mom didn't think it was even worth it for me to go to school at a non-Ivy.'

'Dana, they're just grades. Just stupid grades. As far as I can tell, there's no rhyme or reason why any of us do well on one exam and not another. It's just a giant crapshoot.'

'I hate it here. I *hate* law school,' Dana hissed. 'I wish I'd never come here.'

I nodded. 'But then why didn't you just drop out?'

'Why haven't you?' Dana countered.

'What?'

'You're just as miserable as I am. Maybe even more so,' Dana said.

'No, I'm not. I'm here because I want to be.' And even as I spoke, I recognized the lie.

And Dana was shaking her head, not buying it. 'You used to be different when I first met you. Happier. But then it was like school started to drag you down. You almost never smile anymore. I can't remember the last time I saw you joking around with anybody,' Dana said. The words were coming out in a great tumble, and she paused to suck in a breath. 'I thought that of all people, you'd understand how . . . how . . . *trapped* I feel.'

As these words hit me, I leaned back in the chair, my lower back suddenly aching. I couldn't bring myself to look at Dana, to focus on the slight young woman swathed in bandages and white hospital sheets. Seeing her there made my throat feel like I'd been swallowing glass. Suddenly, I was aware of just how numb I was. And had been, for a long, long time.

'So,' I said softly, finally looking at my young friend. 'What do we do now?'

I stayed at the hospital with Dana until Renee gently kicked me out a half hour after the visiting hours had ended.

'If you stay any later, it'll be my hide,' she said, smiling broadly as she changed Dana's IV. 'And, hon . . . your parents called.' Renee's voice became softer and twangier, and she took Dana's thin hand in her own. 'They're going to be here in the morning.'

I'd thought Dana would react with fear or anger, but instead the tension slipped away from her face. She looked almost peaceful.

'Thanks,' Dana said.

'Is there anything you need before I go?' I asked.

'No. Just don't forget about Holmes,' Dana said.

I patted my pocket, where I'd stashed the apartment key she'd given me.

'I'll go get him right now,' I promised. 'What do you want

me to tell the others tomorrow night at study group? They're going to be worried if you just don't show up.'

'Tell them the truth,' Dana said.

'They don't have to know if you don't want them to.'

Dana shook her head. 'I want you to tell them.' She smiled faintly. 'I'd rather that they heard it from you than through the law-school gossip chain.'

It wasn't until I had picked Holmes up – letting him lift his leg on a forlorn rosebush in the front yard of Dana's apartment building before he hopped up into my Civic – that I remembered I'd turned my cell phone off when I entered the hospital. As I hit the power button on my phone, it immediately began to beep, signaling that there was a voice-mail message waiting for me.

I knew who it was. Graham. We hadn't talked earlier, as we'd planned to. I typed in my password to retrieve the message, and a minute later Graham's voice was in my ear.

'Hey, it's me. Sorry I missed you. I was thinking about flying out there next weekend. While I'm there we could call my parents and your aunt and tell them the news. Give me a call when you get this.'

As I listened to Graham's voice, I felt . . . numb. I thought of Dana, lying in her bed, talking about feeling trapped. It should have been ridiculous – a gifted young woman who had the talent and ability to mold her life into whatever she wanted it to be, talking about feeling cornered. It wasn't like we were trapped in the Gulag, or trying to raft our way through the turbulent waters of the Atlantic in order to escape from a communist dictatorship.

But I knew exactly how she felt.

And I knew what I now had to do.

I reached over to ruffle Holmes's black curly head, and he licked my hand with a slurping pink tongue in response. And then I turned the ignition key on my Civic and drove home.

My parents once went two whole weeks without speaking to each other. Not one word. Not even a *Please pick up a gallon of milk while you're out,* or a *Did I get any mail today?* It was a complete and total wall of silence that neither breached for fifteen days. They'd had their share of fights over the years, but never as bad as that one.

I don't even know what the catalyst for the argument was – even in the white heat of their fury, neither one told me – but the conflict bubbled out into every other area of our family's life. My mother's eyes flashed when my dad was late coming home for dinner, while the tuna-noodle casserole (my father's least favorite meal) dried out in the oven. My father cursed under his breath when he discovered that my mother had turned his favorite golf shirt into a dusting rag.

Evenings were the worst. We'd sit around the dinner table, and they'd each talk to me – their voices artificially bright – asking me what I'd done in school that day or how cross-country track practice had gone, or if I'd yet narrowed down the list of colleges I wanted to visit that spring. I played my part, chattering to fill the silence until I'd scraped the last bits of spaghetti and tomato sauce off my plate and could escape upstairs to my homework, leaving my parents behind to carefully avoid each other.

And then one afternoon I got home early from track practice. Our coach had let us off with only a short run so that we'd be rested for the meet the next day. I ran into the house, chilled as the frigid autumn evening air evaporated the sweat from my skin, and was just about to head into the kitchen when something made me stop. Maybe it was the sudden realization that I'd forgotten to kick off my running shoes by the front door and had tracked mud in across the polished maple floors. Maybe it was to listen for my mother, to see if she was upstairs or down. But whatever it was, I didn't go bursting into the kitchen as I normally would to pour a glass of juice or crack open the oven door to see what was sizzling inside. Instead, I stopped just short of the kitchen door and found myself looking in at my parents.

They were standing in the middle of the kitchen. My mom's hands were entwined around my dad's neck, her ash-blonde head resting against his shoulder. His arms were wrapped around her waist. And then I realized that they weren't just hugging, they were dancing, moving slowly in a well-worn circle. Louis Armstrong was on the radio, crooning 'What a Wonderful World,' a song that has forever since reminded me of my parents. As they rotated around, I saw the silvery tracks of tears on my mother's cheeks.

And I stood back, unseen, and watched them dance.

The more I talked, the quieter Graham became.

'I'm sorry,' I said for the umpteenth time. And I was: sorry for hurting him, sorry for backing out of our engagement, sorry for breaking up with him over the phone. I was sorry for all of it.

'You're sorry,' he repeated, his voice flat.

He was angry. I could tell by his voice, which had taken on a cold, hard tone. Graham wasn't a screamer. When he was mad, it was as though his entire personality was dipped in ice. His tone would grow haughty, he'd cross his arms, and he'd speak in short, biting phrases that made me cringe. I'd always thought it would be easier if he had been a yeller, if it would burn up some of the anger. That would be preferable to the coldness, which could last for days, weeks even.

In this case, it would probably be quite a bit longer than that.

'Yes, I am,' I said. 'I know this sounds trite, but I never meant to hurt you.'

Neither one of us spoke for a minute. And then Graham asked the question I'd been dreading.

'Is there someone else?' he asked.

I hesitated. I know that there are some who stand firmly in the Whole Truth camp and think that a person – particularly a jilted fiancé – has a right to know the complete story. That it would be better for him to know that it wasn't him, or even us, but some unknown third party who was at least partially responsible for the rift.

But it has always seemed to me that these sort of confessions are a cheap way to make yourself feel better. *Yes, maybe I cheated, but at least I was truthful in the end*, you tell yourself, wrapping your conscience in the shabby comfort.

And I knew Graham well enough to know that hearing I'd had a one-night stand would not make him feel better. In fact, I was pretty sure it would make him feel quite a bit worse. So the least I could do was spare his feelings on the matter.

'No, there's no one else,' I said gently. 'It's just . . . it's just me.'

'You don't love me,' Graham said.

God, this wasn't getting any easier.

'I do. Of course I do. But . . . just not enough.'

I winced, knowing that the words were going to cut into his already bruised ego. But this was one area where lying wouldn't make the reality go over any easier.

There was a long pause, and for a horrible moment I thought Graham might have started to cry. But when he spoke again, his voice was clear and colder than ever.

'I think you'll make a great lawyer, Kate. You have a knack for stabbing people in the back.'

I sucked in some breath. He had every right to be angry,

of course. But this was no way to leave things.

'Graham, I don't want –' I began, but he cut me off.

'Spare me. I have no interest in what you want. FedEx the ring back as soon as you can,' he said. And then he hung up.

He hung up on me.

A four-year relationship ended by a hang-up.

And yet I wasn't angry. Instead, I had the same mix of feelings I'd had all those months ago when he moved to Arizona. Yes, there was sadness. Sadness and grief. But there was also the warm, soothing pulse of relief.

I padded back to put the phone on its base and noticed for the first time that I had messages on my answering machine. The first two were from Graham – prebreakup, obviously – and the third was from Jen.

'Kate, you have to come out tonight. There's a Bar Review at the Maple Leaf. We're going to all meet up at Nick's and head over together.'

Were they all downstairs? I wondered. Actually, I could hear music, the dull thump of the bass coming up through the thin walls and floorboards.

I got into bed and pulled the comforter up over me while I decided what to do. Holmes hopped into bed next to me, stretching his body along the length of my thigh and sighing as he fell into contented puppy sleep. I was so tired, the exhaustion lapping over me, but I knew I wouldn't be able to sleep. I thought of Dana lying in her hospital bed, along with other random memories: the anger in Graham's voice. Hoffman's cold stare. Finals looming closer, like a great, gaping mouth, ready to swallow me whole. Nick's face just before we kissed, when he was so close that I could see the flecks of green in his blue eyes.

Nick.

Suddenly, I just knew: I wanted to see Nick. I wanted to tell him that I'd left Graham. I wanted to tell him that I couldn't stop thinking about him, that thoughts of his face and voice and touch were constantly swirling around inside me.

I took in a deep, shaky breath and tried to ignore the swollen feeling in my throat as I climbed back out of bed, hooked Holmes's leash to his collar, and walked out my front door and down the dark, narrow staircase. It was dark out, although I had no sense of time. It felt late. Nick's house was lit up, and I could hear music playing, but there didn't seem to be that many cars lining the street.

He must not have invited a large group over, I thought, relieved.

There was a couple on the sidewalk, just at the bottom of the front steps, embracing each other. The woman's back was to me, and her arms were wound up around the man's neck. It was too dark to see what exactly they were doing, although I could hear wet smacking sounds and see that his arms were in constant motion, traveling along the curves of her body. She gave a little moan, and they stepped away from me, stumbling into the light from a streetlamp. And that's when I saw that the wavy hair falling down her back was auburn red.

Jen.

I opened my mouth, about to say her name, when it suddenly dawned on me that the man she was kissing wasn't her husband. Sean was a big man, tall and broad. This guy was gangly, his shoulders narrow. And then they shifted again, tilting their heads in the opposite direction, realigning their lips, and I saw that the man had spiky hair and a beaky nose.

Addison.

Of course. How I could have been so thick not to figure it out? Addison's secret girlfriend . . . Jen's odd behavior. They'd arrived and left together at any number of study-group sessions or classes, too many for it to be a coincidence.

Addison and Jen were so caught up in each other, they didn't notice me. I turned, crossing the porch to Nick's front door, pulling Holmes's leash along after me.

Jen and Addison, I thought. Wow.

I raised my fist, about to knock on Nick's front door, but then I paused, listening for voices and laughter, indications that the preparty was still going on. But the music was too loud, drowning out all other sounds. No one would ever be able to hear my knock, so I finally just turned the knob and pushed the door open. The music grew louder, although the door between Nick's office and bedroom was closed, muffling the stereo.

Nick's office contained an L-shaped workstation, a desktop computer, and a bookshelf. The only light shone from a green-glass-shaded banker's lamp sitting on the desk. The room was deserted, I assumed, because Nick was so freakishly neat, he probably didn't want anyone to mess up the carefully organized sticky notes he'd written to himself and arranged along the top of his desk. *Outline Con Law chapters eight through twelve*, one read. *Career Center orientation on April 15*, said another.

I crossed the room, figuring that I'd find the others in the living room at the far end of the apartment, where the *boom-boom-boom* of the bass from Madonna's 'Like a Virgin' was blasting from.

Nick hates Madonna, I thought.

I expected that Nick's bedroom – which I had to pass through on my way to the back of the house – would also be dark and closed off, that Nick would keep everyone herded into the living room and kitchen.

I was wrong.

Instead, when I grasped the glass knob and pushed the door open, causing a sliver of light to fall across the otherwise-dark room, I saw that there were two people in the queen-size bed.

I could see the square pale outline of a man.

Female legs were entwined over male ones.

Hips were thrusting forward.

There was the huffing of labored breathing and a breathy female groan that sounded rehearsed, too much like Meg Ryan's fake-orgasm scene in *When Harry Met Sally*.

I still didn't hear any voices, just the stereo blaring in the living room. I knew I should leave, but I couldn't seem to make my feet retreat or take my eyes off the bed. My interest wasn't sexual; I was not fulfilling a secret voyeuristic fantasy. It was more like the sensation of watching a slasher film, when even though you're squirming with dread, knowing the clueless blonde is about to get jumped by a knife-wielding maniac and you really, really don't want to see her get gored, you can't stop watching until her mutilated body comes swinging down from the attic to scare the crap out of her friends.

As I watched, my hand still resting on the clear-glass doorknob, the couple rolled over in the bed, so that she was now on top, sitting astride him. She leaned back, her arms down at her sides, her fingers intertwined with his, and as she did, her small breasts jutted forward and her glossy dark hair grazed the top of her narrow back. He leaned up toward her, and I heard the wet smacking sound of lips on skin.

'Nick,' she said, the word a throaty, guttural sigh. 'I'm going to come.'

Nick.

I stepped back just as the Madonna song came to an abrupt end, and in the brief moment of silence before the next CD track queued up, the thin floorboards squeaked under my feet. Holmes whimpered and reared up, dancing on his hind legs, begging to be picked up. It was only then that they noticed the light cutting across the room, only then that they turned to look at the doorway where I stood watching them, unable to speak and yet not turning away. I gaped at them, the skin on my cheeks tight and hot.

Nick looked at me with an expression of shock and bewilderment. And the woman . . . She'd gone quite still, no longer rocking her hips over his, announcements of her impending orgasm forgotten. The crescent of light shining in from the office was casting a greenish glow on her face.

Lexi.

24

It was Lexi who came upstairs to find me. I knew one of them would, of course, so when she rapped on the back door, I was curled up on the sofa in my darkened living room, waiting for her. Holmes was ensconced in my lap, and I took solace in the comfortable heat radiating from his small body while I plotted what glittering barb I'd toss into the air, waiting for its hooked ends to draw blood.

But when Lexi came in – I opened the door for her and wordlessly returned to my seat – she wasn't apologetic. She followed me into the living room and stood in front of me, her eyes dark and angry, her entire being bristling with righteous indignation, as though I were the one at fault.

'What the hell was that about?' Lexi asked.

'I was looking for Nick,' I said. 'Although now I wish I hadn't found him.'

'You should have knocked.'

This rebuke caused my rage to shift into an even higher stratosphere, one that drained the blood from my cheeks and made everything around me come sharply into focus.

'Obviously I didn't think I'd be walking in on my friend fucking the guy she knew I was not only interested in but had slept with barely two weeks ago.' I shook my head with disgust. 'All that we need now is to find out that we're both pregnant, and we can all get on *The Jerry Springer Show*.'

'What right do you have to be angry at me? Or at Nick?'

Lexi asked coolly, crossing her arms in front of her and staring at me. Her hair fell in perfectly straight, glossy sheets around her face.

'You and Nick weren't in a relationship. And how was I supposed to know that you had feelings for him?' Lexi continued.

'Wasn't that obvious? You knew that he and I had just slept together!'

'You're *engaged*. To someone *else*. Do you think that you get to call dibs on Nick forever? Or do you just expect him to sit around on the sidelines for a year, like the first runner-up in the Miss America pageant, waiting to fill in if Graham has to drop out?'

Ha fucking ha, I thought.

'As a matter of fact, Graham and I broke up. That was after I got back from the Tulane University Hospital, where Dana is currently a patient. She tried to commit suicide, incidentally. Slashed her wrists with a razor,' I said.

I bit my lip, instantly regretting using Dana's hospitalization to lash out at Lexi. It was a shitty thing to do. For the first time that night, Lexi seemed thrown off balance. Shock flitted across her face, softening her sharp features.

'Dana tried to . . . commit . . . suicide?' Lexi asked. She sat on the edge of my ottoman, staring down at the ground in front of her. I noticed that she wasn't wearing a bra under her black tank top, and the sharp bones of her clavicle were visible. 'What happened?'

'She cut her wrists.'

'And, is she . . . Jesus, do her parents know?'

'She's going to be okay, and, yes, they'll be here in the morning.'

'I would never in a million years have thought she would do something like that. She always seemed so . . . together. So goal-oriented,' Lexi said softly.

'Well, that's part of it. She didn't do as well on her finals as she expected.' I glanced at Lexi, who was still staring down, her hands clasped together. A crushingly heavy weariness settled on me. 'Look, Lexi, I've had a long day. I'd like to be alone.'

'You're mad at me,' Lexi said flatly.

'You think? I mean, God, Lex ... why? Why Nick? Of all of the guys you could hook up with, why him? Was it just because you knew he was interested in me?' I asked.

'That's what you think of me?'

'I think you're the kind of woman who flirts with every man in the room,' I said. 'You have to be at the center of all male attention, all the time.'

'And you're the kind of woman who always has to have a boyfriend. You no sooner dump your fiancé then you're already knocking on Nick's door – no, excuse me, breaking into his apartment,' Lexi said. Her eyes were glittering, and her mouth had thinned into a mean, narrow line.

Her words felt like a slap. Was it true? I'd never really thought of myself that way. Sure, I'd had a string of monogamous relationships, and yes, I liked the safety of that. But it wasn't like I planned it out, any more than I'd planned to stay at my postgrad Cornell job for seven years. It was just the course my life had taken.

'That's *not* what happened – well, okay, maybe that's what *technically* happened, but I didn't go to Nick's because I have to have a boyfriend. ... I went to see him, because ... because ... ' I trailed off.

'Because what?'

'Because I wanted to talk to him,' I said lamely.

'About what?'

'Nothing. Never mind.'

'Let me guess: You were rushing in to declare your undying love for him?' Lexi asked sarcastically.

I swallowed and looked away. Lexi's words swelled within the small room, gaining meaning in the silence. She stared at me.

'That was what you were coming to tell him?' she asked incredulously. 'That you're in love with him? Wait – is that why you and Graham broke up?'

'Just forget it, okay?'

'You're in love with Nick,' Lexi repeated.

I didn't answer. I just looked down at Holmes, who was letting out little grunts of pleasure as I rubbed the edge of his ears between my thumb and index finger.

'What about you?' I finally asked.

'What about me?'

'You and Nick . . .'

'I'm not in love with him, if that's what you're asking,' Lexi said frankly. 'And I didn't come over here tonight planning to sleep with him. But . . . I'd be lying if I told you I hadn't thought about it. Nick's an amazing guy,' Lexi said.

I nodded. 'I know he is,' I said. The words felt thick in my throat.

The morning sun was already cutting into my room, filtered through the fitted muslin drapes on my French windows, when the phone rang. I ignored it for a few rings, but then, worried that it might be Dana calling from the hospital, I grabbed the portable handset from my bedside table. I'd burned a lavender candle the night before while I tried to relax into sleep, and the melted wax had dripped down the sides and pooled in the crevices of the wicker tabletop.

'Hello,' I said into the phone.

'It's me,' Jen said. 'Can I come over?'

'This really isn't a good time,' I started to say, but when Jen cut me off, I could hear tears breaking in her voice.

'Please,' she said. 'I need to talk.'

Jen knocked on my door a half-hour later. I'd had just enough time to let Holmes out and get halfway through my first cup of coffee when she arrived.

'Thanks for letting me come over. Would it be okay . . . would you mind if I slept on your couch tonight? Please?' Jen said. She was carrying a canvas tote bag with pink handles and her name embroidered in matching pink thread. It was stuffed with clothes and a cosmetics bag, and a black bra was spilling out of one side. It looked like she'd packed enough to stay for a week or more. I found this disconcerting.

'Of course. What's going on? Have you been crying?' I asked.

Jen's eyes were red, as was the tip of her snub nose, but the rest of her face was pale. She walked into the apartment and dropped her bag on my desk.

'Why is Dana's dog here?'

'Long story,' I said.

'Do I smell coffee?' she asked.

'It's in the kitchen. Help yourself,' I said.

I followed Jen back to the kitchen and waited while she poured her coffee and then added milk and sweetener to the mug. She sat down heavily in one of my ladder-back kitchen chairs and sighed deeply.

'Sean and I had a fight,' she finally said.

'About Addison?'

Jen's head swiveled toward me. 'You know about that? How?' she whispered. Her round eyes were wide with shock.

'I walked right past you two on the sidewalk,' I said. 'I probably should have figured it out a while ago. How long has it been going on?'

'Since October,' Jen said.

'*October?* That long? But . . . how? I mean, how did it start?'

'I gave him a ride home from study group one night, and we ended up sitting in my car for a long time, talking, and then kissing. It just sort of happened.' Her face was sheepish; she didn't look me in the eye.

'And Sean found out,' I said, jumping to the logical conclusion.

'God, no. He has no idea. That wasn't what we fought about.'

'So, what happened?'

'Toast.'

'What?'

'Toast. We fought about toast.'

'You mean, like, "Leggo my Eggo"?' I asked.

'Not even. I was making toast for breakfast this morning, and I had a wee bit of a hangover and so I wasn't paying attention, and the toast burned and set off the smoke alarm,' Jen explained.

'Uh-huh. And how exactly did this lead to your moving out?'

'I didn't move out. I just want to get away from him for a day or two. Anyway, the alarm woke Sean up, and he was furious because he worked last night and didn't get to sleep until four in the morning. So he came charging downstairs like a bull and starting yelling at me for waking him up. Like I burned the fucking toast on purpose,' she said, rolling her eyes.

'And . . .?'

'And we exchanged some harsh words – I told him once and for all that there was no fucking way I was getting pregnant while I'm still in school, and he told me that was just as well, because someone who can't even toast a piece of bread isn't responsible enough to be anyone's mother. So I threw the toast at him, and it hit him right in the face.' Jen sounded gleeful at this. 'And that felt so good, I threw the toaster at him. But I missed that time. It just hit the ground and broke apart, the cheap piece of shit. Sean's sister gave it to us as a wedding present – I bet she picked it up at Wal-Mart for twelve bucks.'

'You threw a toaster at him?'

'It didn't hit him,' Jen reminded me. 'Anyway, we both said some ugly things, and then I said, "I'm leaving," and he said, "Good," and that's when I called you. This is really good coffee, by the way.'

'Um, thanks,' I said. 'What happens now?'

'Nothing. I'll hang out here, and we'll both cool off, and by tomorrow everything should be fine. Do you have anything to eat? Bagels or doughnuts or anything like that? Fighting always makes me crave carbs.'

'No. The cupboards are bare,' I said.

'Then let's go out. My treat,' Jen said.

We waited in line for a half-hour outside the Camilla Grill until two vinyl-covered stools at the counter opened up. A harried waitress handed us sticky laminated menus.

'I'm starving,' Jen said. 'I'm going to have pancakes and eggs and a pile of greasy bacon. You?'

My stomach felt shrunken and tight, and I realized that I hadn't eaten in twenty-four hours. Even so, the idea of food wasn't at all appealing to me. 'French toast, I guess,' I said, and handed the waitress the menu.

I hadn't yet told Jen about Dana, or Graham, or Lexi and Nick. It was hard to believe that so much had happened in such a short period of time. Some days just tumble into the next, completely unremarkable. You brush your teeth, talk on the phone, buy a carton of milk at the grocery store. And then a day comes along where life seems intent on wringing every last second out of it.

'Where were you last night? Did you end up going to the Bar Review?'

'No. I had . . . stuff to do.'

'Like what?' Jen dumped some sugar into her coffee and swirled it around with a spoon.

I took a deep breath. I didn't want to get into all of it, but she was going to find out anyway.

'Graham and I broke up.'

'You broke *up*?' Jen yelped, loudly enough that people sitting around us looked over.

'And now the whole restaurant knows.'

'What happened?'

'Well, it's sort of a long story,' I said. And then I told her everything – going to the hospital, seeing Dana lying there, looking so small and vulnerable, realizing that I'd agreed to marry Graham for all the wrong reasons, going to see Nick and finding him in bed with Lexi. Our food arrived while I was running down the day's events, but neither of us touched our plates. Jen sat staring at me, absentmindedly twisting a lock of burnished red hair around her finger.

'I can't take it all in . . . Is Dana going to be okay?' Jen asked when I'd finished.

'I think so. I'm going to go over to the hospital to see her after breakfast.'

'Can I come?'

'Sure,' I said. 'Her parents will probably be in sometime today.'

'Well, that's good, I guess. They must be devastated. Do you think she's coming back to school?' Jen asked.

'I hope not. Not if it makes her so miserable,' I said.

'And you and Graham . . .,' Jen said.

'We're through.'

Jen was quiet for a few minutes. 'And what about you and Nick?'

I hesitated but then shook my head. 'Also through.'

'Are you sure about that?'

'I saw him in bed with someone else. And even if I don't have the right to be angry about that, I am. I don't think I can get past it,' I said.

'And Nick and Lexi?'

'God, this is starting to sound incestuous,' I muttered. 'I don't know what's going on with them. Lexi says they're not together, but who knows, really.'

'I had no idea they hooked up last night.' Jen was incredulous.

'What happened? I thought Nick was having people over last night. That's why I just walked in. I didn't expect . . . you know,' I said.

'He invited a few people over, but everyone else – everyone but Add, Lexi, and me – left when the Bar Review started. Lexi and Nick were flirting, but when Addison and I took off, Lexi said she was going to leave right after us. I had no idea they were going to sleep together,' Jen said. 'And you saw them? Actually in the act? Naked?'

'Yeah. They were certainly . . . naked. And I really wish I hadn't seen it,' I said.

'I bet,' Jen said.

We were quiet for a few minutes. Jen cut a piece of her pancake off and popped it into her mouth.

'So. You and Addison, huh?' I said.

'That was smooth,' Jen said.

'I'm too tired to be subtle.'

'Addison and I are . . . look, I know it's not going anywhere. We both know that. It's mostly been a physical thing. I was lonely,' Jen said. She picked up a piece of rubbery-looking bacon off her plate and nibbled at it. My French toast, still untouched, was starting to bloat with maple syrup. I pushed the plate away.

'Are you going to keep seeing him?'

'I don't think so. My marriage isn't going so hot right now as it is . . . and I don't want to lose my husband,' Jen said, and I could see that her eyes were wet.

'Are you going to tell Sean about Addison?'

'No. What good would that do? It would just hurt him.' Jen sighed, and pushed away her plate too. 'I've really fucked everything up, haven't I?'

I nodded. 'Yeah, you really have,' I said. I reached out and squeezed her hand. 'But it happens to the best of us.'

'Are you going to finish your French toast?'

'No, I'm not hungry.'

'Me neither. Let's go see Dana.'

Dana's parents were at the hospital when Jen and I got there. They'd flown in from Ohio the night before and looked as though they hadn't slept. Their eyes were ringed with dark circles, and their faces were creased with fear. Dana had her mother's wild curls and her father's round brown eyes, and when she introduced us, they seemed to know who we were.

'You're in Dana's study group,' Alice Mallick said.

Jen and I nodded, and I handed Dana a bouquet of sunflowers and daffodils wrapped in cellophane that we'd purchased in the hospital gift shop.

'Thanks,' Dana said. The smile on her face was strained. 'They're beautiful. How's Holmes?'

'He's fine. He misses you,' I said.

'I miss him too.'

Jen and I didn't stay long. We didn't want to intrude on the family, and the conversation kept taking awkward turns, like when Mr Mallick asked Jen if she enjoyed law school more than Dana did, and when Mrs Mallick asked what my father did for a living. And the entire time we were there, Mrs Mallick was perched on her daughter's bedside, holding Dana's small hand in her own and stroking it with her thumb.

'Mom, please stop,' Dana finally said in a small, pleading voice, and Mrs Mallick stood up abruptly, walked over to the window, and burst into ragged, hiccuping tears. Mr Mallick stood to the side, not moving to comfort either daughter or wife, just rocking back and forth on his sensible brown lace-ups and staring at a sign bolted to the wall that laid out the emergency exit route, should the hospital be evacuated.

'We should go,' Jen whispered in my ear, and I nodded.

'Dana, we'll come by tomorrow,' I said, and I leaned forward to squeeze her ankle, while Jen planted a kiss on Dana's forehead.

'You girls should call before you make the trip,' Mrs Mallick said, still staring out the window. She sounded stuffy. 'We're hoping that we'll be able to take her home in the morning.'

'I can't, Mom. They have a rule that when someone attempts suicide, they admit them for a mandatory psych evaluation,' Dana said matter-of-factly. At the word 'suicide,' Mrs Mallick recoiled, as though Dana had slapped her. 'They've already told me. I have to stay for at least seventy-two hours.'

'Well, we'll see about that,' Mrs Mallick said briskly, turning back around. She must have wiped her eyes when her back was still to us, because her cheeks were dry, if a little red. 'Arthur, you go talk to them. Tell them we don't consent to a psychiatric evaluation.'

'I don't think that's a good idea,' Mr Mallick said, his eyes not wavering from the emergency-exit-route sign.

'Arthur!' Mrs Mallick said sharply.

'Are you just going to pretend that it didn't happen? Again?' Mr Mallick said.

Again?

'We should go.' Jen grabbed my hand.

'Bye, Dana,' I said. 'Good-bye, Mr and Mrs Mallick.'

'Bye, everyone,' Jen said.

Dana gave a small wave as Jen led me from the room. Mrs Mallick didn't say anything as we left – she just stood at the window, her lips pressed together – although Mr Mallick said, in a kindly, vague tone, 'Nice to meet you, girls.'

'No wonder Dana's so messed up,' Jen muttered in my ear, as soon as we were safely outside in the too-cold hallway. I looked for Renee when we walked past the nurses' station, but she wasn't there today. Instead, a nurse with a square build and short burgundy-red hair was manning the desk. She had the phone tucked under her chin while she rifled through a pile of folders, and didn't notice us when we passed by.

'Did you hear what Dana's dad said – whether her mom would admit that it happened *again?*' Jen pushed her heavy auburn hair back behind her ears as she shook her head. 'I wonder what the story is there.'

'Poor Dana,' I said. 'I just wish there was something I could do.'

'I know, I feel . . .,' Jen began, but then stopped, searching for the words.

'Helpless,' I offered.

'Yeah. That's exactly it. I feel helpless.'

*

It was a beautiful night. It was cool and clear, and the spring humidity hadn't yet descended. Jen had gone to meet the others at study group, but I – for obvious reasons – didn't go with her. Instead, I sat outside on my little porch, my Property book propped up on my lap and illuminated with a portable book light. Holmes had tried to hop up into the chair with me, but there wasn't enough room for him, so he finally gave up and sank down by my feet with a grudging sigh.

I was having a hard time concentrating. I'd be in the middle of a case when an image of Dana's delicate wrists swathed with bandages would intrude on my thoughts, or I'd see Lexi sitting astride Nick, her head thrown back.

I was just about to give up on Property when I heard a noise at the back door, which I'd left open for Jen.

'I'm out here on the balcony,' I called out.

Footsteps echoed hollowly against the wood floor, and then the French door behind me swung open. But when I looked up, expecting to see Jen's freckled face and long auburn hair backlit by the lights in my bedroom, I found myself staring up at Nick.

'I thought you were Jen,' I said stupidly.

'I'm not,' Nick said. He smiled uncomfortably. 'Although I just saw her at the Rue. She wanted me to tell you that she's spending the night at Addison's.'

'Why am I not surprised?' I said. I closed my Property book. 'So I take it you know about those two.'

'I just found out a few days ago. Add asked me not to say anything,' Nick said. 'And, for the record, I told him I thought he was making a huge mistake.'

'I can see he took your advice to heart,' I said.

Nick sat down in the other plastic deck chair, his long legs sprawled out before him.

'He says he's in love with her,' Nick said.

'As though that makes it okay.'

Nick shrugged. 'I don't think he's thinking about it like that.'

'You mean he's not thinking with his brain,' I said. 'What a surprise.'

There was a weighty silence.

'Something tells me we're not talking about Addison and Jen anymore,' Nick finally said.

I looked at the boarded-up Cuban restaurant across the street. Teenagers had spray-painted their names in bubble letters across the front. A group of tourists walked by, the expensive cameras clutched in their hands and fanny packs strapped around their ample waists making them appealing targets for any would-be thieves.

'The tourists seem to think that the entire city of New Orleans is like an adult Disney World. They come here and lose all common sense,' I commented. The tourists across the street were now standing in a knot, consulting a guidebook. I wondered what clued them in to the fact that they'd wandered off the route for their self-guided tour – the gang graffiti or the neighborhood crack house?

'Lexi told me why you came over last night,' Nick said abruptly.

Oh. Shit.

'What did she say?' I asked sharply.

'She told me . . . well . . . she said that you told her that you're . . . sort of in love with me.'

My entire body went still. My hands lay heavily in my lap, my shoulders stiffened, and my lungs seemed to lose the ability to squeeze out any air. Only my cheeks, which stretched and tingled with a mortified heat, seemed to retain any feeling. I watched the tourists flag down a cab and clamber into the backseat.

'Kate . . .' Nick said.

'Why did she tell you that?' I'd assumed Lexi had gone back down to Nick's apartment after talking to me the night before. Now I imagined them lying wrapped around each other in bed, giggling over how I'd tried to throw myself at Nick in desperation, before commencing with their second screw of the evening.

'Because she thought I should know.'

'Why, so you and Lexi could laugh at me?' I asked, my voice laced with acid.

'What? What are you talking about? Why would we laugh at you?'

'Because the two of you are together now,' I said simply.

'No, we're not.'

'But I thought –' I started, and then stopped. I didn't know what I thought.

'Last night was just a one-time thing. For both of us,' Nick said. 'Honestly? I think Lexi was just trying to make herself feel better after everything that happened with Jacob. That whole thing with him really hurt her ego.'

'And you're how she made herself feel better?'

'Something like that.'

'And why did you do it? Is Lexi really as irresistible as she seems to think she is?' I asked. I couldn't resist the cheap shot. 'I thought you'd stopped sleeping around.'

Nick just looked at me for a long moment. 'I did. I had.'

'So, what, you just fell off the no-sex wagon?'

'I slept with Lexi, because . . . well, because I wanted to hurt you,' Nick said simply.

'Oh. Well, congratulations. It worked,' I said.

'I'm sorry,' Nick said.

I sighed deeply, and the anger drained out of me. 'Don't be. You don't owe me an apology. And you had no reason to know that I'd be bursting in on you when you were . . . well, you know. Otherwise engaged.'

'But my motivations were shitty.'

'For that, you should apologize to Lexi.'

We sat quietly for a few minutes, watching the traffic creep by below.

'So,' Nick finally said.

'So,' I agreed.

'Rumor has it you're in love with me,' he said. His smile was tentative and full of hope.

'Nick,' I said softly, and he leaned forward and grabbed my hand. He held it between his, looking down at it as if it were a treasure, and then peeled open my fingers and kissed the scar I'd gotten when I was five and fell off my new pink bike with the banana seat and streamers on the handles and a rock had lodged in my hand. As his lips brushed against my skin, I shivered.

Nick stood up abruptly and pulled me up with him, and then he lowered his head down to mine. Our lips touched. In that moment, I forgot about everything that had happened over the past two days. All I was aware of was Nick – his touch, his smell, the solid feel of his back as I slid the palms of my hands down over the soft cotton of his T-shirt.

Nick stepped forward, trying to mold my body against his, but the balcony was so narrow that he'd pushed me right up against the wrought-iron balustrade.

'Wait,' I said.

'Mmm?' Nick asked, as he trailed a line of kisses across the hollow of my throat.

'I don't know if this is going to hold our weight,' I said.

Nick looked over my shoulder to consider the iron railing. 'You're right,' he said, and he turned to go inside, pulling my hand so that I'd follow him through the open French door.

We stepped into my bedroom and landed on the bed, kissing. Nick pulled off my T-shirt and then shrugged off his own, pulling it over his head in one smooth movement before falling back toward me. I pressed against him, reveling in the glow of his skin and the warmth of his body against mine. Nick's hands skimmed over my waist and trailed up to my breasts, touching me through the lacy fabric of my bra.

The next thing I knew, he'd rolled back, pulling me on top of him, so that my legs were straddling his hips. Nick fumbled with the clasp on my bra, before pulling it down and tossing it to the side. He kissed me again, his lips trailing from my mouth down to the curve of my neck.

I was suddenly struck with the familiarity of the scene.

Lexi.

On top of Nick.

Her back arched, so that her shoulder blades pinched together, and her breasts pushed out. And Nick had leaned forward, just like he was doing right now–

'Stop,' I croaked. And when Nick didn't immediately

respond, I braced the heels of my hands against his shoulders and pushed him away.

'Stop,' I repeated, my teeth clenched.

'Jesus. What's wrong?' Nick said. His breathing was uneven and heavy, and his eyes had darkened. I climbed off him, off the bed, and grabbed my discarded T-shirt from the floor.

'You have to go,' I said coldly.

Nick stood up and looked at me. The zipper on his jeans was undone, and his hair was mussed. I couldn't tell from his expression if he was angry or confused.

'What's going on, Kate?' he asked softly.

I shook my head and walked out of the bedroom, across my office to the living room, pulling my T-shirt on as I walked. Holmes followed me, his nails clicking on the floor, and when he saw that I was heading for the couch he gave a little yip of pleasure and jumped up ahead of me, turned three times, and then lay down on the middle cushion with a contented sigh. I sat next to the poodle, drawing my legs underneath me, and held a plaid throw pillow in front of me like a shield.

Nick hung back long enough to locate and put on his T-shirt and pick up the sneakers that he'd kicked off when we fell into bed. He carried his shoes with him into the living room. Now he definitely looked angry. His cheeks were stained red, and his eyes were still and dark.

'So that's it?' he said. He sat down on the ottoman and started to lace up his sneakers. 'You're just going to kick me out, without a word of explanation?'

'Just now, in there . . . when I was on top,' I said, biting out the words before I lost my nerve. 'It reminded me of last night.'

'Last night? You mean . . . with . . .'

'Uh-huh. Lexi. On top of you. You were –' And then I stopped. Did I really have to go through an anatomical description of what I'd seen? Of her hips rocking against him as he pushed into her? Of his head bent over her breast?

I closed my eyes, willing the images away. When I opened them again, Nick was staring at me. And I knew then that he'd been replaying the scene too, remembering rolling Lexi onto him and just now realizing he'd used the exact same play on me.

'How do we get past this?' he asked, his voice hoarse.

'We don't,' I said.

'Kate –' Nick began.

But I shook my head firmly. 'I can't do this . . . I just can't,' I said. 'And I'm not going to change my mind.'

And since there wasn't anything left to say, Nick stood up and walked past me into the kitchen and out the back door. As soon as he was gone, I got up and dead-bolted the lock behind him.

I was supposed to have a brother.

I'd asked my parents for a sibling the way young children do: 'I'm going to tell Santa I want either an Easy-Bake Oven or a baby sister for Christmas.' The preferred gender and species of the requested sibling vacillated, depending on what my dad and I were reading for my bedtime story. When it was *Charlotte's Web*, I wanted a sister just like Fern. When it was *Stuart Little*, I wanted a mouse brother.

By the time I'd reached kindergarten and no brother or sister had arrived under the Christmas tree, I started to go off the idea of being a big sister and instead focused my energy on begging for a kitten. But then my mom started retching and running to the bathroom whenever she smelled roast chicken, and my father walked around looking pleased with himself.

I can't remember how they told me, but by the time my mother's waist thickened and her belly began to swell, I knew. There was a baby in there. Our baby.

Mom spent a lot of time in bed, first driven there by exhaustion and later sequestered by a strict obstetrician. I'd lie down next to her, and while my mom read to me, I'd press my small hand against the tight drum of her stomach and wait for its mysterious occupant to reach up to me, rippling under her skin like a monster.

But then one morning I woke up and knew the house was empty. Or, at least, my parents weren't there, which was really the same thing. I lay in bed, staring up at the horses galloping across my walls (I was in the throes of my horsey phase and had picked out the wallpaper myself), and listened. But I didn't hear my mom's heavy footsteps as she made yet another trip to the bathroom, or my father's whistle as he dressed for work. It all felt different than it had when I went to bed, as though something had happened to shift the very air around us.

I scrambled out of bed and padded downstairs. Gran – my mother's mother – was in the kitchen, standing in front of the stove, staring down into a smoking frying pan. She was a little woman, short and slight with wispy blonde hair, but as I stared at her, she looked even smaller than usual, as though she'd somehow diminished. I must have moved, because she suddenly looked up, and just before she arranged her face in a careful smile, I saw that she'd been crying.

'Gran?' I asked uncertainly. I was wearing my favorite nightgown. It had a high neck and long sleeves, and the soft flannel was covered in tiny blue flowers. It was what I imagined a princess would sleep in.

'Hi, pumpkin,' Gran said. 'I made your favorite ... pancakes.'

She set me up at the table with a stack of lumpy pancakes (cooking had never been Gran's strength), milk, and a sliced banana. I liked the way she fussed over me – making sure I had my favorite glass, the one with the big red flowers on it, sprinkling sugar on my banana slices.

'Where's Mom?' I asked.

Gran hesitated and bought herself time while she sipped a cup of coffee. She always drank coffee from cups with saucers, not out of mugs like my parents did. Whenever I asked her why, she always replied, 'It's a lady's prerogative.' I poked at my pancakes; they were raw in the middle. Finally, Gran said, 'Your parents had to go to the hospital.'

This didn't immediately strike me as bad news. After all, The Hospital was the place where babies were born. This I knew from my friend Kimmy Sawyer, who'd had a baby sister of her own a few months earlier. She'd stayed with her grandmother then too, and when she went to visit her mom and new sister in The Hospital, she was allowed to wear Mary Janes, even though it was February.

'Is it a boy baby or a girl baby?' I asked, hoping then for a little sister, who I could teach to French braid my hair.

'Oh, honey. The baby . . . is gone. He's gone,' Gran said. Her voice sounded weird, like a piece of pancake had gotten lodged in her throat.

'But *where* did he go, Gran?' I asked, my forehead knitting into a confused frown.

Kimmy, who was the resident expert on babies at kindergarten, hadn't said anything about them going anywhere. My mom sometimes teased me that she and my dad found me in a cabbage patch, and I suddenly had an image of a Beatrix Potter-esque vegetable patch full of little babies playing hide-and-seek behind enormous green cabbages. They'd giggle and scamper about on fat little baby feet.

Even at the age of five, I knew this was unlikely.

And Gran never did answer me.

26

'Why exactly are we here?' I asked Armstrong, when I reached him at the front gates of the Audubon Zoo.

It was ten o'clock on Sunday morning, and Armstrong had left a mysterious message on my answering machine instructing me to meet him there. I complied mostly because, after spending the past two weeks feeling miserable and only leaving my apartment to go to class or over to Armstrong's, I needed to get out, to get away from my problems.

'I went on down to the Audubon Zoo, and they all asked for you,' Armstrong now sang. 'Research, darlin'. We're doing research.'

He handed the gate attendant our tickets and escorted me in.

'Research? Research on what?'

'The mating habits of alligators. Who approaches whom? And from what direction?' Armstrong said, his eyes twinkling.

'Of course. Because there were alligators all over Normandy when the Allies landed on D-Day,' I said dryly.

'Everything's always work, work, work with you. You need to learn how to relax. We're here because I like the zoo.' Armstrong tucked my arm under his. 'And because I'm tired of watching you mope around. I thought it was time to air you out.'

I smiled wanly. 'I'm sorry. I know I've been a drag lately.'

'Is that what you call it? You've been making Elvis look positively ecstatic in comparison.'

'Are you comparing me unfavorably to your dog? Because if so, I have to say, you really suck at cheering people up.'

'You can't let men get you down. They're not worth it.'

'You're a man.'

'That's how I know,' Armstrong said, reasonably enough. 'Come on. I know what will make you feel better.'

A few minutes later we were standing in front of a display of two white Bengal tigers. The mighty cats were pacing around their cage, wearing a path in the packed dirt. Back and forth they walked. Back and forth. Again and again and again.

'Aren't they gorgeous,' Armstrong said.

'That's the saddest thing I've ever seen.'

He gave me a sidelong glance. 'What?'

'These majestic creatures are stuck here . . . trapped in a cage . . . pacing and pacing and pacing . . . waiting for death to release them from their captivity,' I said sadly.

A pigtailed girl standing near me turned to her mother. 'Mom, are the tigers sad? That woman says they're just waiting to die. Is that true?'

The girl's mother shot me a dirty look. 'Come away from the crazy woman,' she muttered, taking her daughter's hand and pulling her gently away from me.

'You're frightening children. I think that means you've reached rock bottom,' Armstrong said. 'Which actually may not be such a bad thing. You can only go up from here.'

But I wasn't paying attention to him. I was watching the tigers pacing around, watching their muscles ripple under white fur, and I thought I'd never seen anything so beautiful or so depressing in all of my life. My eyes filled with tears, and before I knew it, the tears were pouring down my cheeks.

'Oh, shit,' Armstrong muttered when he saw me. He pulled a handkerchief out of his pocket and tried to force it into my hand.

'Trapped,' I sobbed. 'They're trapped here with no hope.'

'That's it,' Armstrong said decisively. 'There's only one thing we can do. Jazz brunch, it is. Come on, Kate, let's go.'

'But we just got here. I haven't seen the monkeys yet,' I sniffled.

'The monkeys will wait. This is more important.'

Twenty minutes later we were standing in front of the maître d' at Commander's Palace while Armstrong attempted to sweet-talk his way into getting a table.

'You must have something available. It's just the two of us, and we don't take up all that much room,' Armstrong said, turning on his full-wattage Southern charm.

The maître d' looked at me dubiously. I wasn't dressed for Commander's Palace. Most of the women I'd seen coming in were wearing silk dresses or pale sorbet-colored suits. They wore high heels, and jewelry, and red lipstick.

I was wearing my favorite khakis, faded and soft from use, a gray T-shirt, flip-flops, and no makeup. Worse, my face was red and streaked with tears, and my eyes were puffy. I'd dug around in my purse and found a cherry Chapstick, but that alone wasn't enough to fix the damage.

Still. It wasn't every day that a world-renowned historian – one who frequently appeared on television, no less – showed up, and the maître d' was clearly swayed in Armstrong's favor.

'The last time I was at the White House, the President told me how much he liked Commander's,' Armstrong persisted. 'Told me it was his favorite restaurant in all of N'Awlins. Of course, I told him I was in complete agreement.'

That did it.

'The President?' the maître d' said, suddenly standing taller and straighter. He reached for two menus. 'How kind of him. I believe we do have a table available, Professor. Please follow me.'

'Wonderful,' Armstrong said. He turned and winked at me.

'The President?' I whispered to Armstrong as we followed the maître d' up a narrow flight of stairs. 'Did he really tell you that?'

'I'm sure he would have if the subject had come up,' Armstrong whispered back.

And for the first time in two weeks, I laughed.

Armstrong was right about one thing: It was awfully hard to feel blue during a jazz brunch at Commander's Palace. The maître d' sat us upstairs by the windows, looking out over the courtyard. While we sipped spicy Bloody Marys, a jazz band roamed around, playing 'It Had to Be You' and 'What a Wonderful World.' We dined on turtle soup, eggs Sardou, and bread pudding soufflé.

'I can't eat another bite,' I moaned, still picking at my soufflé. As stuffed as I was, I couldn't force myself to stop eating. It seemed a shame to leave even a morsel of the fabulous soufflé uneaten.

'There's nothing in the world quite as good as bread pudding soufflé at Commander's Palace,' Armstrong proclaimed. 'Tell me this didn't cheer you up.'

I smiled at Armstrong and patted his arm. 'Yes, it did. You're awfully good to me,' I said fondly.

Armstrong blushed – a first that I'd ever seen – and stirred at his Bloody Mary with the plastic straw. 'I know what it is to have your heart broken,' he said.

'My heart isn't broken,' I said, finally laying my fork down in defeat. I saw Armstrong's dubious look. 'It isn't,' I insisted. 'I'm just a little ... sad, I guess. Sad at how everything's turned out.'

'Darlin', you just burst into tears at the zoo. Which, I might remind you, is supposed to be a happy place,' Armstrong said.

Now it was my turn to blush. 'I'm sorry,' I said.

'No reason to apologize. I'm just worried about you.'

'Do you ever wonder if you're on the right path in life?

Wait, why am I asking you of all people that,' I said, rolling my eyes. Armstrong was probably the happiest, most self-confident person I'd ever met. Also the most successful.

'I don't so much now, but everyone wonders about that when they're younger. My parents wanted me to go to medical school and were devastated when I refused.'

'Really? I can't see you as a doctor.'

'Neither could I. The sight of blood gives me the heebie-jeebies,' Armstrong said with a shudder. 'But for a long time I wasn't sure I did the right thing when I chose to study history instead.'

'But in the end you know you made the right decision,' I said.

'Given enough time, yes.'

'So maybe what I need is a time-traveling machine. I can zoom into the future and see how I'm doing. See if I'm happy, if I'm successful,' I said.

'I don't think you ever told me why you decided to go to law school. I'm guessing that it wasn't some sort of deeply ingrained love for the source material,' Armstrong said.

'No. I don't love it,' I admitted. 'But I always thought that a law degree would give me a certain amount of security. There aren't many out-of-work lawyers out there.'

'Did you ever consider that there might be something else you'd enjoy doing more?'

'You mean like being a ballerina? Or an Olympic equestrian? I think those ships have sailed,' I joked.

'How about becoming an historian? You show a lot of aptitude for the research. And God knows you're a hard worker.' Armstrong snorted. 'A slave driver is more like it.'

'I don't have the credentials.'

'So go to school and get them.'

'You mean, after law school?'

'No. I mean now. Instead of law school. Tulane has an excellent graduate-school program.'

The jazz band began playing 'Hello, Dolly.' The lead

singer sounded just like Louis Armstrong. All around us, heads were bobbing and feet were tapping in time with the trumpet and bass.

'I can't do that,' I said, shaking my head once. 'It's too late. I chose to go to law school, and now I have to see it through.'

'Sometimes, Katie-belle, it's braver to admit you've made a mistake and to start over fresh than it is to keep going down the wrong path,' Armstrong said.

Katie-belle. It was my dad's nickname for me, and I hadn't heard it in years. And suddenly I felt like I might burst into tears again. I stared down at the starched white tablecloth and willed the tears away.

Finally, when the threat of weeping had passed, I fixed a smile on my face and turned back to Armstrong. 'Tell me the story again about the time you sat next to the Queen during a state dinner and kept drinking out of her water glass by mistake.'

'Now, that is a good story,' Armstrong said, raising his hand to catch our waiter's attention. 'But I think we're going to need another round of Bloody Marys first.'

I spent all of my time at law school alone. Even when I walked through the halls or sat in the middle of the library reading room, I felt like I'd been encased in glass. I spoke to as few people as possible and openly flouted the dictates of the seating chart by sitting in the back row of the classroom during lectures.

The few times I saw Lexi or Nick, I was polite but distant, and after a few awkward attempts they stopped trying to talk to me. Sometimes I'd sense that Nick was looking at me during a lecture, and when I glanced up, our eyes would meet for a second before his flickered away. This attention didn't bring me any pleasure. I wanted more than anything for Nick to just go away forever, so that any feelings I might still have for him would once and for all dry up and blow away.

The one person I would have liked to talk to was Dana,

but she had withdrawn from school. She'd called me the day she was released from the hospital.

'Dana,' I'd said, when I recognized the thin but steady voice on the other end of the phone line.

'My parents are taking me home with them tomorrow,' she'd said.

'How do you feel about that?'

'Good. I guess. I mean . . . I'm depressed, and that's not going to go away overnight. But I think it's probably good that I get away from here. It hasn't been a healthy place for me,' Dana said.

'Are you dropping out altogether or just taking some time off?' I asked.

There was a weighty pause.

'I won't be coming back,' she finally said, her voice soft but resolute.

'I'll miss you. School won't be the same without you.'

'Would you do me a favor?'

'Sure,' I said.

'Will you keep Holmes for me? My mom is allergic to dogs, so I can't bring him home with me.'

I looked down at the little poodle, who was at that moment curled up in the middle of my bed, snoring softly. My attempts to acquaint Holmes with the makeshift dog bed I'd fashioned out of a spare pillow and blanket hadn't been successful.

'I'd love to have him. Until you're ready to take him back, of course,' I said.

'Thanks,' Dana said. 'Bye, Kate. Good luck.'

'You too, Dana.'

Jen was the one person who seemed impervious to my efforts at self-imposed solitude. And while some days I welcomed the company, other days I'd find her constant prattle about Addison and her attempts to bully me into going to the last Bar Review of the year exhausting.

'I can't think of anything I want to do less,' I said. I'd been in bed reading the Property assignment when she called, and now I burrowed down under the covers, the phone tucked under my ear.

'Oh, come on,' Jen begged. 'No one wants to go out anymore.'

'Why don't you get Lexi to go with you?'

'She won't. She started dating some Two-L, and she's practically living at his place,' Jen complained.

'She and Nick really aren't dating?' The question popped out before I could stop it. Even though both Lexi and Nick had insisted that their night together wasn't the start of a relationship, I still half expected to run into them at school holding hands or sitting close to each other on one of the benches in the outer courtyard.

'No! I thought you knew that. Well, you're never around anymore. Addison was just saying he hasn't seen you in weeks,' Jen said.

I groaned silently. As soon as the subject of Addison was introduced into the conversation, it would spread like a weedy vine, twisting around and taking over everything.

'I should get back to studying,' I said, in a vain attempt to sidestep the inevitable.

'I know, I know. You don't approve,' Jen grumbled.

I said nothing. We'd been over this so often, we'd worn grooves into the subject.

'You think I should break things off with Addison,' Jen continued.

I remained silent.

'You think that if things are so bad with Sean, I should leave him before entering into another relationship,' Jen said. 'Or at least tell Sean that I might be pregnant with another man's child.'

'*What?*'

'Ha! I knew that would get you to talk.'

'You're *pregnant*?'

'No, no chance of that. I'm on the pill. I was just trying to get your attention,' Jen said blithely.

I shook my head, closed my eyes, and counted to ten before I spoke.

'Are you still there?' Jen asked. 'Kate?'

'I have to go,' I said as calmly as I could.

'Okay, okay, fine. I know when I'm not wanted. But before you go, let me ask you one question. And I want you to answer honestly,' Jen said.

'I'm listening,' I said.

'Addison has a summer job clerking at a firm in Los Angeles, and he wants me to come visit him. You know, fly out for a few days and hang out. What do you think?'

'What do you think I think?'

'Ummm . . . you think it's a bad idea?'

'Bingo.'

'But I've never been to California. And don't you think it would be fun? I'd love to see Hollywood,' Jen continued. 'Maybe I'll meet some movie stars.'

'Bye, Jen.'

'You're no fun,' Jen complained.

'I know. But I've come to terms with it,' I said, and clicked the phone off.

Finals seemed less stressful this time around. Maybe it was that they were no longer an unknown quantity. Maybe I was too emotionally drained to get worked up over hypothetical test questions about merchants who'd breached sales contracts or whether the misfiling of a property deed would result in a house being snatched away from the original owner's great-great-great-grandson.

Or maybe I just didn't care anymore.

Hoffman's exam was, yet again, the last one of the semester. I'd hardly seen him since the day he kicked me out of his class, and then only from a distance.

When I arrived in the large, first-floor lecture hall next to the student lounge, the same room where the Con Law class had been held, the flutterings in my stomach surprised me. I hadn't even realized I was nervous about taking the exam. I was certainly prepared. I'd studied the material, copied Jen's notes fastidiously in case Hoffman snuck in questions that only those who'd attended class would know, and I'd resolved not to hand in my completed exam until the end of the three-hour test period, when Hoffman would be so deluged with blue books, he wouldn't have the chance to flag mine.

But even so, as I opened the heavy wooden door and walked into the lecture room, I could feel my whole body tightening with anxiety. My shoulders rose up until they were practically brushing against my silver hoop earrings, and my spine felt like it had been buttoned too tightly under my skin. I looked around for an empty seat in the almost-full room, my hand tucked under the strap of my knapsack. Hoffman was already there, sitting behind a table that had been set up where the podium normally was. His arms were crossed in front of his chest, and his flat, pale eyes were scanning the room. When Hoffman's eyes fell on me, and I saw the faint trace of a smile curving his thin lips, the hairs on the back of my neck stood up.

'Kate!'

I looked down and saw Jen waving to me. She was sitting to the left of the lecture hall, flanked on either side by Addison and Lexi. Nick was sitting next to Addison, and when Jen called out my name, he turned to look at me. Our eyes met briefly, and my heart thudded against my rib cage. I waved back at Jen, but quickly turned away and looked around for somewhere else to sit. There were empty seats in the front right row, and although I didn't relish the idea of taking the exam all the way up there, practically right under Hoffman's nose, it was better than squeezing into the back row between Berk and Simone Parker, whose nickname among the One-Ls was 'Jitter.' She was always tapping a pencil against the desk or running her fingers through her dirty-blonde hair or bouncing her foot. But when I got down to the front right row, I saw that there was folded piece of paper with the word RESERVED printed on it.

Great, I thought. I'll have to take the test sitting next to Jitter.

But just as I was turning to climb back up the stairs, Hoffman's voice rang out, stopping me cold.

'Ms Bennett. Glad you could join us. I've saved a special seat for you right up here in front.' When I turned slowly around, my cheeks burning, I saw that Hoffman looked smug. 'You too, Mr Crosby. I thought it would be fitting for you to sit apart from the rest of the class.'

I glanced over at Nick. He was frowning down at

Hoffman, but then he stood up and gathered his things together.

'Right this way, Ms Bennett,' Hoffman said, and with a silky wave of his hand, he motioned for me to sit at the table marked RESERVED.

Why am I not surprised? I thought. He's just doing this so that he can try to keep my blue book – and Nick's, apparently – separated from the others, to make sure he'll get a chance to flag it.

And it was then that the fury started to roil inside me. My skin tightened and prickled with an angry heat.

Nick reached the front of the room and sat down next to me, leaving an empty chair between us. He glanced over at me, but I just shrugged and started to pull out my test supplies. Yet again, Hoffman hadn't allowed us to bring in scrap paper, and he'd restricted the size of the outline we could have to one page, so all I had in front of me were my pens, earplugs, a bottle of water, and the one sheet of lined yellow paper where I'd outlined the basic concepts of Constitutional Law. This time around, I hadn't bothered – as I knew so many of my classmates had – to type out every last rule and case holding and then shrinking it down to a six-point font. I wasn't going blind over a damned grade.

'Ladies and gentlemen, this is the Constitutional Law final examination.' The room hushed as Hoffman began to outline the instructions for the exam, including his admonishment not to cheat, adding without the least bit of irony, 'I take violations of the Honor Code very seriously.'

Nick and I exchanged an incredulous look at this. I rolled my eyes, and Nick laughed. I smiled back, biting down on my lower lip in an unsuccessful attempt to suppress my amusement. But then Hoffman slapped down a stack of blue books on the table in front of Nick with a loud crack, and the smiles slid off both our faces.

'Take one and pass them along, Mr Crosby,' Hoffman said. 'And from this point on, there will be no talking.'

Nick grabbed a blue book and slid the pile toward me. As he did, he mouthed something that I thought might have been 'Darth Vader,' confirmed a moment later when Nick breathed loudly in an unmistakable imitation of the *Star Wars* villain. A lame joke, yes, but I snorted with laughter and had to turn quickly to hand the stack of blue books behind me to Brian Chesney before Hoffman saw me. Brian's face was the color of plain yogurt after it's been left sitting out on the counter overnight – a sickly shade of green-tinged white – and he was breathing so quickly, he sounded like a panting dog.

I turned back around, just in time to receive a copy of the exam, which Nick was passing over to me.

CONSTITUTIONAL LAW FINAL EXAMINATION, *PROFESSOR RICHARD HOFFMAN.*
THURSDAY, MAY 5
9:00 A.M.-NOON

Instructions

1. This examination contains three questions. They are of equal weight.
2. You are limited to a one-page outline for reference. Consulting any other materials will be considered an Honor Code violation.
3. You should consider yourself honor-bound not to discuss this exam in any way with any of your classmates until after the entire examination period has ended. You should avoid remarks that may seem innocuous, such as assessments of the difficulty of the exam.
4. If you are typing, begin your answer to each question on a new page.
5. If you must write, do so legibly.
6. Your complete set of answers should not exceed

> 3,500 words. That is 14 double-spaced, normal-sized pica typewritten pages or the equivalent. Anyone who substantially exceeds the limit will be penalized.
> 7. Write your student identification number clearly on the cover of your blue book. Do not write your name anywhere on the testing materials.

How in the hell are we supposed to know if we've exceeded 3,500 words? I wondered. And what does he mean, *if you must write*? I glanced around the room. Most of the class had chosen to write, rather than peck away at one of the old-fashioned electric typewriters available in an upstairs room for those students who preferred to type. It wasn't like he was about to let us take the test on laptops, not when we were so limited in the materials we could refer to.

Hoffman is such an asshole, I thought, as I had so many times before. It had become my One-L mantra.

'You may start your exams . . . *now*,' Hoffman barked, and I put the balding professor out of my thoughts as I folded back the instruction page and began to read the first exam question.

I finished the exam only a few seconds before Hoffman called time, dropping my Uni-Ball down on the desk with a plastic clatter. It had been an exhausting three hours, and I shook out my hand, which was now cramping and sore from the nonstop writing. I looked up and saw that Hoffman's pale eyes were resting on me.

'Time,' he said, and his eyes flickered away as he stood up. 'Mr Berkus, if you continue to write, you will receive a failing grade.' Hoffman stood up and reached for an empty brown box sitting on the edge of his table. 'Put your exam inside your blue book. When I walk by your seat, place them both in this box. You are to remain in your seats until all of the exams have been collected.'

Hoffman started off at the first row, but on the other side of the room from where Nick and I were sitting. I glanced over at Nick. He looked exhausted. His skin was pale, and the circles under his eyes were as dark as bruises. In an odd way, it highlighted his eyes, making them look even more vividly blue than usual. Law-exam chic, I thought wryly. How to look good when studying wrings all of the life out of you.

Hoffman walked slowly down the first row, holding the box out in front of him, and each student in turn dropped the exam into it. When he got to our table, he held the box up for Nick, but when it was my turn, Hoffman simply held out his hand, fingers outstretched, waiting for me to hand my blue book directly to him.

I hesitated.

'Is there a problem, Ms Bennett?' Hoffman asked, his tone so icy, I knew that if I said or did anything other than hand him my exam, there would be a battle.

'You said we're supposed to put our blue books in the box. I'm just waiting for you to hold the box out,' I said.

Hoffman didn't move. He continued to stand there, waiting for me to hand my blue book directly to him. I could sense my classmates around me growing restless, stretching their arms out in front of them, wriggling against the hot material of the green task chairs. Everyone was eager to get out of the frigid lecture hall and into the muggy hot spring afternoon, to finally begin the summer break. I wondered if any of them saw what Hoffman was trying to do.

'Ms Bennett, do not try my patience,' Hoffman said quietly, biting out each word, and for some reason – perhaps a masochistic curiosity to see what would happen – I relented and placed my blue book in his hand.

I knew it was a mistake as soon as I saw the look of triumph flash over Hoffman's face. He even allowed himself a smile as he gazed coldly down at me. And then, very deliberately, still holding the blue book up so that I'd see him do it, he folded back a corner, dog-earing it before dropping it in the box. It all happened so quickly and was so stunningly brazen, all I could do was stare up at him.

Did he just? . . . Oh, my God . . . he actually flagged my exam book right in front of everyone . . . He openly violated the Honor Code! Please tell me that someone saw what just happened . . .

It all buzzed through my head in a whirling, spinning mass. And then, as Hoffman started to step away, one thought crystallized: Say something – anything – before he gets away with it.

I opened my mouth, gaping like a fish, as I tried to speak. But before I could form the words, I heard a voice clearly say, 'I saw that.'

Both Hoffman and I turned, and I realized that it was Nick who had spoken. He was standing up, looking right at Professor Hoffman, his eyes dark with anger.

'Excuse me, Mr Crosby?' Hoffman asked.

'I saw you bend back the corner of Kate's blue book,' Nick said loudly, pointing to the box. His voice carried over the lecture hall. I could feel our classmates' attention pique, the weight of their eyes shifting toward us.

'I don't know what you're talking about,' Hoffman said smoothly.

'I think you do. And I can assure you, the administration will be hearing about it,' Nick said levelly.

The two men stared at each other, and then Hoffman smiled silkily and moved on, brandishing the box before him.

'As you wish, Mr Crosby. Although I doubt anyone will be interested in listening to your outlandish accusations,' Hoffman said, turning away.

'I think the search committee for the new dean will be interested,' Nick said.

Hoffman's back stiffened and he hesitated for a moment. Too far, Nick, I thought. But for once, Hoffman didn't have a retort. Instead, he moved on, continuing to collect the exams. I looked at Nick, my eyes wide with worry, but he met my glance and shook his head once, warning me not to talk. *Don't give Hoffman an opportunity to accuse us of breaching the Honor Code*, his face said, as surely as if he'd spoken the words aloud. I nodded and swallowed hard, not sure if I was trying to keep down tears or rage or just shock at Nick's challenge.

It seemed to take Hoffman forever to finish collecting the exams, and the lecture hall remained tensely quiet as he did. But finally the last blue book was in the box, and when Hoffman said, 'You are now free to leave,' our first year of law school came to an end.

28

M ost of my classmates were heading to Mid-City Lanes to drink and bowl, a tradition having been formed at the end of the previous semester. Nick, however, went straight up to Teresa Sullivan's office.

'I have to talk to Sullivan right away, before Hoffman gets to her first,' he'd explained when I tried – and failed – to find the words to thank him, and he'd hurried out of the room, leaving me behind to scoop my exam debris into my backpack.

Jen, trailed by Addison and Lexi, hustled over, keen to get the details on what had just transpired between Nick, Hoffman, and me.

'Hey, tiger. Rough morning?' Addison asked.

I smiled wanly at him.

'What happened?' Jen asked, in a dramatic whisper that was just loud enough for the entire class to hear.

I shook my head. I didn't want to do this in front of everyone. 'Nothing new,' I said shortly.

'Did Hoffman really mark your exam again?' she pestered. I glanced back over my shoulder and saw that Hoffman had already left, perhaps racing Nick to Sullivan's office.

'Right in front of me,' I said, nodding.

'What's going to happen?' Lexi asked.

I shook my head and shrugged. 'For starters, I'm going to go home and take a nap,' I said.

'No way. We're all going out; you have to come with us,' Jen said.

'Yeah, come out with us,' Addison chimed in.

'Thanks, but I can't,' I said, and lifted my knapsack to my shoulder.

'Are you sure? Well . . . I'll call you later,' Jen said.

'Okay,' I said, and I walked past them and slowly ascended the stairs, behind the mob of students also departing. More than a few of them looked back at me before dropping their heads into whispered discussions, the subject of which wasn't hard to figure out.

'Kate, wait up, I'll walk out with you,' Lexi said, and before I could refuse, she'd fallen into step with me.

'How's it going?' she asked, and when I looked at her, my eyebrows raised, she smiled ruefully. 'Stupid question, I guess.'

'Yeah, I've had better days.'

We pushed out of the lecture hall and made our way through the clumps of chattering students clogging the halls as they called out to one another, 'What did you put for number two?' and 'Did you get the procedural due-process angle in question three?'

'They're just winding each other up,' Lexi groused.

'It never ends. When I was coming in this morning, I heard a couple of Two-Ls bragging about how many hours they'd studied yesterday for whatever exam they had today. I'm surprised they didn't just whip out rulers and measure their penises.'

Lexi snorted with laughter. We walked around the corner, passing through another group of chattering students. I saw one of them – Jasmine West, the Sweaty Girl – point at me. She tossed her long, heavy hair over her shoulder and whispered in the ear of her friend and fellow gossipmonger, Angie Russo.

'I seem to have caused a stir,' I remarked.

'Don't mind them. They act like teenagers. Immature

ones, at that,' Lexi said. 'And law school is just a high school do-over for them.'

'I'm starting to think that's human nature. It's like we just get older, not more mature.'

Lexi and I walked out to the back courtyard. Many of the die-hard smokers had beaten us outside and were huddled over to keep their lighters from blowing out as they lit up. I stopped, looking at a tall, very ugly sculpture just to the left outside the door. It was sea-green and looked like a stack of giant Tinkertoys.

'Has that been there this whole time?' I asked. 'I've never noticed it before.'

Lexi laughed. 'Are you serious? How could you have never noticed something this big and this ugly? Especially after all the time we've spent sitting out here.'

'I have no idea how I could have missed it,' I said.

'So . . .,' Lexi said, and then hesitated in a way that made me want to brace for impact. After the exam and my run-in with Hoffman, I was running a bit low on emotional reserves and nowhere near in the mood to have a big scene with Lexi. But instead, she just said, 'Do you want to get something to eat? We could go over to the student union.'

'Now?' I asked. 'But aren't you going to the Rock 'n' Bowl with the others?'

'No, I don't think so. I'm meeting Ian – he's my new boyfriend. I don't feel like sitting in a smoky bar until then,' she said.

'Lunch –' I said, and just then my stomach gave a great rumble and I realized I was ravenous. I'd been existing on little more than sugar and caffeine since finals began. 'Lunch sounds good. But on one condition.'

'What's that?' Now Lexi looked a little nervous, as she pushed a swath of glossy dark hair away from her face.

'That under absolutely no circumstances are we to talk about anything serious. I don't have it in me,' I said.

Lexi laughed. 'It's a deal.'

*

We had a leisurely lunch of greasy pizza and limp salads. True to her word, Lexi steered clear of heavy conversation, including Nick, Hoffman, Dana, and finals. Instead, Lexi told me about her new boyfriend, a Two-L whose name I didn't recognize, although Lexi assured me that I'd know him if I saw him.

'He's gorgeous,' she declared. 'The hottest guy in the school, by far. He's Swedish, and has blond hair and green eyes. Seriously, he could be a model. And he has the sexiest accent.'

'I don't think I've ever seen him,' I said.

'Yeah, you wouldn't be able to miss him,' Lexi said dreamily, while she picked at the label on her bottle of beer. 'And he's so sweet, and so thoughtful. He's like the anti-Jacob.'

'I'm happy for you, Lex,' I said, and I was surprised to realize that I really meant it.

After lunch, she walked me back over to the law school. 'Are you going to be around this summer?' Lexi asked.

'I honestly don't know. I haven't decided yet.'

'Well, I'll be here. I'm interning at the district attorney's office,' she explained. 'So give me a call if you get a chance.'

'I will. Bye, Lex,' I said.

'Bye,' she said, and then she darted forward like a bird and hugged me. I squeezed her back briefly.

And after I watched her walk away, her fashionable leather knapsack slung over her shoulder, I turned into the law school and went to find Assistant Dean Teresa Sullivan.

The reception area for the administrative offices was empty, and the gatekeeper nowhere in sight, so I walked straight through and rapped on Sullivan's door.

'Come in,' she called out. I opened the door and immediately wished I hadn't.

Hoffman was sitting there, in the same visitor's chair I'd

occupied on my earlier visits. Sullivan sat across from him, her large cherry desk between them. She was wearing a jade-green silk suit jacket that brought out the hazel in her eyes. Peeking out from under her desk were a pair of gorgeous alligator brown pumps.

I have to find out where she buys her shoes, I thought.

'Ms Bennett. Extraordinary timing,' Dean Sullivan said.

I thought she might have been joking, but then I saw her expression. Her eyebrows were furrowed down over her eyes, and her lips were tightly pursed. A red stain covered her chest and neck, creeping up to her cheekbones.

'I can come back later,' I offered.

'Please come in and sit down,' Teresa Sullivan said.

I stepped into the office, shutting the door behind me with a final click, and sat in the chair next to Hoffman's. He was so close that, when I glanced over, I could see three moles on his left wrist, nestled under dark arm hair.

'Ms Bennett, one of your classmates has made an allegation that Professor Hoffman breached the Honor Code at the conclusion of your Constitutional Law examination this morning,' she said. 'Specifically that Professor Hoffman marked your blue book by folding a corner down. As you are no doubt aware, all testing at the Law School is strictly anonymous so that a professor's favor or disfavor will never affect a student's grade. If such an allegation was true, this would be a very serious matter.' Sullivan glanced at me, and I nodded, letting her know I understood. She continued.

'I've asked Professor Hoffman to come in this afternoon to discuss the matter.'

'And, as I've told you, this accusation is ridiculous,' Hoffman butted in. His tone was as snide as ever, but I thought that I could detect just the slightest whine of concern at the edges.

'Ms Bennett here,' he continued, spitting out my name as though it had an unpleasant taste, 'has had a chip on her shoulder all semester. In fact, she's had trouble controlling her emotions and her mouth all year, which, as you may remember, led to her being removed from my class.'

This wasn't even why I'd come to Sullivan's office; the last thing I wanted to deal with was yet another face-off with Professor Satan. But as he spoke, I could feel my exhaustion falling away, and a flickering white fury began to burn in its place.

'Ms Bennett, do you have anything to add?' Dean Sullivan asked me.

I looked at her, and she raised her eyebrows, waiting for my response.

'It's true. He folded back the corner of my blue book. The same way you do with a library book, only he bent back all of the pages,' I said.

Hoffman snorted with derision. 'That's a lie,' he said flatly. 'There's no proof, and if it comes down to her word against mine, I'd hope mine would carry a bit more weight. I've been teaching at this school for twenty years, Teresa.' He leaned back in his chair and crossed his arms in front of him. Hoffman stared at Sullivan, his light gray eyes challenging her.

'Actually . . . there is proof,' Sullivan said slowly. She opened an innocuous-looking manila folder sitting on the middle of her desk and withdrew a blue book from it.

It had a prominent fold on the corner.

'What's that?' Hoffman asked.

'Ms Bennett, is this your student identification number?' Sullivan asked, handing me the blue book.

I glanced down at it, already knowing the answer. I recognized the handwriting in black ink scrawled across the cover.

'Yes,' I said, handing it back to her.

'And, as you can see, Richard, there is indeed a fold across the corner,' Sullivan said.

'That doesn't prove anything,' Hoffman said. 'Bennett probably folded it herself so she could accuse me of trying to mark her down, the same way she did after she scored poorly on her Criminal Law final.'

Aha, I thought. So he had known about my complaint.

'Perhaps,' Teresa Sullivan said slowly. 'But then, it's not just her word. . . . I've had three students come to see me this afternoon. They all told the same story – that they saw you bend the corner of her blue book down when you collected the exams.'

Three? I wondered. I'd assumed that Nick had been the only one.

'Friends of Ms Bennett's, no doubt,' Hoffman said.

Teresa Sullivan just looked at him. She finally spoke. 'As you know, I don't have the authority to reprimand a professor. But I will be referring this matter to Dean Spitzer immediately, and I anticipate he'll take action on it before his retirement.'

This time it was Hoffman who flushed, his face going purple with rage. The cold eyes bugged out a little, and specks of spit foamed on his lips as he spoke. 'I've got news for you, Teresa,' he sneered. 'Spitzer's not about to fire me on the word of a few students. Especially when the student in question is already on probation.'

'Perhaps not. But you can be sure the search committee will hear about this,' Teresa Sullivan said quietly, but with just as much force. 'You're never going to be dean, Richard.'

'You . . . you . . . bitch!' Hoffman snarled, standing up suddenly, towering over Sullivan.

The room was suddenly far too small and warm, and Hoffman's hands were curled into fists. The spittle still hanging on his lips gave him a deranged look, and his features were twisted into an expression of pure, malevolent fury.

But Sullivan seemed completely nonplussed. She sat calmly looking up at him, one eyebrow arched. 'Are you planning to hit me, Richard?' she asked mildly, tipping her head slightly to one side.

Damn, she's tough, I thought admiringly.

Hoffman took a step back, knocking into the visitor's chair with the back of his legs. His fists uncoiled, and I could see him struggling to smooth the anger from his face. But his face remained florid, highlighting the pale silver of his eyes. Tufts of grayish-brown hair rose up from his head, and he'd shut his mouth into a thin, drawn line.

'Of course not. Don't be ridiculous,' he said, his voice cold but controlled.

Sullivan continued to gaze at him until Hoffman finally broke off eye contact. He strode to the door and wrenched it open so hard, I half expected it to split off its hinges.

'You don't have the final say on the search committee,' Hoffman said, glancing back at Sullivan. And then he looked down at me, his eyes like two ice chips. I stared back at him. A moment later he was gone, the door banging shut behind him.

'Asshole,' Sullivan muttered, sinking back in her chair. She glanced over at me. 'You didn't hear that.'

'No, ma'am,' I said, although I couldn't stop the grin from blossoming on my face.

Sullivan pressed her fingers to her temples and closed her eyes. She held this position for so long, looking like the before picture in an aspirin commercial, I thought she'd forgotten I was sitting there.

'Um . . . should I go?' I asked.

Her eyes flew open, and the hands dropped down from her face. 'No, I'm sorry. It's just . . . I really thought he was going to hit me.'

'I did too,' I admitted.

'Anyway, we should probably talk about what happens next,' Sullivan said, slipping back into her professional mode. 'Now, as far as your Constitutional Law exam goes, no matter what Dean Spitzer decides to do about Professor Hoffman, I can promise you that a neutral party will grade your exam book. And I think there's ample evidence of bias to warrant having another professor look over your Criminal Law exam book from last semester, to see if the grade you received in that class was fair.'

But before she had finished speaking, I was already shaking my head.

'That really won't be necessary,' I said.

Sullivan frowned. 'But you have an excellent chance of grading onto Law Review. If you do as well on your exams this semester, that is. I would have thought you'd welcome a chance to have your Criminal Law grade reviewed.'

'It's not necessary because ... I'm withdrawing from school,' I said. I was amazed at how calm and clear my voice was. 'I won't be returning in the fall.'

'**Y**ou're dropping out? But why?' Teresa Sullivan asked. 'Is it Professor Hoffman? Because Two and Three-Ls get to choose all of their own classes. You don't have to ever take another course with him.' She paused. 'If he even remains at the school, that is.'

Hoffman really made a mistake screwing with her, I thought. She wasn't going to forget what he'd done – or how he'd towered over her, his face purple and his hands clenched in fists.

'No, that's not why. I'm not leaving because the work is hard or because of Hoffman. I'm leaving because I finally figured out that the law isn't the right path for me,' I said.

Dean Sullivan nodded and looked thoughtful. 'It does get easier, Kate.'

'I'm not looking for easy. I just want to do something meaningful with my life. Meaningful to me. And I know that the law will never be that. If I stayed here, it would only be because I was too afraid to admit I'd made a mistake. Too afraid to leave. And I'm tired of being afraid.'

'Are you sure you don't want me to revisit your Crim grade? If nothing else, I'd think that you'd want to know if another professor thinks it warrants a higher grade. Don't you want to find out if you made Law Review?'

I shook my head again. My hair was tied back in a short pony-tail, and the curly ends dragged against the base of my neck.

'No. If I did grade onto Law Review, it might make me

want to stay. But I wouldn't be staying for the right reasons,' I said, wondering if it made as clear sense spoken out loud as it did in my head.

Sullivan looked at me levelly, and then finally she smiled and closed my file shut.

'Good luck, Kate,' she said.

'Thanks,' I said, returning her smile. 'I'll take all the good luck I can get.'

The thing about huge life changes – breaking up with a lover, leaving a job, dropping out of school – is that there isn't always a clear future to fall into. As much as you might want to think that you're moving toward a different and better future, there's always that one lucid moment when you suddenly realize that you don't have the first clue about what's going to happen next.

Which is pretty much exactly how I felt when I stopped at my locker after leaving Sullivan's office. My hands were shaking as I twisted the combination on my lock and then pulled the door open and stared into the space that had, for the past academic year, housed the flotsam and jetsam of my life as a law student. I pulled out the extra legal pads and pens I'd stashed there, the casebooks and the mirror with a magnet on the back that had hung on the door, the textbooks and Nutshells, and stuffed them all into the enormous camping backpack that I'd been dragging around all year like a punishment. I leaned down and grabbed my bag, and then heaved it up onto my shoulder for the last time as a student at the Tulane School of Law.

Nick was waiting for me on our front porch when I got home. He was sitting on a folding beach chair, tossing a football up into the air.

'Hey,' he said.

'Hi.'

Another storm had blown through and moved on, leaving

the sticky hot humidity in its wake. It felt like we were living inside a clothes dryer. Sweat beaded up on my forehead, and the green T-shirt and khaki shorts I was wearing had wilted, molding damply against my skin.

'Did you talk to Sullivan?' Nick asked.

I nodded. 'She told me you'd been to see her. Thanks for that,' I said. 'And for sticking up for me in front of Hoffman.'

Nick shrugged and looked down at his football. 'I don't know what good it will do. Your word, my word . . . we're not exactly the administration's favorite students. I doubt they'll do anything.'

'They already have. I was there when Sullivan confronted Hoffman. She pulled my exam book out of the stack and saw for herself that the corner was folded down,' I said.

'No way! Really? What did Hoffman say?'

'He was pissed,' I said. I smiled at the memory. 'His face went purple, and that vein on his forehead was throbbing.'

'Oh, man, I would have given anything to see that!'

'He and Sullivan really went at it. She told him she was going to scuttle his nomination to be the new dean, and he called her a bitch and stormed out of her office,' I said. I leaned against the railing that enclosed the front porch.

'Then you're off the hook!' Nick said, delighted. 'They can't let him grade your exam now.'

I nodded, not yet ready to tell him about my decision to drop out of law school, not now when we were – for the moment, anyway – back to the easy companionship from which our friendship had originally sprung. And I didn't want him to think that what he'd done for me, standing up to Hoffman in front of the entire class, had been for nothing – because it meant so much to me.

'What if we both make Law Review? Wouldn't that be amazing?' Nick said. He grinned at me.

'What are you doing this summer?' I asked.

'Going back to D.C. I'm going to work at my dad's firm,' Nick said.

'That's fantastic. It's hard for One-Ls to get summer associate positions,' I said.

'That's nepotism for you. It's going to be awful, but at least the pay is decent.'

'Are you staying with your parents?'

'No, I've got a buddy in the city whose roommate is going to be away for the summer, and I'm going to sublet his room. How about you? What are you doing?'

'I have absolutely no idea,' I said honestly.

'I can have my dad ask around and see if anyone's hiring interns,' Nick offered.

'Thanks, but I think I might stay here for the summer. My lease runs through August, so I have to pay rent on the apartment no matter what. I'll see what summer in New Orleans is like.'

'Hot,' Nick said.

I laughed. 'Yes, I expect so.'

Nick tossed his football up in the air, caught it easily, before tossing it to me.

Nick stood. 'Throw it back.'

I looked at him. All I wanted to do was dive into his arms and feel his body wrap around mine. In fact, I wanted it all – the cinematic ending, complete with crashing waves, a thunderous drumroll, and a fireworks spectacular. And for just a moment, as we stood there staring at each other, I could sense that it *was* there, just a heartbeat away.

I tossed him the football.

One step forward, I thought. One step, and I'll be able to touch him, to brush my finger down the angle of his cheek. One step, and I won't be alone.

Nick opened his mouth, about to speak. But I shook my head, stopping him.

'Have a good summer, Nick,' I said, turning to unlock the door to my stairwell.

I didn't look back. I didn't want to lose my nerve.

Epilogue
Self-Study

At first, I wasn't sure whether I would stay in New Orleans. But I loved working for Armstrong and was thrilled when he offered me a full-time position as a research assistant for his new book. I spent my days holed up in his book-lined library or trolling around the D-Day Museum, downtown in the Warehouse District.

'Blasted Internet,' Armstrong would mutter, peering at the blue computer screen over his bifocals and pecking at the keyboard with his index fingers. 'My editor sent me a list of websites she thought would be helpful, but I can't understand how the damned thing works.'

'Give me the list, and I'll look them up to see if there's anything useful,' I'd say, and leave him to his writing while I tracked down bits of history, like a detective chasing clues.

I loved every minute of it.

One Sunday afternoon, while I was walking through the Quarter, I saw a sign hanging on a house on Chartres Street that read: THE BEAUREGARD–KEYES HOUSE. Something about the place intrigued me, so I typed the name into Google when I got back to the office, and a moment later I was reading all about the house's racy past. It turned out that the original construction had been financed with the sale of the pirate Jean Lafitte's plunders. Over the next one hundred fifty years, it housed a chess champion, a Confederate general, the writer Frances Parkinson Keyes, and, in the early 1900s, when it was owned by the Sicilian Corrado Giacona, it had been the scene of a bloody gunfight.

Suddenly I was envisioning writing the colorful history of the house as a kind of biography. Coaxing out the words, smoothing over the passages, laying out the rich details. Or maybe, I thought, with a thrill of excitement, I'd write it as a historical narrative. When I closed my eyes, I could practically see the French Quarter as it was in 1828 when the first bricks were laid – the dusty streets lined with horses twitching their tails and stomping their feet, the rattle of carriage wheels, the swish of the colorful silk dresses favored by the Creole women sauntering down the narrow sidewalk, the steamships clogging the Mississippi River.

And before I could even think it through, I had fished out a yellow legal pad from the box of school supplies I hadn't bothered unpacking and started to take notes.

When the lease was up on my Magazine Street apartment, Armstrong overheard me on the telephone with yet another landlord advertising in the classified section of the *Times-Picayune*, trying – and failing – to convince them that, yes, I technically did have a dog, but Holmes was so small he wouldn't damage whatever shoddy property they were renting.

'Why don't you move into my carriage house? Rent-free,' Armstrong offered.

'No, I couldn't do that,' I protested.

'Absolutely. It'll help make me feel less guilty for the truly paltry salary I'm paying you,' he'd insisted. 'Really, it's disgraceful how underpaid you are.'

'I have a dog,' I warned him.

'He can keep Elvis company.'

For my part, I was glad I took Armstrong up on the offer. The little carriage house had a working fireplace, high ceilings, and was furnished with squishy armchairs and antiques that glowed with lemon oil. Tucked away in the back house, which was shaded under ancient oak trees and perfumed from the honeysuckle vines creeping up the east brick wall, I sometimes imagined that I lived in an earlier, less complicated age. And Holmes loved chasing lizards around the yard and barking at bigger dogs walking by, from behind the safety of a wrought-iron fence. It very quickly felt like home.

'How's school going? What's it like being Two-Ls?' I asked Lexi and Jen when I met them for lunch at Martin Wine Cellar, a deli housed inside an enormous liquor store.

It was the first chance the three of us had had to get together. I missed them but understood that they were busy with school.

'Same old, same old,' Jen said.

'Except that now we finally get to choose our own classes,' Lexi said, as she took a delicate bite out of her turkey club sandwich. 'Thank God.'

'Have you heard from Dana?' Jen asked. 'I got a postcard from her a while back, but that was ages ago.'

'We've talked a few times. She checks in from time to time to find out how Holmes is doing,' I said. 'She really misses him.'

'I assume she's not coming back to school,' Lexi said.

'No,' I said, shaking my head. 'She's going to start working on her master's degree next semester, though. I think she's planning to live at home and commute in to school.'

'Good for her,' Lexi said. 'What's she getting her degree in?'

'Psychology,' I said.

Jen whistled. 'That's ironic.'

'And she's dating someone. Dana said they're taking it slow, but I think he sounds pretty special.'

'Good. I'm happy for her,' Lexi said.

'Hey, have you heard the news about Hoffman?' Jen asked.

I shuddered. Just hearing his name made my stomach feel sour. 'No, I'm totally out of the law-school loop,' I said.

'They *fired* him,' Jen said. She leaned forward as she dropped this bombshell, her eyes sparkling. 'And Professor Legrande is the new dean.'

'No? Really?' I gasped.

'Yup. Our national fucking nightmare is over,' Jen said.

I looked to Lexi for confirmation.

She nodded. 'It's true. Officially Hoffman's on a leave of absence, but Jacob told me that he's being forced to take an early retirement.'

'Jacob?' My eyebrows rose. 'Are you and he . . .?' My voice trailed off in a question.

'God, no! I just bumped into him the other day at school. But he did ask me what I was doing this weekend.' Lexi smiled coolly. 'I laughed and told him that he'd missed his chance.'

'Are you still seeing that Swedish guy?'

'Ian. Yeah,' Lexi said, nodding. 'Things are going really well between us. You should meet him.'

'I'd like that.'

Jen had become uncharacteristically quiet during this exchange, focusing all of her attention on her ham-and-brie croissant.

'What about you, Jen?' I asked gently.

'Sean and I separated,' she said flatly.

From the shocked expression on Lexi's face, I guessed this was news to her too.

'What? When?' Lexi asked.

'Because of Addison?' I asked.

Jen laughed humorlessly. 'No. Addison and I broke up – is it breaking up? I don't even know if that's the right thing to call it, since technically we weren't ever really a couple – anyway, we ended it over the summer. I thought I told you.'

'No,' I said. 'I think I would have remembered that.'

'Yeah. Well.' Jen sighed. 'The night before I was supposed

to leave to visit him in Los Angeles, he called to tell me that he was seeing someone.'

'Ouch,' I said. I reached across the table and rested my hand on her arm. 'I'm so sorry.'

Jen shrugged. 'I couldn't care less about Addison. I'm more concerned about my husband. And the internist at the hospital I think he's screwing,' she said bitterly.

'Sean's having an affair?' I asked, careful to drop the 'too' from the end of the sentence.

'He says no. But then last week he came home from work and said he wasn't happy and was going to move out for a little while.' Tears flooded Jen's eyes. She picked up the toothpick that had been holding her sandwich together and began stabbing at the croissant with it, leaving a pattern of tiny holes in the flaky crust.

'Why do you think he's having an affair?' Lexi asked.

'I sort of followed him one day after work. He went to the Bulldog with some coworkers, and I saw this doctor he works with. Her name is Indigo – Indigo! – and she was at our Thanksgiving party last year. They were flirting.' Jen looked like she felt sick to her stomach. 'You know, I really don't want to talk about this right now.'

'Okay. We don't have to talk about it,' Lexi said.

We sat for a few minutes. Lexi and I ate our sandwiches; Jen continued to poke holes in hers.

'I just wish I knew that everything was going to work out,' Jen said suddenly. 'Do you know what I mean? I just want to know that it will all be okay in the end.'

I nodded. 'I know. We all want that.'

I knocked softly on Armstrong's open office door. He looked up and brightened when he saw me.

'How about if we blow off working for the rest of the afternoon and go shopping?' he said. 'I need new china.'

I happened to know that he did not need new china. There were five different sets of tableware downstairs, from his mother's good wedding china still housed in an ornate, gilded cabinet to the plain white Crate & Barrel plates he used every day.

'Do you remember a while back you told me about Hunter?' I asked.

Armstrong sighed and put down his pen. 'It's going to be one of those conversations, hmmm?'

'We don't have to talk about him if you don't want to,' I said.

'No, I don't mind talking. There's just not much to say. He was on the faculty with me at UVA. We had some good years and some bad years, and when we split we were both sure it was time. I'm over him now. I have been for a long time.'

'But the night that you mentioned him, you told me . . . well, you told me I should be careful with love,' I said.

Armstrong looked surprised. 'I did? When did I say that? Had I been drinking?'

'Of course.'

'Well, that explains that.' Armstrong grinned. 'You should never hold anything a man says while under the influence against him. It's unseemly.'

'It's just . . . I'm worried that I wasn't. Careful with love,' I said. 'I'm worried that I made a mistake.'

'Not the academic?'

'No, not him.'

'Thank *God*.'

'It's just that for so long, I was always trying to do the safe thing. I stayed in relationships that I should have left because I didn't want to give up the security. But now I'm worried that I've gone and done the opposite,' I said.

'Well, I'll tell you this. Once you meet the right person, it's harder to be apart than it is to be together. Someday you'll meet someone you feel that way about. And you'll just know,' Armstrong said. He looked distant for a minute, and I wondered if he was thinking about Hunter or some other long-ago love.

'I think I may already have,' I said softly.

*

As soon as I walked in the back door of the law school, the all-too-familiar smell of the place hit me: a combination of institutional floor cleanser and freshly printed newspaper. It was a Saturday afternoon, and the hallways were mostly deserted, save for a few students who had ventured downstairs on a study break. I didn't recognize any of them.

One-Ls, I thought. I could tell by their expressions of fear mingled with exhaustion.

I climbed the stairs and, once I reached the second floor, turned right. I walked past the administration offices and my old locker, down to the end of the deserted hallway. I veered left and then stopped at the first door on my right.

There was a brass plaque mounted on the door:

TULANE LAW REVIEW

I drew in a deep breath and then pushed the door open.

The Law Review office was humming with activity. Two rows of cubicles – most of them occupied with former classmates that I recognized, including Scott Brown and Jasmine West – were lined down the center of the room, and a cluster of tables littered with case reports and stacks of papers were set up at the front. Doors on the right and left led to tiny private offices for the editors. There was a laser printer and copier and fax machine, along with a water cooler and a coffeepot set up in the back.

I stood at the door, hoping that no one would notice me, while I scanned the room. And then I saw him.

Nick.

We'd only spoken a few times since the end of our One-L year. Those conversations had been pleasant, congenial even, as we'd chatted about his summer job and my decision to leave school. We were careful to stay on safe ground, both of us pretending to ignore the undercurrent of everything that had happened between us.

Nick was now at the back of the office, standing with a petite woman with thick dark hair and a big toothy grin. They were laughing as they talked, and the woman kept finding reasons to touch Nick's arm or hand. She was pretty, I thought, with a stab of jealousy.

Nick looked so familiar ... and yet somehow different. Maybe it was his hair, which was shorter than it had been the previous year, the waves cropped close to his head. His face and arms were a golden brown, the last traces of a fading summer tan.

He looked up, smiling at something the brunette had said, and saw me. When our eyes met, I felt a jolt of excitement, quickly followed by a small tremor of fear. How was he going to react to my coming here? I had no idea what to expect. For all I knew, the woman he was talking to could be his girlfriend. Or, if he was back to his old tricks, yet another of his conquests.

Nick broke off his conversation and started across the room toward me.

'Kate,' he said. 'Hi. What are you doing here?'

I smiled nervously. 'I wanted to see if the rumor that you'd made Law Review was true. Congratulations.'

'Thanks. It's a mixed blessing. It takes up a lot of time. I feel like I never leave this office,' Nick said. He rolled his eyes comically.

'Uh-huh. So you love it?'

'Maybe "love" is too strong a word, but ... yeah, I like it. And they keep telling us that it's the key to getting a judicial clerkship, so it's worth it.'

'Is that what you want to do after graduation? Clerk for a judge?'

He nodded. 'But the positions are competitive, so who knows if I'll get one.'

'Still, that's great. I'm really happy for you.'

'Hey, you too. I heard that you're still working for Armstrong McKenna.'

I nodded. 'Full-time. And I'm doing some research of my

own. I'm thinking of writing a book . . . and maybe going back to school for my master's degree.'

'Wow. That's amazing,' Nick said approvingly.

The silence was awkward and heavy with expectation.

'Is that why you stopped by? To say congratulations?' Nick asked. He was still smiling, but his face was guarded.

'Do you feel like taking a break? Maybe we could go for a walk,' I suggested.

'Sure. Let me just tell Josie that I'm taking off,' Nick said.

Josie. The brunette, I presumed, with a sinking dread. I waited by the door while Nick disappeared into one of the offices. When he came back out, he had his messenger bag slung over his shoulder.

'All set,' he said.

'Hey, Kate,' a voice called out.

I looked over Nick's shoulder and saw Scott grinning and waving at me. A few of my other former classmates were also watching me curiously. I waved at Scott but hung back, feeling suddenly shy. I was an outsider here now.

'Everyone's been asking about you,' Nick said as we walked out of the office together.

'Have they? I honestly didn't think anyone would notice I'd left.'

'Are you kidding? The One-L who took on Hoffman? You're a legend.'

We took the stairs down a flight and then went out the back door. As usual, a few smokers were out there, hunched over on the uncomfortable benches. The entire courtyard smelled of smoke, and cigarette butts littered the ground.

'Where are we going?' Nick asked.

My heart started to skitter around. I hadn't planned this out – what I would say, how I would say it. I'd thought – mistakenly, I now realized – that it would be better to just wing it. But I had no idea how to begin. And I had no idea what Nick was thinking. His expression was mildly curious but at the same time shuttered.

'I don't know,' I admitted.

'Well. There's always P.J.'s. Or we could take a long walk over to Audubon Park. Or, if you're feeling really wild, we could mosey over to the Boot and grab a beer.'

'The Quarter. Let's go down to the Quarter,' I said impulsively.

A half-hour later we were sitting on a bench in the center of Jackson Square in the French Quarter, next to the statue of Andrew Jackson.

'This is where you wanted to have a personal conversation?' Nick asked. He gestured around. Unsurprisingly, considering the glorious weather, the Quarter was teeming with tourists. They passed by in loud clusters, wearing New Orleans T-shirts and fanny packs and, of course, the ever-present Mardi Gras beads. Zydeco music blared from the souvenir shops that sold alligator heads and overpriced sun-screen.

'I know this doesn't seem like the most obvious place,' I admitted. 'But bear with me.'

Nick nodded.

'So, um, who was that woman you were talking to back at the Law Review office?' I asked, trying to sound casual. I had to know what I was up against.

'Who? Josie? She's the editor-in-chief of the Law Review,' Nick said. 'My boss, basically.'

'Are the two of you dating?' I asked, not looking at him. Instead, I stared at a couple strolling by, their fingers entwined. She had big, blonde, feathered Farrah Fawcett hair, and she was wearing a midriff tank top and the shortest denim cutoffs I'd ever seen. The man leaned over and kissed the woman's bare shoulder, and she tilted her head toward him, smiling happily.

'Dating Josie? God, no,' Nick said, and he laughed, as though it were a ridiculous idea.

Relief flooded through me. Maybe I still had a chance.

'Oh, hey – guess what?' I said.

'I give up. What?'

'I found out why New Orleans smells like burned toast,' I said. 'Armstrong told me. It's the Mississippi River. On humid days especially, it wafts up and carries over the whole city.'

'Mystery solved,' Nick said. 'Excellent. Now why are we here again?'

'This is where we were the first time we kissed,' I explained.

'I remember. I kissed you, you blew me off, and I ended up getting drunk and singing Captain and Tennille songs at a karaoke bar on Bourbon Street.'

' "Love Will Keep Us Together"?'

'No. Even more embarrassing: "Muskrat Love." '

'Oh. Well. That's why I wanted to come back here. I . . . I made a mistake that night,' I said.

Nick went very still next to me. Goose bumps rose up on my skin from where his shirt brushed against me. Somewhere off in the distance, a jazz band started playing 'When the Saints Go Marching In.' The more-drunken tourists whooped and began to dance.

'What are you saying, Kate?' Nick's voice was so soft that at first I wasn't even sure he'd spoken.

'I'm sorry. For everything,' I said, studying his face in profile. His nose slanted down a little just at the end, and there was a faint white line on his forehead, probably a scar left over from a childhood accident.

'You're sorry,' Nick repeated. He still didn't look at me. 'You brought me here to tell me that you're sorry.'

My heart felt like it was stalling in my chest. What was he thinking? Was he happy? Annoyed? Embarrassed?

'And that I'd like a second chance,' I said. The words wanted to stick in my throat, but I forced them out.

'Excuse me, would you mind taking our picture?'

I looked up. A chunky blonde woman in a cherry-red cardigan sweater was standing there waving a disposable camera at us. Behind her was a man with an impressive beer gut, wearing a Steelers baseball cap. Off to the side, trying hard to look like they weren't really vacationing with their parents, were two sullen teenagers.

'Sure,' Nick said.

He stood up, and the family grouped together in front of the Andrew Jackson statue.

'Say cheese,' Nick said.

'Cheese!' they called out.

Nick snapped a few photos. The teenagers even smiled for one of the pictures, baring mouths full of metal braces. The mom thanked him effusively when he handed the camera back.

And then Nick turned toward me.

I looked at him, and he gazed back at me with those vivid blue eyes. And in that moment, just as Armstrong had predicted, I knew. I stood up, and we moved toward each other. I wrapped my arms around his waist. His hands caught in my hair, and then he bent down to kiss me.

'I can't tell you how many times I've wanted to come find you. But I didn't think you'd want to see me,' Nick murmured, his lips so close to mine, I could feel his breath against my skin.

'I just had to know that I could be alone. That I really don't need to have a boyfriend to feel safe.'

'And?'

'I don't need a boyfriend. I just want to be with you,' I said simply.

I kissed him again, pressing my hands against his back, breathing in the scent of his sun-warmed skin, feeling the slow rise and fall of his chest. Nick held me right back, his arms encircled around me like a promise. I had a feeling my bad-luck streak had finally come to an end.

Pick up a *little black dress* – it's a girl thing.

THE BACHELORETTE PARTY
Karen McCullah Lutz

A wickedly funny novel from the co-writer of *Ten Things I Hate About You* and *Legally Blonde*.

'A raunchy, raucous joyride of a book' Jennifer Weiner, author of *In Her Shoes*

0 7553 3271 7

HEX AND THE SINGLE GIRL
Valerie Frankel

Do you think that access to magical powers would help your love life? Who doesn't?

'Had me laughing to the last magical page' Meg Cabot

0 7553 3674 7

Pick up a *little black dress* – it's a girl thing.

0 7553 3722 0

SINGLETINI
Amanda Trimble

Singletini (noun): A glamorous and increasingly common type of girl, possessing an unusual fear of growing up and settling down . . .

A delicious and more-ish cocktail of glamour, fun and true love, this is a sparkling romantic read that's not to be missed!

SPIRIT WILLING, FLESH WEAK
Julie Cohen

Welcome to the world of Julie Cohen, one of the freshest, funniest voices in romantic fiction!

When fake psychic Rosie meets a gorgeous investigative journalist, she thinks she can trust him not to blow her cover – but is she right?

0 7553 3481 7

little black dress

brings you
fantastic new books like these
every month - find out more at
www.littleblackdressbooks.com

And why not sign up for our
email newsletter to keep
you in the know about
Little Black Dress news!

Now you can buy any of these other **Little Black Dress** titles from your bookshop or *direct from the publisher*.

FREE P&P AND UK DELIVERY
(Overseas and Ireland £3.50 per book)